For my dear friends; through bowling, band, and beyond-- I only wish that I could have made you as happy *as* DM, as you make me with your DMs.

And somehow, all of this has come of that...

A city fitting for the simple, short lives of men, Argoth sits at the foot of the Cordol Mountains along the Argothian River flowing with spring water from the mountain highlands. A fine dwelling for a city of men.

Beyond, the greater Argothian Kingdom stretches north to the Midrosh Mountains, south to the Great River Web, and west; through plains, rocky peaks, and dusty flats. Diverse in lands, and varied in is people who settle the different regions, across it all, is the kingdom of men. A fine kingdom for mankind stemming from this city, under a mountain, near the sea from which the founders once came. The streets are almost always loud with the racket of commerce. Heroes, people of business, and adventurers; vagrants, urchins, and do-gooders. No paradise as a whole, but it's a place that hosts all. Even elves and gnomes, close neighbors to this kingdom. Many of their kind dwell here. A gathering place of all kinds, creeds, and morals; and a fine city of men.

But she is not human, *or* elf. She is both, and she is neither.

And she is alone.

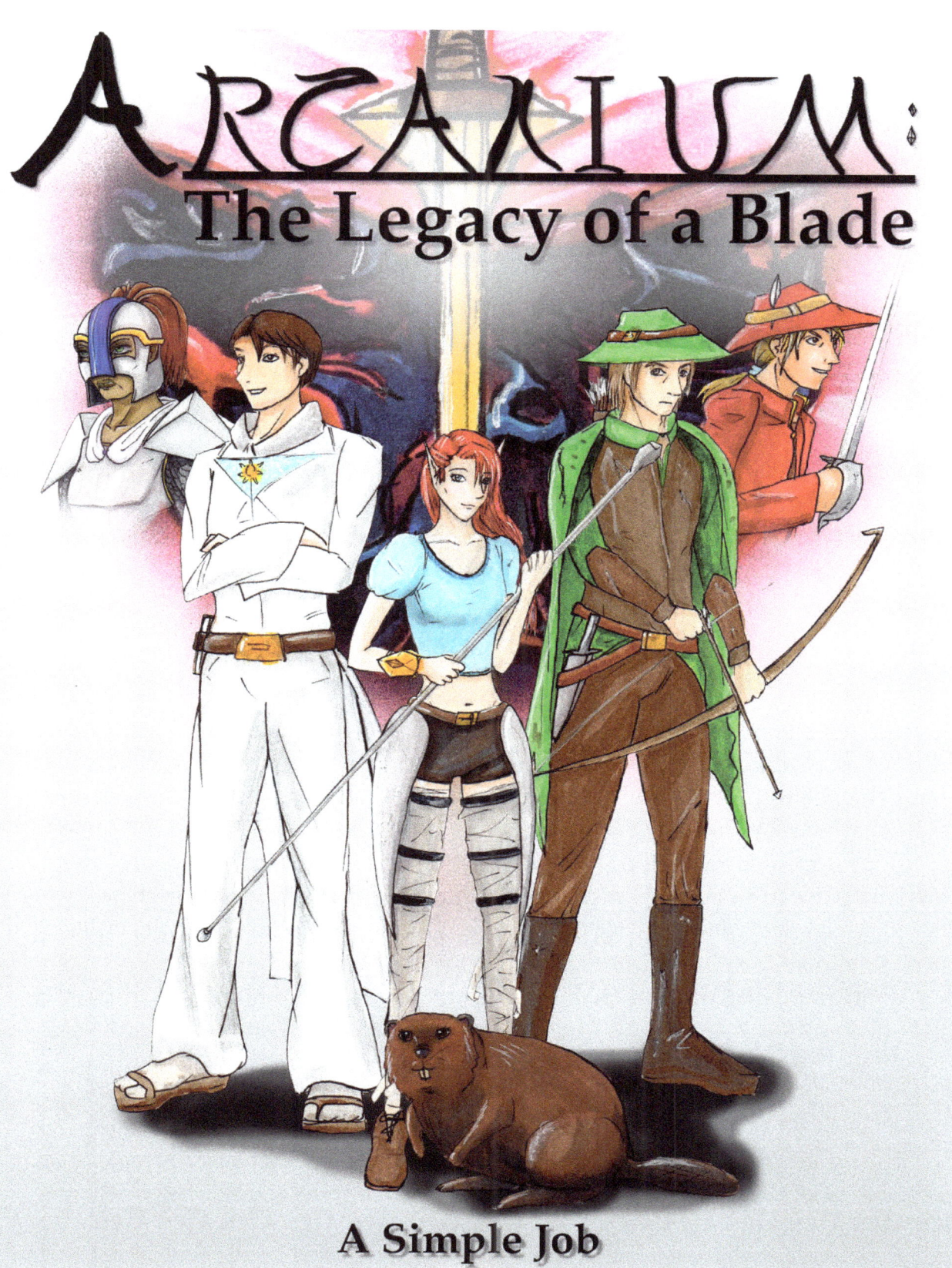

1

It's been a long day. It's not such a warm day, as it is sunny. The benefit of more people out and about certainly outweighs the tax on her fair, elf-like skin. Still, they could offer more than the few pennies she's received. Some give out of genuine wonder, others pass by and simply give as courtesy, others certainly out of guilt, and of course there are more than a few lecherous men.

She counts the coins in her tip basket. As Goldday, it's the last day before the week's end, and many people have been paid, and lucky for her, that it sometimes trickles down. Like in the case of the last person, he gave a few extra coins and told her, 'drink one on me'. She might just do that. *Fifteen copper, one silver.* She tallies as she slips it into her small purse bag. It was once a single use seed sack, just a testament to the elites and how uncaringly they do their business that something yet so functional would be trashed in the rubbish bins behind their shoppe. *Just another week.* Or so, she hopes. But at this rate, by the time she can afford the darn blanket it'll already be spring. In light of her current acquisition of currency, her stomach reminds her that it's been some time since she's had a proper meal.

If she manages to get through town without running into any guards, or just damned lecherous men, for which are often one in the same, she'll be lucky. But for now, she has something. Enough to visit one of the seedier taverns in what is not her favorite part of town. As if she has a favorite part of this city, a city that's done nothing for her, a city she'd leave in an instant if she could. For every penny she earns from some well dressed woman or leering old man, she is both grateful, and disgusted. Nothing to them is everything to her, and it's not fair. It's not fair that even the children have more to spare than she. Still, all she can do in this rotten city is hope they spare her something, anything. Alone, it's all she can do for herself.

She looks around, and it seems that none of the Ar-Guards are stalking around. She can leave her things here for now. She heads for the tavern, stepping through one alley, and another to a different street, her hands carefully holding onto her small, precious bag of coins.

"Hey…" he's almost passed out, and she tries to ignore him as she squeezes past him and the rubbish bins he's propped on. "Hey!" He grabs her arm. And hiccups, "How much, dolly?"

"Let go." she snaps as she jolts her arm free from his drunkenly lax grasp, and as her head flicks as well, she sees a guard not too far off. *Shite.*

And he's not taking 'no' for an answer; made too obvious by his making an obnoxious, drooling kissing movement towards her general direction. "Here's a bit…" he holds out a sludgy coin of some sort.

"Stop it!" she shouts through her teeth. She knows full well she could burn him and he'd let go in an instant, but even as she thinks that, she cannot. Instead, she continues to groan and hiss as she pulls herself away. Too loudly, here comes that Ar-Guard. *Shite!* Her jaw clenches tighty as her eyes dart around looking for a place to run to. There *is* a tavern just across the way that she could duck into. With one last pull she manages to yank free from the grabby sard without breaking her promise and she wastes no time sprinting across the street and into the tavern. In which, a seat in the back will do nicely.

Nestled in the taverns in the city of Argoth are heroes and ruffians of all kinds. Rangers, merchants, those like herself, doxys, and apparently, even clerics. Nothing extra, but they are often a halfway pleasant place to find a warm fire, smooth beer, or just some real food. And perhaps coerce some company for the night as many men often try to do. Especially in a more rough place like this, she's dealt with that before. But at least here they don't kick her out over smells offending their elitist noses. By her nose, she's probably of little concern compared to many of the men there, and maybe some of the women. Admittedly, this place seems a bit nicer than her usual choice. She'll have to be careful though, nicer is all too often linked to price.

She grabs a small ale from the center bar, it's yellow, and likely will taste like piss but at only a few copper a half, she'll take it. Still wary of that guard outside, she spies a quiet looking corner in the back. If it'd just been one of the pretentious Ar-Guards trying to get her on vagrancy, she might fess up and try to appeal to their chivalry. But in this case, if there's a chance they think she might have been selling out, well then she's no recourse but to hide. *Pigs*.

A moment later a woman in a regal suit of armor enters the nameless tavern in this small corner of Argoth. Little notice is taken to the tall, fit woman in Storm Knight's armor, holding a large glaive, and her white robe and mantle contrasting strongly with her rich skin tone. Little is clearly visible of her face with the large nose guard, though two distinct scars on either side of her lower lip can be seen. At least by her with her shaper half-elf eyes and low vantage point. But everyone is just enjoying their drinks, and pay her no heed. Except for her, she shuffles a little further back in her booth and tries not to be seen.

"Ahem!", the Ar-Guard, or rather, the woman knight grunts. There are no responses. Still, the elf just keeps her head down, and hides her hair under the shadow of a support beam.

"A-HEM!", the louder disturbance gets more attention as some patrons turn to her. "Hear ye, hear ye, the Royal Guard of Argoth is currently seeking some adventurers to take a task of great, *national* importance!" At that many of the patrons stop listening, however, around the room a couple of people still look on her intently. She looks up, if they aren't after her, she may as well listen. "Is anyone interested? For your reward could be great!"

She's heard of things like this. Often from drunken bastards trying to get into her leather boyshorts, but sometimes there are bounties put out by the guard. And as she knows all too well, sometimes they'll pay for people to hunt monsters near the city. But her spells aren't that great, and she's no interest in following *that* sard's footsteps.

"Nobody?" the woman knight scoffs demeaningly, as if to call every patron a coward for not sacrificing themselves for the damned noble elites of this city. Judging by that ornate suit she's a high rank, probably with a nice home outside the main barracks.

Still... she considers as she takes another sip of her pissy drink, what she might do with some money. She'd be able to drink better than this slop. She almost would be better relying on the elven half of her blood and risking some tainted stream water. She takes a deep breath, and sighs, her mind now fluttering with all the thoughts of what she really could do with money. Not only that, but *if* she learned and leveled up her magic, she might be a force to be reckoned with. No elitist sard in a suit would *dare* haughtily snort at her again. But reality hits hard, she's never left the city, she couldn't do such a thing alone, whatever it may be. And again, her promise. But she also considers, *When else might such a chance come again?*

"You, She-Elf?" the woman knight says, projecting her dark voice right to her.

She tries not to be intimidated, but after another fast round of thought, she decides.

After taking a large sip of her drink, she is the first to go forward; despite that she is very petite, very young, and dressed in the scrappy rags that were once street performers' clothes. She brushes her red bangs off of her eyes, and tucks one side behind one her considerable ears. "I am Avrel Lavian." she curtseys timidly, upon closer inspection, this *might* actually be the Ar-Guard from outside. "I perform magic shows." she adds, that she might be assumed to have a profession of some sort.

The knight's eyes narrow, and she inspects her thoroughly by the shifts of her shadowed green eyes. Avrel can imagine her thinking hard about her, a small, skinny half-elf. Or, perhaps she's already bullying her in her mind, she is an Ar-Guard after all. Or something like it. Her eyes linger long on Avrel's hair, or perhaps just sizing up her lack of height. By her reckoning, the woman seems to have her doubts about the she-elf. The woman then sort of stares off towards another part of the bar, but then the woman nods to affirm Avrel as the next person comes forward. Avrel steps aside as a clean cut man with short dark hair and light colored robes strides over to the knight. He has a pleasant face, with a warm smile.

"I am Geric, a cleric" he bows respectfully, "I study healing magic as an apprentice at a local Healers' Guild." he says with pride.

The woman looks like she has a better feeling about this one.

He's tall, even by Avrel's reckoning. And taller than the woman knight even, and she's head and shoulders taller than Avrel herself.

Immediately following him is a rough looking man in a dirty, tattered, green mantle, a woodman's hat, and a thick cloth armor tunic. He smells, not outrightly bad, Avrel almost likes it for its natural, earthy quality.

"I'm Zanvan." he slurs before spitting into a spittoon, "I'm a ranger..." he grunts.

The woman seems at first annoyed at his impudence but then seems amused. He's a little shorter than the cleric, perhaps still slightly above average. He might be a little older than the cleric.

And Avrel is suddenly afraid. She suddenly is unsure of her decision to take this job, no matter how simple it could be; not if it means being such easy sport for these men. She calms herself though. She's learned to handle this city, and she can probably handle herself with them if she needs to. Besides, she can only guess that the woman knight will be joining them.

Finally an overly clean-cut mage comes forward sporting a bright red robe, and dashingly attractive red hat.

"I am Rufus of the Redshirts!" he exclaims.

The woman's face lights up, "You mean... THE Redshirts?" she asks.

"THE Redshirts!" he replies showing her a crest on his robe, "Learning a balance of white and black magic, I have sworn an oath to always take part in any journey that might further knowledge of our great world, even at the cost of my life!" he claims triumphantly as he gestures grandly towards Avrel and the others.

Avrel's never heard of 'The Redshirts', but he looks very well dressed, all in rich reds. They must be important, and she doesn't want to seem ignorant. Just the same she tries to get a feeling glance from the ranger, and the cleric. The cleric shrugs, and the ranger looks dismissive.

The woman knight smiles. "Well, you've certainly found your journey, it puts my mind at ease knowing that one of your order will be part of this quest."

The ranger seems indifferent and the cleric even moreso. The woman knight shares a quick nod with the Redshirt, and then, thumping her glaive to the floor, she grabs all their attention.

She then huddles them towards an empty booth in the corner of the tavern. Avrel is still cautious and has to fight a gut feeling as she follows along. The others seem fearless, especially the guy in red who has taken up a spot beside the woman knight. It looks like they are conversing, but even her elf ears can't pick it out in the crowd. A moment later, they get into a booth.

Unfortunately, after they are all situated, the cleric gets up and announces that he's leaving a moment to visit the chamber pot, during which time the woman knight goes to order some drinks. Avrel is fine with letting hers waste, but she and the others are left awkwardly sitting together without much to say.

A moment passes when a small child comes to them asking them for a copper piece to hear him play a song on his tambourine. The ranger seems uninterested, same as the Redshirt, but Avrel takes pity on the child, for she knows what it's like to dance for pennies. Despite a look of annoyance from the ranger and the Redshirt, Avrel smiles to the boy and pays him his fee with one of her last disposable copper pieces.

Much to all of their horror, the child has no rhythm and creates an ungodly racket which echoes all through the otherwise quiet corner of the tavern, turning heads from the more crowded middle section. It's piercing, especially to her elf ears. Just as it seems the ranger is about to silence the child, the child slips and falls and runs out of the tavern, crying. While Avrel is concerned for the child and is almost about to go after him, the ranger scoots his chair back, which happens to block her way.

"Hmph..." he hums, "Gold tooth."

She almost gasps, "You wouldn't kee--" He does keep it. Despite Avrel's protests, he takes it and stashes it in his pocket.

"Gold is gold, kid." he says coldly. And full of contempt, Avrel is about to lash out, just as he beats her to speaking, "Any kid with a gold tooth doesn't need your pennies."

She settles back into her seat, and rests her jaw in her hand, her elbow supported by the table. By this time the cleric and the woman come back, bearing drinks.

"Shame the kid slipped." the cleric says with a shitey grin. A *really* shitey grin.

Avrel's eyes narrow, *He wouldn't have...?* She looks, but there really isn't anything to slip on, *Was he tripped?* It reminds her of the time that some boys kept running by trying to trip her on her own cloth leg wrappings. 'Boys will be...' the stupid old bitch laughed as he took his time to even see if she was okay. It still riles her up just to think about it. But thinking about it helps give her resolve to go through with this job, to rise up, and in time, that she can find some way to make all those passerbys pay. If for nothing else that she will be in a position to aid them only to deny it, pandering to some archaic construct as her reason. *That...* she smiles as that questionable cleric hands her a drink, *Will make it worth it.*

After handing out the drinks, the woman knight unrolls a large, old looking scroll over the table. It looks mostly to be a map, but an old one. "My name is Lethia" the woman knight states, "I've been sent out by the Royal Court of Argoth to recruit a small group to gather info for us." she says briskly. "Specific information."

"Why not do it yourself?" the cleric interjects, drawing Avrel's ire a bit, he's threatening her bread.

"You see these mostly crimeless streets?" the woman knight, Lethia asks, "Do you want them kept that way? We don't have *time* to run around the kingdom, scouting rumors from dark alleys and trading hutches. Does it not make more sense to simply hire people like yourselves-"

She is interrupted by the cleric once more, "Didn't you just say, you didn't want to scour dark alleyways and bars for information, yet here we are?" he says with a snide look.

He folds his arms and leans back, twitching his sandaled foot with eager self satisfaction. *He's that type.* Avrel almost moans. *Next, she'll have an idea and he'll repeat it louder...* she scoffs to herself, not sparing a slight snort.

"Well, as I was about to say, Cleric, we decided to simply delegate this job to people like yourselves who might be familiar with such places. Or... " the woman knight scowls turning to Avrel and also the ranger, "Maybe could use a little help in supporting the kingdom's *healthy* circulation." Her somewhat dark voice gets downright growly. "Or maybe I should find someone else?"

"Excuse me ma'am." the tall cleric interjects, "I am Geric the cleric, not 'Cleric'." Geric, the cleric corrects her with a sneer.

The woman knight sighs under her breath as she leers, as does Avrel. "No ma'am." Avrel is quick to say, defending her self interest against the sardonic arse's sabotage. Not that she herself gives a damn about 'supporting the kingdom's healthy circulation'. "We'll do it."

The ranger tips up his green, wide brimmed hat. "Just get on with it, what are we supposed to be looking into?" He leans back and takes a sip, Avrel then finds herself seated next to his smelly boots as he leans back and props them up beside her.

The woman knight's scarred lips twitch, turning as if she's expecting the Redshirt to say something too or something. But he doesn't. "A rumor reached our information network suggesting that Nerfendör, the King of the Orken Kingdom of YordäsVvin is currently searching for the Runeblade of the Ages and its counterpart the Everlasting Aegis." Her pronunciation of the orc king's name is startling out of her low, dark common. Avrel's not heard much orken speech, but she knows it's a deep, fricative language, and the knight is showing off. Just a typical flex the elitist types like to make. "If he came into possession of these relics he could pose a very real threat to our sovereignty." the woman says imperatively. "The orcs..." she adds, "Could easily make an offensive against Argoth not seen in centuries." Her voice frys in a low tone, "They're ripe for it."

The cleric raises his hand, "Excuse me, but those two relics are just legends aren't they? And even if they are real, everything I've read states that they were lost when the Diablo was cast into the Great Chasm." he prattles on, "Well, the Aegis that is. The *Runeblade* was lost during-"

"You're well read for one so brash." the woman knight replies, "While nobody is sure of the existence of those relics, that point is moot; if Nerfendör is looking for them, it means he's up to something. And if they do exist, it's best we find out about that as well."

The ranger spits, "So it's an arms race and you want us to do your dirty work. *Fun.*" He sighs, lighting his pipe. "The princess must be bored."

The woman knight takes a moment to react. "Even if they are but legends, it'd be worthwhile to know if the orcs are showing any interest in such things." she says.

"Sounds shifty." the cleric shrugs.

"No! Tis a noble quest given by our King! As a Redshirt I see nothing ill in the intent of such a quest!" he blurts.

Avrel and the cleric roll their eyes simultaneously, the ranger simply raises an eyebrow, and sighs smoke from his nose.

"Moving on, and to summarize..." the woman says irritatedly, "We believe it to be beneficial to know whether these whispers are true, first off. And secondly, if such weapons exist and can be recovered before the orcs get their hands on them." she pauses as if to give it a moment to sink in. "Will you take the job?" she asks.

Avrel still has her misgivings, but she nods, and subtly mews, "Yes."

The ranger briefly removes his pipe from his lips to rasp, "Sure."

"Hail, and well met!" the cleric says, everyone guessing that it means 'yes'.

"But of course!" the Redshirt says with a tosting motion with his mug. He's left hanging.

"Good, find out as much as you can over the next few months, when the time comes, return to this tavern and ask for me. I'll be around." she says. "I also have a few other contacts elsewhere, so if needs be, I'll find you." She almost sounds as if she's threatening them. Avrel wouldn't put it past her, after all, she's just a well dressed Ar-Guard. "Here." She hands them each a pouch with 150 gold pieces. "I can give you this much in advance as an investment so that it may ease your supplies. When you return, you'll receive the rest."

"Hot damn!" Avrel exclaims in awe of the leisurely handling of such an amount of coinage. She almost isn't sure how to compose herself, it's more than she's ever held at one time. She's lucky to accumulate as many *pennies* in a season.

"Now the midget dame can stop wearing those horrid rags!" the cleric says nudging the ranger who is having none of such an intimately friendly gesture.

"Was that *necessary*, Master Cleric?" the Redshirt says inquisitively.

"Mmmm... Only as necessary as being a decent height" the cleric grins, "I mean look at her, we might be fighting orcs and she'd barely be able to take on a gnome!"

Avrel's about to bite his haughty, well groomed head off, but catches herself, barely. "I can see this is gonna be a fun job..." she sighs, "These 'rags' are suitable for the dancing I do for my magic shows, forgive me if they aren't the fine linens you clerics get in your stuffy monasteries." she says with a leer as she crosses her thin arms. "*Must be nice!*" she snorts, not jealous at all, her magic is good as it is, and not limited to healing and blessings.

"Oh, it is." the cleric says.

"Alright! Enough bickering about!" the woman knight intercedes. "Lest I reconsider your employment."

"Nay, and indeed!" says the Redshirt. "We have a quest given by our noble King! I suggest we start by arming and dressing ourselves for the journey. Especially you Miss Avrel, modesty is one the greatest armors of them all." the Redshirt pontificates.

Avrel's arms tighten. "Is it?" she mutters. Yes, her pale skin is shown, but certainly not flaunted. *Besides...* "Modesty, or a lacking of it, is just an excuse used when you men can't control your damned urges. So bugger off." she allows herself to almost bark.

"....Yep" the ranger says, shaking his head and blowing smoke out his nostrils. "You three should prepare, I really don't need anything, I'm used to roughing it, my knife and bow are always ready."

"Good for you?" Avrel sighs, "I'll be out getting prepared, meet me in the square in a few hours when you guys are ready." She briskly relieves herself of them. And it seems that the ranger and cleric follow only seconds later, leaving the Redshirt and the woman knight to discuss the bill. That's fine with her, they can afford it.

Avrel goes back to the alley where she performed her magic shows earlier. Just another of Argoth's many streets cross sectioned by houses, shoppes, and alleys. She finds some children who'd been waiting for her next performance, it's a nice feeling that at least someone appreciates her endeavor. What's more, no Ar-Guards are waiting to harass her for having left her things setup on the side of the street. It's but a few bits and bobs, a basket, and a ragged piece of cloth to sit on. But they are her wares, and they are all she has.

"Hey lady! Ya gonna do another show?!"

"Pleeeeease??" another chimes in.

There must be at least a half-dozen children pleading, but Avrel quietly goes about picking up her things much to the children's dismay. When she sees how disappointed the children are becoming, she reluctantly puts down her bag. Even if they aren't going to pay, she still can't say no. It'll be a while. Maybe she'll never even have to dance again.

She smiles, and begins to dance. And as she does, they stop their chatter and watch. Despite her weak and hungry physique, her dance isn't entirely without grace. Not to the bst that she can manage anyway, she only needs only to imagine moonlight and rain.

After a few moments, she begins summoning a spiral of light like white doves around her, much to the children's glee. She twirls a small 'magic wand' and begins channeling some small ice crystals catching the sun to create a dazzling display.

The children 'Oo' in awe in unison, always a good sign. One or two look well dressed too, if the job goes rough, she might get a birthday party off of this. She can dream anyway,

Before she can finish by evaporating the crystals into a fabulous mist she's startled by a harsh shout. "Hey, you!" What are you doing to our children!?" a slightly overweight human woman steps forward, as the would be mist instead falls like rain. "Haven't I told you before? I don't want you doing your lewd shows back here behind our apartments in front of our children!" She's serious. And the cooking utensil held in her hand looks like a painful weapon to contend with. Avrel stops her channel, and picks up her bag, not saying a word. "Yeah, just get out of here you half-bred tatterdemalion!" the woman yells to the young half-elf. Avrel shrugs it off and walks away, familiar with the exchange.

She's taken aback by the amount of volume and hullabaloo in this part of Argoth, given, she's rarely been there during the afternoon of Goldday, and never with intent to shop. Still, the buildings are far better cared for, and there are wagons of goods all around.

Avrel makes her way into the loud, craftsman circle in search of suitable traveling clothes and armor. Never in her young years has she had the opportunity to buy such nice attire. Her eyes widen to take in every vivid color as she looks upon the beautiful dresses in the windows. Not just dresses; cloaks, bonnets, corset tops, and shorter skirts of various flavor. All dreams she can now afford even before doing any bit of this job. It even crosses her mind that she could run with the money and be good for sometime, how she'd love to stick it to those noble sards in their tight purses.

No... she scolds herself, *That wouldn't be right. Or wise.* Maybe not *right*, but certainly *fair*, at least in her judgement. She thinks it over once more, but resolves to do her job.

For now.

Reclaiming her focus, she puts her focus towards the more utilitarian clothing until she spies a fetching blouse pattern demoed in the window. *But will it fit?* She enters the shoppe and quickly finds versions of that blouse on the display rack. A certain blue catches her eyes that are by her best guess, nearly the same shade.

"Ahhh... You like that, do you?" the shoppekeeper asks, making his way toward her. He has a slight lisp, but a kind face.

Even so... she reminds herself, *He's a man.* "Yes, sir." she responds shyly, guardedly.

He looks down at her coin purse and then back to her, "Royal coinage?" He asks, "Doing some adventuring are ye?" he inquires with a friendly wink.

"Mmhhmm." she hums. That *is* what she's planning on doing. A strange feeling comes over her, *Finally leaving this city...* she grins, *Me, on an adventure...* She touches the blouse with the cleaner of her dusty, rough hands, "Can I try this on?" she asks as she timidly points to it.

"Well... You don't look too underbathed." he chuckles, "If'n you turn it down, nobody need know a halfbreed wore it, hehe." the man says with a shrug. "Come inside." He leads her over to a changing booth.

"Thank you..." Avrel says guardedly. She timidly follows the stranger man and goes behind it.

"Yea'." he says as he takes a smaller version from a rack and holds it out for her to grab "Truth be told, I'd made it for young tweens perhaps barely of cycling age, but ye can't deny that it'll fit ye small half-elf frame pretty well!" he chuckles.

Avrel nods, if she had a gold piece for every time she's heard that... "Excuse me, sir, do you sell a corset to go with this?" Avrel says peeking her head out of the curtains.

"Oh hoho, sorry, I wasn't sure ye'd need one, being a scrawny one and all. Here ye go." he says handing it to her through the curtains, no doubt trying for a peek.

Avrel shifts her clothes around, the corset barely does anything as there is little shape for it to hold. "Nevermind, eh?" she says disappointedly as she passes it back out, "D'you have a breast wrap?" she asks, her hand held out through the curtain. She's only standing there for a moment but Avrel becomes nervous over it, "Sir?" she calls. The owner replies with a stretchy tube of cloth to her liking. She quickly pulls it over her boney ribs and pulls on the blouse. It's a pretty sky blue, with cute puffy shoulder sleeves, and a bit of lace around the neckline. "Thanks. Seems pretty good, I'll take it." she says coming out of the fitting booth.

The shoppekeeper smiles, "Very well, lass." he says, grabbing his finance file.

She inspects her bare legs, "Do you have any sort of leg guards?" Avrel asks meekly.

"Hmmm..." the man considers as he looks at her legs, "Did ye want pants?" he asks, but then dismisses. "I have these." the man says as he holds up two shiny leather pads. "I have skirts too." he laughs.

She's grown fond of the convenience of her makeshift leg wrappings. Adjustable, replaceable, and very cheap. "No, maybe just some fabric to make fresh."

"Sure thing then." The man forwardly grabs Avrel's thigh, "Now those, ye strap et on like thes." he explains. Avrel tries to not be bothered by his hands gripping her thighs.

"Umm..." She just wants to hurry it up. "Sure, I'll take those as well."

"Very well, lass." he chuckles warmly, "Ye might trim the excess strap off, your legs bein' so narrow."

"Yeah, ok." Avrel replies, rolling her eyes. "Do you know a guy who could sell me a staff?" she asks, handing him his fee. "I dunno, me cousin got staph from a mistress a few years back, but that's another story. Try the shoppe three doors down, they might find something for ye."

"Thanks, Sir" Avrel says with a little bow. She checks out and clutching her package, she exits the shoppe.

The crowd has thinned a bit, the sun has started to lower over the rooftops. She follows his instructions and walks down the square towards a craft shoppe.

Hmmm This looks to be the place. Avrel thinks to herself. Opening the door she sees a man with long, blond hair behind the counter polishing a cutlass. "um... Um... excuse me, the man in the clothing store said you sold mage staves?" Avrel sits in the doorway for a moment and is met only with silence. "Excuse me sir, I wish to buy-"

"I don't wish to show my wares to a mongrel such as yourself, kindly leave my shoppe." the man barks, leaning up his pointed ears are revealed.

Avrel becomes very apologetic, her hands wave as she says "Oh I'm sorry, I didn't mean to-"

"I said leave!" he exclaims, thumping his hand against his desk. "Whore-daughter!"

And so the small half-elf does, slamming the door behind her. Someday, she's going to break her promise on one of these sards. *One of these days...* She sits on the stoop, simmering for a moment when she sees that ranger, Zanvan, coming towards the shoppe. He walks up to the door before taking notice of her, though she imagines her hair is hard to miss. "What's wrong she-elf?" he mutters in a disinterested tone.

"Don't be such a rag, Mr Zanvan." she says turning her head away. "I'm not exactly a 'she-elf', as if it weren't obvious. That's my problem." she rasps, shifting her eyes towards the door to the shoppe.

"Well." he straightens his hat in some kind of 'cool guy' gesture. "I'm not one for paying too much mind to people's skin. A warm body is a warm body, to me." he says, but his eyes clearly look over at her ears. He pauses to light a pipe he holds up to his lips, "But some people are sards. Get over it or get under it." Zanvan says, stomping his match.

"I've become numb to it." she admits with a sigh, "But numbness doesn't help when my kin don't recognize me, eh? Not even so much as to allow me to buy something."

"Then I would suggest not referring to yourself as his kin." Zanvan says with a cough.

"Well, excuse me." Avrel counters, as she stands and turns to him. "I'm certainly not one of your kind either." Given that she's an elf of bleeding age and she's not at least his height, that alone should stand up to even the densest person's scrutiny. "Tell me, do I seem all *human*?"

"Stop trying to categorize yourself." Zanvan says quickly, though she can tell that his eyes trace up and down her ears. "You want that staff? You go in there, look him straight in the eye, and put it on his counter with his price."

"But, what about..."

He puts up a finger in a shushing, halting motion. The same *all* men seem to do when they see fit to explain things to the fairer sex. "Outside of complete self reliance, there's two great equalizers, elf: Money, and Death." he cuts her off. "I don't suggest you kill him, so bloody pay him. If you put it in front of him, he'd be stupid to turn it down."

She'd never thought of it that way... But that elf is still an elitist shiter, but he's still a bully and a sard, but it won't change how he thinks, "But!"

He doesn't hear her out, he simply opens the door for her and says nothing. She looks up to him, the tall, dirty, dirty blond haired, roguish looking man, and she's afraid. But, he might be right. He gives her a 'would you please hurry up?' sort of look as he holds the door open for her. Finally, Avrel takes a deep breath and hesitantly reenters the shoppe. She then goes about doing exactly what he'd said, and with the staff, she stands at the counter waiting for the elf to notice her.

But he chooses not to. "Ahem!" she finally gets tired of waiting.

The elf's eyes flick up to the sound but then try to ignore her, until it seems it hits him. "You bloody vagabond, I thought I told you to get out!" he shouts angrily.

Avrel stands there silently holding her ground until the elf man stands up and grabs her by her raggy shirt, "Listen you insolent wench, I'm not sure what you're trying to accomplish, you're garbage! *Human* garbage! I'll lower myself enough to sell to men, but never will I sell anything to the gene polluting likes of you!" he says, spitting in her face. She's unnerved, but she's had worse things of bodily origin cast upon her.

"Wow, what a sard." the ranger says, laughing as he leans on a beam in the doorway. "Here, *Knives* I'll buy it, since I'm only slightly inferior." Zanvan says tauntingly. Avrel watches him as she wipes the elf's spit from her cheek. The elf accepts the money, begrudgingly and forcefully tosses the staff at Avrel. If she'd not been so quick to catch it, it would have hit her in the face.

"Now please, leave!" he scowls as he goes back to polishing the cutlass.

Zanvan groans a sardonic, "Hmph." as she exits to the pointy eared sard's wishes.

Once she is outside Avrel breathes a sigh of relief. "Damn, how does he stay open, eh? Arse..." she mutters, but seeing the craftsmanship of the staff, she can sort of see how. He won't get her money again though.

A moment later, Zanavan is out too. Apparently having heard her. "He *is* on the elf side of the merchant square, I'm not sure what you were expecting." Zanvan says coldly. "I would think a mixed one like yourself would know of their disdain for you. Here."

He tosses her an over-the-shoulder holster for her staff. "Oh, thanks" She'd not thought of that. "Elf side?" Avrel asks after hesitating a minute, she hates to sound so ignorant.

Zanvan looks surprised, but then he appears to maybe understand that she's not had much experience shopping. "The elves have their own Merchant Guild here, since they are so few, they stick together. In this circle, this half is mostly their shoppes." the ranger says, pointing around.

"Oh..." Avrel coos, *It makes sense...* she supposes. "Wait! So that old guy in the dress shoppe set me up?!" Avrel asks resentfully. "He said I'd get what I was looking for three doors down, stupid old geezer!" Avrel says stomping her foot in angst. *Just like you men...*

Zanvan smirks, thumbing up the brim of his hat, "Well, young lady, did he say which way?"

Avrel's eyes widen as she feels her cheeks warm with blush. "...Oh."

Zanvan points to a shoppe across the way, "Yeah, a lady smithy runs the weapon smith shoppe over there, he probably meant for you to go to that one." he says.

"Get wrecked, mini-magus." says an only freshly familiar voice. Zanvan and

Avrel turn around to see that cleric standing there grinning ear to ear, his short dark hair contrasting with his white robes.

"When did you get here?" Avrel asks, taking a slightly defensive pose, she doesn't like when men seem to sneak up on her.

"Oh," he grins, "I was shopping too, I got this great deal on some ink!" The cleric proceeds to open a large sack containing dozens of ink phials and a large amount of parchment. "Check it out! Since *some* of us actually have to study and write down our spells." he says leering at Avrel with obvious jealousy. "Anyway, I have unused armor and a mace that I got in the monastery, so I figured I'd use my money to help get some general supplies." he adds.

"That was thoughtful..." Avrel sighs, not appreciating the assumption of her magical innateness based on her racial characteristics. Though it's true.

"Well." another freshly familiar voice chimes in, "He probably figured you'd have to spend most of yours on basics." the redshirted mage says from a ways off, coming towards them. "So guys, are we all ready to go on this glorious quest given to us by our king?"

"I think Avrel here still wanted to go to some other shoppes first, right?" Zanvan says looking towards her.

Avrel nods, "Yeah, the store I was supposed to go to-"

"Whatever." the redshirted mage says, tipping his red hat. "I'm going to get a room in the inn on the edge of town, see you all on the morrow!" He moves like he's very much in a hurry, and is quickly joined by another woman.

"Bye." Avrel waves passively.

Zanvan pays him no mind and leads the two across the square. Soon they find themselves under the shoppe's sign. Avrel stares at the words for a moment before Geric pushes her to the side. She'd almost gotten an idea of what it read.

"Kryptonite: Smithing and Enchanted Jewelry." the cleric reads aloud. He looks puzzled, "Enchantment?"

"Enchantment!" Avrel exclaims, "Mother told me certain jewels can enhance one's own magic power, or other things."

"...Neat" Geric says unenthusiastically. "You two have fun with magic gems, I'm gonna go get some rest." he says as he gives a slight bow and walks away.

Avrel then goes into the shoppe, followed by Zanvan who'd said a word to the cleric, and is greeted by a tall, dark haired lady with toned arms just as she's putting down a mallet.

"Can I getche' somethin' miss?" the smithy asks.

"Umm..." Avrel says shyly, "Yes, please, I uhh-"

"Hmmm I see, yeah, you're at least par' elf aren't you. Betchar lookin' for m'jewelry then?" the smithy says wiping the sweat from her brow," 'Sover there, by the belts an' bracers."

"Thank you." Avrel says appreciatively walking over to that corner of the store. Already she prefers this shoppe by far. Through a forest of racks holding knives and swords, axes and hammers is a display of jewels and jewelry. "Hmmmm..." *I suppose fire spell enhancement could be good.* she briefly considers, *But... the Lazulite of Levitation would be cool too.* And less offensive, she knows why she'd want a powerful fire spell. "Hmmm..." Avrel thinks out loud. *Storm Sapphires...* "Miss, can I get *these* please?" She points to the lazulite.

"Sure theng, an'thing else?" the smithy says chipperly.

"Well." she pauses as her eyes fall to some fancy vambraces and bracers. Some of them would make a pretty wristband if they weren't so aggressive looking. "These bracers are cool, but they're all very.. Weapon focused, do you have anything more decorative and less spiky?" Avrel asks.

"Hmm..." the smithy hums, "Eh might have one in the back, don't get many request for more *casual* bracers, they aren't ver'much in style." walking into a back room.

"What's the point of a *casual* bracer?" Zanvan points out adamantly. "You could literally get anything else more useful! A gauntlet, a magic medallion, or something! Just wear a bracelet if you want something pretty." he shrugs.

"But it might look nice". Avrel answers simply. "And it's better than just a band or circlet or something. I never had much money for decorative clothing like this before." she adds defensively. *None of your business what I wear...* almost makes it past her lips.

"Whatever." Zanvan sighs as he shrugs once more. "It's not my money." he mutters, not exactly for her to hear, but her ears pick it out just the same.

"Ahh, he'e et is." says the smithy as she comes back out. "Had one left. Bit o' gimcrack, but it sounds like that's what ye wanted." It's small, sort of a copperish tone with golden ridges along it's angles. She rather likes it, despite what the scoffing eyes of the ranger say. "That all fo' ye?" the smithy woman asks, handing her the bracer and lazulite earrings.

"Nope, that's all, thank you." Avrel smiles, handing over some gold pieces. "Here you go."

Outside, Avrel is looking through her bags when Zanvan bids her, "Goodnight." and turns and starts walking away before turning back once more. "We're meeting at the fountain by the southern gates, at dawn."

"Oh..." Avrel says with an insecure smile, "Okay then, see you". She was a little afraid he might put some movement on her, he seemed to talk very knowingly with the smithy before she left.

Zanvan makes his way away to his sleeping quarters across town, out of town, or wherever. He's a ranger, he'll find his way. Going her own way, Avrel keeps an eye out until she sees an old stable on the corner. She figures that it'll do, and heads towards it, sticking to the street torches when possible, but wary of any Ar-Guards.

There are none around, and she makes it to the stable and finds the door slightly open and with several empty corrals. Only two have horses sleeping in them. Avrel stacks up some hay and lays in it, dragging her new blouse across her body as a blanket.

2

  As the kid goes to wherever she's off to, he finishes going about his business. Obviously she's buying clothes and very basic things she needs, and the cleric has his particular spending habits too. All he himself needed in that area were some fresh arrows and a new string, which he now has. He opens the coin purse the knight had given him. *I suppose I can pick up some foodstuffs in the morning.* Not that they'll need much, they can hunt whatever else they'll need. But the kid obviously didn't have that on her mind, nor the cleric, and who knows what the fruity red mage is thinking. *Thinking...* Thinking over the whole group, he rather quickly concludes that it might be best if he plans their actions for the morrow, it doesn't seem to him that they will be. He'll need an up to date map, and while he's at it, he might as well start on any rumors to follow. 'Well begun is half done' and all that. He checks over his shoulder for hints of the sun's whereabouts, and once he has his barings, he sets off for a place to think.

  "Good evening, Zanvan!" the barmaid says warmly. He tips his hat and takes a seat in the back. She follows him, apparently it's not very busy for a Goldday. "Your usual?" she asks, leaning slightly on the side of his table in a very particular way. The lady with access to the tap is more thirsty than he is.
  "Please. And, Lavae..." he adds with a come-hither gesture, "Ask around, I need a map." he says, placing his hat down across from him and airing out his sweaty hair.
  "Whatever for?" Lavae winks. "I'd have thought a ranger wouldn't need one."
  "Yeah, yeah." he says coldly, "Just be sure that it's *up to date*."
  "Of course!" There are a few other patrons, she drops off his drink before it seems she attends to that other matter he'd asked for. But sure enough, she returns. "Here you are."
  That was fast. He sets his drink aside. "Thanks." he says, and he gets right to work. But she lingers, watching him as she leans invitingly over his table. Finally he takes his queue and looks up to her, "Yeah, I might not be back for a while."
  "Oh don't tell me..." she laughs, "They've got you on vagrancy?"
  He can't help but chuckle, "Yeah, as if..." he pauses to look around, just in case there's any 'off duty' Argothian City Guards, "Like that doddering old fool, Markell actually gives a damn about guys like me."
  Lavae lets out an all too familiar, flirtatious laugh. The kind looser women let out when something isn't especially funny, but they don't want their query to lose interest. He'll get to that. "Well, maybe not The King, but I bet The Princess would!"

He almost spits his drink over the map over her choice of words. "What makes you say that?" he asks as he quickly steadies himself.

"I heard just yesterday that Princess Catarina has taken over some of those things in The King's stead."

"That's not surprising." he agrees as he takes a deep sip. Hell, he's surprised that none of her cousins have tried to take the throne. "But no, Lavae." he finally corrects, finishing the mug and lighting his pipe, "I just have a little job, and it's always good to have *all* the routes at my disposal." If not for him, for the others.

"Smuggling?" she asks.

"Well, not exactly, it's just..."

"Well, don't be gone too long." she says breathily, "You know you're my favorite." She comes around and gently massages his shoulders.

"Well..." he might as well ask, who knows, she talks to half this side of the city. "I don't suppose you've heard any news about a 'Runeblade' or an enchanted aegis or anything, have you?"

"Can't say I have." she says with a feminine shrug. "But you know, there's the trading post on the east side of the forest, I've heard *tons* of fellows say they've gotten tips out there."

"Hm..." he hums, "I'll keep that in mind." *It was worth a try...* he sighs to himself, he can hope that the others will do their part in kind, maybe not the kid, but especially the two mages. "Bring me another mug and the stew." he says finally, "And... come get me after you close up." he smiles.

She flashes her eyebrows with a lidded smile, and finally leaves. Lavae is pleasant, but the nature of her particular figure is such that she's almost more attractive to watch from behind as she swayfully walks away from him. In any case, she's a warm body.

And with that, he can finally get to planning their route. And with a quick study of the map, Lavae's input might be onto something. He's been there a few times. East of Argoth, along the river, not too far from Ranger's Ridge, not far from Wraugroth as the black falcon flies. And, if that turns out nothing, it's just a hike north to Manitäria, and damn if the gnomes aren't just as talkative as they are traversive.

As he figures out how much miscellaneous supplies he'll have to pack in the morning, he smokes his pipe, and waits for Lavae.

***

"Cockadoodledoo!" screams some nearby rooster, and soon the quiet early morning sounds of a sleeping city turn into the bustling ballyhoo of milk carts and morning commerce of Market Day. He supposes it's time to get up.

    Geric rolls out of bed and dresses before quickly packing his things, including his recent accumulation of ink phials. He sees himself out of the loft, along the way down the steps from its small balcony coming by the owner.

    "Any time, Mr Cleric." the old, toothless lady smiles as she looks up from her pile of swept dust. "Men of The Gilded's work are always welcome to stay."

    "Thank you." he smiles as he tries to step by. She's a little clingy and close, almost like she expects some sort of blessing on her old bones in return. He does *not* have that much blessing to offer.

    "Have a blessed day!" she adds as she resumes her sweeping as he passes her by.

    "You too." he waves from the stair bottom.

    He gets his barings, and takes a good stretch as he looks into Argoth's busy streets. As he stands there figuring out which way to go, almost everyone passing tips a hat and bids him a good morning. He chuckles, *Amazing what some white robes can do.*

    First, he smells it. Then he sees it. Up across the other side of the street is a wagon of cured pork, surely heading to one of the Marketday breakfast bazaars. He can almost taste it as he rubs his palms together, just thinking about it with a side of good bread and a few eggs.

    With a lull in the crowd he prepares to dart across the street and follow the blessed wagon. However, as he's about to make his grand departure for breakfast and adventures beyond when a small stoogette in a black coat nearly knocks him over. Well, they might have if he weren't himself a holy beacon towering among mortals. She bounces off, quickly and fluidly picks up a fallen loaf of flatbread and a rolling bottle of wine, gives a rushed, staccato curtsey, and hurries away.

    "Watch it--" he shouts as they pass into the crowd. "My child?" He couldn't really tell her age, she seemed nervous, and had hopefully *bought* that wine at like barely ten bells in the morning.

    "Oh my." the old lady calls down, apparently still at work. Why she doesn't sweep the dirt off the side is beyond him. "Are you okay, Sir!?"

    "Yeah, thank you!" he turns and waits for another gap, hoping to follow the smell.

    "I swear, kids these days…" he can hear her quivering with indignation. "No respect for our guards, or men of the cloth, the girl's can't make a home proper, they just taste Midrosh cheese and wafers!!"

    "Okay, Broomer." he sighs to himself as he finds his traffic gap, and rushes through. He waves back one last time as he follows the smell.

The cleric's chase leads him to a food market, and after only a minute he locates the pork wagon. He waits while they refill the stand with the precious product and is first in line as soon as the stock is refilled.

"Just a moment!" the guy says.

"No trouble, my good fellow." Geric knows he must have had ordained timing to have gotten here just as they restocked from whatever smokehouse this wagon is from, so he doesn't mind waiting. He people-watches for a minute while he waits. A typical crowd, it looks like; some nobles, mostly common folk-- then, much to his dismay, he also spots that red suited mage, What's-His-Face, approaching his very same meat stand. "Not him..." he groans under his breath. He wants to say Dufus, but he knows that's not quite it.

"'Ere ye go!" the guy says. Geric promptly pays for his bacon, and while he wants the other accompanying sides, he's in no mood for that red mage guy right now, it's too early and that old lady already drained him.

The mage hasn't seen him yet, and short on time, Geric ducks under the nearest table.

Which immediately becomes occupied. But it's no matter to him, unbeknownst to the other, top-side occupants of the table, Geric enjoys his bacon. And solemnly enjoy the company of some fine maiden ankle with it. *Not exactly fitting of a cleric...* he admits to himself, but that's his own matter. He's on his knees, he figures that counts for something. So far, all things considered, he's having a fine morning, if a little unusual.

He's about half way done his slices of bacon when a small rat crawls up through his shirt and pops its little nose from his wide sleeve. At first he's able to stay calm, it's not a spider, just a little street rat. He'd prefer something more noble, perhaps a tick-eater, but confident in his skills, he fears no rat's bite. The rat crosses the line when apparently, the small varmit is making eyes at a strip of his illustrious bacon. His rather peaceful under-table breakfast quickly becomes an uncomfortable situation. The way he sees it, there's little chance of not creating a ruckus if he's to defend his bacon, which he certainly will. Quickly, he devises a plan to seem like an honorable hero in all this under-table bacon and ankle-beauty consumption, and it might just work.

"HAHA!" he yells as he bursts up from under the table, toppling it, and giving a bit of a surprise to the people who were seated there. He clutches the rat at arms length that they all might see it and bear witness to him and his apparent heroism. "*You*, I've tracked you far and wide, yon evil wizard! You who have schemed to peep and steal from many a young maiden, I have finally caught thee!" He tries to make his voice deep, his manners noble, but in the end it's a rather contrived signal of virtue, even by his standards.

"Shite!" the rat exclaims.

He's preparing what to say next when it sinks in. "....MmmmnWhaaaaat." Geric says taking a closer look at the rat who is now firmly in his grasp. *Maybe my plot wasn't so far fetched as I'd thought.* he grimaces.

"Is it so much to ask for a lonely old man to scrounge up some cheap meat and admire a little foot now and then?" the rat asks. The former occupants of the table draw back in disgust. Geric would too, but somebody has got to hold the darn rat.

"Well-- uh…" He's not sure where to go from here. "I uh… Demand that you transform yourself back and present yourself to the authorities!" Geric says, trying to regain his composure.

"Heh." the devious rodent chuckles. "Like I'm gonna listen to some quote-unquote 'cleric' who was sneaking peeks the same as me."

Geric breaks a sweat. "Lies, lies and slander, I'm not the the one on trial here, I demand-"

"You demand what? A whole thigh!? Chippu chippu chippu!!"

Geric then tossed the perverted varmit into the air, leaning all his weight back and bursting forth in a mighty punch, launching the pipsqueak into the air. At just that moment, a black-falcon promptly snatches him up by the tail. "You haven't heard the last of me, Cleric!… Ahhhhhhhhhh! So very high……..!" the rodent squeaks as he's lifted into the distance.

He smiles as the rodent and bird fade from sight behind the rooftops. *It's gonna be a good day.* he tells himself. Geric then turns toward the lady whose table he has ransacked with a bow. Only to immediately be slapped by the young maiden and whacked over the head by her suitor. Did he deserve it? *Probably.* But he also knows he's done his good deed for the morning. He pulls his bacon from his inner sleeve and bidding them a blessed day, as a cleric should, he sets off.

After such an eventful breakfast, Geric uneventfully goes to meet his new business comrades at the fountain near the city's southern gates. The red guy and green guy are there waiting for him, the ranger in green is chowing down on a deer leg, and the red mage is pacing. Had he foreseen this, he might have stopped for seconds along the way. He'd forgotten about that whole 'dawn' bit, but it seems so did the red mage and the stained-haired half-elf. He finds a stone, takes up a seat, and opens one of his pages of spells he copied from a book last night. He might as well commit these new spells to memory while they wait.

He's almost memorized one as not a word is spoken until the red mage asks, "Where is that rather trampy girl? She's late! What a tardy tatterdemalion she is, what an impure blooded-"

"Tiny." Geric adds to the list.

"Give it a break." the ranger chidingly cuts them off. "Although, she does seem rather late, even for a woman…" he comments as he's tossing away the bare leg bone. "Could be comin from the far side of the city, and it being Marketday…" he adds, "Just a thought, I don't actually know where she stays at night."

"Or with whom, dare I say." the red mage says dusting off his collar.

"Somehow I feel like she's not up for all that stuff." the ranger says, "She was pretty tense."

"If I were that tiny and scrawny, I'd be too!" Geric laughs, "I mean, she's so tiny, *she* probably fits inside the man, aren't I right?" he says, nudging the ranger, who seems unamused.

He pushes Geric away firmly. "You… Are a *cleric*, right?" he says in a confused tone.

"Ehhhh… More or less." Geric shrugs with a smirk.

"Ether way…" the red mage interjects, "Dare I say I hope she comes soon. It's not as if we can leave without *her*."

"I mean…" Geric grins, "*We could.*"

***

Avrel awakens when to a familiar nudging from a wet nose, followed by a hard slap from a flat tail.

"Candice?" Avrel says, her voice froggy, as it is in the morning. The fluffy brown blur comes into her half-elf eye's sharp focus.

"Chippu chippu!" says Avrel's happy familiar. Her saber-like, yellowed incisor teeth smile as her little nose twitches with affection.

"Yeah well, I thought…" that quick she loses her train of thought. Avrel rubs her eyes, and yawns, "Did you find yourself some food?"

"Chippu chippu!" the happy, brown beaver says, flopping her tail around eagerly.

Candice always did like a good aspen log. "That's good, eh? Sorry I haven't been able to give you food myself recently." Avrel says, petting her beaver behind her tiny round ears.

"Chippu." she squeaks, inquisitively sniffing and waddling around Avrel's packages and new clothes.

"Thanks for being so understanding." she smiles as she taps the beaver's dark little nose. "That… reminds me, I've got big news! I--" Suddenly it hits her, and suddenly she's aware that it's far past dawn. "Oh! OH!!! I'm gonna be late!" Avrel says attempting to jump to her feet, instead flailing onto the floor. "Wait!" She catches herself mid panic, this isn't the stable she'd bedded down in the night before. *Where am I?* Avrel picks up the strange blanket she was wrapped in and starts to shudder, "Where did I get this? Why was I sleeping in this canopy!?" She looks around at the foreign deck, she's used to sleeping in various nooks and crannies around the city, but she's also accustomed to waking where she'd laid down the night before.

The dress shoppe owner comes out of the back door to greet her, "Oh, hi little miss, would you-"

"*Ah!*" Avrel shrieks, her ruddy hairs on end as she thinks out all the things he might have done to her.

"I guess ye don't want 'ny breakfast?!" he says in a sad tone.

"Why am I here?" Avrel says furiously, with a subtle, magical tingle around her fingertips. She looks around and it seems as if Candice scurried away.

"Ah, I saw ye sleeping in that stable and thought you'd deserved better." the man says with a friendly smile. "So I took you here and made y' comfortable."

Avrel looks at him suspiciously, she's not sure if it's a real smile. "You didn't do anything funny, did you?" she asks acquisitively.

He chuckles. "Young miss, I'm an old dressmaker, if'n I *really* wanted to grab a feel now and again, I could. And to that end, you need worry not."

That fact doesn't comfort her much, in fact it sounds like what she'd expect of a man. "...Ok." Avrel says cautiously.

"Ye want some breakfast?" he asks again.

The glowing tingle around her fingers subsides, and her stomach growls. "Sure." she sighs, "But I'll shoot fire if you try anything untoward." she lies, but she'll make him pay just the same, she has a metal staff now.

The dressmaker laughs and pats her head, "No need, lass. Come."

It goes against her better judgement, but with a heavy sigh, she goes over to him. It feels wrong, but she'll try her best to be courteous. A free meal is a free meal, and she's in no frame of mind to be picky.

"Chippu?" she hears from behind a flower pot.

Avrel looks to Ralph's back, as he heads for his kitchen, thinking about how she's occasionally seen beaver-pelt hats and the like. "Maybe stay here." she says softly.

Candice nods, and hides once more behind the flower pot.

Aside from his startling her and Candice, he's fairly nice, for a man especially. Attentive, and a very good cook it seems. As they are most of the way through a nice morning meal the man introduces himself as Ralph.

"Nice to meet you Mr. Ralph." she replies in kind. "I'm Avrel Lavian. I uh... I do magic shows, street performances, that sort of thing." she explains shyly. She has no shame in what she does, save that others often look down upon her for it. Elitist shiters.

"Fancy that." he says warmly, "Thought you looked familiar, prolly seen ya around. If'n you do street shows, why the traveling clothes?" he asks. "Saw ye purse, got a king's quest or something? Do ya?"

Suddenly Avrel jumps up, barely able to contain herself, "*Shite*! I need to meet those guys! And I still haven't changed into my new clothes!" She gulps down the rest of her porridge and runs for the door, "Thanks, Sir!" she turns briefly to yell back to him.

"You're welcome lass!" he replies, sounding like a humorous smile. "Oi! Fat rat!" she barely hears him yelp, and a moment later she's joined by Candice. Together, they make a long, southward run through Argoth. After the first several crowded squares of rushing wagons, Avrel picks up the beaver, and carries her most of the rest of the way.

Short of breath, and her ears screaming with the rushing of blood, Avrel nears the fountain to overhear Zanvan talking to the cleric. "You... Are a cleric, *right*?" he asks.

The tall cleric replies, "Ehhhh... More or less." he sneers with his cocky, shitey smile.

Zanvan sighs and face-palms. She feels like she's missed something. But then, obviously she has, she's *late*.

She goes right up to them and then drops her head. She bows over a long minute trying to catch her breath before she can utter, "Sorry I'm late!" She's not had a run like that since being short almost ten coppers on a meal, and given the part of town, she had no interest in what manner of work she'd be asked to do to repay it.

"The hell is that?" Geric exclaims. She looks up and he's pointing to the breathless beaver standing next to her. Zanvan seems a little surprised by the cleric's colorful language.

"What?" Avrel questions, "Oh, Candice? She's a nature spirit who came to me as a child." she explains. "I was bathing in the river not long after my mother passed and..." suddenly the warmth is gone. *Mother...*

"But why is it a *beaver*?" the cleric asks, his tone is dry, unamused, and somewhat critical. Just the type of subtle judgmentalness she'd expect of a cleric.

"Because... She's a beaver?" Avrel says with a touch of heat, "She swam up to me, and since then she's been my friend."

"Hmph…" Zanvan sighs. "That stands up to scrutiny."

"And" Avrel quivers, "You can't just ask why somebody is a beaver, arse." she retorts under her breath.

"MmmI just didn't know you had a familiar, is all." the cleric shrugs with a tone, "Much less a smelly water-rat."

"She is not a--" Avrel strides up to him only to back off, she doesn't even come up to his shoulders. "Jealous?" she asks from a safe distance.

He gives her an intense look over a pregnant pause. If she recalls, a lot of humans who use magic have to recite words of power and memorize spells. His reaction tells her that she's guessed right.

"Are we ready to go?" the redshirted mage asks, having been tapping his foot all the while.

"I am." she apologizes once more, even if she's been here for several minutes now. "Sorry for making you wait." But it seems nobody is really paying her any mind.

"Alrighty then!" the cleric exclaims, "let's go already!"

She crosses her arms, "So Mr Zanvan, any ideas on where to start?" she asks.

The ranger nods down as if he's about to say something when the redshirted mage gets very close to her. Too close for her liking for a man she doesn't know. Shite, for a man in general. "Miss Avrel… Lavian was it?" he asks, but doesn't let her respond, "Tis an elven artifact, mightn't you know something off it?"

She steps back, "Can't say I have." She'd never even heard of those things before yesterday, but she doesn't want to seem ignorant.

"Truly? Never before seen a blade of pure arcane crystal around a hilt?" he follows.

"No." she grunts, "I haven't." And he's really getting on her nerves.

"Mother or… Father? They never spoke of --?"

"Bug off, like he did!" she finally says with a strong shove.

Zanvan finally puts an end to it. "Stop." he commands, just before she'd have made the Redshirt stop.

"We could check around town." Geric comments, "Hard to say, we don't know how much she already has been sniffing out."

"Tell me, Master Geric…" the Redshirt asks, "Does your healer's guild bear any insight? T'would assume you've asked."

The cleric shrugs, "MmmNot really…?"

"Are you sure, elf?" he asks.

And just as she's about to test her new staff on him, Zanvan again intercedes. "Well, what about you, Rufus." the ranger asks, tipping his hat up by it's brim "According to that knight, you Redshirt mages are something special."

"And rightly so!" he arrogantly answers, "But as I harken all the way from Astaroth, across the sea, I know very little of the whispers on this shore."

The cleric grabs their attention with a hand wave, "Well, if The Aegis was supposedly lost in a 'Great Chasm', I suggest that we start with your mother!" the cleric heartily laughs to himself, only stopping when he comes to realize that everyone has stopped simply to give him a look. "But in any case, that'd put it in the far north."

Avrel takes a seat on the edge of the fountain, and here she'd rushed, only to be surrounded by fragile, male egos afraid of making a wrong decision, and jokes at womens' bodies' expense. "So what? Back to the taverns?"

"No." The ranger answers, "I think it's safe to say we won't find out much here. If it were that easy, she'd not be outsourcing it to other people. And I did a bit of that last night already."

"True, true." the redshirted mage nods, "And ever looking to do good, I've heard nothing within this city, even with my ear close to the ground for such things. I suggest we look elsewhere." Yet again he looks over at her. "From whence did your elven heritage come? Any relations there?"

"Listen, you--" she spares her more cutting insults, "My mother is gone. Her family cut her off when she married my father, even after...." she doesn't care to get into all of that either. "As for *elves*..."

"Enough!" Zanvan puts a pipe in his mouth and then lights it. "I think a good bet would be to visit the gnomes." he says with a smooth sigh of smoke

The gnomes? Avrel questions. She's seen a few in her life; small, about half a typical human's height, usually driving a wagon. "Why them?"

"Among other things..." he begins to explain with a smokey sigh, "Gnomes get around, many are travellers and traders. It's possible they might know something. Or perhaps know someone who might."

The cleric snickers, "Sounds like a plan that requires very *little* thought." he puts in. "Speaking of which, Advil, what do you think?"

"*Avrel*." she frys, lowly.

Zanvan shows them his map, "If we take a route I have in mind, there's one other stop we can make." he says pointing to something that's doubtful the others could make out. "Unless anyone has a better plan, I'm going to insist we start there." he says.

"So... East?" the cleric asks.

"South." Zanvan quickly corrects. "Then east, and north."

"Through the woods?" Avrel catches, "But..." She looks to Candice, "I've never been very deep into the woods..."

"Well, elf." Zanvan sighs, smokily, "It's time you have."

"Tis decided!" the Redshirt exclaims.

"But--"

The cleric gives her an unwarranted pat, "Come on, knife-ears." he says as he goes to the ranger, who is apparently in charge. "Let's go already!" he waves. Zanvan puts his pipe out, and the Redshirt goes too. Through the woods it is.

The three men set off at the ranger's word, and she does follow, but she follows slowly, looking back towards the city once more before heading steady on towards the city gates. She fears this city, she even *hates* this city, but she knows it. It's still home, which the wilderness is not.

But it if affords her the opportunity that is promised, she'll do it. She must. Cautiously, timidly, and hesitantly she goes into the wilderness beyond Argoth's gates.

***

As the four of them and the kid's pet make their way out of the Argothian city gates barely a word is spoken. She tries to sure up their names, and such, but that's about it. Which as a man of the woods, and a lover of soft, sylvan quiet, Zanvan can appreciate. After listening to the cleric and that gaudy red mage chatter while waiting for the girl, he was a bit afraid of what this journey might entail.

He leads them down the main road heading southward out of the city towards the Argothian River. Along this way they pass a few carts that are heading towards the city before reaching the first of several bridges. The kid's beaver takes the opportunity to swim across, merely because she can. He would guess that with her owner living in the city, the beaver might not swim as much as it'd like to. But then, if the creature is magical, all bets are off. With three magic users in this party, he's not going to inquire, what he needs to know will surely come out. And hopefully, he can keep it straight when it does.

Upon reaching the far side of the next bridge Zanvan pulls out a map, not that he particularly would need one for his own purposes, but for the others' sake. He's not sure why, they've barely left the city, and there are still a few cabins and such scattered along this way, but the kid especially seems wary.

And the cleric of all people, *ornery*.

"Hey Zanven!"

"-*van*" he corrects

"Vän" he enunciates, almost with an exaggerated elven or some accent. "If we're heading into the forest, maybe Anvil should go first." says the cleric. "MmmBeing a knife-ear and all, they're all about those trees, you know.."

Zanvan looks over to the cleric with a look of wonder. Wondering how long he might be able to put up with that. The little half-elf girl blushes as she dismisses the suggestion. "I've never been very far outside of the city, only to a few of the nearby streams." she says, still somewhat to Zanvan's surprise. He'd have thought she might only go into the city for whatever work she does and live outside, almost like himself. "And my name is Avrel!" she fires back. "Av-rel."

"Mmm... Yeah, whatever." the cleric shrugs.

The kid, Avrel, blushes and looks up at the cleric with a bemused glare. He can't blame her, Zanvan finds himself doing the same. He's got to be the least cleric-like cleric he's ever met. Not that he has spent very much time with them, only that he keeps them occupied with the confessions of young women.

Thus, they cross the final bridge heading south into the dark, old forest. The sounds of creatures can be heard all around, punctuating the constant trickle coming from the small creeks. To him, it's nothing, music to his ears, in fact. The cleric seems to pay it little mind, same as the red mage. The kid, despite her elven half, still seems a little wary.

Despite her natural attraction to the woods in her blood, the wilderness very clearly fills the girl with fear. If the city is much of all she's known for her life, he can imagine that she might feel very strange. "So, elf." he says.

"Half..." she replies.

"Kid." he scoffs, "How old are you, might I ask?" Admittedly, it's not an uncommon question of him to any decently attractive young body, however, in her case, it's genuine curiosity and little more.

"*Avrel.*" she first insists. "And about..." she seems so confidently ready to answer, but she takes a long pause to think about it, and counts fingers.

"Damn, Zanvan." the cleric nudges, "She's *old.*"

"Even at a hundred she'd be young for her kind." Zanvan says, brushing off the cleric. "Well, *half* her kind." Not that age ever matters for elf-kind, from what he's seen, they'll look like a matured twenty-something for all their long lives -- nearly ten times that of humans.

"I think..." the girl, Avrel finally answers, "Somewhere just under twenty?" So she's a bit to go, he'd assume. Time to fill out maybe. He's no interest in her anyway, she's all bones, not the *elegant* slenderness of the average elf. And certainly not the pearly-fair skin or hair.

"You *think?*" the cleric scoffs, haughtily.

"Ahh." the red-shirted mage chimes in, "Therefore, she *is.*"

"Predictable that you'd ask the only *woman* her age." she pouts, "As if for men, it doesn't matter." She crosses her arms, "Men are just big children anyway."

"Says the one the size of a big child!" the cleric says quickly, there going the chances of a thoughtful rebuttal. He might have at least quoted the old adage of the aging of milk and wine.

"I was only curious." Zanvan answers, ignoring the cleric. "Your kind are hard to tell." Still, an elf- a half-elf of almost twenty and almost no experience of the woods, he finds it a little sad.

A few moments of later he motions to them to slow. "Watch where you walk." he quickly warns the party, "It gets swampy in here sometimes, don't go getting stuck." Likely it's the kid that'd be in the most danger, but he won't go there.

"What exactly are we doing here anyway?" Avrel asks. "I thought you said the gnomes were to the east."

"If I remember correctly…" and he knows he does, "There should be a very old, giant tree down this path, once we find that, we take the fork heading north." Zanvan explains. He'll double check the map later.

***

They continue on until a brief lunch, and then on until evening and at night they stop, and eat once more. That night, she makes sure she is distant from them. They talk some amongst themselves, and then they sleep. If she's honest, she knows she fears them. And she should. She knows what men can and *will* do when they want something. It's a simple job, and that's all. She has Candice for company. Men will leave, but Candice will always be there. She never uses the bedroll, instead she falls asleep against a tree petting her dear friend, who ends up sleeping on her lap until morning.

The forest grows darker as they go deeper, but it makes little difference to her eyes. And as the initial fear fades away, Avrel finds it eerie but beautiful. Like an old friend welcoming her back from the war of survival in that horrid city of men. The cleric and Redshirt seem as if they couldn't care less. And to Zanvan, it seems routine. Of what little she really knows of ranger life, that does seem like something she should expect.

But this night, Candice urges her to be less distant. There's a bit of a clearing, and Zanvan has made a small fire, over which he cooks some roots he dug up along the way. It's a long and hard thought, but the beaver is very insistent, she's like the mothers she's seen trying to get their children to make new friends.

"Okay." she finally agrees after unrolling her bedroll. "But I want you ready to bite them." she commands.

The Candice chatters her chippus, and nods before grinning with her incisors very visible. Despite the assurance, Avrel keeps her staff ready.

"See?" She hears the cleric even as she's still a few feet off, "I knew if you cooked some vegetable roots she'd join us."

Suddenly she's more than a little off put by their attention. The ranger who is puffing away at his pipe waves, as does the Redshirt. "Care to join us?" the ranger says, not sounding much like he cares one way or the other.

"Yes," the cleric says in a nasally voice, "Miss Leavening, please grace us lowly humans with your divine, elven presence."

Already she has a mind to leave, but Candice thwaps her ankle, and takes a spot by the modest fire. She herself sits in a wider gap between the redshirted mage and the ranger.

"I saw you fall asleep on that tree last night." the Redshirt says.

"Yeah, sorry." she says, "I was…. Tired."

"And here I thought elves didn't *need* sleep." the cleric says. Apparently he's been reading a book as she watches him turn a page.

Before she can answer for herself, Zanvan corrects the cleric. "They don't need *as much*."

"Half-elf." she further corrects. Maybe it depends on how they are raised, but she carries on the typical pattern of her human mother.

Avrel can tell the redshirted mage is trying to catch glances at her, if he does it again, she'll call him out on it.

He does. Just as Zanvan hands out the cooked roots, of course. Shitey timing, but the root isn't half bad. "Thank you." she says.

Zanvan nods as he gives the others out. "You'd be surprised what's edible in the forest, kid."

But somehow, she's not surprised. It seems that with every moment in this place, a soul memory long locked away and forgotten is being uncovered. She'd say maybe it's her elven half, but then, she wonders, *What's his excuse?*

She catches the Redshirt making one more quick look. "Got something to say…" she pauses, "Rufus?"

"I?" he asks, "Nay." But obviously he lies, he's flushing with guilt.

"Oh…" the cleric looks sly as he leans over to the redshirted mage's ear, "You like to 'nibble the knives', do you?"

"Certainly not!" he says abruptly, disgustedly almost. More like, if anything, he finds elves repulsive.

"I mean, I can't blame you." the cleric says, sitting back straight, "I mean Avrel here isn't even a good specimen; short, ill tempered, and…" he pauses. "And whatever it is with the stained hair."

At least he got her name right. "It's not stained." she rebutts coldly, just the same. "My mother had copper hair, I-"

"That's *not* copper, knifey." Geric says as he quickly reaches over with his tall body arms and plucks a hair from her head.

"I *did not* give you permission to touch me!" Avrel barks, swatting his hand away. Candice already has made her way to the cleric's sandal, ready to put a bite through his big toe.

"Calm your points." the cleric dismisses as he begins to look at the hair. "Hm." he hums "All the way down to the roots."

And then he bloody hands it back to her. "*What* the *hell?*"

"I don't want it." he shrugs.

She finally throws a look at Zanvan, who's been kind enough to step in before. He's sharpening a knife and smoking, he's not paying them any mind.

"Tis a beautiful shade." the redshirted mage comments. "Like crimson flame."

"Well, here." she leans over and plants it in his hand, "I'll make more." she scowls as she glares at the cleric, who seems sardonically amused.

"Alright, cleric--" Zanvan starts to say.

"Geric." he corrects.

"*Geric.*" he grunts, "Leave the kid alone."

"Thank you." she says, nodding.

The ranger scoffs, "I don't feel like dealing with him losing an appendage." Zanvan says, pointing out Candice whose jaws are widened and ready to bite the whole of the cleric's big toe cleanly off.

"Yikes!" he retracts his foo, leaving his sandal behind.

Avrel's had enough anyway. "Come on, girl." she pats the side of her leg guard and the beaver comes. She's about halfway to her bedroll when she turns back to them, "She's watching you." she warns, "And she'll take off more than a toe if you all act on your sick instincts!"

They are good and silent for a moment after having their innate toxicity called out and the source of it threatened, so she goes to her bedroll and lies on it. As her eyes fall shut she can hear, and practically see the cleric waving, "Goodnight, dear."

She repeats it, lowly, "Goodnight... Dear." but to Candice, who snuggles under her shoulder. The night is quiet but for a deep, far off rumble she only hears when her ear is to the ground. Through that, Candice's soft, rhythmic breaths draw her to sleep, just as her mother's had on those first terrifying nights on the street.

On the morning of the third day, she is as tends to be, a little behind the others save for Candice, who is by her side. But up ahead, she can see that they've stopped. Coming into the wide clearing herself she can see that they've at last reached the massive tree. It's a very old tree, fully demanding the respect of the path makers who laid the paths around its proud and prestigious girth. As wide as a city row house at least, Avrel briefly fantasizes of living in such a tree, wondering if perhaps it's great years of wisdom would be imparted to her. It strikes her strange that she's so seldom had feelings like this, having lived in that city. Strange, and a little lonely, for surely these men don't understand. And surely to Candice, it's merely the beaver's equivalent of a fatted calf.

Perhaps her thoughts of food are influenced by the men preparing to stop for breakfast. They've barely begun for the day, but they stop just the same. Apparently they aren't used to pushing through mild hunger.

"Alright." the cleric says, "Now we just head east, right?" he asks as their simple meal of bread and preserves comes to a close. Simple maybe by their standards, but a delight to her.

"Dare I say..." dares the Redshirt. "Which way is east, good ranger?"

Zanvan dismissively brushes them off, with a special attention towards Avrel, it's like he could tell she was unnerved a bit, and he goes to circle the tree. "Most of the moss is on this side, this should be north then." he shouts, calling them towards him, "Eastern path should be over there." he says confidently, and very surely.

Avrel's conflicted. One one hand he's a man, but she does find it in herself to respect his more naturalist ways. She might even be envious, the darkness of these woods fills her with fear as much as wonder, but he has peace with it. *How did a man become more attuned to nature than a...* her thought stops, and she sighs, *Half-- elf.* The sylvan green though, it tugs at her heart. And many trees are still dormant, how much more will she feel this deep calling to see them when they are all lush?

"Pack up, let's go." Zanvan tags her. She still has half a biscuit left, but it seems everyone else has packed while she was lost in thought. But better that than lost themselves. Alone in the woods with a bunch of men is one thing; *lost* in the woods with a bunch of men is something she doesn't even want to think about. She sighs in relief as Zanvan shows them his map before they set off, but she is a little nervous still.

Not that the bloody cleric does any part to help. "Aww, don't those ears tell you how to navigate the forest?" the he asks as he flicks one of Avrel's points.

"You are rather cunning, Mr Zanvan." the Redshirt praises, "Despite being a ruffian ranger, you've earned the respect of a Redshirt." he says with his hand held to his chest in some gesture.

"...Great." Zanvan sighs, as he takes the lead once more.

A few miles down this eastern path, Avrel's half-elf ears catch some rustling in the nearby brush. She reacts, but it seems the others don't hear it. "Guys?" she says softly. They turn back and give her a look before continuing, as usual, men don't believe women. A moment later, she hears another rustle, and Zanvan raises his hand ordering a halt.

"Shh…" he hisses, and holds a hand to his ear.

"I didn't hear anything." says the cleric.

A moment later, Candice scurries back from further up ahead and sits by Avrel's leg. "Should we run?" Avrel whispers as she lowers herself.

"I'm not sure." Zanvan whispers back as he crouches, "Just stay quiet." It seems that ranger hears it too, the other men listen. Typical.

It stops for a moment and it looks like Zanvan is about to continue on when they hear an inhuman, cat-ish chatter from the bushes after a sharp twig snapping there abouts.

"I for one am not afraid." the Redshirt exclaims in a proud and boisterous tone. "Come at us you ravenous brutes!"

At his words, a pack of small, thin, lizard-like humanoids emerge from the bushes surrounding the path. They have scales, but also tufts of brownish fur around their snouts, and dark eyes. They are armed with primitive spears, but spears nonetheless. "You come for our candles, yes? We no let you take candles! You no take candle!" the largest, about her height, cries out.

Zanvan draws a bow, and an arrow from his quiver. It seems everyone else is quicker to draw their weapon than Avrel. It takes some finesse for her to pull her staff from its holster on her back.

"Hey now!" the cleric protests, "We don't want your candles… I mean… not unless they sell for a lot or something!"

"We just want to pass through!" Avrel says fearfully, "We swear!" Having never seen a kobold before, She'd rather not have to fight one, especially if they are intelligent enough to speak.

"Don't bother." Zanvan orders, "Kobolds always give trouble to woodland travellers. Paranoid idiots."

"Then let their paranoia be their downfall!" Rufus, the Redshirt sneers as he flourishes his rapier, drawing the kobolds attention onto him. He tauntingly pokes his rapier around the air in front of him and shouts, "Come at me foul beasts!" In his hand it seems he's brandishing a spell that looks almost like a fire made of shadow. "Ha! Curs! Have you not the courage to face a Redsh-?" His words are suddenly silenced as a kobold javelin pierces his throat.

"Rufus!?" Avrel cries out. It has happened so suddenly that she is unsure of what to do. He twitches, he gurgles something, and he falls, spilling blood into the earth. The other two seem not to care, they stand guardedly, and readily. As the kobolds attack, the cleric holds up his mace and Zanvan pulls the arrow in his bow.

And yet she is still, her companions are fighting, and one lies dying, gasping about a place in a coming kingdom until he simply--- stops. She is stricken by fear as she touches the body which has already gone pale, he's dead. Barely a week into their quest and he's dead. She should think it right, his own bloated masculine ego left him open to the strike, but she's not thinking it. She's sad, and terrified. He heckled her, but he *talked* to her unlike so many. Bewildered, she turns to her other companions.

Zanvan dispatches the leader kobold with an arrow between the eyes but is quickly chased back as he can't seem to distance himself from the kobolds for a clear shot. Coming to her senses as the shock of Rufus's death wears off, Avrel pulls herself up, and quickly moves to Zanvan's aid, as does the cleric after he smashes one who'd singled him out. The kobolds can speak, but they aren't intelligent. And while she hasn't much experience in fighting, she manages to block their strikes and serve as a distraction long enough for Zanvan to take easy shots at them. Or for the cleric to bash them over the head, even the cleric proves a better fighter than she is, it seems. But no matter how skilled they are, they can't overcome the numbers. About six had initially surprised them, and now there are at least twice that. If nothing changes, they'll be overrun. And she dares ask herself how often she's heard of the fates of women captives.

But she has her own way to answer that, even if it means breaking a promise made to her mother long ago. She's no choice. Use her magic to attack another living thing; or die, or worse.

"Back!" she yelps as a tingle in her fingers is joined by an orange shimmer.

Candice chatters a protest, but Avrel ignores it. It *must* be done.

"Guys! *Back!*" she warns again. She can feel the heat as she puts her anger and her resistance to fate of death or pain into her magic, a flame spell she'd use in sparing amounts in shows or to light a candle. It burns brightly as a ball of arcane power in her hand, she tries to aim it though her arms are shaking, and she releases it.

The flame spreads out like a dragon's breath, scorching the kobolds nearest to her, and closing her eyes from the brightness of the fire, she lets out a second burst. A third is cast, and a fourth is stayed by the cleric, who lowers her hands and snaps her from her intense focus.

"Hey!" he shouts at her, giving her a startle. She shudders, and looks at him. And slowly the fight of flight fades. "Not bad, knife-ears." he says with an uninvited pat to her shoulder. "MmmMaybe look where you cast next time." he smiles.

She looks to Zanvan who is using his cloak to beat out some brush that is beginning to catch fire.

"Yeah, kid." Zanvan groans, "I'd appreciate it if you don't burn down our woods."

She can only nod, but Avrel nods sincerely. She's never used her magic so directly at another person, or being. Not with intent to kill. "I'm sorry..." she says to them and the woods, but also her mother. She looks to one of the streams hoping to rectify her mistake. "I'll get some water!"

"No!" Zanvan barks. "The last thing I need you to do is go ripping the streams from their beds or something."

"Yeah, he's got it anyway." the cleric shrugs. "No need to show off." he bends over her with a sardonic grin before going to help the ranger himself.

"Candice!?" Avrel calls after her eyes linger on the bloodied body of their companion.

"Chippu." the beaver chatters back, popping from an unscathed bit of brush.

"Oh good." she sighs as she sits on a stone and takes the beaver onto her lap, *You're safe...*

She sits to the side trying to regain her composure as the two men also take a moment. It's strange, she cares nothing of him and barely knew him, but his death is unnerving. She's dealt with deaths both fast and slow, even her mother, but she'd not expected anything so soon, nor so sudden. They all might have died had she not broken the promise to her mother. Avrel wonders, *How many times will I have to?*

"So." Zanvan says, only slightly less strongly than his usual self, "What about the stiff?"

The stiff? Disgustingly callous are the hearts of men, of that she's quickly reminded. Likely, the Redshirt, Rufus would not have cared at all if it'd been her passing. And even if the cleric's assertion was true, men care nothing of women they lust for; only that they dutifully accept their seed until their bodies wear out but his line is preserved. Men know only how to dispose, and nothing of disposability. Should she take the highroad, she wonders, or treat him as he would her?

"I can preserve his body if we want to carry him back." the cleric, Geric suggests.

"That's doubling back." Zanvan quickly shoots down, "If you're going to cast a spell over his body, cremate him and be done with it."

The cleric nods evenly, but Avrel speaks her piece, "Return him to the soil." She'll take the highroad. She'll choose to care, at least a little.

The men share glances but after the cleric shrugs they get to work. Avrel and Candice find some rocks in the stream as the men move some of the softer dirt, and they bury Rufus the Redshirt by the side of the path. It's marked only by the river stones making up for the shallow grave until Zanvan sticks the mage's thin sword above the gravesite. For a moment they are all silent for their fallen comrade. She herself, still putting to rest her distresses, puts his red hat over the handle of the blade for as long as it might stay. She steps back and looking down at the earth, she sighs. Aside from that, it seems that the whole forest is silent for a long moment.

Then, she hears footsteps, and she looks up to see the cleric's back. "Really..." he says calmly, "No sense in wasting a good hat."

At first she doesn't quite trust what she thinks she's seeing. "Geric!" she gasps, "P-put that back right now."

He just goes ahead and puts it on. "Fits well too."

"Zanvan, I-" she turns for help, but he's just smoking his pipe.

"Kid." he says, "Haven't you ever wished you had a hat for those ears of yours on a cold night?"

"Well, of course." she answers, "But--!"

"Rufus doesn't need it."

He has a point, but she has a better one, "Well yeah... But It should go to someone who needs it!" she turns to the cleric, her jaw locking to a grit, "Not some cleric who-" She stops. *What's the point?*

The cleric just raises his shoulders, "Hey, it's a nice hat." he says matter of factly. "Waste not, want not." He takes it off and just for a second hovers it over her, briefly covering her eyes in dark, red shade. "See, it wouldn't fit you anyway."

She steps back as it's removed, and walks away wordlessly, still trying to make sense of Geric, the cleric's actions. He's half right and that's part of what bothers her.

After a few moments of deafening silence, Zanvan tags them each. "Come on, let's keep moving."

She can't imagine him being so cold, so emotionless. He's *dead*, and they are to just carry on? Not that she knew him, Rufus, more than a few days, *But still.*

"Come on, knife-ears, the beaver's out pacing you." the cleric calls from ahead.

She glances back once more, and thinks no more of it. He's not the first she's ever laid to rest in a nameless grave in the woods outside of Argoth. And, it's not as if she didn't take what she needed from that body, even if then it was more rightly hers to begin with. Just the same, maybe that's what's hurting her so, that it reminds her of that; that it reminds her of other graves in similar Argothian woods.

"Cleric..." she asks. "Geric." she adds, more personably.

"Yeah, April?"

She'll bite her tongue on that, his voice sounds sincere for once. "What about his family?"

Geric turns to her rather straightly, and puts his hand on her shoulder. "Don't worry about it." he says, and then turns, "He probably barely knew them." he says, almost happily, but all around in a very ambiguous tone. And she couldn't see his face. Candice is up by Zanvan already, so Avrel quickens her pace, and leaves what transpired to lie.

3

Having finally made it to the other side of the forest, they've stopped for the evening, and Zanvan is making them a fire. Avrel lies back into the grass along the roadside and breathes deeply the fresh, open air. Not so stagnant as the depths of the inner woods, and not so dirty as Argoth's. It feels wonderful.

"Care to do the honors, Geric?" she hears Zanvan ask. She looks over and his firepit is all done save for the fire itself.

The cleric, lost in a book, takes a moment to respond. "mmWhat, me?" he asks, as if only now the words reached him.

"No." Zanvan scoffs, "Rufus."

"He's dead." the Geric shrugs. Zanvan looks unamused, and Avrel is still unnerved by his cavalier attitude. Finally he closes the book, "But seriously, I don't know an ignite spell. I'm more on the healing side of things than harming."

"Shame you couldn't heal Rufus." Avrel interjects.

The cleric gets an uneasy smirk. "There's no healing back from that." he comments. "Well, legally anyway." he adds cryptically.

As she thinks about it, the ranger hasn't asked for help starting a fire since they began. "Zanvan, why can't you light the fire?" she asks.

"I'm low on strikers, and in a hurry." he says dimly.

"What about your rocks?" she asks.

"The fairy." the cleric chimes in.

At least it wasn't more kobolds... she thinks to herself, but she does remember now. It also explains why Zanvan has been rubbing sticks together since then. And that does take a good deal longer. "Alright." she agrees, "I'll light the fire."

"Thanks." Zanvan says.

"Hmph." Avrel hums as she lights the fire with relative ease, wondering what the cleric meant by, 'legally'. "I'd have thought one of you haughty, schooled up clerics would have no issues raising someone."

He looks at her with darts as he smacks his book shut, "That my dear is called '*Necromancy*', and is illegal, immoral, impractical, and most importantly -- very hard to come by." The way he says it implies that he's maybe tried. "From what I know of it, we'd need a lot of... *Material* to revive that guy." He stands up, "I once read about some ancient sorceries that involved crafting dead bodies into big golems of flesh!" His fervor is unnerving to say the least. "And that's, in part, why it's unlawful to practice it."

"You sure read a lot." Zanvan scoffs as he lights a twig in the fire, and then his pipe. Much to Avrel's dismay, it takes all the freshness from the air.

"Well you know." The cleric glares at Avrel, "Magic is hard work for most of us."

She lets that slide, him assuming that she's automatically good at magic due to her elven side. She has to work at it too. He's almost seated beside her and so she moves, lying in some grass upwind of Zanvan and the fire's smoke.

Her ear low to the ground she faintly hears that same, deep something that she heard a few times within the forest. It's distant, like a rolling thunder from the other side of the Cordol Mountains, but closer now. As she leans up, she can no longer hear it. She lays back down, this time pressing her large, pointed ear to the ground. It's stopped for a moment, but then resumes once more.

"Okay there, knife-ears?" the cleric asks.

Knife-ears. Knife-ears. *Knife-ears*... She throws herself upright. "Eh, I have a name you know, cleric!"

"So do I, tiny." he chuckles "So do I."

She sighs, he's getting under her skin just for the joy of it. She'll be the better person. She's a woman and he's a man, anyway. "I have a name, Geric." she says firmly, "Avrel."

"I know that." he smiles, "I'll try to keep it in mind."

"What *were* you doing?" Zanvan finally asks, it looks like he's preparing the pheasant he shot in the woods this afternoon.

"I heard something." she answers. "A distant rumble in the ground."

Zanvan finishes his cut and then sitting the bird down, he presses his ear to the ground. His eyes move back and forth as he looks to listen very closely. "I hear... something." he dismisses. "I doubt it's anything to worry about."

"Yeah, Avrel." Geric says with an unwanted nudge, "You're an elf, you'll hear all sorts of nonsense. It's probably nothing."

"You don't believe me?" she asks.

"Well, I can't hear it." Geric shrugs, "Zanvan *barely* thinks he can." he waves off.

Avrel can feel her face tighten with indignation. "I'm not lying." she grunts, "Sounds to me like you're just jealous, and don't believe women."

His stupid smile fades to a look of confusion, "Wait, what?"

"Would you two just stop?" Zanvan orders as he puts bits of the poultry onto small spears of wood.

"Yes, Father." Geric smirks, returning to his shitey grin.

Avrel crosses her arms, and silently complies. Whether she's believed or not, she knows she heard something. That's enough for her. She doesn't care if they believe her or not. She calls over Candice and waits for the bird to cook.

"Don't worry." Zanvan comments, "The trading post is near. I'll get some more stones there."

She lies back down, letting the grass tickle her gently as a soft breeze blows over their little camp by the northward path. "I don't mind." she says softly.

Zanvan skewers the bits of meat and stakes them by the fire to cook. "You're not still thinking about Rufus, are you?" he asks, almost sounding annoyed that she might.

"No." Geric scoffs. "She's just sad that she won't get to show off her elfy powers."

"It's not that." she half rolls over to look in their direction, and stops with a long sigh. "My mother made me promise that I'd never use my magic on another person. Not ever." she admits.

"Seems arbitrary." Zanvan shrugs off, coldy.

"My father was a monster hunter… I think." she tells them, "I can understand her wanting me to be nothing like that sard." She barely can contain her feelings, and so she stops with that, at least for a minute. "I've only ever used it for practical things, or entertainment. My shows, or cooking, or-" she points, "Lighting fires."

"I'm sure she'll forgive you for scaring off those kobolds." Geric mumbles, preoccupied by his book.

She can see that they aren't listening, and that's fine. But the cleric is wrong. She's not just upset at breaking the promise, she's sorry that she hesitated. Rufus might live had she not, but instead she tried so hard to keep it that someone perished. He died, and she *still* broke that promise.

"Well." Zanvan says as he flips the skewers, "Explains why that spell was a bit wild."

She nods, not sure he can see it. But she is sure that she'll likely have to use her spells like that again. She looks down beside her to the beaver snuggled under her hand, and her big, dark eyes. "She'd forgive me, right?"

Candice warbles and nods evenly, but it's not a very direct answer, not what Avrel had hoped for. "Yeah." she concedes, "I guess."

"Food's ready." Geric calls, "If you're done talking with the rat…"

She rises from her grassy bed. If the ranger's sense of direction is to be believed, they'll be at the trading post soon. And there, an inn. She'll decide by then how she'll proceed.

It's a very standard sort of inn for the countryside, she imagines. Unlike the larger, more ornate ones within the city, it's more of a big cabin. It's rustic, but certainly an upgrade from the outdoors, and the warm firelight after coming from the darkness of the woods is just too inviting.

Aside from the small trading market, a few small homes, and the inn itself, there is a tavern in the inn's lower level. Zanvan handles trading the pelts from the woodland monsters while she and Geric wait. He comes back with some money and presumably some fresh supplies in his pack, and gives them each a share of the coins.

"He's heard nothing." Zanvan says darkly. "We can *try* the tavern."

"I was kind of hoping we'd be staying here for the night." Avrel says softly.

Zanvan looks to the in, and to the already half setting sun. "I guess." he concedes.

Geric seems to share her relief. "I wonder if they have a bestiary?"

Zanvan shrugs. "They might." His eyes sort of fall to the side, "Anyway, I'm getting a drink." he says before he heads for the inn.

Geric follows, but she holds off a moment, not that they notice. "Candice?" she calls as the beaver waddles to her side. "Maybe you should stay out here for a bit." Surely other people keep animal companions, and rarely those as sentient as Candice, but still, people are prejudiced against rodents.

"Chippu." she chatters.

"Yeah." Avrel turns, wondering that for herself. "If there is a bath, I'll call you in." she promises, and Candice looks much happier.

Inside, Zanvan already has gotten them beds, however, Avrel insists that she have a private room. He complies, but takes no time to check it out first, he instead goes right to the tavern below. She doesn't either, and follows him. It's not especially crowded, and they are able to get their food and drinks served to them quickly by the barmaid.

After they eat, Zanvan quickly finishes his drink. "Hookah?" he asks them, abruptly.

"Goddess bless you." Geric replies with a snide grin.

Zanvan looks unamused

"No, thanks." the cleric clarifies.

"Avrel?" the ranger asks, turning towards her. She looks to Geric, and tries to get an idea of what he means, and not knowing what it is for herself, she lets him go alone.

"Maybe another time."

As he shrugs and leaves them, she can see where he's going. 'Hookah' appears to be some sort of group smoking, she notes as she takes another glance. She's not seen it in her days, but she's only been allowed in bars for a couple of years, and nothing even as nice as this one. *If it can be called 'nice'.* she comments to herself as she looks around. Hunters, traders, another ranger or two by the looks of them; it's maybe a bit more refined than what she's used to, but not *very* much.

She has no interest in smoking, so Avrel stays with Geric. For a while, she watches him read and write and copy from the book the host of the inn gave to him. She can't read a word of it, but judging by the ink sketches inside, it looks to be about beasts and monsters. He's very quick, very active, and his strokes evoke an almost rhythmic music-like sound. It's a strange observation to her, that Geric is actually so serious in his work. She almost asks, but instead she guesses he's trying to prepare for any monsters they might face, as to not be surprised again. Which reminds her, she has some thinking to do.

"Hey elfy!" a patron calls to her, he sounds drunk, and looking up to him it's more apparent. "You wanna make some quarter-elves?"

She looks to Geric who seems completely tuned out, "Not especially." she frys darkly. "I'll make some quartered humans if you don't leave me be." she smirks as she takes a sip of her drink. At this, the cleric leans up and looks at her with a raised brow before returning to his work. He's not going to help her, obviously, so she looks to Zanvan who is occupying himself with some other company. *Fine...* She's had enough of this, and there are better ways to unwind and think when she has a little money to spare. The tap ale is pissy and light anyway.

She finishes her drink while raising a lewd gesture to the drunken sard, and promptly goes upstairs, checking along the way that she's not followed. She's passing the inn's front desk when the scent of a burning aspen tree wafting from the fireplace reminds her of Candice. It's a longshot, but she sees the host. "Do you have baths?" she asks.

"Yes, actually." the host answers, much to her delight. "Three silver." he holds out his hand, and Avrel quickly hands over her pieces. He ducks under the desk a moment and then hands her a towel, "Down that hall, past the rooms. I'll get the boiler started." he says. He moves a bit more spryly than she'd expected given his age. He's easily old enough to be her father, Zanvan's even, if she were to guess. His beard is scraggly and streaked of grey. He also staggers a bit, and he does have a half empty mug of beer by his desk.

But it matters little so long as the door has a lock. Avrel wastes no time in taking the towel and making for the bathing room. She opens the door which does have a lock, and a small window facing to the empty woods at a height that nothing can be seen and only supplies moonlight. She looks around, the older guy is gone, and no one else seems to be about. She undoes her shows and focuses, beckoning her familiar to come. The beaver stealthily makes her way from the hall into the bathroom, so much so that it almost gives Avrel a start. She shuts the door behind her friend as she unwraps her leggings. Candice eagerly sniffs out the knob until

Avrel draws the water and neatly folds her clothes while the tub fills. It's good and hot too.

"I smelled the aspen, I assume you took a little snack?" Avrel asks, waiting for the tub to fill up enough to be worth stepping into.

Candice chirps her chippus.

"Yeah?" Avrel considers, "I doubt it though, they won't miss a few logs." She finally gets in, no sense in catching a chill while waiting. Aside from the towel given to her, it looks like there's tiny, coin-sized drops of soap too. Really not a bad deal for three silver, by her judgement. The bathhouse she patronized in Argoth charged extra, prohibitively so.

"Hmmm... It's been a while, eh? Not since I got paid to do that birthday party last winter." she says lathering up and scrubbing her fingernails.

"Chippu chippu!" the beaver replies, cannonballing into the spacious porcelain tub.

"Ehh..." Avrel says, petting Candice's head, leaving a powdered wig of bubbles, "Sponge-baths once a month with river water really aren't optimal for humans... Elves-- Whatever the hell I am..." she sighs under her breath as she goes about her business. It's not long before a prime insecurity of hers makes itself known. If she'd just had the hair of an elven shade, it'd be a small matter, but with her scarlet locks, it's something that brings her outright dread. Even while lathering her upper arms she can feel the stubble already. "Alright, have at it." she says as she holds her arm up in the air, exposing her armpit.

Candice chatters as she grins, and nods eagerly, and then uses her sizable teeth to trim her underarms.

"Ahh... that tickles." Avrel giggles, involuntarily. The wet, leathery nose and its whiskers tickling as they always do. "I really should buy a razor. I have the money for it now." She considers as she closes her arm.

"Chippu!" the beaver chits evenly.

"Yeah..." Avrel smiles, "But then, you'd be out of a job."

***

Down in the bar, most of the patrons are shite faced and loud. Too loud for Geric who sits there trying to enjoy his drink and copy down useful information. Eventually the rowdiness of the bar gets to him, it seems the calls on the elf were but the start of it. As he reads the same paragraph for the third time, he swears that if he's asked again about clerics and the right of drinking he'll give them a bar flashing they won't soon forget. He's seen what a dia spell can do in a confined, dim room, and he'd have it that the only twinkles they see are the sparkling flecks against the purple blobs.

And he becomes aware that he himself has lost him his place. He chugs down the rest of his drink angrily as he begins reading once more. <u>'The West Argothian Woodling is a 4 cubit tall woodland beast which often disguises itself as a-'</u>

"Hey there." a bosomy bar maiden says to him. "Can I refill your drink?"

He slams his palms against the table as he quivers. "I don't know!" he screams stressfully. *"Can you refill everyone else's drink with sleeping drugs so they will shut the hell up so I can get this done?!"*

The bar maiden takes a few steps back. "...I'll uh.. See what I can do." she mutters and walks away looking like she might cry. He hadn't meant to do *that*.

Zanvan comes up to him a moment later, at which point Geric just slams the bestiary closed with an iron fist. Not that he actually has an iron fist, but he rather wishes he did, it'd be quite useful in lifting his mace. Maybe less so for administering medicine.

***

Zanvan ignores the cleric's slamming of the table. "Y'know, bars are generally loud places." he says, "Most people don't do their transcriptions here, just go up and do it in the room."

"Yeah." Geric nods. "But there's no *booze* in the inn!" the cleric says sarcastically.

Zanvan lightly slaps him over the head and goes back to the emptied hookah corner where he flags down the bar maiden.

She has a nice smile, and a nicer figure. And he makes sure his eyes convey his interest in that. "Sorry about my comrade, he's kind of an idiot." he says.

She seems to welcome the admiration. "No, it's fine." she says cheerfully. "I get lots of people yelling at me, comes with the job. Can I get you anything?"

He might as well test it further, "I can think of a few things." he says with an inviting smile, and a strong posture.

She bends down over the table in a provocative way that accentuates and displays her buxom figure. "Were you asking for a different flavored shisha, a drink, seconds? Or something else?"

She's coming on stronger than he'd expected, all the better. "Can I get some *dessert*? Is that on your menu?" he asks, more or less directly.

She looks down at his tight pants, and smiles, "Yeah." she nods as she stands back up, "I might be able to get you *breakfast* once I'm off duty here." she says sensually.

He smiles back, favorably. "I look forward to it." as he exhales some vapor. "I'll just have another drink in the meantime."

She takes his cup and goes, and he leans back. He supposes it's not so bad that the other two wanted to stay here for the night. He feels a slight hit to the brim of his hat. Geric from pretty far across the room glares at him, disapprovingly of course. The projectile is on the table and he picks it up. There's writing on it. '<u>You're welcome, rebound-catching bedswerver!</u>' it reads.

He tips his hat to the lonely cleric and his books.

***

Upon hearing a loud shout and thump from somewhere else in the inn, Avrel is quiet for a moment and hears something like breathing. "Hey…" she whispers as she drops herself deeper into the water, "Candice, check the door." Although the noise a moment before sounded like it might have even been from the bar, this sounds close, closer than snoring from another room. As Candice quietly waddles out of the tub and across the room, Avrel quiets her mind and body and listens hard. "Well?" she asks.

Candice nods, someone is outside of her door. Avrel debates, is she getting peeped? Is someone else waiting? Or are they after Candice? In any case, she quietly gets out of the tub and wraps herself in the towel to which she hears a muffled giggle. She quickly starts charging a fire spell in reserve and sneaks across the room and throwing the door open. There sits a portly drunken man with a wide toothless grin on his face. The host, but he's obviously had a few more to drink.

"Heh… heh!" he smiles, "I waited all night up here to see something good", he burps, "But then then I see ye, and yer not more than a slightly fat boy!" the drunken man says with beer filled drool dripping from his scraggly beard. "Not even any fat…" he adds to her dismay

Avrel is incensed, while she doesn't throw the fireball at him, she kicks him in the face. "Candice!" she points, and the toothy familiar sicks on him, distracting him long enough that she can grab her clothes and run to her room. It's nothing fancy, but that's of no concern at the moment. She looks for security and finds it in locking the door and barring it with a chair. After some time, she undoes it long enough for Candice to join her. Safe with Candice, she goes into a light sleep, unwillingly, but drowsy still from the tub and the late hour.

Avrel is awoken early before dawn by a knocking at the door. *About time those guys came up.* she grimaces. "Geric? Zanvan?" she says softly slightly cracking the door.

"Hey…" she hears half burped, "Sorry for insultin' ye figure, please, keep an old man company!?"

He's still there. "'No' means *no*, you debauchee!" she says as she shuts the door in his face, catching a bit of his beard in it serves him rightly. Still with no sign of the guys, she packs her things up, and dresses.

Once her leg wraps are good and tight, she and Candice climb out the small window and onto a ledge. Her petiteness finally being something of an asset. She crawls along the edge until she comes to the communal sleeping area. Through the crude glass, where Geric and Zanvan's beds were supposed to be, she looks.

She only finds Geric.

She tries to open it from the outside, until with a little work of an arcane hand, she twists the latch from the other side. Once opened, she goes to Geric.

"C'mon, we're leaving!" she whispers.

"But my sleeping experience!" Geric whines, eyes still half shut, and louder than she or anyone else would probably like. "I need a long rest to regain my spell stamina…"

"I'll explain later, just come on." she says insistently while Candice tugs on his shirt.

"Okay…" he sighs, rolling over in and then out of his bed. He's so tall it doesn't seem that he could be comfortable anyway.

She has no trouble tiptoeing through, but Geric it seems has heavier feet. "Where is Zanvan?" she inquires once they are out of the room full of hopefully still sleeping patrons.

"I dunno." he yawns, "He was talking to the lady at the bar." the cleric says in a tired stupor.

***

She's let him in the back.

He stands in the corner while she finishes off the last few mugs. He'd offered to help, but she declined. Perhaps she's trying to create suspense but he cares not. Or maybe it's just as she said, her slovenly cook of a brother's messes aren't Zanvan's problem. Whatever her reason, it's late. But she's about done.

"Do you have a private room?" she asks as she wipes her hands on a dishtowel.

"My friend insisted on one for herself." he says, "But not I."

"No trouble." she smiles as she walks by with a pinch of a tug on his hat. She leads Zanvan to her room and shows him to her futon bed.

He takes a seat. It's soft and worn in. "Going somewhere?" he asks, curiously as she continues for another door.

"I'll be right back." she winks.

He yawns as soon as she shuts the door behind her, and looks out her window from where he sits. It's at least several hours past midnight, he hopes he won't drag too much in the morning.

"Zanvan." he hears from out in the hall. It doesn't sound like the barmaid, it sounds like the kid.

"Zanvan?" he hears, this time definitely Geric.

Why the hell are they up? he curses, *Unless...* that thought is quickly thrown away. He looks to the door to what he guesses is her powder room before he quietly walks up to the door to the hall. "Yeah?"

The kid throws open the door with the cleric looking still half asleep behind her. "We're leaving!." she says far too loud for the hour.

"No, no, guys I-" Avrel and Geric start pulling at him, and struggle him out the door, "But guys I really, she- OUCH!" he yelps as even Avrel's damned beaver gives him a solid bite.

After fighting them off as long as he can without coming to blows, he finally gives in. For them to be so insistent there must be a good reason, and painful as it is, he leaves her alone.

4

"I feel…" not quite dead inside, but Zanvan laments as they gather themselves some distance outside of the inn. His disappointment isn't immeasurable, but nonetheless, his night is ruined. What was left of it anyway. "So what was so important?" he asks, trying both to stay calm, but also awake.

"Hey, don't look at me." Geric says, with a shrug, "It was Avrel's insistence that we leave so immediately."

She flushes at the accusation but says nothing in her defense either. Already Zanvan's long hope that it was truly important is somewhat dashed. "Why?" he asks as he firmly plants his hand on her shoulder.

"Get your bleeding hands off me!" Avrel hisses, throwing off his grip and forcing him back. "I've had enough of touchy men for a while."

'As *if there's much to touch, scrawny-*' Zanvan catches the words before they leave his lips. Ale and a lack of sleep, not to mention the interruption, he's finding it hard to be civil. "Hmph." he hums as he pulls out his pipe, striking a match and proceeding to walk past her.

"So what even was it?" the cleric asks with a yawn.

Avrel looks to swallow hard. Whatever it is, it's important to her, but it seems she lacks the courage to say it. "The host…" she looks away.

"Out with it." he says, scoldingly, with a sigh of smoke.

"He was creeping on me." she says. Her eyes and voice, it's almost like she might cry.

But at whatever small hour it is he doesn't care, and he gives her a look to make that very clear.

"*Really?*" Geric's lack of restraint for once finds itself on his side, "You had your own room!" he groans, "With a lock!" he adds.

Avrel's mouth purses into a pout, and under her elven cheeks he can see how tightly her teeth are gritting as she crosses her arms. Tightly, and with her slim shoulders tensed and raised.

The conversation is over, and for all intents and purposes, so is the night. They might have three, maybe four hours before dawn. "Come on." he creaks. Geric seems ready, but Avrel and the beaver by her feet seem steadfast. "We'll rest in that grove up ahead, just hurry up." he catches himself short of a snarl. He just hopes the kid isn't going to be so much trouble at every stop.

After a few hours of rest, they continue northward on the road. Given the night and early morning prior, there's a definite, awkward silence and an air of tension. The trees thin again, and again they are in the wide open, with only tall grass along the road. Zanvan frequently checks to find Avrel lagging behind. Somehow, even the beaver is keeping a better pace.

"So ummm..." Geric starts to ask. "How much longer till we get there?"

Falling behind again... he notes, as the cleric's question was followed with a tug to his mantle. "A day or two straight." he answers *"If we keep a good pace."* Zanvan adds with a glance back, not by accident making eye contact with her.

The kid looks as if she was going to say something, but she simply looks away onto the treeline to the west. All for the better, it's much too early still.

By mid morning the road comes to a small brooke at which they refill their canteens and have a small meal.

While they break fast, the kid breaks her morning-long silence. "Sorry... to have inconvenienced you guys." she says. "I was probably overreacting. I'm just... Touchy about that sort of thing."

The words barely leave her thin lips when Geric's question is strung and ready to fly in reply, "Were you a rape baby?" Geric says, munching on a bacon strip.

"Hell no!" she jolts, "I just... I..." she mutters, pausing like she's a little unsure, "I'm just touchy, okay?" she retorts.

"I don't see why it's relevant that you bring that up now." Zanvan says, capping his waterskin. "The night is spent, and we've begun anew." She can't undo it with explanations.

But she seems to think otherwise. "Alright, my father... I guess he wanted more children, or something and my mom didn't!" says the kid. "I grew up watching him hurt my mom like that until the damned day he finally left us." She's flushed by now. "I know that look *you men* get when you are carnally driven and it scares me. Deeply. OKAY?!"

"Cool story?" Geric says as he's finishing his food. "If it makes you feel any better, I was 'touched' by a priest in the Cordol Monastery." he chews.

"Ok...?" Zanvan grimaces, "That probably doesn't make her feel better." he adds, rubbing his tired eyes before looking to the kid. He's made the correct assumption.

"I was lying to make her feel better." Geric laughs. "At least I tried." he stops for a second like he's pondering a memory. "Mistress Erin was a bitch though." the cleric's colorful words have not yet ceased to surprise him. Or the elf.

"Hey." he scoffs, "At least I'm not the one who messed up the group's whole morning just because she's scared that an older guy is attracted to her." Zanvan says leaning down to her as he scoops a piece of bacon from the pan. He takes a bite, "Next time, deal with it. Okay, kid?"

Avrel quickly stands and slaps him. Hard, his hat is almost jostled loose. "Son of a bitch." he hears her grumble as she picks up her pack and her staff and goes on without them.

"Anvil wait!" Geric yells and waves to her, to which she just raises her hand in a lewd gesture as a reply. The beaver seems reluctant to follow her, pausing momentarily to look dimly at the two men, but goes on as well.

A moment passes, as if she'll get far anyway. Especially with that attitude. "*Anvil?*" Zanvan groans.

"Nice going, *idiot*." Geric says, grabbing his things and dodging the correction.

"She needs to simmer down." Zanvan says calmly, feeling no blame.

"It's not my fault she's sensitive and has daddy issues or something." Geric shrugs before putting his pack on his shoulders, "But now who am I gonna tease?"

Zanvan shakes his head as to say 'I don't know.' More so that he doesn't care, she needs to get a hold of herself. "Come on let's get going." he says, lowly as he grabs his pan and things. *Still*, he considers that he might have been harsh. "I hope she doesn't get into trouble…"

The pair goes the next two days of their journey not knowing if they and Avrel had gone their separate ways for good. Although, assuming she continues on the quest, they'll likely cross paths sooner or later, Zanvan reasons.

They are nearing the gnomish city of Manitäria when a heavy storm hits them, slowing them down, though they can see the giant mushroom capital building in the distance. Given how low the other houses are leading the way into this territory, it's hard to miss the larger, fungi structure even in such rotten weather.

"This's all your fault! I'm not sure how, but it is!" Geric yells over the howling winds. So *he's* the one the cleric will tease now…

***

Avrel is sitting in a warm tavern within the gnomish city, sipping a drink and trying to understand the other patrons. Despite the tavern being understandably made for gnomes, the ceiling is around seven feet tall to accommodate most human travellers. Avrel, a good half cubit shorter than most adapts more easily than most to the seats and table height.

"Er, der storm! Yer comparnerns er gernner ber serked!" the gnomish bartender cries. Even in argoth there is a diverse array of accents one will come across, but she's not heard one like this. And she can't even begin to try and read their lips as under their beards, the lips hardly move any more than it sounds like their tongues. But, if she can understand the squeaks of a beaver, she can learn this, and roughly has, at least for words here and there.

"Yeah, soaked" Avrel frys with a mean smile. Underneath the bar counter her hand clasped around a gem. Being infused with weather magic, it glows from being channeled. It's mildly therapeutic, she finds, as she focuses her anger into the storm. A keepsake of her mother giving her a little more gusto, she's only ever created little clouds for her shows, she's ever tried to wring every drop from a storm onto someone.

"Ser yer loorkern fer ar 'Rurnblerd erf ther Aergers ernd ther Erverlersterng Aergers?" a traveler inquires. His little beard is stained with some beer.

"Yes, supposedly they were lost when the…" She pauses to think of the cleric's words, "Diavolo supposedly fell into the Great Chasm of Eternal Death… Or something." She can't quite remember it right. "But we've heard that they may be real and recovered. Have you heard anything at all about anything like that?" Avrel asks, and explains. It occurs to her, she's very ignorant on the subject and really just jumped at the chance to leave that damned city. A nervous chill comes over her as she realizes how alone she is and so far from home, *What am I doing…?* She never really did take her time in that inn to rethink this over.

"Hrmmm" the traveling gnome strokes his long beard, "I hevern't, bert I der't traver fer, Er bert a tavern orver ther merchenrt guird mert harv sorm'ern therre thart mert kner sermthirng." he ponders.

Avrel thanks him with a nod after taking a moment to digest his words through his accent, and gets him another round. Even the larger gnomish drinks are somewhat small, even for her.

"CHIPPU CHIPPU!" The rain soaked beaver bursts through the tavern door and sits beside Avrel.

"ERMERGERD! ER BERVER!" the patrons cry. Candice is almost half most of their heights. The other animals are all pygmies fit to the gnomes' heights, she hadn't thought about that.

"She's with me" Avrel assures them. Too late now, she's invited her in.

"Errrrrrr" they all moan.

"Come on." she says, calling Candice, "Want some corn whiskey, girl?" Avrel invites, patting her hand on the seat next to her, opposite the traveller.

"Chippu chippu!" the beaver squeaks, snuggling her legs a moment before taking the seat.

"Alright, *one* shot" she tells Candice. "Hey!" she says raising her hand.

"Yers merm?" the tender replies.

"A shot of corn whiskey and a corn muffin for my beaver here." she says as the beaver turns and squeaks at the bartender, accidentally frightening him.

"Yers.... Yers ma'arm!" he shudders as he walks into the back room. He returns with what to him is a small cake which to Avrel is merely a muffin and places it before the hungry rodent along with a small shot glass of whiskey.

"Chippu Chippu!" Candice squeals with glee, again frightening the short gnome.

"She says 'thanks'." Avrel relates to him.

"Yer wercorm." he says, keeping his distance.

Candice chatters after downing the shot. "Oh?" Avrel says, and then sniffs the glass herself. "Very woody." Definitely what she's heard called Lumberjack, or just a 'Jack', whiskey. Candice's favorite, and not unlike what her mother would mix with a dark syrup to give when Avrel or he had a cold or something. To this day, she's not a fan of the taste.

She finishes her own drink, but with no sign of her party after a few hours, Avrel pays her tab and finds an inn. For Avrel, she has little trouble finding a bed she can fit into due to her short stature. She wishes that sardy cleric were here, just so that she could give him the miniscule aggressions he so often casts on her.

Her door locked, she takes off her clothes and hangs them to dry. She sits on the bed and looks out the window to the inviting rain. Be it something in her blood, or not, she longs for the feeling of the rain on her naked body. She always has when it rains, or better yet, the smoothness of silvery moonshine. Rare though are days when she's comfortable in going through with it.

No... Not in a strange place. she says to herself. Still, the sound of the rain invites something in her soul, and the men of this small place are barely a threat. She debates it, even talking it over with Candice, but even still firmly against it, she considers the dark, back streets near the inn. Back streets not so dangerous for a small woman as Argoth's.

Once she's sure everyone in town is asleep, she sneaks out to dance and cleanse herself in the warm air and cool drops of the early spring storm. Clinging to what she knows of the ways of her elf blood, she attempts to take in rainy days as much as she can in this manner, rare as it is. "You keep a lookout, eh Candice?" she whispers.

"Chippuuuuuu..." the beaver squeaks tightly.

Avrel continues her rain-dance as she starts to tear up. In her solitude her mind fills with the lonely thoughts that she'd started to leave behind for the past few weeks with her companions. She finds that that heart movement makes her dance become more intense, and then it becomes more sloppy and slow until she eventually stops. And she breaks into tears.

Just as a flash of lightning illuminates the sky, reflecting off her smooth wet skin, she falls to her knees and relents her anger towards her companions.

"I'm sorry guys... I'm sorry Mr Zanvan, I shouldn't have done that and left you guys so briskly. Will you forgive me, my companions... My..." she pauses as a smile comes to her frowning face, "... Friends..? Have I... made friends?" she whimpers. *Nah, just companions on this simple job.* She reminds herself, and after this, perhaps not even that, and even if still, never 'friends'. "Still..." she sighs, "I was wrong...eh?" she asks as her eyes meet Candice's. Why does she lament freedom from those men? It's a puzzle to her, and a painful puzzle at that.

She eventually gets herself up and sneaks back into her room where she dries off, and lays down to sleep. "Mother... For the first time in so many years since you passed, I didn't feel so lonely." she cries, as her beaver comes and cuddles under the quilt with her. "Well, I know, Candice... You'll always be with me." she smiles. But even as men, she enjoyed the conversations not tainted by the poison of their masculinity. They aren't friends, she has Candice for that, but they were human company.

Soon, her thoughts fade and flicker before taking shape, and she drifts off to sleep.

***

"It must be midnight, should we keep going?" Zanvan asks Geric, the rain still pouring around them.

"I dunno, I suddenly feel stricken with exhaustion." Geric complains.

"Hmm..." Zanvan isn't especially full of energy himself. The storm is breaking now though, surely they can make it into town. "It's not but a few miles." Zanvan encourages.

"Ugh... Fine" Geric says gathering his strength as he looks ahead. It really is very close. It just seems far, even to the ranger because of the weather, and as darkness came earlier than evening, time has seemed longer.

They make it into town after just a little bit longer. It's too late to ask about their companion, no one it seems is out. Everyone appears to be asleep, or if they're smart, indoors at the least.

"If we're looking for her in a gnomish city we're going to have a bad time." Geric yawns.

She's not that short, but even Zanvan can't help but crack at that one. "Let's just find an inn that can accomodate us." he says, returning to his serious demeanor. "Then I might get a drink, if there's a tavern still open." He looks around, there might be one.

"If the gnomes are as composed of mixed dwarvish blood as they claim to be, they should be hearty drinkers." the cleric agrees. "Whatever of those old stories can be believed."

"Yeah." He shakes his head, only this cleric would know of stereotypes of races long extinct. "Come on, I think I've stayed at one down this way when I was here once before." he orders. He starts to go but turns back to the cleric who is playing with his hat. "What?"

"See, it was good that I took this hat!" he smiles.

Zanvan shoots him a glare for what it's worth in the dim darkness. "Come on."

They get to the inn, and they are able to put some beds together for them. However, they can't help but both sit in a silent unease. And Zanvan to a greater degree.

"It's a good thing that the ceiling is tall enough for you to stand, otherwise you wouldn't be able to pace like that." Geric comments as he lies in his beds and turns the page in his book, just as unable to rest as he is.

"I'd feel better if I knew she made it here." Zanvan finally stops and sits on the side of his beds, lighting a smoke. "If she's headed home, I'd hope she'd know to go straight west from here."

"I wouldn't worry." the cleric dismisses, turning another page. "Knowing elves, she's probably why it rained so hard."

Zanvan finds himself rolling his eyes, but maybe the cleric isn't wrong. "Maybe I just need a drink." he concedes. "You think there's a tavern still open?"

Geric pauses, and closes his book. "You have some bad habits." he comments, never failing to inject his bizarre tongue and cheek piousness where he can. "And I think we passed one that was open on the way in here." He rises up, "Let's get going."

He might have guessed that was coming.

"Herrler! Wercorm trarverrers!" the gnomish bartender welcomes them. It occurs to Zanvan that it's more than possible that gnomes would have places open at all hours with how commercial they can be. He tips his hat and takes a seat, the cleric follows suit. "Drernks?"

"Yeah." Zanvan answers. "And have there been any other humans here today or yesterday?" he asks directly.

"She's not human, Zanvan." Geric corrects, making points over his ears with finger gestures like a damned fool.

"She doesn't consider herself elf either." Zanvan reminds him.

"Heh." Geric snarks. "You can consider yourself anything you want, that doesn't mean you are the thing." he says, proudly stroking his soaked cleric robes.

And here I thought pride was a sin... Zanvan sneers to himself. "She did have pointed ears." he concedes, "And hair that was red like a brick."

"ERRRRR!!!" he yelps in a moment of insight, "Yer lerk lirke ther mern thert errf gerl wers loorkerng fer." he says happily.

"Oh wow." Geric says as he leas very far over the small bar and inspects the bar's tender. "You're a freaky little shite."

"Hurr?" the tender says with a shocked look on his face.

"So wait, you've seen *Avrel?*" Zanvan inquires before things escalate the wrong way.

"Yers, sher wers irn here earlier ternert." the bartender says while polishing a glass. "...Her arnd thart berver." the gnome shudders, with good reason, a rodent that is that proportionally large is intimidating.

"So are all of you this disgustingly short? Or--?" Geric tries to insert between Zanvan's conversing.

"Do you know where Avrel is staying?" Zanvan asks.

"Hrrrrm", the gnomish bartender strokes his beard, "Erm nert sure, bert there arr nert arlert erf plarcers thert terk terller ferk."

"Can't have been the same Avrel, she's no *terller ferk.*" the cleric inserts sardonically, only to be ignored by both of them.

"Do you have a directory or list? Zanvan inquires.

"Also, have you ever heard of elevator shoes?" Geric adds, and if he adds again, he might get smacked one.

"Yeahr, Er'll merk yer er cerpy erf the wern Er gerve ter her." For a few moments they hear the scratching of paper, and then the little bartender hands them a list of inns to try.

"Thanks" Zanvan says with a smile before he empties his mug.

"Yer, herr yer ger."

"Thanks again." Zanvan smiles as he leaves a sizable tip. "Come on." he says, grabbing Geric who is doing the same.

"Berr!" the gnome waves as they make for the door. As the cleric turns back, probably to make some sardy remark, he nearly hits his head on the door frame.

"So where first?" Geric asks as he shuts the door behind them. Zanvan is already looking at the list, carefully to keep the rain from affecting it.

"Avrel is short enough, she could probably go to the first place she saw." he says thoughtfully.

"She's so short, there aren't a lot of places she can't go, amiright?" Geric says with a poke.

Zanvan sighs a stressful sigh and starts walking, not particularly caring if the cleric follows. But of course, he does. "Let's just get back to the inn." he says, it must be at least two, maybe three hours past midnight by now. "She's safe, we can find her in the morning if we want to."

The cleric shrugs, agreeingly, and they trek back to the inn. The rain is only now letting up to a drizzle as they turn in for the night.

***

As the rooster screeches with particular shrillness, Geric and the ranger awaken. The ranger spares no noise as he gets himself out of bed and dressed. Geric finds himself a bit more sluggish, but he manages to get out before the obviously oh so motivated ranger starts bossing.

At least until he's almost done getting his robe on. "So, should we look for her?" Zanvan asks, handing him his brilliant, red hat, but not without a look.

"*Shall* we find her." Geric corrects with a sneer as he takes his hat. "And I suppose we can take a look."

The ranger looks like he's thinking long and hard, finally, he says something. "She's just a kid." he says briskly, "If she's going her own way, that's fine, but I want to make sure she's set to go before we part ways."

"How considerate." Geric dismisses, he probably just wants to bed her.

"Come on." Zanvan says coldly as he leaves the room. Geric follows and they quickly pay their bill before heading out.

They start looking into the other inns on the list the bartender gave to them with no success. Geric's going to insist this be their last stop as they come to one on the edge of town, near the bar from the night before.

"Huh." he scoffs, "How did we miss this?"

"It was dark." the ranger dismisses and heads for the door.

Still, there's no doubt they would have stayed there had they noticed it. *Too late now.* he shrugs.

"Hellerr there strerrngerrs" the host welcomes as they enter.

Geric pushes past Zanvan. "Hello Tiny, is there a short half-elf woman staying here?" he grins as he leans over the gnome because he can.

The gnome is obviously intimidated, and is cautious of disclosing this information two two strange men. Geric *is* dressed like a cleric though. "Errmm... Yerrs? Err thernk. She cerm en larst nerght." the host says timidly.

He's content to stand over the gnome until Zanvan pulls him back, to the host's relief. "May we see her?" Zanvan asks.

"Errrm... Sure!" the gnome hops off his chair and leads them down a tight hallway to a room. "Thers wers ourr herrny-moorn suirt, she fournd the berd to ber birg ernough fer her."

"Thernks, I mean thanks!" Geric says, unironically as he tips his hat to the little host.

"Thernk Yerr Mirster." he smiles to Zanvan. "Ther clerirc irs ern arrs though." Geric hears him mutter as he walks back to his front desk.

They both stand there a minute, it seems they each expected the other to open it. "Oh come on, what's the matter Zanvan?" he asks. "I'd hardly think you'd be afraid to open a woman's door."

Zanvan's return glance is equal parts resentment and agreement. He maintains that glare as he turns the door.

As it opens, the two men see the little elf sprawled out on the tiny bed with the water rat sleeping peacefully across her scrawny thighs. There are petals all about the room and a suspicious sponge beside the bed. Geric can assume its intended use.

The beaver twitches as it becomes alert to their presence. It looks somewhat uneverved, but then starts flapping its tail. He can't help but notice the gnome sized hip pillow that the wee-elf she-elf has got around her neck. "Hey, you'd know..." he mutters to his side, to Zanvan, "Is that pillow--?"

Zanvan's glare finally softens as he almost cracks a grin after a quick glance. His eyebrows flash an amused expression. 'Yeah.' he mouths.

Sun knows where that's been, but he'd rather not. And the darn rat is taking too long to wake her up. "Wake up, tiny!"

***

The crust breaks from her eyes as the blurry white and green shapes form into her two companions. In her doorway, in her room.

Immediately she shivers, and bites her tongue. She knows she shouldn't let her guard down, she should never, but they are still across the room. As her tunge is almost bitten through, she manages a courteous, "Guys?" in an early morning frog as she leans up from her bed.

"Hey kid, how are you?" Zanvan asks reservedly.

"I'm fine." she says as she quickly catches her blanket, remembering she'd gone to bed without undergarments. "Oh my." She's a sitting duck. No. she reminds herself, she's not, but safety demands that the two strong and tall, and easily overpowering men get out. "Eh... would you guys give me a moment, I'll meet you outside."

"Oh?" Zanvan says coldly, crossing his arms. "You're still coming with us?"

"Yeah?" she answers stiffly, but she won't let the fear of these men rob her of what will be hers. "Now would you go?"

"Sure thing." the men say in unison tipping their hats and filing out the small door, shutting as they go.

And she breaths a long sigh as she lets the blanket drop from her chest. "Candice?" she calls. The beaver waddles from the foot of the bed, she'd gotten ready to bite them, if it had been needed. *Good girl.* Avrel sighs. She's still uneasy, but so far, these men have not accosted her. They are friendly at times, and she figures, so should she be.

The two are waiting for her as Avrel comes ducking out of the small inn with Candice close behind. Avrel bows slightly, "Sorry, I hope it wasn't too much trouble to find me, I-"

"No, it's fine." Zanvan interrupts with an assuring tone.

"Well, actually--" Geric interjects. Zanvan turns to him with a stern look and shushes him. "Never mind" Geric shuts up for a short moment. "You were able to stay at a normal non-travelers' inn because of how short you are" Geric finally belts with a hearty laugh.

Zanvan facepalms and Avrel just gives him a glare. *Friendly at times.* She reminds herself. "Anyway, I'm sorry I ran off, and I'm sorry for slapping you the way I did, Zanvan." Avrel says as she looks at the ground, not able to look him in the eyes. He deserved that, she's more concerned that the storm enhancement was too far. But that, she'd rather not say.

Zanvan tips her chin up. "It's fine, I shouldn't have gotten in your face." he says, oblivious to the offense of his unconsented touch, but she'll let it slide.

Geric chimes in, "... And I'm sorry you're not taller." His apology seems terrifyingly genuine, so is she. "Now let's get information scouting!"

Avrel shakes her head, and rolls her eyes. "Yeah, let's go."

Having made up, the group spends the morning going to several bars and places of interest trying to gain info on the objects of their quest. It's not long until they make their way to a tavern near the city's merchant guild, as apparently suggested by the bar owner to the men the previous night. Just judging by the vestibule, it's fancier than most of the others they've been to. It's quite ornate and it has a pleasant aroma about it. It must be nice for the wealthy merchants who can afford to frequent it.

"Herr yer!" the tavern host yells at them as they stand, half ducked in the vestibule. "Yeahr! Yer gartta payr er corver ferr irf yer nert pert erf the guird!"

And there's the elitism. she grimaces, finding it even outside of Argoth's upper class. Lucky that the Ar-Guard gave them money for things like this.

"Hey come on. "Geric says jocularly. "The lady here is *almost* as tiny as you guys, can't you give us a break?"

"N*er!!*" the host gnome screams, "Arnd fer yer Irmformershern, I'rm er wermern!" she says unbuttoning her shirt and hopping up and down in Geric's face.

"Good Gilded Goddess!! Make it stop!" he wails as her chest hairs looks to scratch his cheek. Avrel covers her mouth, She'd be impressed by how high the gnome can jump if she weren't trying not to heave.

"Enough!" Zanvan booms, holding out a handful of silver chips. "Will this cover it?"

"Cover it! Cover it!" Geric screams.

"Hr... Alrert." the she-gnome says as she buttons her shirt.

The group passes by her as quickly as they can, all of them wanting to forget what they've seen. Avrel and Geric follow Zanvan as he leads their way down the tiny hall into the tap room. There aren't any human sized accommodations.

"Hey, over there!" Avrel points as she finds a corner booth where she is able to sit. Geric and Zanvan both can't fit under the table and simply resign to stand on their knees beside it.

"So Avrel." Geric sneers, "How's it feel to fit in a gnomish nook?"

She's about to come up with her comeback as he yelps in pain. "Damned rat!" he says as he shakes Candice from his foot.

"Candice!" Avrel crawls from the still very cramped table, and restrains the beaver. "Candice, it's okay."

"Oh yeah." Geric scowls, "Just grand." he mutters as he waves a healing spell over the bite.

"Kid." Zanvan tells her, "Muzzle the beaver and lets get to work."

As if she would even use a leash. "Just sit tight, eh Candice?" her dark ebony-brown eyes shift to the cleric and back before she nods. The obedience is awarded with a pet, and she slips into the corner of the booth.

"Good enough." Zanvan dismisses, but it doesn't seem good enough for the cleric. He'll have to deal.

They begin asking nearby patrons about the relics they are questing for. Avrel has very little success, but after a while, Zanvan calls her and Geric back to the table. He's got a gnome in traveler's clothes with him. Avrel answers his call and slides into the booth. In addition to the traveller, the bartender comes over as well.

"Sor, whert exerctler er yer loorkerng for?" he asks. Zanvan waves for the tender to pour the gnome a drink. The others get their's filled as well.

"We're looking into the ancient relics." Geric quickly puts in, "The Runeblade of the Ages, and the Everlasting Aegis." Geric replies, surprising the group in that he didn't make any comments about the gnome's height.

"Hrmmmmm" The gnome scratches his beard. It's clean and mostly white with streaks of light brown.

Avrel wonders if they maybe gray early, he doesn't look very old. "We- we aren't even sure if they exist, are you familiar with the legend or anything at all?" she says shyly.

"Errrr... Cern't sayr Er harve. Burt, erts possirber the errves mighrt knerr sormtherng." the gnome says sipping his drink. "Therr lerve very lerng, lergernds erren't ser dersternt terr therm."

"Figures, our elf doesn't know." Geric says nudging Avrel who forces a playful giggle. He's half got her there, but Rufus has already played that point out.

"Sor, heres's the dear; Er do traird wirth the errves. Burt recerntler, sorrm orf the giarnt marrmerts erf the south earstern plairns harve cerm nerth ernd merd the road murch mere mouterners. Erff yer courd herp me scarre therm erff, E'rr lert yer traver irn mer cart ter the errves. Sournd goord??"

Avrel and Zanvan listen intently to the proposal and try their best to understand the accent laden mumble they just heard spoken, but Geric's eyes glaze over. "Oh by the Gilded Goddess and all Hazell's dragons." says bewilderedly, "The the hell did I just listen to..." Geric replies.

Avrel tries to diffuse the tense silence that followed Geric's statement. "Sooo, yes. We'd be more than happy to help you with your ummm... marmot problem, right guys?"

"Sure." Zanvan sighs, lighting his pipe.

"Herr, ner smorrkirng!" the bartender yells.

Zanvan shakes the match out, "Ugh... I'll be outside." he says with a grimace as he scoots his seat out and makes for the exit.

"Chippu!" Candice chirps, making a very good and topical point on the subject.

"That's true, you might." Avrel says giving her a pat. "So when would you be leaving?" she inquires.

"Tomorrerr irf yer gurrs arr readerr." the traveler says happily, "Merr nerm irs Berb!" he says holding out his hand to shake her hand. "Berb Ertharns"

"I'm Avrel Lavian." pleased to work with you." she says graciously.

"I'm Geric, a cleric, and I'm taller than both of you." Geric says standing up over the two as they shoot him a scowl.

At least we have each other. she figures, at his size, he's no threat.

"I'll see myself out." the cleric sighs, leaving she and the gnome together to close out the arrangement.

"Well, we'd best be going, we'll be staying at the inn on Chanterelle Street if you need us. Shall we meet you at…?" Avrel says as she shakes the gnome's hand.

"Dawrn." Bob replies.

"See you then!" Avrel says as she drops some gold pieces on the table to cover the tab. She quickly finishes her mug of ale, it's not very good. "Enjoy your drink!" she smiles to him as she scoots from the booth. He smiles, he seems more accustomed to gnomish ale, as she'd expect.

"Gerd-berr!"

"Good-bye." she waves, "Come Candice!" she bids, and as the beaver joins her, they make their way out of the taproom.

5

Avrel and Candice come out from the building to see Zanvan as he's chatting it up with a lady with very dark, bronze skin. It's the deepest tan she's ever seen, and it makes her jealous, she herself just freckles and peels. She's quite pretty, her hair is dark like ash, and her almond shaped eyes are like fine garnet.

And Zanvan seems to have noticed.

"So, are all easterlings' skin so marvelously rich as yours? Or is the sun just gracious to you, my dear." he says as he kisses her hand.

She blushes and looks at Zanvan with sly eyes. "Well…" she says coyly "I don't know, you see-"

"Wife!" A deep, brooding voice barks. "Let's get going, I can't abide by the smell of these mushrooms everywhere!" A tall, strong looking man with a sheathed scimitar beckons from across the street.

"Oh… Yes sir…" she says submissively, "Maybe if our paths cross again…" she whispers sliding her hands across her feminine curves.

"… Sure thing." Zanvan sighs.

"So much for hookah and a hookup." Geric says as he comes out of nowhere.

"Did you set up the deal?" Zanvan asks, preparing to light his pipe once more.

"More so than you did, apparently." Geric snickers.

Avrel feels bad for her though, as she does for all women shackled by some man's wedding band. But then, she'd not be much better off free to be taken by Zanvan either.

"Jähöroth to Avrel?" Geric startles her, she'd spaced out.

"A what?" she answers, putting her concerns for the stranger to rest.

"Forget it." Geric shakes his head.

"Did you set it up with that gnome?" Zanvan asks.

Avrel nods, "Yeah, he'll meet us at dawn."

"Well good." Zanvan says dimly, sighing smoke as he speaks, his eyes linger on her across the street as she is helped into a large supply wagon by her husband.

"Huh." Geric comments, "I've never actually seen an easterling before. They're certainly far from home."

"Yeah." Zanvan scowls, "She's heard nothing of the Aegis or the Runeblade."

Avrel's eyes narrow, somehow she doubts he actually asked. *Easterling, huh?* She takes another glance as the wagon goes on its way. The world sure is vast.

"Hey, let's be off then." Zanvan says with a tag to Geric. He refrains from touching Avrel, which she appreciates.

They head back to the inn Avrel had stayed at the previous night to see if Geric and Zanvan can find suitable rooms. The longest bed is just over five feet long. It's *perfect* for Avrel and for Candice, but it doesn't suit the taller men.

And, this place charges extra for putting them together.

"Erm sorrer, Sirs, Therts hewr irt ers!" the host says with finality to Geric's haggling.

"Forget it, Geric." Zanvan scoffs, "We'll go back to where we stayed last night."

Avrel can't help but be delighted as the cleric's prized height actually comes against him, and she has no shame in letting it show. "I'll meet you in the morning." she grins.

"Come on." Zanvan insists as he leads Geric away.

Avrel watches down the hall until they're out of sight, and once that show is over, she grabs her doorknob.

"Herr, wert!" the host says, "Cern Er gert yer sermtherng ter ert?" he asks, she thinks. They always sound as if they are asking a question.

"Something to eat?"

He nods. "Er'll breng ert ter yerr!" he offers.

She's heard of room service inns, now it's no wonder it was so expensive the night before. "Um… I'll just have whatever."

"Er'll gert yerr therr serp?" he, she thinks, asks.

"Yeah." she nods. "Sure. I'll be inside, just knock, I guess."

"Shurr!" he says, with a little bow, "Merr plersure!"

Eventually he comes to her door with some soup. She wasn't sure that's what he'd said, but she's happy to have guessed right. It's supper by the time he arrives anyway, and she's determined to not be late tomorrow. Bob said 'dawn', *she hopes*, and she'll be ready. She enjoys the soup, and then promptly goes to bed.

The following morning Avrel wakes up way before the rooster rises. Not wanting to waste the morning, she decides to go ahead to the dining room to get some breakfast.

"Serry Mer'm, wer dern't stert urntir servern Er'clerck." a host calls after her as she heads for the dining room.

"Oh." she pauses. *Seven would be far too late.* "Damn."

"Serry ferr erny erncornvenernce." he says with a little bow.

She smiles and brushes it off, but she was looking forward to it. The soup was damn good. No matter, she can go elsewhere to find something to eat; for her *and* for Candice. It's a feeling that's strange to her, and she ponders it as she returns to her room to clear out her things and get Candice. No waiting in a back alley for stales to be thrown out, no haggling for fruits or vegetables that fell from a cart and were noticed by the owner, no desperate run to claim them before they could be noticed.

"Chippu?" Candice chirps.

"Come, girl." she says with a pat, "Maybe we can find some firewood for you."

She flaps her tail as eagerly as one might expect from a beaver, and her smile is just as toothy. "Chippu!"

After checking out, Avrel and her hungry beaver head out into the morning light. She's not sure of what day it is, but whatever day, it's already surprisingly busy with supply carts. Little gnomish men, and maybe women riding little wagons all about. If this were in Argoth, she'd assume it is either Goldday or Marketday, but that's just a hunch.

Having forgotten the need of her stomach, she's taken quite a bit of a walk through the little city, it being the first she's ever seen outside of Argoth. And again, the peace of feeling no threat from the tiny gnomish men gives peace to her casual walk down the dark, fore-dawn street. Eventually, there's a rumble from her abs, defined by lack of fat, and not so much by muscle, as she has little of either.

"Oh yeah." she sighs, and takes a look and listens around. Her elf ears hear the sound of quacking and she follows it, where there are birds, there may be eggs. Sure enough, in a little alley is a cage next to an old gnome with a cart of farm goods.

"Hellerr! Carn Er herp yer firnd sermtherng?" the old man asks. The vegetables are all vibrant and colorful roots. Somewhat typical fair this time of year, she supposes.

"Um... yes." Avrel says looking over the cart with Candice sniffing the aroma of the sweet beets, radishes and other treats. "Could I get a parsnip for my companion here?"

"Anerthirng fer yer?" the gnome says as he grabs a thick one.

"Do those ducks lay eggs?" she asks, pointing to the cage.

"Erm... yeahr, how marnerr?" the gnome asks, opening the cage. Before Avrel can answer he's suddenly overwhelmed by the proportionally large duck.

"ERRRRR! ERRMERGERD!" he cries as he's knocked over and pecked by the angry fowl.

"Umm, Candice, you wanna get on that?" Avrel gasps, turning to her furry friend, not sure of what to do herself.

"Chippu" Candice replies as she then works to subdue the deranged duck. Within a moment the beaver nips the duck into submission, and the gnome catches his breath. He's not *too* badly pecked.

"Here" Avrel says, offering a hand to the man.

"Thernks." he pants, "Hrmm... Irf yerd lirk, fer yer herlp, Err'll threr irn the derk ers ar bernous!" he says, happily holding up the limp, bitten up duck.

Avrel blushes in thankfulness, and sympathy. The poor thing just wanted to get out of its prison. She's the kobolds trying to kill her for leaving Argoth. "A bonus duck, eh?" she thinks she heard him right. "Umm.. Well thank you! It's just that, it's um-" She's cut off by a hard snap as the gnome breaks the duck's neck over his knee. "...Well, okay then." Avrel says with a hint of sadness. "You can sit it on Candice's back I suppose."

"Shure!" he says as he places the dead duck over the beaver's back.

"Thank you" Avrel says with a slight smile as she pays the man. She hands Candice the parsnip, and takes her eggs. "Will you be alright? she asks, noticing that a few of his wounds are bleeding. "I have a cleric friend that-"

"Ner." he smiles, "Er'll ber firn!"

Avrel nods. And notices the hints of sun breaking over the horizon. "Come on, we'll eat when we get there." she says to Candice, though it appears Candice made quick work of the pale root.

The two make their way back to the inn, and it finally hits her why she feels so at ease here. *It's a little strange*, she thinks as she walks down the street, *I for once don't always have to have my head up-tilted*. Outside of feeling immune to threats, she's also amused at how she's somehow a tall person. She wonders if this is how Geric must feel most of the time, with the almost eye-level shoppe signs and a strong sense of presence. But of course, she won't be an arse about it.

When she and her familiar come to the inn, her companions are nowhere in sight. *Good.* she smiles, and wastes no time to consider how to prepare her eggs. Unlike Argoth, Manitärian roads are gravel, not cobblestone. She can't just crack it onto a smooth stone and blast it with heat. "Hmmm..." she thinks hard, *Zanvan has all the cookware...*

"Chippu?" Candice suggests.

"Boiled eggs?" she asks. That was how her mother would often make them back when... And they never knew when he was coming home. Funny that Candice should suggest that, but it might work. After a moment she starts looking for and finds an old flower pot filled with rainwater the alley behind the inn. "Think this'll take the heat?"

Candice just shrugs with a quiet "Chippu", so Avrel proceeds to blast the pot with a fire spell.

"And just leave those in for a few minutes..." she sighs.

"Chippu!" Candice shakes her back, drawing attention to the dead duck.

"Yeah, I'm sure Zanvan and Geric will like that, just hold on to it a little longer." Avrel says, petting the beaver's head. And she obliges.

Avrel's seldom had chicken eggs, much less had duck eggs, but they seem larger. Though, even chicken eggs are larger than some she's seized out of desperation. She only can hope they taste better.

***

Zanvan is awoken by Geric who has apparently been up for some time.
"Ugh.. Is it time to meet her?" he groans. He'd be half worried if the room weren't still dark.
"Yeah, we should head on over" Geric replies.
"Hmmm.. What are you doing up so early?" Zanvan asks. Usually this is quite the opposite, with the cleric dragging his arse.
"Ah you know." Geric dismisses "Taking a walk, grabbing some bacon, enchanting a few ducks to be easily angered, just normal, clericy, morning things."
Zanvan leans up, and grabs his pipe from the bedside table. "Yeah… 'normal, clericy, morning things.'" he scoffs as he lights it. "Well, we should go then." he sighs. With Geric ready to go, for once, and not surrounded by bits of paper, he grabs his pack heads out. After they pay the inn owner on the way out, Zanan sets his bearings for Chanterelle Street.
"Are you not going to eat something?" Geric asks as they are making their way downtown.
"I'll find something on the way." he dismisses. "Besides, we usually get attacked by some animal with a decent pelt, I need to be hungry for that stuff." Zanvan replies. He takes a longer stride hoping the cleric might take the hint. He doesn't. *It's only natural…* he supposes, he loves waking to the soft sound of the forest, the cleric would be more used to bombastic hymning and all that lot. It doesn't make it much better though.
"Yeah, but salted pork!" Geric pleas.
"Come on, I'll eat when I want." Zanvan says upping his pace even more, simultaneously trying to put his pipe away.
"You know, I've heard it said that these little folk eat *constantly*." Geric informs him. "Now really, shouldn't we have a second breakfast for that full Manitärian experience?"
"Last I checked…" Zanvan stops and smiles coyly, "You were pretty proud about being nothing like these gnomes."
The cleric doesn't seem to have a counter to that, he just stands there a moment. "Maybe I've been shown the light?" he says at last.
Zanvan gives him a stern look as is done with it. As he makes a swift turn he feels his cloak fan out in the breeze. It's the swift breeze that flows as the warmth of

the sun sends the chill of night into retreat, dawn is coming, and they have laces to be.

He finds the kid's inn, but checking with the host, it seems she's left on her own. "Did she say where she was going?"

"Errr…" he scratches his beard, "She werrs arsking abert brearkfarst, bert sherr serrd sherr nerrded ter berr sormwherre. Sherr courdn't wert ferr ourr brearkfarst."

Geric butts in, "I don't suppose that her complimentary meal is transferable?"

"Nerr."

"No?"

"Nerr!"

"Nerr!?" Geric twists out, making an utter arse of himself. Or rather exposing the fact.

"Thank you." Zanvan says, putting a not abrupt enough end to it before he turns for the door.

He waits outside and lights his pipe until the cleric follows out a moment later. "MmmI swear." Geric says, lifting the side of his hat to scratch just above the ear. "All we do is look for and wait for that elven shrimpette."

Zanvan rolls his eyes. *There's that ever holy patience of yours.* Still, he's not wrong, the kid is far too illusive and impulsive for someone so vocal about her fears. "Why don't you just pray for a sign or something you clerics do?"

"I once prayed for patience, you see where that's gotten me." the cleric scoffs. And then after a snort, he sniffs. "Do you smell duck?"

He does. "What of it?"

"Argh…" the cleric moans, "If I'd pray for anything right now it'd be food."

"Do it, maybe we'll find--" he pauses. He hears a familiar, girls' voice, and an animal's chatter.

***

As Avrel is softly humming to herself as she sits cross legged by her makeshift boiling pot in the back alley of the inn, she quickly glances up to the sound of approaching boots.

And sandal type things with thick woolen socks. It's Zanvan and Geric, so she resumes retrieving her eggs from the boiling flowerpot of water. "Ten minutes right?" she tries to recall, not that she has much to go on but her own internal hourglass.

She's aware that Zanvan and Geric are watching her, their faces are peculiar. "Umm... You okay there?" Zanvan asks in a confused tone.

"Yeah, I put them there." she replies as she peels one.

The men share a glance. "Ok aythen." Zanvan says, sighing out some smoke. "Glad you weren't too far."

"No." she says, "I made sure I was here. Oh, Candice has a present for you." she says chomping down on the egg.

"Chippu!" the beaver squeaks as she offers up the duck.

"Oh... Nice. Thanks. I'll make some jerky or something with it." Zanvan says, seeming distracted by Geric's fixated glare. Zanvan picks it up by its flaccid neck and takes a close look, "How did you come by this?" he asks.

"Long story short; the duck got angry and attacked the guy I bought these eggs from." she smiles as she begins peeling another egg. "And I helped him so he gave it to me, pretty nice, eh?"

Geric finally stops leering and instead seems to try to change the subject. "Where is that 'Berb' guy?"

"Bob?" Avrel says in a shushing voice, "His name is 'Bob Ethans'."

"Well?" Geric asks again, still not having been answered.

"He should be here soon." Avrel insists, as she peels her third egg. By this third egg, she wishes she had some salt. Still, she's thankful for the food as it is. Yet, she is still a little sad for the duck.

"Well, thanks." Zanvan says as he leans down and pats her head.

She finishes eating while they pace to and fro, and after that, they all wait for a few more minutes. Then, just as the streets begin to glow with dawn's first rays of light, she can faintly hear the sound of a wagon pulling up to the front of the inn. Zanvan reacts to hearing it a short moment later.

"Come on." he says as he and the cleric go, leaving her and Candice behind. "Just a second!" she says before dumping the water from the flower pot. She heard the wagon first, and yet she's the one left behind!

As she catches up, the gnome is just bringing his horses to a halt. "Hellerr!" he says cheerily, "Here yer ger, arl abord mer swerrg wergern."

"Swag wagon?" Avrel asks.

"Wer yers, Err gert mer swerg frerm ther errves! Arnd Err trarnspert ert orn thirs wergern!" Bob replies, "Arl abord!" he yells beckoning them to get in. Avrel happily gets in while Zanvan and Geric study it for a moment. Aside from the smaller pearch, it's quite a good sized wagon. The horse is full sized too, many she's seen in the Manitärian streets thus far were pygmy ponies. *But, she supposes, I guess that'd not work well for larger hauls.*

After her, Geric and Zanvan get into the back of the wagon and settle. "We're good back here." Zanvan shouts, giving him the ok to start moving. Though largely empty, he has some goods to trade back here, notably some sort of preserved castor's jaw.

"Look away." Avrel says, turning her beaver around.

"I am glad that this is a full-sized wagon and not some gnomish sized cart." Zanvan says, as he puts out his pipe.

"MmmmProbably wouldn't bother Avrel." Geric says with a nudge, he's seated right beside her. "Am I not right?" he says with his shitey grin. For all his prodding, at least Rufus's questions were genuine.

Avrel looks at him with somewhat sarcastic fury and sass, "Was your mother beaten up by a short person or something?" she asks.

"MmmNo, not as far as I know." he laughs loudly. "Besides, they'd be too small to beat her up, because they'd be by definition, short."

"Ugh..." Avrel says resting her face in her palm. *I'm small and I bet I could beat you if I needed too.* She'd try anyway, no man will ever have at her without a fight.

For a while they all sit silently with only occasional sounds and squeaks made by Candice or the wagon. Over the morning and into the afternoon, Manitäria and it's many mushrooms fade into the grass of the Argothian plains.

"I'm bored!" Geric says loudly breaking the silence. It seems he's out of books.

The silence resumes until Avrel stirs. "I have some cards.." she says, reaching into her pack. "What do you guys like to play?" she asks. Before either of the men can answer she takes the band off and shuffles the deck in a flauntingly arcane manner, just to set the cleric and his shitey, masculine ego off. "I once got a whole silver piece for this trick." she comments. "Got to eat pretty square for about a week, eh!?"

Geric is unamused, but Zanvan flashes her a polite smile. "Are we betting?" he asks as the politeness turns cocky.

Avrel shrugs, almost dropping the cards from her arcane grasp. "Sure."

"You talked me into it." Geric says, spryly.

Zanvan balks, "I'd have thought this would be the part where you tell us, 'gambling is wrong!'"

"It's okay, my son, we all make mistakes." the cleric says in his most snooty, clericishly holier than you voice.

Avrel finally starts dealing out the cards into four piles when Geric takes notice of the fourth pile. "Is Bob gonna join us?" he asks, rather confusedly.

"No." Avrel shakes her head. She savors the look on his face as he watches Candice make her way to the card pile and start messing with the cards, chirping with glee.

"No!" Geric says staunchly.

"But why?" Avrel questions.

"Because I'm not playing cards with a *beaver*!" he shouts, pointing to the rodent, sitting on its rump and holding up a fan of cards.

"Just play." Zanvan says in an annoyed tone.

"But... C'mon, how is it even holding them like that? She hasn't any thumbs! It's just not as The Gilded would have it!" Geric continues, pointing at Candice.

The four sit there silently for a few moments. "Candice and I play a lot, she knows the rules." Avrel smirks, knowing full well, that's not his protest. And they sit another long moment

"*Fine.*" Geric gives in at last and they begin to play. After a few hands Candice wins a small majority of them, and Geric visibly becomes suspicious of his toothy opponent. "You're awfully lucky for an overgrown muskrat!" he says in an accusatory tone.

"Chippu chippu chippu." Candice chatters in a laughing sort of way.

"Hey listen, you little varmit, you can't be that lucky.... I'm supposed to be that lucky!" Geric says folding his arms and staring hatefully at the beaver who stares snidely back.

"Why do you carry cards around with you anyway?" Zanvan asks, though he tips his hand that he was barely paying attention to her before, and it's plain he knows it as soon as he says it.

She sighs and begins to reply "I use them in my show someti-"

"AHHA!" Geric yells abruptly, "You're cheating using your natural born magical stuff to cheat! You are aiding this beaver and conspiring against me!" Geric continues.

"Geric... You lost a few hands of cards to a familiar in the form of a beaver..." Avrel says as she's gently petting Candice behind her tiny ears, "Calm down and accept it, it's a game."

Geric stares intensely at the both of them, her and Candice.

"I see the kid isn't the only one with paranoid tendencies." Zanvan scoffs.

"*Excuse me!?*" she snaps back.

"I said, 'I'll deal the next hand', okay?" Zanvan says as he tries to settle both of them down. She'll let it work, just because she knows it's not paranoia if it's true. If she's recalling the definition right.

"I refuse to play with a beaver! One time, they stole my shoes and made me watch as they added them to one of their little twig huts!" Geric yells, and throws down his hand before recrossing his arms. It sounds rather unlikely.

"Fine, if you're going to let a beaver win your money, then so be it." Zanvan says brushing Geric off. Candice gives Geric a toothy look, much like a smile.

"Mmm... Okay, fine!" Geric shouts as he picks his cards up. "*I won't lose my money to a rat.*"

Seeing just how mad he is, Avrel leans over to Candice and whispers, "Hey, let him win, do us a favor, let him win his money back." She's seen what men can do when they are angry.

"What are you conspiring now?" Geric asks inquisitively.

"Nothing." Avrel replies, starting to lose her cool. "Just shut up and play."

Zanvan deals out the cards and they all take a look at theirs. After trying to get some better cards, the beaver folds. The pot adds up to quite a hefty sum when finally Zanvan folds leaving only Avrel and Geric. They raise each other back and forth until both their coin purses are empty. As they are about to lay down their cards, the cart is bumped and everything is shaken up.

"ERRMERGERD! WERVS!" they hear Bob cry out. The cart is again shaken as Bob brings it to a sudden stop. "Plerrs, gert the wervs!" he yells. The three hop out of the cart while poor Candice is pinned in the back of the cart by a large length of heavy grade rope. But Avrel can't help her at the moment, and at least she's safe.

The encounter is short as Zanvan quickly shoots the wolves. He and Geric gather their bodies so he can harvest their pelts while Avrel checks on Bob who she finds alright.

All seems well and they get back into the wagon. Despite the sudden stop, everything seems alright. *Except...*

"MY MONEY!" Geric cries out. Indeed, the pot had been scattered by the shaking and had been tossed around for the length of time between the wolves first bumping the cart and the eventual stop. "I gotta find it all, I was gonna win!" he cries.

"Well hey." Avrel says patting his shoulder, "At least you lost your money to some wolves and not a beaver." she says trying to cheer him up, though she's not without pain of her own. "Besides, we'll get that money back when we sell these furs."

"It's not fair." he grunts with a scowl, "I just wanted to buy something fancy and gloat in front of that little floppy-tailed shite, is that too much to ask?" Geric asks the wind.

"Awfully *material* minded, aren't you?" Zanvan asks.

"*Justice* minded." the cleric corrects, defeatedly.

"Herr!" Bob shouts back to them, "Cern Err gerr?"

"Yeah!" Avrel says as she frees Candice. They settle into the wagon and begin again towards their destination. With no more card games.

They go about this for several days, defending the cart, getting the cart unstuck, and listening to Geric complain. It's about high-noon and yet again, they hear Bob's call to action.

"Ermergerd!" he cries, "Ar chargerng berrnerrcern!"

"A what?" Avrel asks, usually she can make out the gnome's words.

Zanvan stands up and looks forward, over Bob's perch. "Bonnacon." he says grimly. And then smiling smugly as he grabs his bow, he leans out the back of the wagon. "Hope you guys like steak!" she hears him say.

"Sharl Er sterp?" Bob asks.

"Nope." she hears Zanvan say with a hint of strain, "Steady on. Buggers have skulls harder than our cleric."

Geric seems unaffected by the sleight. "I suppose he doesn't need us, bonnacons aren't very large."

"Bonnacon?" she can't see by cranning out the back.

"Bull-horses." Geric says.

That she's heard of, but the look on Geric's face is one of elitist snobbery let down by her lack of vocabulary. "Some of us haven't had the privilege to read bestiaries all day." she scoffs.

He doesn't deny it, he just smugly shrugs.

She crawls over to the front of the wagon and takes a look over Bob's perch, for what she can see on her toes. It's a slimmer beast than a wild auroch, but heftier than a horse, to be sure. And sure enough, a single arrow through its head downs it, even from a distance. She shifts to look out the open back as she hears Zanvan jump from the side. If he's at all consistent, he'll be retrieving his arrow.

And he is.

"Hey, Bob." he says as they pull to a stop, which she is unprepared for. "These things are good eating, but you have to cure them fast, mind if we stop?"

"Err..." Even hanging halfway out the back of the wagon she can hear the gnome scratching his beard.

"I'll let you keep the mane."

"Err serperse." he concedes.

She doesn't concede to Geric's offer of help. She just drops into the grass in lieu of being often down like a child. "Why can't we just save it for later?" she asks as she walks over to the ranger, who is already arms deep into the creature's flesh.

"Their shite is caustic, it'll rot them inside of an hour." he grunts, throwing another long strip of meat beside him.

She can already see it's rump area shrivelling away. "Gross."

"They taste great." he says.

"Unless it kills you." Geric comments as he joins them. "One wrong cut and all its bile floods out, burning your skin down to the bone."

Suddenly, she's not so interested in trying it. But, Zanvan is going to a lot of trouble for them, so she figures she will anyway.

"I just wonder..." Zanvan says as he cut meat off the thighs, carefully not touching the already decayed parts. "Usually they graze in herds."

"Something must have separated it." Geric shrugs, "Good thing for us too, I'm tired of eating grass." He quickly raises a finger, "And I don't care what you say, I won't eat wolf."

Avrel crosses her arms and shakes her head at them. They are amusing at times.

"Chippu chippu!" Candice chatters as she leans out from the wagon, looking rather far back into the distance in the sprawling field.

"How can you tell?" Avrel squints but even her elf-eyes can't see what the beaver's nose can smell. "Alright, be careful, and stay away from wildcats." she says tenderly.

"Chippu!" the beaver squeaks as she leaps from the wagon.

"You're just gonna let it leave?" Zanvan asks, lighting his pipe.

"Yeah, she does this from time to time, she'll go out for a while, a few days even and come back. I remember one time there was a suspiciously coincidental damming of the Argothian River when she had left."

"Wonderful..." Geric says with a sigh.

"She just wants to find something to eat." Avrel shrugs, "Aspen probably."

"As do I." Geric sighs.

"Well." Zanvan says as he lifts up a string of meat strips, "Let me hang these to cure and I'll cook some later."

"Yer, cerm ern ner!" Bob sounds a little impatient.

Avrel gets back into the cart while Geric and Zanvan string the meat as they often do. Already, she misses Candice as they take up their favored spots, and once again, the wagon begins to move.

"I'll just leave this mane back here." Zanvan says, wrapping it in a spare rag which turns bloody very fast.

"Thernks!"

Zanvan tips his hat, though Bob won't be able to see it, and sits back and lights his pipe.

"Cards?" Avrel asks after a little while, "I only lost a few face cards, we could play Old Crone, or something."

Geric jumps at the chance. "Without the rat, yeah sure!"

Zanvan sighs, wiping his hands on his cloak. "Yeah."

As she deals the hand, Avrel feels vulnerable. She sighs softly to herself, *Candice will be back. It may not be the stagnant and well explored city, but she'll be back.* She glances at her two companions. She's *probably* safe until then.

It's the next morning and Candice is yet to come back. Unlike the thick steak-like fillets Zanvan made the night before, for breakfast he made thin strips almost like bacon. Most of the time she can take meat or leave it, especially for its price, but this bull-horse is rather good.

After their morning meal, they continue east. Geric looks to be rereading a book, Zanvan sharpens his knives, and she sits back against a crate. She wishes she could read. She wishes she had a weapon to maintain. She wishes Candice would return, but she also wants to respect her autonomy. She said she smelled some yummy trees a few miles away, and so Avrel will let her enjoy them. Even then, she wonders how far away she can call, in Argoth it never could have been more than a few miles. She doesn't *really* understand familiars at all. *Would Geric know?* she asks herself, but hesitates to ask him.

Around supper time, Candice still isn't back, and with everyone so silent, it's all that's on her mind.

"Geric." she says, stiffly.

"What's up, ears?" he replies, nonchalantly from behind his book.

"What do you know about familiars?" she asks. Geric doesn't react, and only moistens his finger to turn the page.

Zanvan who has been staring into space looks halfway interested. "Worried about your pet?" he asks.

"A familiar isn't a pet, ranger." Geric is quick to correct.

"Well, obviously." Zanvan says in his typical cold smugness, "I've never seen someone's pet beat a grown man in cards."

"A familiar is a nature spirit, or wayward spirit or some shite that bonds with some animal after making an astral link to the host mage." Aside from the colorfully un-cleric-like language, he says it as if he's reciting it. "And only those with strong, natural or innate connections to the magic can have them."

"So *you* can't?" Zanvan prods. And Avrel begins to get it, Zanvan wasn't being a bore by taking over her question, or he-peating, he's playing off of Geric's toxic, male ego. Of course it would take one to know how to play with one.

"Not typically." Geric answers, finally looking up and over his book.

Still, all she can think of is Candice. In the city, she knew generally where Candice would go, and that it was safe. With each passing mile she worries more. Candice's rat-like nose is strong, but what if the distance is too far?

"I hope she's back by supper." Avrel mutters.

"Or maybe she was somebody's supper." Geric says with his shitey grin, "I've heard that those rat's tails are quite the delicacy.

Over her own disgust Avrel hears Zanvan confusedly ask, "But you won't eat wolf?" To which the cleric shrugs.

Her concern unresolved and their discourse going nowhere, they fall silent as Zanvan pulls some dried meat from the back of the wagon and he passes it out to each of them, and Bob. They aren't stopping for supper then, she accepts, and she sits in still quietness but for the tearing of the leathery, dried meat. All Avrel can think of is Candice, and how she'd teasingly gnaw such things, or hardtack, stale breads like her toothy friend. *Please come back... Please make it back.* She moans inside.

Until all of a sudden they hear a deafening squeak, far too loud to be Candice, or any other rodent of her size.

"*Werr!!!*" Bob cries as he brings the wagon to a skidding stop, "Here der arr! Der virmerts!"

The company gets out of the cart to see that there are large ridges in the earth making passage impossible. They turn to a large hill that is cracking open and watch as a giant marmot comes burrowing out.

As it rises out, it lets out an ear-piercing squeak, and like the others, she covers her ears. Or what of them she can, her hands aren't that large. As it stops, she notices Zanvan drawing his bow and quickly she motions for him to put it away as she steps forward. He seems to oblige for the moment, and she draws her staff only in reserve for defense.

"Hey Bob, do you have any dried pepper?" Avrel asks, warily glancing around. She doubts their pelts are worth much, and she'd rather not hurt them.

"Er do, Zarnvern was yersirng irt for hirs jerker." Bob replies.

"Zanvan, where is it?" Avrel says holding her free hand out behind her.

"Here!" Zanvan grunts as he drops a satchel of dried peppers into her hand.

"Okay, hopefully this'll work" Avrel sighs as she starts twirling her staff. "Geric use your mace and grind it into a powder." she commands.

"Why me?" Geric whines. "Can't I just whack them?"

"Because you're the one with a mace, idiot!" she shouts, rolling her eyes. But she hears him getting to work, so at least he's listening. She turns back to her front and focuses and gathers her power, and she can feel she's almost done as a marmot nearly the size of a bear comes out of a mound and charges for her. But she's almost ready.

"Avrel, if I'm not allowed to shoot them, you gotta do something!" Zanvan yells to her, as he puts an arrow to his bow.

Before he can let it fly, Avrel swings her staff and clangs it against the metal wheels of the cart, making a horrendous noise, cringe inducing for man and beast, and painfully loud to half-elves. The incoming marmot turns about-face and runs for the burrow hills.

"Alright is this ground enough for you?" Geric yells over the cacophonous clanging as she strikes it again.

Avrel looks and nods. "Yes." She closes her eyes and begins casting her spell as a heavy magic wind takes up the ground pepper and disperses it over the area. She guides the wind, she can feel the wind around her. She can feel them turning away, and hear them as well.

"Ermergerd! Yerr dird ert!" Bob cheers.

Avrel opens her eyes and stops casting her wind spell as the marmots run away in a loud and squeaky stampede. *It worked...* she sighs in relief.

Zanvan lowers his bow. "That went surprisingly well." he comments, patting her shoulder.

She looks to Geric, smugly as she waits for his response, she knows he has one.

"Mmm... I'd still rather have wacked them." he shrugs as he throws his mace back into the cart and claps the pepper dust from his hands.

"Herr dird yerr knerr ert'd werk?" Bob asks, after sneezing.

I didn't. she has time to admit herself as she too sneezes. "Candice hates pepper. Apparently most of her kind do." Avrel smiles.

"I've heard gardeners say it works for rabbits." Geric adds.

"Well, maybe just give us a heads up." Zanvan says with a tint of sternness. "If you have an idea, share it with us before the time comes, hm? If that hadn't have worked, that bloated whistlepig might have trampled you."

On one hand, she sees where he's coming from, on the other, he's assuming she planned it. She didn't. Of course, men always assume women are conniving and planners. *Maybe we often have to be.*

"Errg! Gert irnterr the wergon!!" Bob yelps. She'd ask why, but turning with a jerk is suffice; all the piled, churned and loose earth comes crashing down sending waves of dust and dirt into the air. And despite her releasing the spell, the air is still quite lively.

"Oh shite!" Avrel curses as she pulls her blouse up over her mouth. Zanvan does the same but with his cloak. Geric, having been in the process of putting his mace in there, is already in the wagon

As they all get into the back of the wagon and close the flaps, the debris fuzzes against the canvas top, and the ground settles. It feels like it might last forever.

"I still don't get it!" Geric yelps over the noise, "The really large ones usually keep to themselves and avoid more travelled ways!"

"Bert Er terk mer ewrn shert curts!" Bob replies. "Bersirds, irt's nert lirk Er'm bersed irn Mirdrasherth ern cern hirre guerds!"

"Yeah, I suppose all the military escorts Midrashoth's merchants have access to, this wouldn't be a big deal." Zanvan agrees. "Or Argoth."

With one last crackle of dirt, things sound still and settled. "It sounds clear now." Avrel says, breaking off the conversation and putting her ear to the side of the wagon.

"I'll check." Zanvan says. He'd just gotten his pipe out, but he puts it back. He puts his head out the back, observes for a moment, and pulls back in. "You mentioned gardens, cleric?" he asks. "The plains out there look like a tilled up garden."

"See, if we'd just whacked them…" Geric snidely puts in.

"Shouldn't you have a sleep spell?" Zanvan says as he opens the curtains and jumps out.

"Nobody asked." Geric utters as he follows.

Avrel stays a minute. Maybe they're right, she just acted without any plan, not considering what would happen if the marmots were merely driven away. *Oh no…*

"Mrs Arvrel?" Bob asks as he's about to pass through the curtains.

"Oh…" she composes herself. "Nothing." Nothing except that she hopes to goodness she didn't drive Candice away too.

"Come on out, tinies!" they hear Geric call, and both sharing a mutual sigh of reluctance, they follow.

As she looks out from the wagon, Zanvan's description holds. It looks quite like a tilled back-alley garden in long strips stretching almost as far as her half-elf eyes can see.

"Looks okay." Geric yells as he inspects the surrounding landscape, "But I'm not sure how we'll get across all this soft, churned earth!" he adds as both he and Zanvan sink in as they step on it.

Avrel has no such problem, and Bob doesn't seem to either as he goes around and sits up on his driver's perch. "So..." she asks. "How *are* we gonna cross?" Looking at how the wheels are a bit sunken in, she wouldn't expect them to roll over that loose dirt very easily, not without getting stuck.

Geric looks at it and then to her, "You could freeze it to hold it tight while we go over it." he thinks out loud.

"That... Could work..." Avrel says placing her hand to her cheek, thoughtfully. She's never done such a large freezing spell, only enough to freeze mist.

"You know, we could just pack it down." Zanvan says in an instructive tone. Geric and Avrel look at each other and agree.

"Hey Bob, do you have any shovels?" Avrel asks. Meanwhile, Geric has already impatiently begun routing through the stuff in the back of the cart.

"Found some!" he yells.

"Oop, never mind we found some." Avrel passes along.

"Hmmm..." Zanvan grunts, sounding rather disappointed. "Shovels weren't really what I had in mind."

"Well..." Avrel asks, "What should we use, eh?" She rests her hands on her hips. It's not like it'd be her first choice either.

"I dunno." the ranger shrugs, "Get a tree and roll it back and forth over the path?" he suggests, coldly. "That's more or less how they prepare roads in towns and cities. Not..." He glances at their tools, "Packing it down with shovels."

"Therers werrn." Bob says pointing to a short, thick tree about a dozen yards off.

"Okay then..." Of course, something inside her shudders at downing a tree, but it looks half dead anyway. "Do you have any axes?" Avrel asks.

"Wernch, yer luckerr Er herd shervers, whyr wourd Er herv axers?!" Bob says in a harsh and sarcastic tone.

"Mmm... then we can't use that idea now can we?" Geric says frustratedly as he crosses his arms and leans on the cart wheel. "What about your spells?" Geric asks, tauntingly, "Or will your ears shrivel up if you kill a tree with them?" He seems to think it's funny.

But Avrel knows best, if you want a tree cut down, there's only one person in their stupid party who is qualified.

As the gnome, the ranger, and the cleric go through all the tools, she sits on the back of the wagon's extended tail-gate and sits quietly with her eyes shut. She knows she's out there, she just hopes that she can reach her. And that she's safe. Maybe it wasn't as bad an idea as it feels, but she'll never make it again. She can feel a tear come to her eye as she focuesall her thoughts on her, and she just hopes the others don't see.

She's elf, or at least half of one. While the men fiddle with tools, she'll do this the natural way.

"You sleeping, she-elf?" Geric asks.

"Half." she corrects. "And--" Maybe she was, the sun is much dimmer, by an hour at least. "I guess so."

"Well come on, Zanvan's cooked up the last of the bull-horse flank."

It's strange, and she has a lingering feeling she can't quite describe. She feels as though she was asleep, but also, she feels very aware. The crackle of the firepit, the wind through the grass, the age of the wood and stone. By the time they are finished eating it's receded, but it's damned peculiar just the same.

"Shall we try again?" Geric asks.

Zanvan puts his pan over the flame and smothers it. "I suppose, unless the kid had any bright ideas during her naptime." he scoffs.

She opens her mouth to chide that remark, but just then, a distance chirp is heard.

6

"Chippu." they hear again, this time coming closer. Avrel opens her half-elven eyes, and in the distance they see a small brown creature making its way through the grassy plain. As she stands off of the tail-gate she clearly sees the dark, ebony brown eyes, the dark, wet nose, and the tiny buck teeth of Candice racing towards her.

"Seriously?" Geric says, laying his face in his hand. "Is that the bleeding beaver?"

"Chippu" Candice squeaks as she makes a flying jump onto Avrel's lap. Avrel flinches briefly as Candice's tail slaps her shin rather hard and then welcomes her wood-loving familiar.

"Oh..." Avrel lets herself moan as she holds her close. "I was starting to worry." she frys, "Let's not do that for a while, okay?" Maybe it's the men rubbing off on her, but she represses the few tears trying to drip from her eyes. She's still not quite sure why she was so worried, but it's over now, Candice is back. She gives her a good squeeze for good measure.

"You know..." she hears Geric say, "I was kinda hoping it wouldn't come back." he says lowly to Zanvan. She also hears Zanvan give him a soft punch.

Jealous arse. But she's said that enough. "So, I hope you're still hungry!" Avrel says petting Candice's head.

"Chippu!" Candice bares her teeth in compliance, apparently, she never quite found the feast she'd hoped to. All the better for them.

Zanvan comes over to Candice and pets her lightly and then points to the large tree in the distance. "Do you think you can-" Candice darts off towards the tree before he can finish. "I'll take that as a 'yes'." Zanvan says, straightening his hat. Everybody but Bob follows the beaver and watches as she so masterfully gnaws into the side of the trunk.

That's her girl, "And *you* wanted to pat the dirt down with shovels..." Avrel says, flexing and stretching, still stiff from her impromptu nap.

"Hey! You agreed to it!" Geric says defensively.

Zanvan points to Candice, "Do you think we should help?"

"Nah." Geric scoffs, "Just leave it to the beaver. Also, why didn't you just take it down with one of your *innately born* spells or something?" he asks pointing at Avrel.

"We're in a plain." she reminds him, "There are like -- no trees around, certainly none this big, eh!? You wanna risk it getting blown up? And, *oh yeah, it* could set the whole area on fire!" she retorts sassily.

Geric raises his finger as if to reply but simply closes his mouth and turns away. Then turns back, "Maybe you should stop gloating over your innate power and learn to control it better." he sneers.

"I know how to control it." she snorts, "It's using it in bigger sizes or for attacking that I'm inexperienced."

"Okay." he brushes off, "You're still blooming into a delicate and deadly, know-it-all elf mage. But one that still lacks control."

Avrel knows better than to get into that, a man lecturing her about control. But she can't say *nothing*, so she hits him with the best reply, which is none but a confident smirk.

After just a few minutes, Candice has most of the tree eaten through and by Zanvan's suggestion, they begin pulling it over until it finally snaps. After Candice has at the few protruding branches, they can drag it over to the path. Or rather, what should be a path.

"I'll get you something nice at the next stop." Avrel promises the beaver as she returns to just beside Avrel's feet. Geric and Zanvan carefully lay the tree down in front of the horses. At long last they can finally lay their weight over it and use it to roll over the loose earth to make it dense enough to at least try and roll the cart over.

"By the Gilded, Avrel..." Geric grunts. "Why do you have to be so scrawny and short? You add like, no weight to this thing!"

Avrel half heartedly giggles it off as they push on, almost clearing the sunken burrow when Zanvan motions for Bob to start coming across. Once they clear the ridge of sunken earth, Zanvan runs up ahead to check if there are anymore blocking the path. He motions that there are none, and so they all hop into the back of the wagon and make their way to the nearby rest stop. It's almost dark.

"What were you up to, beaver?" Geric asks, before opening one of his large books. Candice stares at him snidely from across the cart and holds up a coin which she chews and apparently had chewed on, a fragment of his lost winnings.

What's more, Avrel can tell that her cheeks are full, and have been full -- Of wood, she'd have thought. It would explain how come Candice was still hungry enough for all of the bark she's just eaten.

"Chippu?" In their corner of the wagon, Candice spits out a few and offers them to Avrel.

"Shhh!" Avrel shushes, Geric's mind is in a book, but not for long as it grows dark. But she smiles, Candice went all that way just to get her some of the lost money. "Thank you." she whispers, "I'll take it later." she winks.

As they pull up to a rest stop not far from a village, a young half-elf girl greets them and offers to take and tie up the horses. From what Avrel can tell, this is a nice inn, complete with a covered stable. She'd guess that in the heart of Argoth's plains, it's likely a well travelled area. Not that she's seen Zanvan's reckoning of where they are on a map, but she's aware of the second largest city in the kingdom, Midrashoth is somewhere north, and Wraugroth somewhere south, but not very far, in all likelihood.

Zanvan would know, but Zanvan hops out and offers to give the stable-girl a hand, which she graciously accepts. Avrel and the others, tired from the long ride, stagger in and immediately go to get assigned to their bunks. Of course, it somehow comes to be that Geric is in charge while Zanvan is busy. She's exhausted, and doesn't really care until she hears Geric trying to negotiate at the front desk. Specifically, that they get a discount by having her and Bob share a bed.

"Well." the fair elven lady's eyes fall hard on Avrel. Very similar eyes to that of the shoppekeeper in Argoth. "Muddying the blood quite a bit aren't we?" she says, then looking to the gnome. Her eyes are like a cold, blue, frost and her lips as red as Avrel's hair.

"Well." Geric says, leaning his arm onto the counter, "If that girl working in the stables is any indication, you don't mind that, do you?"

She's obviously taken aback, cold, elven grace even has its limits. "Excuse me." she asks.

"You're excused." Geric smiles, "Now the other guy will be along shortly, so may we--"

Avrel finally has her say, pulling Geric back from the counter with what leverage she can muster against his foreboding size. "Excuse me?" she rounds.

"You're excused too, my child." he says with some pious hand gesture.

"Nothing against you, Bob--" she says to start with, "But *no*."

"Erm marrierd." he adds against Geric's attempt at frugality.

"Mmm... come on, you two are small enough, there's no reason that you can't share a bed!" Geric explains.

"He's a married man, maybe even one with a conscience." Avrel growls, reaching up and trying to lift him by his collar, but barely able to tug it, "I'm a young lady-- Why in hell am I explaining this to a *cleric*?"

"Hah! *Lady*..." he scoffs like the sardy bastard he is when he gets ornery like this. "*Hoyden*, maybe. This lack of thrift is probably why you're poor." he shrugs off cooly as he turns back to the elven lady.

Mother ffff-- "Have you ever had a fireball *up your arse!*?" Avrel growls. She's too tired to produce one, but he doesn't know that.

"No!" Geric squeals.

"Then get me my own bed!" she yells, standing as tall as she can on her heels, and spraying in his face.

"What a waste of money..." Geric sighs. "Little children in the slums could use that money."

"And yet--" she counters, "No matter how you upper-crusties scrimp and save, we never see any of it." she says as she steps away and crosses her arms, "Never once had one of you clerics offer to help me, or my mother!" *Even when she was deathly sick, you just--* she stops, even continuing in her head is pointless.

Candice waddles by gnawing the coin which irks him even more. "Fine, but it's coming from your funds, not the party's." he says, putting money down for three beds, "Let the beaver cough up the rest." he laughs to himself as he goes down the hall.

Bob follows, leaving Avrel and her own bill. "Sorry about my acquaintance." she says softly as she gets her purse out.

"Mother or father?" the elf woman asks.

"Huh?"

"On which side are you of our blood?"

"Oh." Avrel swallows, nervously losing her money count, which is hard enough as it is. "Father." Avrel finally has her coins ready but notices the elf woman looking crossedly at the names written by Geric. "Did he write my name wrong again?"

"Perhaps." she says coldly, "Lavian? Not Laviandöltír?"

Avrel swallows hard, but dryly, and grits her teeth as her lips curl with uneasiness, "Just Lavian." she says, "My mother's family name."

There's a frighteningly bitter look from the elven woman as she reaches for a key. "I see."

***

"Thank you so much for your help." the stable-girl giggles as the wagon is backed into a spot and the first horse secured in its pen. "Most customers can't be bothered to even tip me a hat."

He can't see why, she's cute and despite the smell, fair on all other accounts. "Is that all you care for, just the tip?" he asks. "Or is company welcome?"

"More than welcome." she smiles. "I don't get to talk much, not so much as I might like anyway."

"But you seem to like horses." he puts in, but not pushily, Zanvan's just testing the water.

"Yeah." she sighs with a pleasant smile, "My parents opened this inn around when I was born and I've taken care of the animals since I was eight." she explains as she ties the last horse to its post.

"How long ago was that, if I may ask." Zanvan says, giving her a charming look. "You seem very... proficient."

"You're a sly one." she says drawing closer to him. "I suppose your meaning is to figure out my age?"

"Well, perhaps" he smiles.

"Old enough." she confirms. "My parents are an interracial couple, my mother is from the elven lake village, Järviby, her parents didn't approve of her marrying my father and so she was disowned, so they started this inn." the young lady explains as she presses herself against Zanvan. "Anything else you'd like to know?"

Knowledge, he smiles to himself, but he might have guessed about the inn, the signs out front were bi-lingual, and she has a very elven look-- Which also means ambiguous in age. "Quite the story this place has." he smiles, gently pressing her away, just enough to make her hungrier. "Any excitement happen here as a result of its location?" he asks.

She backs off fully, but without losing a desiring look in her eyes she looks around at all the tied up horses and sensually caresses the knots. "I've spent ten years mastering tying things up, I can't help but wish to know what it feels like. I imagine it a somewhat... Euphoric feeling." she says biting her lip slightly, "But alas, most who come through are stuffy elven or Midroshothian merchants; no ruffians, no excitement." She grabs a spare buckle and pulls it taut.

Zanvan grins heartily, and pulls her back closely to him. She smiles as he takes the straps from her hand, seeming to delight in the force by which he does it.

***

The sun is beginning to set, and it'll come to darkness soon enough. Yet, she's still to hear from them personally, frankly a dissapointment, as silence offers no favorable reports to her superiors.

So, dodging the eyes of some of the other Argothian Guard upon the shift change, she goes to the nameless tavern where this folly began. She'd gotten word that one of the group had fallen, but yet has one of her own underlings ascertained who. She *should* know by tonight, yet her thoughts wander, and she wonders if she herself should have gone. Should she have *insisted*? Her drink has no answers.

"Well hello, *Leth.*" He's dressed in his best medals, and cleanest armor, the perfect image of an Argothian Guard. Frankly, looking to be a might over qualified for his meager work.

"Kain." she says. "Found me faster than I'd expected." she says coldly as she takes another gulp of ale.

"Most people take their helmets off when they drink." he scoffs.

She gives him a glare, he knows better. "So then, did you find anything?" she asks.

"One body, evidence of a fight, burned brush, some kobold remains." he says casually.

"Body?"

"I dug it up, he was dressed in red." Kain says with utter calmness as he hails a drink.

She lets the ale sit and turn bitter on her tongue before she swallows, "I see." she says coarsely. "No sign of another?"

"Just our friend in the red robes." he leans back in leisure. "Sorry." he says, emptily, "I understand pressure from the higher ups is mounting on you." His drink is delivered, but before he can take it, she grabs it and takes a hefty chug for herself. "It seems I'm correct?"

Given his vast decor, she can't give him the lamblasting she'd like to, not in front of so many who don't know better. "It'll work out." she promises.

"I hope so for your sake." he laughs, stealing back his drink, notably not drinking from the same end of the mug, "Word is they're both quite impatient, and curious as to why you're skipping meetings." He reaches out to her, "Care to come with me to tonight's?" he offers with a shite eating grin across his punchable face.

She knows better, he wants to make someone jealous by going to the meeting with her, as if they've met regularly on this assignment. Which gives him far too much credit. "Are you done?"

"I suppose." he scoffs out, "But I'd maybe try to have something to show for next time you show." he warns, "Will Argoth rise?" he asks.

"Argoth shall be *raised*." she responds, and then waves him away.

She finishes the last drops in his cup and goes, leaving her coins on the table. She carries on through the darkened streets as Argoth prepares to sleep, and finds herself on the edge of the city, upon a high overlook from the surrounding city walls. From there she looks out towards her castle, her bond, her duty. None of these filthy meetings by egotists with their own agendas. What she does she does purely for her kingdom. To make it what it should be, what it once was, and shall become again.

For her kingdom.

For her people.

***

Zanvan awakens in some hay next to the half-elf stable girl as a sunbeam crosses his eyes. Still asleep, she's quite a bit frazzled looking, hardly an image of a graceful elven kind, but cute nonetheless.

And still bound up a bit, he notices. As he leans down to undo her hand ties he notices her eyes roll under her lids as she too wakes up. "Oh hey…" she says in a half dreaming frog. "Sure you want to do that so soon?" she looks up at the window, "We've got time." she invites.

"Sorry." he says briskly as he continues undoing the knot and trying to remember her name from the night before. "My companions and I need to be setting out soon."

"Hmmm..." she stretches her freed hands, "Yeah, they ought to be passing out breakfast by now." she smiles to him. "You'd better go then."

He gets up and dresses. "Aren't you coming?" he asks.

"Nah." she sighs, "I have to be ready to untie the horses as needed for any guests leaving this morning." she says as she pulls her girdle on. "Presumably you."

"When do you eat then?" Zanvan inquires, genuinely curious.

"Here and there." she laughs. "Don't you worry about me, just go."

No use in arguing, he prepares to head to the inn, but as he passes she grabs hold and tries for a kiss. A kiss he quickly puts down. "No, thanks." he tells her and continues on his way.

***

Avrel's eyes flutter open as the sunrise brings a new day. Candice is sitting between her thighs making it impossible for Avrel to move without disturbing her. "Candice." she rubs the soft, loose skin behind the beaver's neck. "Psst." she leans over into her little round ears.

"Chippu!?"

"Shhh." Avrel answers lowly. She looks around, she'd gotten a corner bed with a privacy screen in an otherwise communal room, but setting the beaver aside and looking out from it, it appears her friends are already up. "We'd better hurry." She'd est not give Geric any more ammunition for teasing.

She finds them where she'd expected, in the dining room with a few other early risers. "Hi." she waves as she comes to their table.

"Oh, there you are." Geric says, punctuated by a crisp crack of bacon. "I was beginning to wonder if Zanvan had finally gotten to you."

She can feel her face grow hot, as she must be flushed very red. *The very idea!* "No way in hell-!"

She's grabbed, softly by Bob. "Herr's tearserng." he reminds her.

She snorts a deep breath as she sits down across from Zavan's empty seat. "Well, it's too early for it." she snaps.

"Oh!" the cleric says with all the glory of an epiphany, "Because pure-blood elves don't reach *maturity* until what, like, fifty?"

Which is worse, she's not sure, that he claims to know her body more than she, or that he won't leave her alone. "That's not what I meant you egg-headed... *Sacricolist!*"

He leans back, of course with a shitey grin, and slowly chews his bacon. "Big word, I'm proud of you, my child." he almost chuckles; belittlingly, no doubt.

"Derr yer mirnd?" Bob begs, "Irt's earler."

A bowl of hot porridge is placed in front of her by the hostess, and so she drives into it. It is too early, but she didn't start it. All of it though reminds her of her goal, of why this job is so important. She *won't* be beneath those elitist, know-it-all sards forever.

Zanvan slaps the shitey cleric's head through his red hat as he comes around to sit. "Sorry." he says to everyone but Geric. "Nobody here has heard any word of the artifacts." he explains, "An elf described a hunter with a strange blade that she saw one night, but that was more than a decade or two ago."

"That's... vague." Avrel sighs. Though just the thought of monster hunters, bounty hunters and the like makes her think of him, and that's not something she ever wants to waste time on. "Decades?"

"You elves regard decades and centuries as we mere mortals might use years or decades." Geric quickly informs her, again rubbing the salt of his foreknowledge of half her own race into her wounds.

"Dern't worrer! Thirs term tormerrer or serr we'rr ber nearlerr art the errvern lerk towrn." Bob says, happily chugging down his porridge, not minding what sticks to his beard.

"Not to pry but is that where your family is from, Avrel?" Zanvan asks, crunching a strip of bacon. He must have ignored the dozen or so times Rufus asked, not that she'd blame him if he did.

She does blame him for bringing *him* to mind, again. "...I'm not sure where my father was from, it's possible." Then again, there's been a lot of that in this inn.

"Yeahr, morst errves frorm errournd here arr frorrm Jarverrberr." Bob chimes in.

Avrel quickly finishes eating and excuses herself to go pack her things. She doesn't want to talk about him, she doesn't want to be reminded how little she knows of half of herself, and she's not hungry for seconds.

"We won't be long." she hears Zanvan tell her as she leaves the dining room. She lingers one moment on the edge of her hearing.

"So, where were you?" Geric inquires, to which Zanvan is silent. Geric prods but the ranger refuses to answer his incessant questions, and eventually, the cleric stops.

She thinks about that as she goes back to her bed to grab her personal pack and her staff, and of course, Candice, but she'll maybe try that next time she's not up for the shitey cleric's teasing. *Silence.* she considers. But, she's no fool, men far too often take silence as consent, and *consent* to his teasing she does not. "Right Candice?" she asks, not realizing that she hadn't been thinking aloud.

"Chippu?"

"Never mind, let's just get to the wagon, eh?" she sighs.

She treks to the stable and shoves her things into her spot in the hold, after finding a piece of the inn's firewood for Candice to snack on.

"Thought you hated birch." she scoffs as the beaver curls in a circle of rope for bed. "After all your running I guess you are tired." she pets before climbing back out of the wagon.

"Oh, hello." Avrel hears from behind her. She turns around to see the stable girl with one of Bob's horses.

"You're um... Attentive." Avrel says, dropping from the tailgate.

The girl looks at her strangely. "You're half-elf too, aren't you?" she asks, pointing to Avrel's ears.

"Yes, I am." Though, there's hardly any comparison. This one, he looks very elf-like. Avrel has the cheeks and eyes maybe, but- "So far as I know, elves aren't known for being short and having pigmented hair, why do you even have to ask?" Avrel says with a playful smirk.

"Your friend mentioned you last night. It's just nice to know I'm not alone." the stable girl smiles.

"Who, Zanvan?" Avrel asks, a bit surprised, and wondering under what context.

"Yeah, he's um... Quite a man." the stable girl blushes.

Avrel feels her brows raise on their own. "You got a name?" she asks.

"Allura Evëdöltír-Hamon" she says, seeming to understand the mouthful that it is. "What's yours?"

"Avrel." she answers, and then takes a minute. Would that make her own true name be Isisdoltir? But putting together what the elven lady implied, *No*. She is elven from his side, and thus has nothing to do with those names. "Well, it's been nice talking to you, but we've gotta be going soon." Avrel says, realizing she must have been awkwardly paused for a moment. "Thanks for taking such good care of the horses and... stuff." Avrel says heading back towards the inn.

"You're welcome." Allura giggles. "If you're ever by again, tell your friend, I'm always willing to help him take care of..." she winks, like Avrel is somehow complicit or would help feed his carnal conquest, "*Stuff.*"

And of course she can only feel bad for her. "Sure." she says emptily before she goes into the dining room to find her companions.

The three are happily eating and Bob passes Avrel a piece of toasted bread. She accepts it, but then asks "Are we about ready to go, Bob?"

"Yeahr, we sheourd ber gorrirrng." he replies, seeming to regret that fact. The men all at once cram down the rest of their food and grab their personal items and head for the door.

As they all at once leave the inn lobby, Avrel notices Allura waving, and nudges Zanvan to get him to notice. He seems callous, and not to care, intentionally so. He's *ignoring* her.

"I see how it is." she says darkly, "You take the knowledge of her and afterward you don't acknowledge her?"

Zanvan gives Avrel an unconcerned but also unpleasant look before he sighs and reluctantly they both wave back.

Geric notices and turns. He also seems to take note of Allura's ethnicity. "See Avrel, there are other half-elves." he pats, unwantedly, "Although you're still a freak because you're so short." She immediately replies with a slap, though his shitey smile tells her in his mind, it was worth it.

"Arll errberd!" Bob calls as they linger.

Zanvan and Geric hope in with ease, Avrel of course takes a moment to climb up and gets no help but once they are all seated, Bob gives a shake of his reins and they embark once more.

About midday the next day it begins clouding up to the west and coming eastward fast. The winds pick up as well.

"Ohr nerr, thirs mighrt slerr urrs dern." Bob yells to the group as he ducks into the hold to get a raincoat.

"Hey, can you clear this up with some magic, you elves can do stuff like that right?" Geric says poking Avrel.

"Umm well.. I can make the storm stronger, I don't think I can dissipate it." she replies in a down voice. "Besides, it wouldn't feel right to dissipate the beautiful storm nature has made."

"Damn." Geric grunts. "I have no such tree-hugging hang-ups. I could if I had a spell for it."

But you don't. she smiles smugly to herself. Perhaps it's best that innate power among humans is so rare, with ones like him around.

Zanvan sighs smoke from his nose. "Shouldn't you be dancing or something?" Zanvan asks Avrel.

She freezes, is he thinking about *her* like that? He'd better not, she'll make him regret it if he makes a move like that. She resolves to disappoint. "Well... I heard that elves do dances depending on the weather, but.. I don't know that much about it." She lies, blushing quite a bit. Were they not around, of course she would.

"That's a shame." Zanvan sighs, leaning back and puffing his pipe. "I was under the impression that many elves were... were-"

"Pluviophiles?" Geric puts in.

"Yeah, Pluviophiles."

Avrel crosses her arms, feeling violated by his words. Of course, she's not sure what that word means, and like hell she'll ask Geric. All the same, coming from him, and it's ending, she can guess it must be sexual. *Pig.* she thinks to herself, echoed in a quiet mutter.

Still, she looks out through the curtains, at the big, wet drops of liquid sky. Not a rotten, weak mist, but drops -- large, and bearing the power of nature in them. Part of her would just love to open the tailgate and lie in it, and after let the wind dry her.

"Since elves are said to have been born from nature itself." Geric reads, "They often seem to take attunement from the elements. Even now, the elves of Järviby are said to be most attuned to water, the High Elves from that of wood and air, the wood-elves of earth and... *wood*, and of course, orcs like their fire and metal."

She turns to look back inside at him. As much as it interests her to learn more of her kind, or half, it still irritates her that he knows so much more than she.

"I knew that offhand by the way." he chortles haughtily with that grin of his. "I'm reading about 'stitch' spells right now."

"One would think a cleric of your age would know that by now." Zanvan says with a smokey billow.

"One would think." he brushes off.

Obvious that he's gone back to his book, Avrel continues to look out at the storm. Maybe it is her blood that drives her love of it, and of shining stream water. It's not something she's considered much before, but maybe in many ways she is more elf than she realizes. Or wants to be, but she reminds herself that not all elves are by whom she is elven, to what degree she is.

That comforts her, as does the pouring rain.

The rainy day passes slowly and late that night the clouds break, the shimmering moon light can be seen reflecting off of the lake.

"Herr gurrs, we're here!" Bob announces to the group.

"Shhhh... Geric and Avrel's big brown beaver are asleep." Zanvan replies. She's actually not, she's just resting with her eyes mostly closed, and with Candice on her lap.

"Werl werk therm urrp! The errves wirr warnt ourr carrgo cherrcked." Bob commands.

Before Zanvan can even give her shoulder a shake, Avrel snaps her fingers to awaken Candice, and Candice promptly whacks Geric in the face with her floppy tail.

"Ugh... Tired of this beaver..." Geric grumbles. He grabs her by the scruff and sets her aside, "You'd make a nice hat though."

Avrel protectively takes Candice back. "Why the check?" she asks, generally, lest she lay into the cleric. Nobody replies, they instead are quickly grabbing their things. Once everything is grabbed and in order, she joins the others near the tailgate to wait for the supposed inventory check, whatever its reason.

After a few idle minutes of sitting with her pack at her feet and Candice in her arms she decides to ask again. "Why the check?"

"They're arferrd orf smerrglerrs." Bob replies.

"But we're going *in* to their village." Geric says curiously.

"Dern't ersk merr! Err jerst derr trerd wirth therm." Bob laughs.

"Just another reason elves are annoying!" Geric giggles. Avrel gives him a death stare as she is not only offended, but considers just how many, or rather how few he's actually met. "Oh no, you're a half-elf, you're okay. Well, mini, but okay." he clarifies. "You're only *half* as annoying."

Avrel continues to stare for several moments until the cart stops.

"Everybody out!" they hear from outside the cart. It's a very fair sounding voice, strong and articulate in its accent.

They all get out and stand in front of the shifty eyed inspector. He's about Zanvan's height, tall, blonde, fair, and ears like her own. "Submit your bags for checking and allow us to search the cart." he commands.

"I feel like this is invasive..." Avrel whispers to Bob. She'd have expected it of Ar-Guards, they'll insist on a search if an urchin like her so much as bumps a market table. These guys are at least keeping their hands to themselves as they paw through the goods.

"Hey! You there, what are you whispering about!?" the inspector yells towards her, the now cowering half-elf.

"Nothing." she creeks.

"Hey you." Another elf barks, or as close as they can come to barking, it seems to be a trait in elven men that they always seem profoundly bored -- And judgemental. "Rape-born bitch, what's the matter, afraid to be around *real* elves?" another elf remarks while going through her bag. Other guards casually mutter things in elvish while taking glances at her. Mutter, it's almost like a low singing the way their language flows. If it weren't slandering her and assaulting her with words, she could like it.

"Whoa, you've got a lot of gems and stuff in here." he exaggerates to his companion inspector, "What's the matter, mudder, can't do spells without them?" the main inspector asks.

"My mother's." she says grimly.

The surrounding elves all share a haughty nasally laugh. "Oh?" the lead inspector says with a taunting glare as he leans down, his elven brows knitted as he looks into hers very closely. "Have you... shame? Mudblood?" he taunts as he turns. "Search her." he orders the others.

"Mudblood?"

"Shjäít blyté." he murmurs as he snaps his fingers, "There are more direct translations, shall I use that instead?" Two elves pass him as he turns his back to her, and they come at her with intent.

Avrel feels her cheeks grow hot as they must be turning beet red and her pupils dilating. "When you say '*search*'..." she grimaces as she steps back and away, "Am I being detained!?" she yells while she struggles as two of the far taller elf men pick her up from under her shoulders and carry her off towards a small station house.

"*This is why I hate you pointy freaks*" Geric yells to them in protest.

"Shut up, cleric." the inspector says coldly. "You have nothing of suspicion." he begins to laugh haughtily, "Just a bunch of ink and parchment and some *written* spells."

"Whert arbert Zervern?" Bob asks.

"Nah." the inspector laughs "We'd rather not begrudge him, his type might enjoy some of our drinks and hookah. Forgive us, we mind not traders, nor tourists, but we do have our order to preserve just the same."

Geric, Bob, and Zanvan look upon the inspector with disgust for as little as it helps her as she futilely flails in the hold of these jerks.

Away from her companions, and inside the station house Avrel gets roughed up and questioned. It's like her pinching of the harvest months' apple cart all over again, only this time she hasn't done a damn thing.

He paces back and forth just to intimidate her, and she's trying her damnedest to ot let it work. "Why does a half-bred, muddied blood woman come in a merchant cart packing a bunch of magic gems?" the interogating officer asks.

"Because me and my companions are looking for something." she bites out. "I used to do magic shows, and because my elf father and human mother consummated! Now let me go and give me back my stuff!" Avrel yells.

"Well there's your first problem! Whoever the hell your father was, taking a human woman. Nänivíjá." the officer says, getting right in Avrel's face.

"N- 'Nahni-vee...yhau' to you too!" Avrel retorts. The officer chuckles before resuming his inspection. He's casting something over her and is checking all around the lower corners of her mouth as the lead inspector from before comes in.

"Nothing in her teeth?" he asks.

"Nothing." the other reports, finally pulling his long arsed fingers out from her gums. "She doesn't brush much, but she's definitely a mix, otherwise they'd no doubt be rotting out."

"You should see my beaver's." she says, "I can arrange that if you'd like!" she gets out only a second before the other in charge, who had her dragged in here in the first place, puts *his* hands all over her face, and feels up her lower canines from without.

"No." he confirms. "Some freckling, but no sign of green either."

"Naniva yau!" she tries to pronounce again, mangled in discernibility by his intruding hands, to which he does release her, giving her head a forceful throw as he lets go.

"You certainly seem very human, aside from those ears." he concedes "No femininity in your shape, awful pigmented hair, yeah... You probably aren't much of a threat. Certainly no orc." he laughs, looking her up and down, judging her body shape or height; either way, showing that the predatory mentality of the male sex is beyond race. "Though, the presence of a mix-bred heathen might be disruptive to the populous..." the officer considers.

"Are you kidding?" Avrel says rolling her, certainly blue enough, eyes.

He glares at her again with his icy blue eyes, as he strokes his baby smooth chin, "You're free to go." he says dismissively, "Just keep out of trouble, and don't seduce our men... Or women, or whatever you muddied heathens do." the lead inspection officer says as his two men begin untying her from the chair.

Avrel rolls her eyes, exaggeratedly to express her displeasure with them, lest she do something more rash. *Seduce your men? Women?* What kind of freak do they take her for? Just because she's mixed blooded? "Yup, I'm really an indiscriminately diddling, seductressing slut of shite-blooded elven shame..." she frys, saltily, "But after this, I'll do my best to be good, eh?" she adds, with just a hit of phoney cheer.

The officer looks at her with apprehension and then points her toward the door. She gently rubs her rope burn as she gives them a glare from her own piercingly blue eyes, but they seem unaffected, and so she exits the small room and returns to her business.

"Hey Avrel!" Geric happily says to her, just as she comes out from the little staton house. "We're clear to go." Good for *them*.

"Yer orkey?" Bob asks consolingly.

"Yeah Bob, it's fine..." she sighs. "It's not like they felt me up or anything gross. It's not like- never mind, let's go."

She goes ahead, but after a moment they all join her back in or on the wagon. The gate is opened, and they proceed up the road to the lake village.

After a while, Avrel's curiosity gets the best of her. Of course she hated what the guards did to her, but why? Why her? Why the bizarre stuff with her face? Finally, she asks Bob "Why are they such... Such-"

"Arseholes?" Geric interjects, of course. She could practically sense him just waiting for that.

"Well, sort of." she admits, "Why were those guys so strict and.. cruel?"

"Werl, they dern't lirk smerrglerrs ernd they dird herv an isher wirth serm orcs caurserng irshues." Bob explains. "Arournd thern, they starrterd wirth the erxtrerr securetyrr."

"That seemed extreme though." Avrel sighs. She gently feels the corners of her mouth and jaw, "Why the face?"

"Don't worry." Zanvan says, patting her shoulder. "I've met other elves within the city and elsewhere, most aren't so angry or outwardly expressive about it."

Geric yawns and blows a raspberry at Candice for no discernible reason, other than that he's him, although, maybe she missed something. Regardless, Avrel settles into her spot and snoozes as Candice comes to her side.

After a short rest, she's awoken as Bob pulls his wagon to a stop at an inn which must be on far on the other side of town from where they'd entered. She yawns and stretches, still half asleep as they exit the wagon and are greeted by a graceful hostess. She doesn't say much, but like the men at the border, her words flow like a song, and with hard to understand, rolled tones that sound almost cat-like. Her silent and graceful way of walking, her glowing fairness, and her cuttingly blue eyes; she is almost like a rich Argothian's white cat. She takes them to their private sleeping rooms, and as Bob is with them, it seems the horses and cart are taken care of. The sheets, as she falls into them, are the cleanest feeling and smelling things she's ever felt or smelled.

The silver moonlight gently shows through the window as she lies in it, along with just the gentlest sense of music, distant, but there. As Candice forms into a ball beside her, she drifts to sleep.

Avrel is awakened the next morning by the sound of what must be elvish chanting and singing. She opens her window and looks out over the lake and the sparkling mist of the cascading waterfall pouring endlessly into the clearest water she's ever seen. She breathes in the fresh air and smiles gently, but sadly.

I feel as though I belong somewhere like this, but... she thinks to herself, remembering the prejudice she faced the night before. Still, there is always that *one* brook in Argoth, "A cabin there would be wonderful." she sighs, the thought is as alien as it is natural; for living away in the woods is barely a life so successful that it would demand the respect of those who've looked down upon her. *And yet*, she considers, *after this job Candice and I can have just that. Or maybe something of both.*

She looks around to find the source of the sound but can't see anything from her current vantage point, not that it's a bad one. More than the village she had expected, they are on a hillside facing another hillside across from a great plateau on the far side of the lake. From the landscape, to the otherworldly lake-elven architecture like spun glass, it's more breathtaking than she could have imagined in the darkness they arrived in.

Avrel dresses and heads out without her friends, and even skips breakfast for the time being. She's determined to find that music before it's over.

She follows the beautiful sound all through the 'village', down the hill, and through the path leading up between the hills until she comes to a gazebo where the choir is singing their music. Though she can't understand a word of it, it speaks to something common to them beyond her pointed ears, like an innate elven love of such things in her inner self. Avrel looks around as the morning sun dances off of the lake, the morning light shines through the mist generated from the streams falling from the plateau on the northern side of the rich, sapphire-like blue water, and spring's generous greens; and she feels overwhelmed emotionally and begins to cry. She can tell that most pass her by, gazing at her in judgement of this mixed breed, muddied blooded elf weeping in the middle of Lake Square, but she can't help it. Others, she shamefully aware feel sad for her, pitying her perhaps for her shite blood, but none offer comfort or kinship. All of them pass her by. Ignorant to the meaning of the mumbling and whispering of the elves around her, finally Avrel becomes aware of herself beyond her emotional influx when she hears a woman's voice finally call to her directly.

"Young ma'am, are you-- is everything... Alright?"

Avrel blushes realizing, more consciously that she is hunched over and weeping in the middle of a crowded square. "Eh?"

"Um... Young ma'am?" the woman asks again, coming closer, she's a bit flushed, as if maybe, just maybe one of the passer-bys told someone about 'the ugly half-human girl crying in the square', though she can't be sure.

"Oh... I.. I'm sorry I just.." Avrel blurts out feeling shaken, she feels like a grand tier dolt.

The poor girl is embarrassed... or something along those lines obviously thinks the elf. "Oh dear, it's nothing." she smiles. "I've seen grown men weep at the grandeur and beauty of our *village*." the woman says handing Avrel a soft cloth to dry her eyes.

"Village?!" Avrel pulls the cloth away from her eyes, "This place is a small city!" she says in surprise.

"It's just a linguistic tradition from ancient elvish, the word for any sort of settlement is 'Vehräghé' which to the common tongue just became 'village'." the woman explains with a warm smile. "An artifact of our closer proximity to Argoth, I suppose."

"That's... Pretty cool." Avrel says, trying not to sniff, "I'm sorry I don't know very much about elves, even though-"

The woman presses her index finger to Avrel's lips, gently quieting her. She studies Avrel's face and looks deep into her eyes. "I understand." she comments, almost cryptically as the breeze fans out her surprisingly dark, almost raven hair. As the blush fades, her skin is an almost pearlescent porcelain, and again, the darkness of her hair also is present in her starkly beautiful brows. The elf woman stands tall and thinks for a moment, still looking at Avrel curiously. "Here." she says handing Avrel a small token, "This should help you find your way around town without much resistance."

"Wow... Thank you!" Avrel says, remembering to curtsy, but her mind quickly coming up with more questions in just that short time. "Um... What is it?"

The elf chuckles warmly at the small mix-breed's ignorance no doubt, but also looks at Avrel with strange familiarity.

Avrel gazes back. Most purebloods in Argoth were wholly indifferent to her. There is grace to this woman's face... And something else.

"You might find the library interesting, small ma'am." the elf woman turns and waves farewell and begins to walk away.

"Miss erg um... Ma'am, I don't even know your name!" Avrel says, taking a few steps towards the elven woman.

She turns back slightly and smiles, "I am Tárjä." she says, her voice as soothing as a melody, "Tárjä Ämëlídöltír" she says, it might be significant, but given how little Avrel could say of prominent names in Argoth, it's worth nothing.

"Thank you Miss Taur- Miss Tarja" Avrel bows her head in gratitude. She inspects the token and slips it into her pocket. She wishes to thank Miss Tarja once more but that quickly, she is gone. Avrel looks down the street both ways, but she's not to be seen. And as the purplish orange light of daybreak fades to the subdued yellows of morning, she thinks no more of it and decides to go back and meet with her comrades.

7

"Hi guys." Avrel says cheerily as she finds the guys in the corner of the dining room of the inn. Who knows why they sat back there, it's not very crowded. "Where's Bob?" she asks as she looks around, thinking she might have merely missed him.

"He went off to procure his merchandise." Zanvan says unenthusiastically.

"What's wrong?" she asks, taking note of his tone which is distant and detached, even for him.

Geric pokes the rather fancy looking roll on his silver plate, "It's all bread… Everything for breakfast is a form of bread!" he laments while Zanvan nods agreeingly. "I want my bacon!" Geric whines.

"What about that bon-bonna, bull cow jerky?" They've eaten it enough, she'd have thought she'd remember it's proper name by now. "You could just eat that if you want meat." Avrel reminds them.

Zanvan folds his arms. "It's in the cart." he grunts, "And Bob is gone."

"Oh… Well.. we can go out and find something that's not bread if you wish." Avrel suggests, though she doesn't see the problem. "May I?" she says, hovering her hand by Geric's roll.

"Be my guest." he sighs.

She tastes the corner, it's surprisingly dense in texture despite how flakey it seems to the teeth. It tastes bland at first but has a subtle fruitiness that's hard to place. Even just the small bite satisfies her appetite to a notable degree. "I don't hate it." she comments, "It's very filling, but if you'd rather go out--"

"But my *free breakfast with lodging!*" Geric cries out. His outburst grabs a few looks both from the calm, collected elves working the place as well as the handful of other travellers.

Zanvan stands, "Bread holds, we can leave it in the room for later." he says as he takes the rolls and places them into a pocket on his cloak.

That she can agree to. And so does Geric, judging by him standing as well, and so they leave the dining room.

As they come into the entrance foyer of the inn Avrel asks, "Anybody know where Candice is?" as just then she hears the flip flop of her tail slapping against the steps.

"Oh, she slept in." Avrel giggles.

***

With the groggy beaver joining the group, Zanvan leads them out into the streets and they take a look around. Between the rich blues of the lake, the white stone streets and glassy walls, and the beautiful trees the city is still striking, even if it lacks a certain sylvan shade.

"So... You guys want meat then." the kid asks again.

The cleric nods, "Yeah, or just anything that's *not* bread." he sighs.

Indeed, not that bread is a bad meal, but not the breakfast he's accustomed to. "Be prepared to pay a pretty penny though, elves don't farm animals like men do, so the only thing we might find is roasted game." Zanvan tells them.

His words seem to spook the kid's pet, and after Avrel gives it a little talking to, the beaver decides to stay behind and just eat the bread. Geric of course reacts with glee, but he just hopes she doesn't eat all of it. She is basically a giant mouse after all.

With that taken care of, they begin to leisurely stroll about the elven city. The high-elves he knows are prideful hunters in their vast northern woods, but he can't be sure the same goes for these lakeside dwellers. But as a ranger, he knows how to follow his nose. After a while of searching they find a place with some smoked redmeat-fish and they have breakfast there. During their meal they discuss possible ways to spend their time.

"C'mon guys, what's the plan?" Avrel asks, "I'd bet the tavern we saw on the way here doesn't open until nightfall, so we'll need to scout for information elsewhere."

He'd thought she was asleep at that time, apparently not. "I don't know. Maybe Geric will want to find a magic shoppe so he can buy some spell scrolls." Zanvan says, turning to the cleric.

"I wanna go to the library." the kid suggests, and he's surprised, that sounds more like Geric's thing. Hell, he's not sure but for a sign or two that he's seen her read a damn thing.

"That works, after we eat, Zanvan and I will go to the magic shop and stuff and then we'll meet you there." Geric says as he's chewing on his food, the fish is a bit chewy. Avrel agrees, and when she finishes her portion she heads out, towards the library he *hopes*. Though in a sea of blondes, she does rather stand out, should she get lost.

He and Geric eat a bit more and then head out themselves. They look at many signs, some underlined in common, many not, and ask around until they find a shoppe selling magical wares.

They enter as a tall, platinum blonde person in flowy clothes, whose gender is not immediately determinable from behind, welcomes them to their shoppe, "Greetings, men." Their voice is soft.

"Excuse me... Miss? Ter... Ter terribly sorry to bother you, but where are your magic scrolls that I may buy one?" Geric asks in a tone unusually humble for him. The shoppe owner turns around from behind the display that was blocking the view of their body revealing that they are an incredibly bosomy elf woman. Her face isn't the most classically feminine, but she seems to know this given the ornateness in the reveal of her bustline attire.

"I'm sorry." she dismisses, "But as most of us born of elven blood have innate magic knowledge, scrolls are something we generally don't need, and thus are not something I carry" she explains with insincere disappointment, typical of a shoppe owner.

"Oh, well, I'm out of here." Geric says as he briskly turns aboutface. "Thanks for nothing, pointy!" he says before storming out.

Zanvan however is taken by both the shopkeeper and a large jewel-studded bastard sword in the corner. "Can you tell me about that sword over there?" he asks. Unlike Avrel's basic arcane jewels, Zanvan can appreciate jewels of true elven arcanery. He's spent enough time using them.

"Ahh, that belonged to my late husband." she explains. "He never kept it with him, he felt it was too pretty and precious to him to risk it being damaged."

"I'm sorry to hear that. It's a beautiful sword." Zanvan says, walking over and getting a closer look at it, guessing by now that it's a momento, and not for sale.

"I had it made especially for him, but since he never took it with him." the woman begins to cry, "He didn't have it when he was attacked by some bandits in the plains!" she wails. Zanvan feels rather surprised at this seeing as though elf women are often known for their grace and composure. But then, being around the kid, he should know better. "We'd only been married for a few *decades* and during that time I always worried that something might happen to him in that time, but he never paid it much mind!" she continues to sob as her legs buckle, and she drops.

Zanvan picks her up off the floor. But for her face, her body is remarkably soft and womanly, her skin smooth as silk. "It's ok, you did what you could." Zanvan says, trying to console her, to say the least.

She holds her hands out as she speaks. "But he was out there guarding the merchant carts because he wanted to make sure my suppliers' stuff got here unspoiled!" she bawls.

"My dear Miss --" Zanvan remembers the sign on the shoppe, or at least as Geric had read it, "Rintja, don't grieve so..." he says tenderly.

"I've just been so lonely ever since he was killed, I try not to think about him but..." she whimpers as Zanvan caresses her cheek.

He's heard tales of the breaking of the stonelike mannerisms of elven women on the infrequent times in which they are fertile. If this is it, as it would seem by all accounts, those men weren't boasting. It's almost laughable.

She leans up and kisses him passionately pulling him on top of her. "Promise me that if only for a few moments, you'll banish the loneliness from my heart, and you'll take his sword and never again let it stand as a reminder of my pain." she moans passionately.
Supposedly, rare as it is for one to be like this, why should he not? Who is he to deny the wisdom of elves? Or gifts? "I will." Zanvan says as he gently caresses Rintja's voluptuous forms, which are even more shapely and pleasant than was hinted by her decorative bustier.

***

By faith in the word of mouth, Avrel has found the enormous library. It's shape is difficult to describe, it's like white marble, spun like glass, and it's lines and shapes flow as beautifully as water.
At least, from the outside.
When she tries to enter, two guards are standing with lances crossed, blocking her passage through the causeway. She sits there for more than a few moments watching as other elves are allowed in and out.
"Excuse me." she tries to assert, but they only give her a cursory glance before staring on ahead once more. She pulls her hair back as if to pull it into a pony-tail to make sure her ears are more than obvious, but they still pay her no mind. In the mirror polish of the wall, she fixes her hair, she despises how pony-tails show off her scrawny neck. She tries to casually pass under where the lances are crossed, only for them to be adjusted for her slighter size. Obviously, she's unwelcome.
 She then remembers the token-like object that Tarja had given her, and walks up and shows it to one of the guards who after sharing a look with the other, reluctantly lets her in. As she passes through one guard mutters to the other something in elvish, but Avrel pays it no mind, she can't understand it anyway. She walks in and gazes on at the massive collection of artifacts and books in every corner.
It's not long before her awe is interrupted by a cold, "May I help you?" Having never to her recollection actually *been* in a library, she replies back in a normal volume, "Actually, maybe... I--"

He raises a brow and makes a slashing motion across his throat. She can tell he's not pleased with her, and she also recalls how angry Geric gets when people are noisy and he's trying to read, or transcribe.

She swallows hard before she speaks softly, "Yes, do you have any books that might have information about the Runeblade of the Ages or the Everlasting Aegis?" Avrel asks. Another thought coming to her while she waits for his answer.

"hmm..." the librarian strokes his chin, "Third floor, and to the right, you'll see a statue of the tree goddess. Around there is where we keep such records. Who may I ask are you?" he inquires snidely.

"Um I'm Avrel Lavian, me and some companions are-" Avrel shyly responds.

"Yes yes yes." he cuts her off, "Go on, I won't hold you up." he speaks while walking back to his chair behind the front desk.

Avrel looks around for some stairs in the maze of ornate shelves lined with countless books. Spying some stairs spiralling up she goes to them. They are steps made of quartz, cut into flat planks, and she makes her way up them to the section described to her. "Beautiful." she remarks, though she's delicate as she steps onto them. Counting her way up to the third level, she eventually finds a section with a polished stone carving of a *very feminine* tree.

"Well, there's the tree goddess, 'Tra-- Trehhh... Treanjia'? Goddess of the Woods..." Avrel sounds out aloud. The common letters she hopes are the same as the fanciful glyphs above them. Limited in literacy, she realizes that she shouldn't have come without Geric or Zanvan, but she might at least gather some worthy looking candidates while she waits. *Hmmm, this book looks good and old.* she thinks to herself looking at a large leather-bound book. The gilded lettering is so fanciful, she can't discern whether it is elven or common, not that it's of much difference to her. She takes the book off the shelf and lays it on a nearby table and pulls up a chair. For what it's worth, she begins gingerly flipping through its pages. Often Avrel would skim flyers and posting boards, using her limited knowledge of the scripted language to augment any indicative pictures. However, in Avrel's mind the elvish runes in the old book seem to speak for themselves to her mind. At first this frightens her, the symbols seem to become voiceless ideas in her mind as she looks at them. They also seem to glisten as she looks at them. More than once, she almost closes the book completely, resolving to wait and have Geric take a look. No... she decides as she opens it up once more. Geric often spoke of a 'contents' or an 'index', perhaps if she can find that... Little words with hashes next to them, she hopes this is it, giving herself over to the words speaking idioms into her as she looks them over.

" 'Runeblade, see Arcanium - page'... " she mumbles to herself looking through the index. She looks through the book until she comes to the desired page which reads, or rather *tells*:

"Arcanium: a crystalline state of condensed magic, also known as 'Mana Particulate' was said to have been used by the great Archmages of ages past to create magic focusing gems of incredible power."

It's strange, but her own mind takes the words and speaks them to her. "Oh! 'For weapon applications see Tiger Knights and Diablo Conflict artifacts on page'... ugh.. This is indirect..." Avrel mutters as she flips through the pages once more, though, she reminds herself, the book is practically reading to her. 'Rubra Magi' catches her eye briefly, she wonders if they were in any relation to Rufus's order. The mental image looks similar. Then, she comes to her desired page. Basic counting she can do. "Mostly..." she sighs.

"During the Tiger Knights' battle against the Diablo, the Tiger-Blood Warrior crafted a sword hilt with Mana Particulate
gems studding either side, when an ethereal bond was formed with the handle, a blade of Arcanium would crystallize
taking the weapon-form desired by the user. Danelijus the Tiger-Blood Warrior Mage and his knights would eventually
defeat the Diablo, casting him into the great Northern Chasm after cleaving the Beast's heart from its body. The heart of the beast,
was nearly impenetrable and was shaved down into a gruesome shield by the knights but it quickly became apparent
that the beast's will still resided within and corrupted the first two knights to try to wield it, and thus it was left deep within the Chasm."

She can't get over how clearly she sees things in her head. She rather dislikes it, but perhaps Geric can better dissect this for her.
"Miss Avrel?" the librarian says laying his hand on her shoulder.
"Eh!?" she squeaks, "Oh... Sorry... Sorry I was just...yeah." Avrel says in a startled and brash tone, "I'm Avrel." she holds her hand to her head. "That was bizarre..." she comments idly. The elf looks at the book, "Ah yes, those older ones are a bit odd, different elves experience them differently." he says coldly as a mere matter of fact. "I'm surprised they work for you at all." he *has* to add.
She collects herself, this man has come to her, "Is something wrong, sir?" she asks.

"Word was sent here that one of your companions requests your presence." the librarian explains in an uninterested tone. "Eric or something I think they said his name was."

"Geric?"

"Yes, that was it." he confirms. "He said that when you got this message, you are to meet him at the Läppílúnt Lakeside Tavern, 'Assuming those pointy eared freaks actually relayed this message and aren't interrogating and, or violating you because those stupid tree-huggers find this to be 'suspicious' or something' were his exact words, or so I was told." the librarian informs her with a grimacing glower.

No doubt in her mind that it was Geric. And unfortunately, no doubt those were his exact words. "Umm... Sorry for my acquaintance's rudeness." she says, bowing her head slightly. "Thank you for relaying the message and for letting me look through your books." Avrel sheepishly expresses to the man as she makes for the exit. Not rushing, but in a hurry to get away.

***

Geric is puttering around town, still disappointed after he has left the magic shoppe when he decides to go see if he can get any information about the relics from some random knife-ears. He looks around and sees a large town square of sorts down by the lake and starts making his way towards there. If Zanvan is held up by what he assumes, he's got between ten minutes or even a whole half-hour to kill.

He gets down into the square and looks around, there's some people singing in a gazebo for whatever reason. *It sounds nice...* he supposes, but he's glad he hadn't picked this square as a spot to read. He walks up to some of the more friendly looking elves, or rather, the least haughty and unfriendly looking ones, that are around and starts asking them about the relics but none have any answers for him, or they didn't understand his common tongue.

He quickly gets bored and looks at the lake and decides that he'd like to wash up in the lake before heading to meet Avrel at the library. What the pointy ears won't share, books certainly should. *At least they aren't so enamored in their own longevity that they forgo written records!* he chuckles to himself.

He follows the shore a long way down until he's behind a small cluster of trees and is somewhat distant from the square and most buildings. He takes his robes and things off and wades into the water. There, he starts washing himself down with a rag. After a few moments he feels something swim by him, he thinks nothing of it, it is a lake after all, there are bound to be some fish in it. He continues to splash his face with the shimmering clean lake water until he feels a sharp and horrible biting sensation on his calf.

"YAHHHHOOOUCH!" he screams loudly, followed by several obscenities and swears, unfitting, he knows, but who cares? Not him at the moment.

"Human-sir, are you alright!?" A svelte elven woman asks him. She must have been walking past, presumably having taken an afternoon walk along the shore calls to him. Of course, with elf eyes she's still a fair distance away. Uselessly far away to be more exact.

Geric has begun making his way towards the shore but feels another bite. "OUCH!!! No, I'm not!" he yells back before being bitten again.

"Oh Shimmers!!" she gasps, "I implore you, get out of the water; it's dangerous!" the young lady cries out, quickening her pace, but not by much. All these elves wear such gaudy, flowy clothing that they make his ensemble look as humble as a cleric's rightly should be.

"*Nice!*" he scoffs, "OUCH!!! Why not hang a bloody sign!?" Geric says angrily as he makes it to the shore he turns and sees a large jawed fish with its teeth stuck in his flesh. "AH! bug off!" he screams as he slaps it off, not even caring what flesh it takes with it. If he knew a damned lightning spell...

"Are you alright?" the young lady asks again.

"No, of course not, what kind of shite lake is this, you got biting fish all in it! What's the matter, do signs offend your sense of nature?? This place is arse! I'm going back to my room at the inn!" Geric says, hobbling over to his belongings and throwing them over his shoulder.

"Oh please don't go!" she begs, "Come back to my house, I'll cure your wounds and you can talk to my brother!"

"No!" he puts down, as he is straight up not enjoying anything about this leg of the journey. "I've had it with this place, the messed up gatekeepers, the haughty shop owners, *even the lake* is a shite hole!"

She's obviously hurt by those remarks about her 'beautiful home', but still, she persists, "Please Sir, don't be angered so! My brother owns the Lakeside Tavern, he'll be opening in a few hours, come with me and let me heal you, he'll give you some free drinks I promise!" she offers desperately.

"Do I not look like a cleric?" he asks, knowing that he of course, does. Unmistakable so. "I can heal my own damned wounds! Consarned fish, I--" Geric stops mid limp, "Free drinks you say?" he thinks it over, "Well, I suppose it is only right that I be paid some sort of reparation for all the pain and suffering this place has brought me. Sure, why not... MmmWhat's your name, my child?" Geric says in a calmer more forgiving tone, haste in all things but judgement and all that.

She smiles. He'd swear she looks a bit like Avrel, but he figures the elves all tend to have the same high cheeks, and such. Her eyes are of a typical light blue, and her hair light gold. "I'm Jänsen, please come with me."

As his sinful, curseful wrath fades, so does his fight-or-flight. And with it, nature's way of dulling the true nature of the pain. The two make their way to the tavern and taproom whose porch has a wonderful view of the lake. Or it would be, were the lake not an infested shitehole. But the place, he must confess, is pretty, well kept, and clean. But rustic and woody compared to most of what he's seen of town... city... *Vehräghé*, he hears in his mind's snootiest elf voice. Surprisingly unelf-like, which Geric does appreciate. "This may sting a bit." Jansen says softly as she enchants a misty cup of potion.

"Eh, if it does just get me another beer." Geric says confidently. She smiles as she pours the potion over his calves and feet, whispering a spell. "Eeek!" Geric chirps briefly as his bite wounds are foamed over by the fluid before the flesh quickly mends. Geric looks down over his limbs with satisfaction before leaning back with a calm, "Neet." He'll have to get the recipe.

"Ah, Júkkä!?" Jansen says after he hears someone come through the door. "Is that you, brother?"

"Yes, sister." the male voice answers, at least Geric suppose, because he did so in elvish. "You're here awful early. Oh, entertaining a... Guest?" the tall, handsome elf man says in a slight tone of disapproval.

She blushes and steps back, "Well, not exactly you see–"

"Not a chance." Geric cuts her off, nothing against her, but *no*. "I got bitten up by your freaky-arse lake and your sister offered me free drinks and healing." Geric manages to get out, taking a sip of his apparently very strong beer. "And believe me, I'm thirsty!"

Jansen and Jukka exchange nods. The elf man's voice and mannerisms change quickly, "You are one of the people who came into town with that gnome, are you not?" Jukka asks as he sits beside Geric.

"Maybe." Geric says, swallowing the last of his drink with a large gulp. "Why do you ask?

"Let's just say there's a reason that as of late our lake is full of these ravenous fish." Jukka says informatively. "And if you and your companions were to *alleviate* the issue we might be able to compensate you in some way."

A *quest within a quest*? he wonders. Sounds to him like a bit of a bunny trail, but then his judgement is just a little impared at the moment. "Sure, I'll tell you where my friends are, if you wanna send word out for me, I don't feel like looking for them..." Geric says motioning to Jansen to hand him another drink.

"S-sure, where might they be?" Jansen asks, handing him another mug of beer. It's not so bad now that he's used to it. He can't feel his legs to say the least.

"I don't know where *Zanvan* would be." Unless he has the *endurance* of an ox. "But *Avrel* is probably waiting at the library, in fact, Zanvan is supposed to meet her there, so yeah, just find her and give her this message..."

"Oh dear..." Jansen sighs to herself as she takes it down on a note as he dictates.

***

Zanvan leans up from laying beside Rintja and a tied off lambskin in a pool of passion's sweat as he suddenly remembers that he is supposed to meet Avrel at the library. She gets up as well and grabs the promised bastard sword, and polishes it with her leggings that she had grabbed off of the floor.
"You handle a sword well." he compliments. "Are you sure you don't want to keep it?" Zanvan asks her as he dresses himself.
"No, take it." she says insistently. "Take it and go."
He thought it was good himself. "Alright, farewell." he says with a shrug.
She's surprisingly silent the whole time while Zanvan dresses, which is a nice change. With a final wave, he takes the sword and heads out the door.
He looks around and decides to drop the sword back in his room at the inn until he gets a proper sheath. He finds Candice there waiting for him and she follows him out as he then heads for the library. He arrives just as Avrel at that time is exiting the library. It seems she sees Zanvan hurrying towards her in the distance, the kid has good eyes.
"Hey!" she shouts waving him down. She informs him as he comes closer, "Hey, Geric told me that he wants us to come to the Lappiland? Lap-"
'*Lap-dance?*' he'd interject if he was with someone he could trust to take such a joke. Avrel, he knows, is not such a person.
"Something or other 'Lakeside Tavern', quickly!"
He goes to her, and nods before looking to get his bearings on where the lake is from here. Avrel briefly turns to Zanvan, probably noticing the intense stench of pheromones as he's deciding which way to proceed to get to the tavern.
"At it again." she scoffs to herself.
He turns as if to ask her, 'what of it?', and the look on her face tells him she gets the message.
"This way, follow me you '*sly*' dog." she insists.
Zanvan chuckles, "Wrong way." he quickly catches up to Avrel, her steps being so small. He turns her around and points. "See, we passed it earlier."
"Oh." she pouts.

"Follow me." he says as he walks past her. He can hear behind him as with a deep breath, she concedes.

***

She follows Zanvan to the tavern where Candice is waiting also. It stands out a bit from the rest of the buildings as it looks more like a dockside building on Argoth's rivers. Not that this detracts from its beauty, Avrel in fact finds the finesse and grace of the woodwork to be almost more awe inspiring than the shimmery, glasslike material used more widely in the city.

It still doesn't look to be open, but Zanvan doesn't seem to care, he goes through the front doors anyway. She follows him, and they sit down at a table. As they start looking around for their friend, Avrel notices Miss Tarja sitting in the corner. Otherwise, it seems that they might be the only ones here. She waves to her.

Tarja warmly takes notice, and gets up and sits next to Avrel. She then looks across the table, and with some sort of gesture, introduces herself to Zanvan. "Hello, your friend will be in shortly. I'm Tárjä, and you are Zanvan, no?"

"Yes, that's me." he says striking a match to light his pipe, "Care to explain why we were called here? I'm assuming you're in on it."

"You're perceptive." the elf woman smiles. "Your days as a ranger have made your senses sharp."

"Apparently the cleric's been talking." he softly says to Avrel, which she's glad for, lest his ego as a ranger swell more.

Another door opens to the side of the bar and Geric enters the room alongside two elves which seems to surprise Zanvan as much as it does Avrel. It also shows just how tall he is that he's taller than not just the woman, but the man. Geric pushes another table to join aside with theirs, and sits down, propping on his elbows and folding his hands over the table.

"I suppose you're all wondering why I've gathered you here." he smiles with great satisfaction.

She'd swear he must have staged it to be as much like something from a story or book as possible. She'd certainly not put it past the egghead. "Well, yeah. But I'm thinking it's more to do with those two having you gather us." Avrel says with a sassy smirk. She's obviously called it by his brief reaction, but more than that, he doesn't let it get to him.

"These are the two owners of this Lakeside Tavern." he motions to the pair of elves behind him, "Due a series of events, I was brought here with fish wounds that have been healed up. We talked for a bit and these two made a proposition." Geric says raising a hand like he invites one of them to take over the discussion.

The fair, slender woman sits beside the cleric as does the wiry but thin man and then she leans forward a bit, "I am Jänsen Énjädöltír." she introduces.

"I'm Júkkä." says the man, "Her brother."

"How much do you know of Järviby?" Jansen asks. Both of their accents are thick, but Avrel can understand them, but she knows little of Järviby.

Zanvan sighs, smokily, "You were some elves who settled around this lake at the foot of the plateau. You found the fishing here to be like the forested river valleys of the north-northeast before the temperature began to drive the northernmost settlements elsewhere." Zanvan replies quite knowledgeably, "And wars."

"Indeed. " Jukka replies. "I'm surprised, we were under the delusion that most of your race give little care to such things."

"I for one support that delusion." Geric says proudly as he raises his hand, most likely jealous that his advanced knowledge wasn't what was spoken.

Eyes roll.

"I went up to the Everwinter Woods about ten years ago." Zanvan says with a puff. "It's where I got my bow. I still have some of the original arrows."

"Alright." Tarja now puts in. "Well, about... maybe a decade ago some of these ocean 'snapping fish' started appearing in our lake and since then, they've taken it over until it's become the inhospitable and nearly unfishable place it is now." she explains. "His father's family, thus mine was one of those who took part in the founding of this city. My father, he and my mother helped establish the fishing guild, a couple of centuries ago when I was a young elfling." she again singles Avrel out for a curious look, "Probably not much older than you."

Avrel tries to ignore it for the moment. "So what, the 'snapping fish' have eaten all the other fish?" Avrel asks softly.

"Yes child, not only that, the larger ones actually destroyed many of the boats we used to use."

"So what do you want us for?" Zanvan questions. "Do you even know why this happened?" There's a moment of quiet as Tarja looks at Zanvan with intrigue, just then her attention is drawn elsewhere as there is a knock at the door.

A more mature looking man that Avrel thinks she might have seen in the library enters the tavern.

"Sorry I'm late." he apologizes. "Some people don't put their books back when they are done..." he says taking a seat near the group. Avrel shrinks down slightly, it's him, and she's now remembering that *she* hadn't put her book away.

"I'm the Headmaster of the Arcane Arts School here in Järviby, I am known as Master Dánníus." he tells them. "Or I believe that would be the equivalent title."

Geric nods, as if he's some authority on the matter. "Yes." he says, as if Dannius needed his approval.

Avrel looks up at him in slight surprise at his name. It's vaguely familiar.

"I once had a student of incredible power." he starts off, and in all her days in alleys and streets and vagrats forming trashfires, things starting off like that are never good. "He was one of the most powerful mages I had ever taught." Dannius stands up and gets himself a drink from the tap, "But I failed him. Just as his father, Jähörä rest his soul, his power was so all encompassing of his being that it began to touch and corrupt his mind, his time in quiet meditation eventually became screams of terror." he continues. "I tried to help him but he began shutting himself away, convinced he could purge his madness with inward focus and expanded power. Power, *power*! He searched to gain, so sure that more power would free him. By that point he isolated himself to all save his familiar spirit, a duck-rat, a platypus."

Duck-rat? Avrel takes note.

Tarja's expression turns sad as her eyes glass over with subtle tears. "You mean?" she asks.

"Yes indeed, My Lady, Tárjä." he says, as if to extend sympathy to her and her alone, "Shäddäi Kriegsön had a thing with aquatic creatures." Dannius continues. "You of course know this."

Avrel can feel her entire body become very tense at the mentioning of the name and looks cautiously to share glances with Candice who is shooting whiskey, but even so, she looks significantly more serious for the moment.

"I've come to believe that Shäddäi has returned from some other territory." the man says, "And by his ill controlled powers, has brought these invasive fish with him from the seas. I have come to the conclusion that he is living somewhere in the wilds of the plateau." Dannius explains, sitting back down.

As all her memories come upon her like a flood, Avrel gets up, abruptly and quite driven. "I'm leaving!" she informs the group, "Come Candice." she commands, harshly.

They all seem startled by her suddenness, but she doesn't care. She's too stricken emotionally for thought or cares of perception. She has things that *need* doing.

"Avrel, where are you going?" Zanvan asks, grabbing her arm.

She grits her teeth, thinking of *him* bringing his wanton destruction to such a beautiful place as this. "Something I've meant to do for a while." she rips her arm from the ranger's carnivorous grasp. "Get your hand off me, debauchee." she replies in a cruel, harsh fry. *Dammit.* she curses. *Goddess Dammit.* It's hard for her to not put her fist through the door as she reaches for the latch. All this time, all this way and he still taints her. He still mocks her, and puts enmity between her and half her race -- Maybe even what should be her true race. *Bastard, sard.* Her limited vocabulary doesn't afford her the words needed to describe her feelings, let alone him.

"I'm going."

***

"But Avrel!" Geric shouts, but the little half-elf gives no reaction and leaves the tavern, slamming the door as she goes. "My child!" he adds. The Master looks the way of her wake thoughtfully for some reason, as if he needs one, but that Tarja woman is very taken back as well. As are Jukka and Jansen a bit, but less in shock, he might at least communicate with them. "Tsk... Half-breeds" Geric says leaning in to the elf siblings.

The Master casts an eye to the dark haired elf woman, "You don't th-"

"Don't know." she shrugs, but Geric can see her lips twitching over hard, gritted teeth. It makes him happy in a strange way to see the haughty reserve of elves broken by the little elf's ill temperament.

Zanvan adjusts his hat after glancing back as well. "Moving on?" If Geric knows him, he's worried, but maybe won't say it, yet. But his tone suggests he'd rather not waste time, he might be curious as to what's in the half-breed's mind, and Geric can't blame him for that.

Finally, Tarja picks up the conversation. "When he began his slip into madness ravenous fish and even beavers, coypu and platypuses nearby would cause issues with increased intensity, that's when we made the connection, all those years ago." Her poise is back and her face is almost stone-like, but for her eyes.

"And so he was cast out." Jansen finishes. Tarja seems quite pained in relating the story.

"He was dangerous." Jukka adds. "Our history is ripe with those unable to control the kind of power he was amassing, unwittingly no less. It's part of why Tárjä's husband's ancestors came to this place."

Geric, of course, is half a walking history book, and he can recall a few instances that this could apply to. It's why to this day some Argothians aren't fans of the knife-ears. It did give them some fine legends of mighty men though. "I see." he comments, stroking his chin for good measure as to make it seem as if he was actually pondering the account directly.

"Do you know where he went or why he'd come back?" the ranger inquires.

"Last we heard, which was decades later, he'd taken up life in a human city." The Master replies.

"He sent his family a letter." the dark haired elf woman, Tarja replies, "He'd met a human woman, and bound himself to her, knowing what that meant should he ever wish to return." she pauses, a few cracks forming in that haughty stone, "But that in her, and his new life, he'd found some sense of peace."

8

Avrel rushes back to her room and grabs not just her staff and her pouch of magic gems. Candice worries as she sees her master maybe biting off more than she can chew. But what can she say? What can she do? Avrel is her master, her spirit bond, and she'd risk no harm to her, not as a beaver, not as a human.

"Chippu?" she chirps, just calling her name in a longing, sorrowful tone.

Avrel glances at her in a wordless reply. Candice sees the boiling anger, the hatred, the rage and confusion. But Avrel is grown up from the girl, and Candice knows there's little she can do to quell her anger, only watch, and guide as she may.

***

Avrel quickly heads out of the town and toward the plateau, not caring who she bumps into while rushing through town, not interested in the music, or the beauty of the lake under the sunset. Just *him*.

The moon is directly overhead in the night sky when she makes it to near the waterfall where she hears a faint screaming in the distance. She continues to climb the incline until she reaches the shear, rocky sides of the plateau. She looks around until Candice gets her attention and runs under a bush. A path? Avrel crawls under the foliage, and follows her. She finds herself on a ledge that overlooks the lake which is now quite a ways down. Even as her singlemindedness has its hold on her, she takes in the view of Järviby's light flickering on the water for a moment. It almost calms her before she hears a muffled, gut-wrenching scream from down the ledge, in the direction of the waterfall. She carefully makes her way closer and closer as the white noise of the waterfall grows ever louder and ever more thunderous. Her pace slows as the rock becomes more slippery and wet but she continues on with determination. Up ahead she sees Candice stop and look towards the rock and back to her, Avrel hurries to find that there is a cave.

The cave is well lit with torches on either of the far walls but doesn't allow much light to bleed out through the opening, concealing it to onlookers below. She looks around, her sensitive ears still ringing from the falls just outside. Candice runs over to a platypus that is sleeping near a deep puddle.

"Shhh!" Avrel commands as she sneaks deeper into the cave, paying the other critter no mind.

She comes to another large chamber where she sees various magical artifacts glowing, and she can almost sense a thickness to the air. She steps inside and finds him, an elven man clutching his head lying in a fetal position, and screaming.

Avrel looks down at him as he lip quivers lest it should sink. She's disgusted, revolted even. She steps forward, drawing her staff. *It... Is him.* she thinks to herself. "Shad Kriegson!!!???" Avrel growls.

The elf in tatters and shreds of clothing startles and flails across the room shouting gibberish. "The falls fish don't summer the green oaks!" he blurts out, hiding his face from Avrel's death-stare.

"I... Never believed I'd find you in my sight again..." she frys, recalling last she saw him. "I never *wanted* to have you in my sight again" she hisses through her teeth, "Not even were I blind and yourself the *only* thing I could see." she shouts harshly at him, her vision distorted with tears, and likely red with fury.

He looks at her frantically, almost like he recognizes her. "Dead... Dead things speak not to the sand from behind the moon..." he blurts before he rolls over crying.

Avrel is filled with a torrent of emotions, he is the man but there is little to communicate with. Her heart aches to see the creature she once saw reduced to its bitter essence. It's not who or what rather that she'd expected. The great subversion adds to the swelling pain in her hurting heart. "Despicable." she growls out, the depth of feeling in the words tearing painfully into her throat. "There is no humanity left, no ghost within that shell is there? You are now what you always were, **an animal!**" Avrel growls.

Shad looks more aware as his eyes widen, like a tutored child who is only beginning to understand a simple concept. His whimpers cease, his breathing eases, "Who... are you...that you torture me like this?" he mutters.

Avrel's legs are planted firm to the floor, her fist is raised and tight as she screams "I am Avrel Lavian, daughter of Isis Lavian, the woman whose heart and body you despoiled!" And she screams it loud, not sparing him any of her vigorous hate.

He looks as a deer in the torchlight. He obviously hears her words, he looks to be trying to listen. "I... Isis... and child. The beaver's child did having done no wrong, why you hate me so?" Shad asks calmly. "Mother still lives in brick forest of her kin, yes?" Shad nods, "Making little twig huts with friends, yes?" He confusedly swings his eyes to Avrel and to Candice.

"Use your words Kriegson!" Avrel screams, stomping her foot. "Mother is *dead*! She succumbed to her grief after five years of a broken heart after you left! You beat her, violated her, and made her bare the full extent of your mad fits! And *still*, she loved you!" she screams, clenching her fists until her flushed knuckles turn white. "Like an idiot..." she growls.

Shad's eyes water up to her surprise, but aside from a screech, he says nothing.

"After all you did…" she murmurs, "She still loved you… And you just left." Avrel cries angrily. "Just left her there!"

"Nicole? Nichole Bach!" Shad shouts. The sleeping platypus awakens and looks to Shad in attention. "Flapper fly the cave away…" The platypus sits there for a moment and then shuffles out. "Isis… Death because of sadness… Blame is… Me?" Shad says gripping his head as if he were in intense pain. He then lets out a shrill scream.

Avrel is unaffected by his boisterous shriek, no matter how it brings a painful fuzz to her ears. "You killed her, and now you're ruining this village's lake. What else have you done?!" Avrel says ragefully stomping forward and positioning her staff in an aggressive manner.

"Enough Avrel!" Zanvan yells from behind. Avrel turns to see that Geric and Zanvan have followed her. She hadn't even heard them, but then, between the falls and the sard's screaming, her ears are ringing.

She turns half around, "Why were you guys listening in on me? bloody hell, this doesn't concern you!?" Avrel growls in response.

During this, Shad begins to crawl to his feet. "Good father, little lady sees beaver, small lady must be killed. Then, my peace." Shad says hesitantly.

"Oh." she snarls, "So you're just fine with bugging over this whole region because you wanna live in peace?" Avrel asks, "Blissfully pretending that you didn't leave my mother to die alone, and leave me as a bastardized orphan!?" She can't help it, her rage boils so strongly inside of her that around her, her arcane power swells, her hair is gently tossed, and her shout rips through her throat. "Well *draw your sword motherfucker!*" Avrel screams, gripping her staff from the very end to maximize her reach.

"Avrel!" Geric calls, "I don't care how angry you are, possibly because you're so darn short, but taking your anger, from wherever it comes from, out on a man who's not even all there isn't gonna fix the past!" he warns, moving up closer behind her with his arm outstretched.

"You two, get back, or so help me!" she yells with fire in her eyes. As if they know her. As if they know the first thing about her, about *him*. About what he did to her, about what he did to her precious mother. Men themselves, they'd never understand. "You could never understand what I'm feeling..." she almost cries.

Avrel turns back, ready to engage Shad when she sees him stand perfectly erect and draw a bladeless hilt-like bar from his robe. It looks to be very old, bronze tipped, a broken sword of past eras. Broken, useless, it's a match for him. And yet...

"Baby cries, baby interferes, baby breaks peace over baby's life." he pants. "One less voice in head. No..." he thinly smiles in twitches, "Kill lake town and the chirp wailing of the sirens will exit the sluice." Shad says in perfect calmness.

Zanvan reaches for her "Avrel?" he yells once more.

"No, this is between us, it has been for ten years!" she yells in reply, No... All her life. "I hate you..." she mouths at the deranged he-elf.

Suddenly the bar Shad was brandishing lets out a blinding flash with the sounds of over a dozen tone crystals ringing out in unison. The air coalesces into a glowing shape, quickly crystallizing into a broadsword of crystal. "Tiny girl visits mother, soon to speak not to the sand from behind the moon..." Shad smiles malevolently.

The flash alone caught her off guard, but seeing what it might be, Avrel, Geric, and Zanvan all stand back in both shock and awe.

"Is that--!?" Geric and Zanvan both shout.

It... *Couldn't be.* she mouths as the words don't come. "Why do you have that!?" Avrel screams frustratedly.

"Voices told me... Would quiet voices... Doesn't." he says,, sadly. "Will quiet yours!" Shad yells taking a battle stance.

Avrel, unsure what to do, reverts to her previous position, even as doom forms a lump in her throat.

"Avrel!" Geric calls, "You can't fight him alone, not if he has that!" he insists. He touches her shoulder only to be shrugged off.

She remains calm, or calm as she can be. "He can barely form sentences, he can't fight..." she frys with a confident sneer. "Let him try..."

Avrel runs at Shad Kriegson and swings her staff from maximum length at Shad's head. Shad weakly raises the sword in an attempt to block it, so weakly that she knows she can plow through it.

But as Avrel's staff strikes the arcanium blade, it lets out an almost musical sound, like a choir of breaking glass. And with the sound, violent vibrations into her own weapon.

"Arrrghhh!!!" Avrel screams as all the energy of her swing seems absorbed by the crystal blade and suddenly returns as a vibrational shock that shoots back from her staff through to her shoulder. She jumps back, cradling her forearm, "What the hell...? Ahh..." She can see already the bleeding under her pale skin.

"Avrel!" Geric yells. "I *really* suggest you let us help you, he's not just a crazy guy!"

"No!" Avrel grunts, with the detering wave of her hand, unwittingly also raising a wave of fire which drives her friends back. "If this bastard has that... All the more that I should deal with him..."

Avrel takes up her staff in her other hand, rushes into him and again swings hard and wide, and once again he weakly raises his sword. Avrel sees it coming and in rage, swings even harder and more recklessly with her non-dominant hand. Spell or not, she'll break him!

***

They can only watch as the heat of her accidental flame still holds them back. The kid still hasn't gotten a hold on those damn flames of hers. Zanvan blanches as again the loud crash and the vibration to her hand force her back, this time she continues to try to fight, the harsh clang forcing her back. Screaming in anger and pain her final swing is hardly deflected, the flesh between her forearm bones is torn open and her fingers are so ravaged that she can no longer grip the staff. The mad elf bats the staff out of her hand and slashes her across the ribs with remarkable alacrity, as if suddenly he's awake. She flails herself, desperately crawling backward away from him, who is now holding the blade to her throat. Her eyes flutter like she finds it hard to keep her eyes open through the intense pain, and that her tears are making it hard to see when they are open.

"Say hello to the meat lady for me..." the elf, Shad sneers as he kicks her in the face. Her nose profusely spurts forth blood which showers her lips as he back-swings, no doubt wanting to cleanly lob her head off.

Just then his arrow whizzes through the air as Zanvan finds a clean shot through the heat distortion, but the elf quickly catches it with his magic and tosses it away. No longer able to wait, heat or flame be damned, Zanvan runs forward drawing his bastard sword as Geric rushes over to and pulls Avrel back to a safe distance.

"Zanvan!" Avrel squeals, "Don't! He can't be beaten with that thing!" she cries as he hears Geric pull out a satchel, hopefully of medical supplies.

"Quite the change in attitude..." he mutters only to himself. Zanvan looks around and waits for Shad to take the offensive, and when he swings wildly at him, Zanvan grabs a torch from the wall and throws it in his face.

Shad wails as he spastically tries to brush the hot ash from his eyes, and in the process, dropping that damned peculiar sword. Zanvan then cleaves Shad's thigh, and it bursts with blood, but as Zanvan goes in for a killing blow, the wounded elf sends him flying back with a spell of pure force. But not just him, it sends rattling waves of energy all around, randomly, and unstable and unfocused in power. Zanvan has had little practice fighting those with magic, but it's no stretch to him that such a spell could have sent him across the lake and back if he weren't bat-shite crazy.

"Give she to us!!!" the elf shrieks, as sparks of flame sputter from his clenched fists. Zanvan cautiously presses forward holding his blade in a stalwart guard for what it's worth. Shad stands quivering, twitching as if energy is jolting across his body uncontrollably when he abruptly lets out an ear-piercingly loud howl. He stomps, and white bolts of energy fan out, cracking the floor and the walls all around the cave. Zanvan easily dodges them, and they miss the kid and Geric entirely. But as he looks back to the elf, he finds himself staring straight into a fireball charging at arm's length. But the elf's other hand is clutching his temple, and his eyes are shut.

He lunges for it, low and fast like a coiled snake, and to that end, landing another deadly strike on the elf's other leg. The fireball shoots straight out of the opening flashing the curtain of water to steam, and the elf shrieks again. But not to compress the wound, but to clutch the sides of his head.

The he-elf falls over and wails and rolls, not minding his bleeding or his foe, or perhaps unable to. But as he reaches, and begins to crawl on his side towards Avrel and Geric. But before he can reach them, and before he can cast another of those terrifying spells, Zanvan stabs him through the side of his ribs, pinning him to the floor where he lay. He flails about screaming gibberish, the vitality of elves preventing what Zanvan had hoped to be a swift passing.

"Daughter!" Shad cries out, his jittering fingers clawing at the air between them, his voice startlingly clear, but desperate. "Forgive me! In leaving, I meant to leave you with the least pain of our connection!" Avrel leans up slightly. "Avréllïä…" Shad mumbles as his eyes glaze over and his flailing becomes a mild twitch. "See me…" he gargles lowly, his eyes fixated upon hers. With a final cough that spews blood in front of him, Zanvan feels the tension around his blade abate, and the glow from the dropped crystal blade dim. As the breath squeezes out once more, the elf, Shad Kriegson passes.

***

As the ranger wipes his blade off with a piece of Shad's robe and throws the now bladeless Runeblade hilt into Geric's pack. Undistracted, Avrel whimpers and hisses in pain as Geric tries to inspect her injuries. He looks carefully at her mangled hand, and her ribs, binding the areas where the skin is broken.

"Your left arm is a mess, if you hadn't had that bracer on, it probably wouldn't be in one piece!" Geric says trying to use positiveness to calm her down.

It doesn't, Geric finds as he begins feeling her bones, "Ahh! What are you doing!?" she screams.

"Avrel, I don't think your hand is broken, but I need to snap some of the bigger joints back in place.." Geric tries to say as peacefully as he can, a verbal trait he's experienced in. "Careful with your elbow. Shite I may have to cut you a bit to set things right…" he thinks aloud.

Judging by how she jolts, he shouldn't have said that.

Zanvan gives a worrisome and slightly doubting grumble. "Can you even do that?" he asks, "Hand surgery is awfully delicate, or so I thought."

"Oh it is." Geric says as casually as he can. "Well, let's snap to it." the play on words does nothing to comfort her as he grips her upper and lower arms by her wrenched elbow. Her pupils dilate as she gasps, and leans up.

"What no! No don't! Please!" she yelps in desperation, and he's barely put any pressure on her yet.

And unbeknownst to her, she's risking more damage. Geric hopes he can save her use, but he also knows he'll need as perfect circumstances as he can get. He has no choice but to carefully pin her tiny frame under himself. "Alright, alright, calm your barely existent breasts…" he sighs, again trying to lighten the mood to no avail. He whispers a brief incantation and then taps Avrel in the forehead, putting her into a deep sleep.

***

Zanvan looked ready to help hold her still, but looks far more relieved to see her go out so easily. He, after all, must be reeling from the fight too. He gets Geric to carry her staff and his sword so that he himself can carry Avrel out. During this time, all Candice can do is weep and squee in her grief. She doesn't want them to leave Shad there, she knows that much is obvious, but clearly they can't bother with that now, and are going without her. Her poor little Avrel, only barely escaping what could have easily been her doom, only by the skin of her tiny teeth. Candice takes one more look at Shad and then no more. She follows the men carrying her dear Avrel.

As they get out to the ledge behind the waterfall, Candice sees Shad's platypus looking very sad, obviously recognizing the loss of her master. She gingerly walks over to the grieving and weakened platypus and offers some comfort. After exchanging some chirps and grumbles, she convinces the platypus to use what strength it has to follow her and the others back down to Järviby.

***

By this time it is late morning, but it's already been a long day, and he's not even the one carrying her down the plateau. As not to waste any more time, they return to the tavern, Zanvan covered in blood with Avrel over his shoulder, and Geric silently preparing himself for the work he must do.

They are still quite far from the tavern's deck, about where there ought to be a sign warning of the cursed fish when all too familiarly, Jansen sees them from afar, and is trying to call to them.

"Goddess, take their eyes." Geric scorns, softly to himself. He waves back, but he is too unrested to waste valuable energy on shouting back. Not if he's to do surgery.

She finally gets the message, and comes to them. "Miss Avrel!" she says, again, still rather far away. "Mr Zanvan too!"

"It's just a scratch." the ranger says stoically.

"Hasn't been a praiseworthy day for any of us." Geric comments.

"Oh... This is awful, I--"

"Miss Jansen." Geric finally says as composedly yet as firmly as he can. "We're going to need some things, rags, spirits."

"Right." she says with a tone of anxious panting. "I'll be waiting!" she says as, yet again, her damned flowy elven attire means she really can't run very fast.

As they come to the door, Jansen who has been waiting holds it open as they enter. She says nothing, but quickly grabs Geric some clean rags and some high alcohol spirits that he can use to clean Avrel's wounds. Zanvan gently lays Avrel down on the floor, and steps aside.

Geric douses his hands in the spirits and muttering a soft prayer gets to work first by removing the haphazard dressing he'd placed on her side wound, and then cleaning and wrapping her chest properly.

Jansen paces by again. "Is there anything more I can-"

"Pillows." Geric grunts, *If things aren't aligned just right.* he cursingly reminds himself.

"Right!" she complies, disappearing into another room.

Zanvan then horns in. As much as it strokes his ego that the ranger is interested in watching him treat Avrel's injuries with such care and alacrity, Geric wishes he'd back off just a bit. "Give me some space." he says softly.

The ranger complies. "Despite being a sarcastic bastard most of the time, you're pretty good at this." Zanvan says casually.

It brings a smile to him, slightly and he nods. "Thanks." he turns to Zanvan, "Don't think I'm a pervert just because I took her shirt off to clean this wound." he quickly clarifies. "And don't you *ever* tell her, she'd kill me."

Zanvan chuckles, "She would too." he agrees, "I wouldn't worry about it, way she's built I didn't even notice, beside there's nothing weird about a doctor type seeing you nude."

Zanvan's point stands, Geric's seen kids with more fatty tissue than this one. She's filled out *some* since they met, but she's still quite cadaverous, and that's not even accounting for her bloodloss. Not that it's easy to gauge that either. She barely had color either. "Well, this girl might, you know how she is..." Geric sighs.

Zanvan chuckles, darkly like this whole situation has made him wonder just 'how she is'. What manner of person is she, really?

It's certainly made Geric wonder himself. He thinks he knows what has happened, but it's been a long night. "For that matter, I would imagine she wouldn't know of 'going to a doctor'." he comments to himself. Maybe he does so a bit abrasively at times, but really, he only ever is trying to get her to lighten up a bit; if her life has been as rough as she believes.

"So..." Zanvan begins to ask, "Any reason you can't just blip it all away with a healing spell, or potion?"

A common, ignorant question, but whatever. "Most potions only work on less severe wounds, I can use those as follow up later." Geric says with a grunt as he pulls the bandages as tightly around her fissured arm as he can. Zanvan steps in and lends an extra hand. "Besides, Avrel's so tiny, I don't know how to dose her." Geric continues as he affixes it, and tears off the excess gauze.

"Umhm." Zanvan nods, "And healing magic?" he asks.

Geric takes a deep breath, damn he wishes he knew stitch. "Again, in this case, better for follow up. I'm not sure if that magic blade imparts any curses on its wounds, and I don't wanna find out." he swallows hard, "In school that was one of the first lessons, they demonstrated casting a healing spell on a wound on a sheep and the sheep's wounded area just blew up. Kaplooossshhh!" Geric animates the severity of the explosion to the best of his ability by waving his hands and twiddling his fingers.

Zanvan comes beside him for a closer look, "Is there no way to check?" he asks in a sigh.

"Not that I *know*." Geric replies, growing tired of Zanvan's questions.

And with that, he realizes the point of Zanvan's questioning, "Not that you know? Or *know of*?" he says, exposingly, "You're a bit young for a cleric, aren't you?" he asks darkly, and not very loudly. "Most men of the medical clergy are at least in their near thirties." he says with an inquisitive stare.

"What of it?" Geric says as he carefully snaps Avrel's right hand joints back into place. It's a startling and terrifying sound.

"You never graduated, did you...?" Zanvan says in a cold, stern voice.

Geric has to stop his work on Avrel's hands for the moment, "Not exactly." he replies dimly. Can he not wait until a better time? He resumes his work, making sure everything is in its place.

The ranger leans back, it seems he got to where he wanted to take him.. "What happened?"

Without hesitation Geric coldly replies "It was a lot of things." Not a lie, but he can tell by Zanvan's mannerism that he's not accepting of the near dodge.

"Like?" he asks in a prodding manner, obviously he won't take a short, painless answer.

"Shite teacher, stupid rules, and obnoxious cohabitants, *okay*?" Geric shouts stressfully, again having to stop his work for a moment.

"That's pretty much what I thought you'd say." Zanvan chuckles.

And what about you? almost makes it through his lips, nobody chooses the wildman, vagrant, ranger's life without cause. "It doesn't mean I can't use spells or treat wounds, so what does it matter?" Geric says defiantly as he returns to work on Avrel's hand. He's happy to find that most of the smaller, more fragile joints aren't injured beyond jamming and sprains. The smaller wounds he had to make, he heals right up with a simple wave of his hand and a few muttered words. Those he knows don't have any elven funny business. He knows what he's doing, if that's what the ranger is so damned worried about.

Jansen comes back with a pillow, handing it to Zanvan as she goes to check something cooking in the kitchen.

"Now Zanvan." He startles the proud and oh so *official* ranger, "Put that under her *head* not her hips." Geric cracks with a crooked smile.

Zanvan leers him back, like he's unsure whether his humor comes from a place of utter love and sanity, or somewhere more sinister, still he obeys, gently places the pillow under Avrel's head.

"Good." Geric pats. "You make a decent nurse."

He can tell that at first, that *really* gets under his skin, but it fades to a cocky smile, "How would you know?"

Geric lets out an unwitting grumble. He might've asked for that. But, if Zanvan's okay, he's okay. "Touché."

***

A moment later Jansen comes out of the kitchen holding up the platypus with great care." Can you guys watch her until I can get Tarja over here?" Jansen asks as she places the billed creature on Zanvan's lap. He supposes she has a business to run, but she might have at least let him say 'yes'.

"Sure." he says, as Zanvan looks into the eyes of the platypus, and the platypus stares straight back. *Shad Kriegson's familiar, Avrel's father...* he assumes, he's pretty sure, but still sketchy on last night's whole affair.

Candice chatters at the creature in his lap, and the duck-rat's duck bill replies with something in kind. Weakly, like it's dying. Candice continues to look at Avrel's fractured arms, still covered in blood and webs of bruising. She herself has looked better. Magic's mysteries being what they are, a convoluted mess, he wonders if her weakness is indicative of the kid's. But then, he considers how often Avrel and Candice spoke, about many things. Everything, at times. *Drove Geric half nuts sometimes.*

And after a few seconds, Zanvan has an idea.

"Hey! Candice" her dark eyes are startled to be sure, his apologies. "Ask this platypus 'Does the Runeblade inflict curse wounds'." he calls to the beaver softly whimpering next to her unconscious master.

Candice replies with her squirrel-like chatter as she walks up and exchanges some squeaks with the platypus. After some lengthy squeaks Candice walks up to a very intensely focused Geric and gives a 'no' nod. He doesn't notice.

"Geric?"

"You know Zanvan, I'm a bit busy?" he scolds back, "If I'm to be questioned and pleaded with while trying to not leave this diminutive damsel a cripple, you could at least send in that Jansen woman." he bites out, "At least her accent is interesting."

Candice slaps Geric's boot with her tail.

"What!?" he stops, just short of a swat.

"I think she said 'the wounds aren't cursed'." Zanvan restates.

To that, the beaver warbles and nods.

"Oh, so the ranger gets to understand familiars too?" Geric was already a bit flushed, but now he's full red. "Oh." he sighs. "Seems good." he nods as he turns to his pack and lifts out one of his books and begins flipping through it. "If this goes wrong, it's on you, Toothy." he says with a curt turn, "I'll make you into a hat."

It would seem the beaver believes him, she steps back.

The cleric takes a deep breath and mumbles a short incantation before touching Avrel's wounds. They slowly start to glow with a soft, minty light. "That should make this much simpler." he smiles, and lets out a heavy breath.

Not bad. Zanvan notes as the smaller wounds have already closed. "She'll be good as new when she wakes?"

Geric wipes his brow with one of his oversized sleeves, "Well, she might be bruised still, she still ought to take it easy for a few days. Especially that arm." Geric replies. "If I can get her some good followup potions, she'll keep her mobility." he winces, "Unless I mucked up. Or missed something. Or was too late already…" His confidence seems to wane as he continues to list possible issues, ending with, "Or she's a cripple. But I have *some* pride in my work." he says returning to a half smile.

For the last few minutes, Zanvan had become okay with the 'cleric' not being so official. That's slightly diminished now. Still, he gives him an affirmind nod as Geric begins washing his hands in a basin that Jansen had supplied him with. He also begins cleaning up his things and placing them neatly back in his pack. He grabs a bottle of spirits that hadn't been entirely used up when he cleaned the wounds, and goes out to sit on the lakeside deck and relax, Zanvan follows, he needs a smoke.

Not a word is spoken, by he, the ranger who cares too much about some urchin, city kid, nor the 'cleric' in practice only. They are a fine pair, the both of them. But Zanvan gives him a hearty nudge with his fist to his shoulder. He's done his best.

After an hour or so Jansen comes out on the deck. She seems very apologetic, but also firm. "My apologies." she nods her head slightly, "I'm sorry to do this…" she says tenderly, "But we're opening soon, so if you could take your friend back to your rooms at the inn, that'd be appreciated."

Zanvan can tell she's trying not to push them out, but all the same, they should go. "Oh yeah, sure." Zanvan says, putting his pipe out, and promptly heading inside. He carefully grabs the kid off of the floor. *Little thing is so pathetically light.* he thinks as a somber smile cuts through his otherwise grim mood in the matter.

Geric follows and picks up his pack. "Watch the arms. Let them hang straight."

"Sure." He's got her fingers all wrapped stiffly, he might have done her whole arm that way. *Oh well.* he sighs, he's a discount cleric after all.

As they are about to pass through the doorway Jansen grabs their attention once more, "Oh, Miss Tarja will be by the inn later to pick up Nicole if that's ok." she informs them. Zanvan nods, and motions for Geric to carry the thing. Obviously, he doesn't want to, but he complies. Jansen nods and waves favorably as they head out into the street. Geric seems indifferent, though if asked Zanvan thinks he might say he tolerated *those* elves. He could tolerate Jansen himself.

"Alright, thanks for everything." Zanvan says as he waves, still carefully balancing Avrel's tiny frame.

"Sorry about the mess on the floor, Jansen." Geric adds.

"No, thank you." she says. For the lake, Zanvan guesses.

They make their way to the inn through the golden afternoon sun lit streets, hoping to see Bob's wagon sitting by the inn's stable, but alas, to their dismay it's not.

They take Avrel to her room, shaking off the accusatory looks the inn hostess gives the two men as they take an unconscious and beaten young lady to her sleeping quarters. Not that he's never carried a woman to her room before, but this isn't the same. Proving that, Zanvan carefully puts her under the covers, and sets Candice on a chair beside the bed, along with the now very weak platypus. He sets a glass of water there too, should she need it, and hopes the 'cleric's' magic does it's work.

Despite the drink after all his work, Geric looks a bit wound, even now. Zanvan feels as though he could eat a shank himself. *About time.* "Hey." he says to Geric who is springing the feather on his cap with his finger, "Since the cat's outta the bag, how about I get you some elven wine?" he offers.

His brows shift, favorably, "Yeah." he smiles, "And the closest thing these tree-hugging sards have to steak."

Probably venison. He pulls him up from his seat on the side of her bead and holds the door for his *esteemed* doctor. "Watch her Candice." he orders, with a strong finger, "And watch the platy- *Nichole* too." Zanvan commands as he shuts the door.

***

Candice just squeaks at the handsome, rugged ranger until the door shuts. She's relieved as she hears him lock it too. He's taking good care of her girl, her master. Both of them, really. That cleric, he's shown far better colors than she'd have expected even a few days past. Having a healer and taking him for granted, she's taken to looking that gifted horse in the mouth, but he's shown his teeth, and they are healthy. Maybe not so very clean, but healthy. Much like her master's.

"Chippu?" she calls Nicole, but the poor dear is far too weak now to reply. *Understandably.* But, she'd hoped to ask a few things about Avrel's father, about everything. But, it's the rules of this form, Shad is passed, and thus Nicole cannot be saved. And all not saved, is lost.

She could do with a good, leafy limb, or maybe some of that 'cleric' boy's syrup, but he took his bag, and there's nothing in this fine, elven room she'd dare nibble at. But it's alright; her girl, her *master* is alright now. She just needs to watch over her now.

She always has.
She always will.

***

In the dining room Zanvan finally gets to try some of the foretold elven hookah. He hadn't become the connoisseur that he is now last time he was in an elven province. He also gets Geric his promised glass of elven wine as he looks through several of his books to try to find the proper potion dosage for a '5'1" half-elf woman', a size he believes to be a slight over estimation, but he's not the supposed 'cleric'. Geric may act like he finds it a trivial pain, but with the good wine and the deer-steak, Zanvan knows he's enjoying himself.

The hookah's taste is unusual but palatable, made more so as he chats it up with a very richly skinned wood-elf from the far west who is also enjoying some. Though she has feminine curves, she has a strong, exercised physique and her clothing does little to hide the appeal therein. Unlike the more plain, muted accessories of the lake elves, she has vibrant jewels and stones around her neck, and through her ears. And a fetching, smokey paint around her eyes.

"So what brings you this far eastward?" he asks.

She smiles, looking him over. "My companions and I..." He instantly switches to more active listening, her accent is very thick, and not one he's used to, not at all. "...We serve as mail couriers to the lands beyond our ancient forests. We just got back from the land of our kin who still clingk to the evergreen forests of the far north." the wood-elf replies as she exhales the smoke through her slender nose.

While the elves sing their lines of words, she hums them, gliding slowly between vowels only to be set apart by a few clipped, sharp consonants. And damned if half the sounds aren't sizzled, lowly. *Geric would have the words for it.* Zanvan admits that he's no linguist.

Not that he *needs* to be. "How are they faring up there?" he inquires, "I was up there several years past and they seemed to be doing okay despite the glaciers' encroachment." he replies in a bid to show his knowledge.

She smiles sensually as she sips her wine, between whiffs of the hookah. "Hmmm, you are quite well traveled, I like that." says the wood-elf. Her accent, it almost is orken, he can make sense of that to a degree. He'll have to. "Yes they seemed to be well, some of the younger ones seem more concerned though. I suppose the older ones care less as most of their centuries are behind them." she laughs. "So it's 'okay doomers, have fun elsewhere'."

He laughs, not so much to be phoney, but enough to show interest. "So, if I may, why did the *most beautiful* of the elves leave their homeland and make their home so far west?" Zanvan asks, pouring on his charm, the darker skin he could take or leave, but there's no denying the shape that it's wrapped around. It certainly has a healthfulness that many women lack.

"The man who later became our leader feared the eventual encroachment of the ice." she explains, "With one of the forest goddess's great seeds, he and some those who believed him followed him to a land he believed was full of promise, also *much* further from those dreadful orcs." she replies giving him a satisfied look. "Not so far from where your race originates, or so I've been told."

Zanvan asks an obvious question, "You're not a fan of the orcs?" he inquires in a smooth voice.

In the distance Geric can be heard muttering, in his apparent best impression of her accent, "Ay'm nöt eVven ze ffan öff elVvesz!"

He pretends not to know him, lest he contend with the other wood-elves in her party as well.

Or any of the other patrons for that matter.

The wood-she-elf shudders, hopefully at their topic and not the rudeness of the individual Zanvan has *never seen before in his life.* "Of course not, since the days of old they've been a mockery of us elves." she replies in a passionate tone, "Their allegiance with The Beast in the past and their continual disregard for the forests deserves dread, do you not agree?" she continues.

Zanvan certainly does, and not just for her sake.. "Well, I suppose they got what for it, cursed in appearance and a spoiled, dead land." Zanvan pauses thoughtfully for a moment, "I'm no fan of their kind either." his voice low, gravelly, pained with things he tries not to think about too often.

"True, brutality and carnality have their places, just not toward the woods of the world." she comments, sighing some smoke. "Carnal thingks...." She gives him a coy look up and down as she says it.

Or young girls lost in the woods, he might say should he choose to dodge the obvious invitation, which he won't. "And where should *carnality* be directed towards?" Zanvan asks in a sensual tone with a raised brow.

She smiles, he hadn't missed it. "*Zanvan* is it?" she asks, standing up with a provocative stretch, "Why not come to my room in a few minutes, I'd very much like to show you."

The ranger pulls off his hunter's hat and slides his hand over his hair, "I suppose that could be arranged." he says coolly but with a smile as he feigns having to think about it, and just slightly hinting at a comparative glance to the other attractive patron in the room.

She looks to Zanvan flirtatiously, and *greedily.* "Third floor, first on the left, don't make me wait too longk." she says as she pays her tab and heads up the stairs. Zanvan leans back with his arms behind his head with a confident smile, eventually he notices Geric glaring at him. Once he has Zanvan's attention he says nothing but gives him a reluctant thumbs up. Zanvan grins and after several minutes he pays his bill and heads for the stairs. He has to wonder if the 'cleric' really hates the elves or how they speak as much as he acts like he does. He wouldn't touch that with a ten-foot halberd shaft.

***

Geric catches him as he passes, not standing, but making a bit of a reach for Zanvan's mantle. "So I'm gonna have to stay here waiting for that Tarja woman?" he asks, admittedly a little perturbed.

Zanvan shrugs, "Yup, have fun." he replies before walking up the steps, no doubt following that rather callipygous wood-elf.

"Ugh..." Geric sighs as he returns to studying his books, and writing notes and equations next to recipes, along with scribblings of the questions his mind throws out, frustratedly. *Why does she have to be small? Why half-elf? What parts are more human? What parts are elf-kind? How old is she? How old is she -- for an elf? Is she ragging? Does she rag yet?* Most of them even she'd not know. Some of them only the Gilded and the Silvered Elohimé would know, and even real clerics aren't invited unto their divine council.

After a while of reading, scribbling, and drafting, Geric's tired eyes wander to a sound coming towards him and he notices a tall, dark haired elf woman coming down the stairs, it's Tarja. He thinks it's Tarja. She's not the *only* elf with dark hair like that, but it does stand out a bit. Maybe she inks it?

He puts a marker in his book and closes it. "Hail and well met." he groans, inviting Hopefully-Tarja to take a seat.

She is somber, her elf eyes look sad and dim. She softly returns his hello and sits down at his table across from him. "I heard from Júkkä and Jänsen about what befell little Avrel." she looks guilty over it. Which *does* kind of make sense. "I'm sorry about that." she says apologetically. "Shäddäi was... I'm sorry about him."

Geric brushes it off, "Hey, it's not your fault." *Not directly, anyway.*

She looks away, as if she may beg to differ. "I--" she stumbles, "I did not know she was his *döltír*."

And that sets off an alarm bell in Geric's mind, suddenly their crazy inconsistent surnaming convention makes sense. It's dumb, but it makes sense. "That Avrel has daddy issues, big surprise he was here though. MmmYou never know who you'll run into, I guess." he sighs, and then downs the rest of the wine in his glass. "On the bright side, she made solving your issue pretty easy. He was gonna kill her, so we took out two sins with one confession." Geric grins, realizing that he'd poured that on *way* too thickly. Ignoring that, he goes to pour himself another glass of wine. "You want some?" he asks, "Zanvan got me a whole bottle. I hate to admit it, but wine is one thing you knifer's do well."

"No." she looks down and away, "No, thank you."

"Yeah, me neither." he puts the bottle down. "I think I've had enough."

"Um... Jänsen said you have Nichole, Shad's Platypus?" Tarja asks gingerly.

Geric's face turns slightly sour. "Yeah, Avrel's beaver decided to invite it to come back with us." he tells her, "Between you and me, I hate that beaver." Geric whispers.

Tarja giggles tenderly for a moment, it's forced, he can tell. "Yes, little Nicole." she says reminiscently, "Shäd always had a thing with aquatic creatures. He didn't fish like his father, but sometimes they'd go out on the boat together and he'd always have some turtle or muskrat swim up to him. Then one day he was down more southward when he came across what looked like a young platypus being attacked by some forest sprites. He fended them off and found it to be a... more magical creature." Tarja sighs, "His father would have loved to see that."

"Yeah, Avrel has that damned magic beaver." he says, not hiding his crossedness with the damned thing. "Bloody thing is a card shark!" Geric says with agitation, "How do you know so much about Shad and all that anyway?"

"Well.. I knew him when he was growing up and for sometime after that." she replies in an almost cautious manner. "I never knew he had a child." she adds like an afterthought.

"So what do you want exactly?" Geric asks as he takes a sip of his drink.

"With Shäd deceased..." she pauses as her lip rolls over trying to hold her clip up, "Nicole probably isn't long for this world, with her spirit link being broken and such. I was kind of hoping that I could take care of her until she passes." Tarja states compassionately.

"Ehh sure." he shrugs, "Take the damn beaver if you want her too, I don't care." Geric says dimly, "I doubt Avrel would want anything to do with her father either, so I doubt *she* wants the duck-marmot." he says as he stretches and stands. "I'll get her for you." The cleric leaves money for his tab and heads up the stairs with his books. Tarja follows him up to the main level but not up to the upper floor, and so she sits quietly in the lobby for a few moments.

He quietly goes in and grabs it, before returning to the elf lady. "Here's the ducky thing." he says as he hands over the sleepy creature to the slightly sad looking elf woman.

"Thank you, Geric." she says with a fragile smile.

"No skin off my nose." he scoffs, "At least I have a nose, unlike that thing." he says pointing toward its bill.

"She certainly is an unusual creature, isn't she." Tarja says, forcing another laugh. "Poisonous too, but... I doubt she has the strength for that now." She shakes Geric's hand and heads out towards. By this time it is quite late and Geric goes back for his books, and retires to his quarters.

9

"See me!!" he tells her. And she does, as the sword rips through him and the light in him fades. Avrel sees him. Avrel saw him. Avrel is still running through that cave, looking for him. Angry, lost, lonely, and tired...

She saw him, but she never found him.

The following morning Avrel wakes up to Candice's worried face after another nudge from her nose, as well as to a feeling of stiffness, and soreness. And she hasn't even moved yet. She barely remembers anything after that fight, *Only...*

"Chippu!?" the Candice moans.

"Yeah yeah, I'm okay... I think." Avrel says in a groggy morning voice, it even hurts to breathe. She leans up to feel a harsh pain in her side and particularly through her forearm. "Ouch.." she shouts, quietly as she's able. She finds her hands and fingers stiff and painful at first but once she flexes them a little, they become more usable, what parts aren't wrapped uncomfortably tight anyway, that is most of them though. "Ehhh...?" she moans "Let's get you your cornbread." she mutters to Candice as she attempts to dress herself slowly, stiffly, and without standing. And with barely any use of her hands. She doesn't need her keen nose to notice a drunken smell nor to realize that it's her, "Eww... Ughh... they must've used alcohol to clean my cuts." she says disgustedly.

Candice chatters as if to laugh, but it's a relieved sort of laugh.

The two make their way down the steps to the dining area where Candice's eyes boggle at the sight of a fresh, steamy hot pile of cornbread buns. Avrel and Candice see where they'd like to sit down, once they get some breakfast on their plates, which is a task in and of itself, it hurts too bad to try and levitate anything. But with a pinky and a thumb, she manages, and once at their choice table, Candice begins gnawing into her cornbread.

Avrel eats her food slowly both due to her pain with movement and being lost in thought. Deep thoughts.

Geric wanders in and sits next to her trying to get her attention but she seems not to notice. "What are you thinking about?" he asks but gets no immediate reply. "Gee, I'm sure glad my friend is a cleric who can heal me up when I go into a patricidal rage!" he says in an attempt at mimicking Avrel's voice, he however, only draws attention from everyone else in the room.

"He attacked me..." Avrel murmurs too quiet for the man to hear. "Good morning..." she frys while slowly putting a vegetable stalk in her mouth.

"MmmHey, you woke from your trance finally." the cleric says with a chuckle, "I thought I might need to get out my spell book, how are you feeling?" he asks.

"I'm okay." she lies with a painful grunt. "My ribs hurt really bad, my forearm hurts worse." she mumbles.

"Yeah." Geric replies, "If it weren't for that otherwise useless bracer you wear, your arm wouldn't be in one piece. Also your ribs are cracked. Don't worry, I stayed up late last night to learn how to make you some potions to help your bones and stuff heal." he smiles, and looks like he's almost about to pat her back when he stops just short.

"Thanks." Avrel tries to smile. "This thing is itchy." She scratches at her chest wraps.

"Don't mess with that!" he says suddenly. "You'll need to keep it on for a few days."

"Great."

A few moments later Zanvan comes down. He seems relieved to see her up, not very outwardly, but she's learned to tell. "Hey, Bob is parked outside, he says we can leave as soon as we're ready." he informs his companions.

"Sounds good." Avrel says quietly. "I'm not hungry…" she murmurs.

"Is she okay?" Zanvan asks, looking to the cleric.

"Can I see your hands?" Geric asks her.

She obliges, stiffly. She feels like a crone, she can hear everything moving and it disgusts her. Suddenly Geric presses what seems very hard into the meat of her hand, making her practically see red. "*Crotchsucker!*" she barks.

"Still a little swollen." Geric answers Zanvan.

"No shite?" she can't help but hiss. "Bloody, eh?"

"Just rest them." Geric promises, "If I can get your potions mixed you won't be wrapped for too long." he pauses to sip some water, "I might have to crack you a few times."

She shudders, she was afraid he'd say something like that. "Can we maybe just go?" she tosses down a vegetable stick she'd been idling gnawing at. "If Bob's done, I just wanna go."

"Yeah." Geric shrugs. "Let's go."

"What about breakfast?" Zanvan asks.

Geric winks and points to Zanvan, "Memory serves, somebody's got some bull-horse jerky." he replies with a smile.

"You're right." Zanvan says happily. "I'd almost forgotten."

They stop a short minute on the way out to pay their bill and grab anything else from their rooms before heading out into the morning sun. The guys are nice enough to carry her things.

A moment later, the familiar cart pulls around and they are greeted by Bob. "Hellerr frernds!" he says smiling and waving from his driver's perch.

"Hello mmmBob." Geric says as he passes by on his way to the back of the wagon.

Avrel finds it hard to say anything, and she can't properly wave either. She forces a smile for Bob, but that's all.

"Lert's gert goring!" he says cheerfully.

Geric easily gets into the back which has a good number of more things in it, but for her, the climb is impossible. "You can go ahead." she says backing away so Zanvan can pass. He first helps Candice up before his large, manly hands are in cup shapes only inches from her waist.

"May I?" he asks, he sounds annoyed maybe, but he does ask her.

"Thanks." she nods. He grips her around her hips and sits her bottom on the tailgate, he lets her stand from there before he himself gets on, and still with both his *and* her things. "Thanks." she says again before she finds a spot, or rather, what spot Candice has chosen for them.

Zanvan looks for his jerky. Geric takes out a book and spreads some papers and little vials of things around him, and finally Zanvan gives the all clear. They hear the reins shake, and they begin to move.

"Sor, Er'm gorner heard south-werst ter the birg mirnerng cirty dern there." Bob yells back to them over the clopping of his horses.

Avrel moans, "What for?" she inquires softly.

"Ther do serm trerd wirth the orcs, ernd ther herv lerts orf prertter germs ernd surch." Bob says happily.

"Thank goodness we're not trading with the orcs directly." Geric asserts. "They are freaky!"

"I've never met any." Avrel says in an inviting way, surely Geric or Zanvan will explain.

"Well, the women are alright." Zanvan explains, of course, that being his first thought, "Aside from the big lower teeth, they just look like tall muscular human women with a darker, olive complexion. The men on the other hand..." his face turns fierce, it scares her a bit, she's ever seen him like that before. "Savage bastards."

"I met an orc guy once." Geric interjects. "He was a total arse. Like you said, the women are bearable and have like an olive skin tone but the guys are almost like a greeny... green. And their tusky teeth are even bigger and they're just hulky arses! Competative loudmouths."

Zanvan described them, but of course, Geric... "You met one, so you assume they are all like that?" Avrel questions.

"Shushh!" Geric quickly replies.

Zanvan seems to agree with Geric's claim, "The men... Are very brutish." he says solemnly.

Avrel concedes by not retorting it. If they've met one, they've met more than she. She'll take their word for it, to a degree, until she can make up her own mind. She'd like to ask more, but she's tired already.

She disengages them and tries to find space to lay down, the cart is far less open than it had been but she eventually finds some space. Her small size has its advantages. She moves a box or two and slides right into her freshly cleared cubby. Candice comes beside her and tags her so she rolls over a bit --

A mistake, Avrel yelps as she accidentally puts weight on her side. It fades fast enough as she falls flat, but for that one minute she was seeing searing red.

"MmmThat reminds me Avrel..." Geric yells out to her. "I've gotta cook this potion I'm mixing for you. Should cut the pain and help you heal, just try to remind me later when we stop."

"Thanks, I will." Avrel mutters as the beautiful elven city slowly fades over the horizon. She can still see a bit of it through the curtains. Beautiful, full of water, and song, and elves. But even so, even there, she is both, and neither. It's not home, and never could be.

And really, she's not sure she'd want to live there just by what's happened, that plateau is so visible. That damned plateau of grief. Still, she has lingering questions, especially for Tarja. She seemed to know Shad very well, but she never knew how. It won't be her home, her beacon of success over the people who looked down on her must be closer, and more present. She pauses though to wonder if that's really worth the effort. Of course, she'd wanted nothing more than the ability to cast off the cares of those who did the same upon her, But... she considers as the last of the blue lake fades over the horizon, *It is beautiful.* And while not permanently, maybe it's a place she'll return to.

Someday.

Avrel remains half awake as they continue on, she reclines, and Geric and Zanvan enjoy the jerky. She's still not hungry, and the scenery turns to plais once more. She can't roll over, but she does manage to get some rest.

That night when they stop to make camp, Geric starts brewing up the promised potion for Avrel over the fire they've gathered around. Zanvan lit it.

"You wouldn't believe how long it took me to figure out how to dose this for you." the cleric humbly brags, "Seriously, I had to look into the dosing for a female elf, reduce it by a two-thirds, and then account for the fact that you're tiny and thin. 5' 1" I hope." he comments.

Oh? Five and one? "Yeah. I guess." Like hell if she knows, how could she? But just the same, she'll take it.

"I had to look through four different books!" Geric says in a not so subtle and braggart way.

"Thanks." Avrel says with a soft gracious smile just the same.

"Hmmmm... Shoot!" Geric shouts in annoyance. "Do we have any Orken Wheat Root?"

"The heck is that?" Avrel asks.

Zanvan tips up his hat, "It's a grain that grows like a weed in the southeast region of the orc's land." he explains. "It grows elsewhere though. The root is really good for your bones, so they say. I've heard rangers say they can 'milk them' after a storm, but I've never tried it."

Avrel can't help but wonder if that's true, *Plants making milk?* It actually makes her wonder when the last time she'd tasted milk was. It's expensive, and she never liked the taste anyway. "You *need* it?"

"Yeah." he confirms after a flurry of page flipping. "This recipe needs a clump of it. Everything else is stuff I have on hand." Geric says, loudly thumping shut his book. "It's a shame, maybe if you'd eaten some once in a while you would've grown at some point!"

Avrel's drowsy-like demeanor changes on that, she's in no mood for his teasing. "Oh my goddess, just cut it out!!" Avrel says as she slaps Geric, only to hurt herself more in the process.

"Learned your lesson?" he taunts as he rubs the stinging cheek. "Hmmm... I suppose I could find a substitute.... Hmmm..." Geric carefully flips through a different book. "This recipe is almost the same, it uses enchanted wolf bones instead." he mumbles prompting Zanvan to look through his pack of animal pelts.

"Hmm..." he hums as he shuffles through his bag. "I remember keeping some because I know they are valuable. Yeah, here." he tosses a leg bone to Geric.

Geric inspects it before handing it to Avrel. "You wanna do one of your elf dances or something over this thing?"

"What?!" she yelps in trepidation and self-consciousness.

"Well, I don't know..." Geric says waving her off, "*Enchant it!*"

Avrel grunts and mumbles for a moment before clasping the bone to her tiny chest and taking a prayer-like pose, she sits like this for several moments until she begins to flush and feels herself sweating, slightly. Finally with a bombastic out-breath she hands the bone back to Geric. "I got nothing..." she sighs.

Geric, unamused checks his book. "Hmm... Enchanted... with moonlight!" he says proudly.

"How does that work?" Zanvan asks.

"No clue!" Geric replies with a befuddled smile.

"Give it here." Avrel says holding out the slightly better of her two hands. Geric hands her the bone once more, this time Avrel holds the bone up above her as she stares to the shimmering silver crescent moon, this time she mutters something to herself and the bone takes on a faint glow.

"How did you do that?" Geric says scratching his head.

Avrel hands it back to him. "My mother made one for me when I was small and afraid of the dark streets. *'Wolves howl to get their vitality from the moon, and so does the howl of your heart draw the night-silver magic into its form once again.'* ." Avrel reminisces.

"...Sounds... Cool?" Geric says taking the bone and unceremoniously tossing it into the pot of boiling ingredients. "Your mom seems to have been quite learned in the Arcane Arts." he comments.

Avrel nods. "Yeah, she *was*." she says wistfully, maybe they didn't know, "I learned a lot from her, that's how I began doing my shows." For a moment they are all quiet, so far as she can tell as she watches the brew's boiling bubbles.

"Alrighty, here you go." Geric says taking the pot off of the fire, "Dab a little of this on your forearm and side once a day and then cover it with a warm compress." he says as he pours it into a bottle.

"Thanks." she replies. "I think I'm gonna get some sleep now, see you in the morning."

"But first!" Geric interjects, his hands all ready chomping at the bit.

She closes her eyes and lets him touch her. Each crack is like lightning striking her hands, wrists and arms, but he quickly cools it with a healing touch. *Thankfully.* she breathes sighfully.

"There you go." he smiles. "Again in the morning."

"Can't wait." she frys sardonically.

∗∗∗

Avrel waves, just a little more limberly as she climbs into the back of the cart with the help of a box, and that damned beaver quickly follows.

Bob scoots in, "Irrs she orrkay?" he inquires.

"I'm not sure, we haven't even eaten yet." Geric says putting a potato on a skewer and suspending it over the fire.

"She hasn't eaten much at all." the ranger puts in, "Not since the incident with Shad Kriegson."

The gnome strokes his beard, "Shourd we prerr mayrberr?" he asks.
"Nah, prying might make it worse." Zanvan replies.

"I mean…" Geric scoffs with a haughty chuckle, "I'm already prying quite a bit as you saw."

"Yeah." Zanvan comments, "That looked painful."

"Hey." Geric holds out his hand, "Look at all those little bits? There's a lot to injure. I hope I never get crunched up like hers was!"

Zanvan touches a twig to the fire to light his pipe. "So then what you're doing is--"

"Yeah." Geric continues, "I've gotta break up the scars where her body is mishealing on its own and reapply the regeneration spell."

"Ferscernerterng." Bob replies.

"She's making good progress." Geric assures them, "I'm sure she'll be fine in a little while."

"Stirr." the gnome nasals out, "Sher seerms erff."

Implying that Avrel isn't off or easy to set off to begin with. "If it's anything at all, she's probably just on the rag." Geric asserts.

The other two entertain it as a possibility, but after a while their discussion turns to other things.

The next few days pass with little excitement, Avrel uses her potion and sleeps, Zanvan smokes his pipe now and again, and Geric sprinkles them with his knowledge and wit between the chapters of his books.

One afternoon the crew stops for a break by the side of a scenic river, and they fill their canteens, and break for supper just a little earlier than normal. Avrel's rather sudden change in demeanor prompts the wee merchant to ask the men about the events that unfolded in Järviby. After all, he was out buying his merchandise.

Geric of course is rather animated and into his recounting of the story, having read so much, he prides himself in his ability to recount such things. "So then Avrel's like flinging her staff at that nutty guy and he blocks her swings like it's nothing! And then her arm splits open and sploosh! Blood goes everywhere!" he describes vividly and energetically. "From there I dropped by to help *that* one." he directs the gnome's attention to Avrel as she sips some wild mint tea, her scrawny legs dangling off the back of the tailgate.

"So then I threw a torch in his face." Zanvan continues. "He was pretty easy to dispatch after that."

"Err merr." Bob croaks, shaking his head, "Sorrer, Er derdn't rearrers erl thert herd herpperned." Bob looks over at her, pitifully.

"Oh, it wasn't so bad." Geric smiles, "Cuz lucky for you people, you're blessed with me!"

"Yeah." Zanvan grunts. "Isn't she going to join us?"

"Sherr mert berr ermberrarssed." Bob suggests. "Werr... arre kirnda gerrsperng abert her."

Geric hadn't considered that, but now that he does, he realises he *might* have taken parts a bit too far, and those damned knife ears, she probably heard him. "Zanvan, you call her." he says.

The ranger rolls his eyes, but after siping some water, he turns towards her and the wagon. "Avrel?" he yells over to her. "You okay!? Don't you want any bread?" "I still have some jerky too!"

"No, I've..." she shakes her head. "I've got a headache... I think I'm gonna lie down." she replies.

He watches her scoot inside the wagon, out of sight, and turning down the elf-bread. It was gross fresh, but as toast it takes on a savoriness and it's not bad. "MmmYeah, she's totally on the rag." Geric comments to the other men, but they don't seem to care for his expert medical opinion.

In fact, Zanvan seems to ignore it altogether. "So what's the deal after we go to Rudaski?" Zanvan asks.

"Err heard thert there irs surrpost ter ber arr turnner throurrgh the mourntern, sorr we'rr gerr threwr there, berk terr Mernerterrrer." Bob replies.

"Works for me." Geric sighs, then he realizes how long a trek that'll be through the plains. *Oh well...*

"While we're in Rudaski we might as well ask about the Aegis." Zanvan says thoughtfully. "I even asked Kylai about it, since she travels a bit, but she knew nothing." he says, sinkingly, "About the Aegis at least." he smiles widely. Very widely; it must've been that callipygous wood-elf's name.

She was alright. he guesses, but moving on... "That's a good point." Geric agrees, "And if we don't find anything there, we can check out Midrashoth."

"Yeah, it's not terribly far from Manitäria." Zanvan nods. "Otherwise, we still have the Runeblade, and not one orc in sight. Sounds like she's all worked up and fretting over nothing." he chuckles.

"That ugly knight?" Geric clarifies.

Zanvan though smirks and shakes his head, "The Princess."

***

Avrel listens as she sits off of the back of the cart while the guys talk and enjoy their meal over a large, table-like rock. But she doesn't join them, she wishes to be alone, and drink some tea.

Even so, they seem to peek at her from time to time. And during a pause in the guy's account, Bob in particular casts a sad, almost worryful eye over to her until Geric goes on with his confident self praise.

But she blanches at every mention of her rage. Of how she lost control, how she almost hurt her friends when she accidentally threw that anger fuelled flame at them. "Candice, I wasn't *really* like that, was I?" Avrel asks.

Candice seems to not want to reply, which in and of itself says a lot. And Avrel knows, she knows how much of a freakout she had. She knows how badly she was hurt.

"Avrel, you okay!?" Zanvan yells over to her. "Don't you want any bread? I still have some jerky too!"

She shakes her head, "No, I've... I've got a headache." she lies. "I think I'm gonna lay down." she replies, chugging down the rest of her tea and retreating further into the hold.

She can still sort of hear them, but she tunes it out, eventually. And soon enough the guys soon finish their meal and get back into the cart. Avrel is curled up in a small bed of rags and daydreams, trying to keep herself calm and unaffected by the torrent of negative thoughts and images that are bringing uneasiness to her mind.

"Chippu?" Candice squeaks as she snuggles in closer to Avrel.

"I... Couldn't think straight, I just had so much rage and energy inside... but I only can feel remorse now. I blew it..." Avrel confides while she pets Candice. "If I'd ever found him, I wanted to tell him how I felt, but not like that..." she pauses briefly as she tears up, "Not like that..." Avrel says with a tear running down her cheek onto the beaver, "And now he's..." Candice looks up at her with worry and of helplessness, which is true. She's just a beaver, and Avrel can only talk to her. She's just a pet, and she can't fix these things that are broken.

She still clings to Candice, and eventually, she falls asleep.

The following days continue in similar fashion, and only twice do they encounter some troublesome wild beasts. In both cases, they are easily dispatched and harvested without her help. Geric still prescribes rest, and limited strain along with his potions and his cracking and recracking, but she wouldn't have wanted to help anyway. Right now, she feels as though she can't.

After a while the sound of wind over grass fades to bumps, and then a most settlingly smooth ride. It's almost smoother and flatter than something paved. It's quite nice until she's forced to roll onto her still sore side to cough. It's dust, it's a lot of it wafting back to her, and it's enough to get her up to look.

"Ugh.." Avrel says grunts as she comes out of the little space she's carved out in the back of the wagon.

"Hello stranger." Geric says, scooting over to give her space between him and Zanvan. "What's crackling?"

Her lungs, but she gets his joke. "The air is so dusty here it woke me up." Avrel says with another cough.

Zanvan breathes out some smoke, "Doesn't bother me." he says, shrugging his shoulders, and pipe in hand. Avrel and Geric both give him a disapproving glare. "But I've heard it's not quite as bad once we're in town. Since most of the dust is thrown up into the air, it doesn't come back down until you are out a ways, and downwind." he explains.

Avrel pulls her blouse up and over her mouth. "Sounds reasonable." she says a bit muffled by the cloth.

She takes a look out the back of the wagon. It's not desolate, but it's dry, and flat but for a ridge to the west. Not many trees, just short bushes and shrubs, and bizarre little possums with shells. It's a change from Järviby -- or the plains for that matter, and it's not one she's sure she likes.

After what Geric promises will be their last little ritual of him manhandling her hands, Bob grabs their attention. "Erlmorst therr!"

Zanvan steps out and looks out the back of the wagon.

"What does it look like?" Geric asks, as he follows, leaning off the tailgate to the other side. "MMmm. Dust." he scoffs, sardonically. "I hate dust."

"I hate dust too." Avrel almost sneezes.

"Heyrr!" they all turn as Bob chides, "Surperserdly, these merntairns were wornce ourr herms!"

"Huh?" she turns to Geric. Zanvan to practical things, but Geric shines in such bookish trivia.

He laughs, he seems to enjoy that she looked straight to him. "Dwarves used to live here before they bred with humans and settled Manitäria."

It feels like she learns something everyday. "I never knew that." she says, trying to catch a look around to the front of the wagon.

"A lot of the mines we use are just old towns." he continues, "The Nether-Naededallir -- *or something* mountains they called them."

Mountains? she wonders, they are more like tall, bald, rocky hills. "Aren't they a bit small for mountains?" she asks.

"Aren't you a bit small for an elf?" he counters, she knew it was coming the moment she said it. "They say they were once tall mountains like Midrosh or Cordol." he explains without further jokes, "Only that in the war that almost wiped out the dwarves there, the battles and orken magic eventually fractured the rock, causing many of the levels of dwarven cities to sink and collapse." He pats her shoulder, "That and the accounts that they were larger were made by smaller folk." he laughs.

Bob shares the laugh, somehow. She thinks about it, and she guesses that she can see the humor in it.

Within another few hours they arrive at the outskirts of this 'Rudaski'. The settled areas are as flat, brown and dusty as the surrounding area, only with a lot of crates and large split rocks tossed about, and a few farm houses in spots where it seems things grow. There are after all some streams coming down from the hills. Avrel hopes, but can only wonder if this rape of the world's beauty is the doing of those settling here, or orcs long before, or that it simply is naturally this ugly.

As they head deeper in, the dreariness of the landscape gives way to more houses, and many shoppes and smithies, and other business. It's the same climate, the same turf, but there is a busy atmosphere that takes away some of the bitterness.

To her at least, Geric seems to have taken a certain liking to it. Maybe he's imagining the quiet solitude in which to read, but she thinks Zanvan would agree that one can find that just as easily in a greener place with trees.

Not long after they've entered, Bob pulls to a stop and they hear him asking someone about things. Financial things, trade things, prices, rumors, things she doesn't rightly understand. Nor does she care to, honestly. Just hearing it irritates her, talk of profit, prices and the like, meanwhile people like her and her mother are left to starve.

"Chippu?" Candice seems to notice her tension.

Is she letting it show that much? "Yeah." she says giving her a pet, "I'm fine." she says as she pulls her lips back, grimacing with a grit, "It's nothing." she says, fully aware she's not hiding it any better.

"Chippu." Candice warbles, softly.

Avrel looks up at them, Geric with his book, Zanvan with his pipe. "I suppose." she admits. Maybe she can trust them, at least more than she might have thought in the beginning. The *both* took care of her back there, not to say she should leave her guard down completely, but maybe, just maybe she should take more chances after this. "Yeah." she smiles back, touching Candice's wet nose.

"Chippu?" she asks with a look, pointing with her eyes to one, then the other with an ornery smile. Ornery, and downright wrong.

"Never!" Again, she'd never drop her guard *that* low. Never, and to no *man*. Male nature is still male nature, she reminds herself, no matter how kind they are to her at the moment and must remind Candice in private. "Nothing more." she says, softly, "That's the way it has to be." she adds, sternly as they begin moving again.

"Yeahr, irt's urp hirgh, kirnd erff erberve merst erf therr cirterr. Er've nerver yersed therm, but I believe it's near serm hert-springs ernd geyrsers." Bob explains to a question she missed. But Avrel latches onto 'hot-springs'.

"Hot... springs? Like naturally warmed spring water?" she says, more excited than she's felt in days.

"Yerp." Bob says, "Birg perrls, lirtter perrls, Er'd jerst berr cerrefer, ert's nert erwned berr ernerwern, serr ert's nert merd erp wirth trerverllers irn mirnd." he further explains.

"There's hot-springs near Argoth, you know." Geric adds, "Up in Cordol they built a bathing room on one."

"Yeah.." Avrel chides, "And the others I'd bet you'd have to pay for."

Geric shrugs, of course. They've met Shad, they saw her before she bought these new clothes, don't they get it? Zanvan is quiet, maybe he does, he might have *some* idea what it's like for her, depending on how long he's been living the ranger's life. *Not like some pampered cleric.*

She forces a smile anyway, "Maybe now that I have money, I'll give it a try when we get back."

They have to lock the tailgate as they start up the hill. After the leisurely, smooth ride they've had, it feels strange but exciting too. Out the back she gets a very good look at the mining town or city rather, and its districts and cart trails moving ore and rock.

Soon, they come to a more leveled off spot as they reach the inn. And at Bob's word, they start unloading their personal items. He seems antsy, or maybe just in a hurry.

"Zernvern!" he shouts, Zanvan answers with his attention. "Yer cherck urs irn, erkay? Erm gerrnerr gert arr heard start ern mer sherpperng." Bob says, tossing Zanvan a pouch of coins before speeding off.

"Sure thing?" Zanvan replies as the gnome heads off. "Where's Avrel?" he asks. She hears but she's already a fair ways away.

She overhears Geric grunt as he lifts both his and her packs, "I think she said something about those hot-springs, probably for her cramps."

Zanvan quickly looks around until his eyes catch up with her as she stands. waiting to know what he wants. "*Hey!*" he yells.

Avrel points to herself. So he did want her. "Me?"

"Yeah, get over here, we've got stuff to do!" Zanvan shouts, waving for her to come back.

Avrel goes back, slowly. "Yeah?" she says with a hint of impudence.

"Geric is taking our stuff in." Zanvan explains. "I'm gonna check us in and then you and me are gonna get some info from around town."

Avrel frowns, "Take Geric, I'm tired of smelling like a drunkard." She demonstratively sniffs her arm, and the offers for him to do the same.

His face says it all, she does smell foul, even by the ranger's standards. "Just come with me, I promise you can do your hot-spring thing later." Zanvan says in a compliant tone.

"Hmm…" It's still early in the day, and if she bathes now, she's liable to be dusty again by the time she sleeps. "Oh alright." she sighs. "Candice, you coming?"

Candice yawns and sits beside Geric. That would be a 'no'. She rather wishes she would, but Candice is her own person, she supposes.

Avrel follows while Zanvan checks them in and gives Geric the key as they pass him, still struggling with the packs, and looking none too happy about being left with Candice.

"We might not be too long." the ranger says in passing.

"Hey, wait!" Gerc calls, but Zanvan is now almost in as much of a hurry as Bob was, for some reason. She questions it. But, she has her guard up, and also she trusts him somewhat. He gets his instincts out on enough other women, far prettier women, she's sure; she doesn't see why in hell he'd suddenly attack her.

"I'll bring you something nice!" she says with a smirk as she turns back to the cleric, and then she and Zanvan make their way towards the governmental district.

Along the way, Zanvan explains a hunch. It's nothing incredible, but he reminds her of how close Rudaski is to the Yordlands' border, and thus how any governing body would certainly know of whispers from orcs before they'd make their way to Argoth. "But even under a royal errand, I doubt they'd talk to us directly." he adds.

"So?" she asks.

"So--" he says shortly, "So we find a watering hole where they go to drink their stresses away."

She kind of likes the plan, the only problem is that while discussing it, they never stopped to ask which way it was, and they are in the commercial district before either one realizes that.

"So much for that otherworldly sense of direction." she snarks with a smile.

"It's my bad, I admit that." he grunts. "I know a relative of the Governor, but I've not actually been here before." he tips his hat as he scratches above his ear, trying to get his rangerly barings.

"Why the subterfuge then?" she asks. "Just ask them directly." she insists.

"Apparently, your ears're picking up some of Gerics words." he comments with a grin, "But let's just say that's *not* an option." She can only guess what that entails. "Traders." he points to a group of people in furs, "You just stay here. I'd bet one of them knows their way around."

Better than you. she chuckles to herself as he walks up and they pass on by. She tries her hand at it with a miner by the looks of him, but he takes one look at her ears and brushes past her. Abrasively. She tries on another, but it's the same. Between this place and some of the elves in Järviby, she's almost starting to miss Argoth. In only that small way of course. If she ever were great and powerful, she'd get all of her mixed sisters together and form their own settlement.

Yeah, all ten of us. she sighs as she's bumped by someone else. Her daydream did kind of leave her in the way for that. Rather than a passerby, she recalls Zanvan trying to coach her into buying her staff; she'll walk up to one of these peddlers and she'll get the info she wants.

Avrel quickly sees a gemstone display on a storefront and starts talking to the clerk there, at first asking about the Aegis, but quickly the shoppekeeper steers the conversation turns toward the gems. The gems which are very pretty, and she does have *some* disposable money. She's honestly not sure where the pivot happened, but *he* has *her* attention now.

Avrel takes her bracer off. "So... do you have anything that you could set into this?" she asks. "It's very special to me, you see--" she points to the still present, but faint bruising on her arm along a more noticeable scar where the flesh was apparently cracked open as she tells a redacted version of the story.

***

Meanwhile Zanvan is standing in the middle of a crowded street, trying to get some passerby to talk with him. Finally, a reasonably attractive woman comes by. Blonde too, something familiar in her fair eyes, delightful fur accents to an otherwise simple but expensive looking dress. Definitely someone worth talking to.

"Excuse me, Miss, do you have a moment?" he asks confidently.

"Hmm?" the pause as she looks him over disconcerts him. "Oh why... Why yes!" she says more than welcomingly. "As long as you're not with any elves handing out environmentalist tripe." she laughs, holding his hands as if they were good friends.

Not quite... he thinks with a half-smile as he looks back, just to see if Avrel is near. She'd be pouting that sour pout of hers if she'd heard that. "Not at all." he replies.

She pauses briefly to look him over once more. "Ah, still a ranger, my mistake." she laughs as if expecting a response.

Zanvan hopes he doesn't look as confused as he is. She maybe looks slightly familiar, but that might just be that he happens to prefer blondes. Best be out with it. "And you are?"

She gives him a look over, with a sort of coy smile as her eyes take him in. Finally she shakes her head almost disappointedly, but still smiling, "I'm Elisé." she curtseys. "And that shorter guy over there is my best friend, Hayden."

Zanvan bends down and kisses her hand. "I am Zanvan, I'm here on a quest and I'd like to know this area." he says, already making her blush. "Would you care to show me around, perhaps I can explain my quest in better detail over supper?"

Elisé is quite blushed, made all the more poignant by a fair complexion that is in contrast with all the sun-darkened and soot dusted skin around her. She mouths his name. "Well, you see." she says aloud. "I'm with my friend there, he was helping me with some errands and then I believe we were going to do something after." She looks a little embarrassed. "He's always trying to spend time with me, poor soul."

Zanvan gets her meaning. Like all men, he's been there at least once. He, not especially often though. "Well, perhaps I can find someone to occupy him." he suggests, looking over to Avrel, and thinking. "This job is rather important."

She glances at the guy again, he supposes maybe she'd find it nice to be seen in town with a man exceeding her own stature, "If you can find a way to have him preoccupied, by all means." Elisé chuckles.

He looks again, it's worth a try, *It'd certainly make the kid's day.* he figures, and she's seemed like she could use it. Zanvan bids Elisé to hold on a moment and then he walks towards her friend who is waiting at the corner.

"Hey kid, you busy later?" he asks, making a strong approach.

"I'm not a k-" he cuts himself off and instead tries to keep his cool. "Kind of. Why?" her friend replies.

Zanvan smiles, "Well, you see that cute little elf girl over there by the jewel shoppe?" to which he begins to question why she's moved... *Whatever.* "I saw her looking this way at you and I'd bet *anything* she'd love for *you* to show her around town this afternoon." Zanvan says encouragingly.

Elisé's friend blushes. "You.. Really think so??" his voice cracks.

Avrel's not his type either, but between him and Elisé, and Avrel with this guy, they can cover a lot of ground fast. "You ought to go offer to take her around." Zanvan repeats. "Don't be shy, she's a friend of mine."

"Hmm." Hayden hums as he looks to Elisé thoughtfully, then his eyes look in a different direction. "Yeah, sure." he replies finally.

"Good!" Zanvan says with a hearty pat on the back. "Go catch her before she moves on!"

Hayden runs after the kid and Zanvan goes back to Elisé.

As Zanvan approaches Elisé, he holds his arms open, head held high like it was nothing, asserting his utter victory. "I'll see you in a couple of hours?" he grins.

She laughs and nods in agreement, "I look forward to hearing all that you've been up to, Mr Zanvan."

***

Avrel is still conversing with the jewel peddler. They are beautiful, but if she put some enhancement jewel in her bracer, Zanvan could never make fun of it again. Not that he has recently, but she might as well deter it.

"So, you don't think any of these are enchanted, at all?" Avrel asks, rather discouraged. Just then she feels a tap on her shoulder as her shoulder blades rear up in response. She turns quickly, half expecting Geric.

"Excuse me, Miss, I- umm..." this guy swallows hard and nervously. "Um... You see, I just was wondering if you were new to town, we could um..." he stutters out, nervously.

"Can I help you?" Avrel asks rather confusedly, and defensively. She doesn't like men sneaking up on her.

"Yes." he says, smiling, awkwardly. "Well, actually no. I want to help *you*, I have some things to do, but as a friend of the chairlady of the Fur Guild, I'd like to... Welcome you and... I thought maybe, I could sh-show you around town a little later." he nervously squeaks out, ending in a massive gulp. Avrel can feel her face warm up like she's turning red at the proposition. Coming from this seemingly sincere younger man, who for once isn't intimidatingly towering over her. But he *is* taller than her. "Would you like to? If you're not doing... anyth-anything else?" he says softly. He doesn't have strong features, not even any stubble. Weak looking in fact.

Avrel relaxes slightly as she slowly nods. "Yes, can you pick me up at the inn up that way?" she says pointing in the direction she and Zanvan had come from. It's a risk of course, but this guy isn't propositioning her for his carnal needs, and she doubts he could take them from her. She'll get them some info for sure. "Rocky Hill Inn I think it's called."

"W-Why sure!" he exclaims excitedly, but giving a lingering glance to her ears. "I'll be by in a couple hours, Miss--?"

"Avrel" softly replies.

"Hayden" He gleefully bows and runs off, leaving Avrel with the brightest smile she's had in weeks. Maybe it's from all the teasing she's gotten from Geric over the last months, but it feels nice to be more positively approached for once. She grabs her bracer and quickly excuses herself from the jewel stand, making a run to find Zanvan who she almost immediately bumps into.

***

The kid comes running full speed, which is either very good or very bad. Either way, at least she's feeling good enough to run like that.

As she comes closer, he sees that she's smiling a little bit. "Hey Zanvan." she says, flightilly, "I uhh... I gotta go get cleaned up, you see this nice guy just offered to show me around in a little while and um..." she says nervously and excitedly, "I kind of... Have a date!" she blurts out.

"You do." he agrees. "I mean, *you do?*" he *asks*, feigning surprise, were Avrel not so excited, she might notice the weak facade.

"Yeah!" she says. "I know it's just to get some info but..."

"Gotta get all prettied up?" he finishes.

"I've never actually had a boy *politely* ask me out before." she tells him, "Not unless you count this one little kid who after one of my shows asked me to marry him... Or the old men asking me for -ahem- *wifely favors*." she frys. There's no doubt in his mind that she has her reservations on the matter, knowing how she is, he's surprised she's *this* enthusiastic. "Perverts." she spits, sounding much more like her old self.

"Well." he falsely contemplates, "I should make you help me gather info, but I suppose I'll let it pass, go on." Zanvan says in an uncharacteristically nice tone. He hates it. "But be sure to ask around."

Avrel nods in response and dashes off.

He runs his hand across his hair, matted under his hat, "Easy."

10

I wish Candice was here... Avrel thinks to herself. She doesn't know much of making oneself up, strangely she thinks the beaver might. Though sometimes Candice acts like an older sister of sorts. She begins to ask herself, *What do girls do?* And she's repulsed, no, this mostly business, and she'll not doll up like a plaything. *That*, she keeps on her mind as she continues down the street.

Eventually, a stand with fresh fruit catches her eye. "Red berries!" A few times she and Candice had found them on the street, forgotten and left behind. Certain kinds always stained her fingers, they might work as a rouge for her cheeks. Avrel checks her purse and stops by the fruit stand where she buys one of those fruits.

"Just one?" the merchant asks, rather surprised. He looks up at her hair, like maybe he, like so many, assumes it's an unnatural stain.

"Yup!" she replies. He takes her money and hands them over. "Thank you!" she smiles as she turns to leave. Gosh, she loves actually having money.

She drops back to the inn and gets directions from the hostess on how to get to the hot-spring pools. She grabs a towel from her pack, and Candice who is done with her nap, and heads up the steep hill from a path from behind the inn. Riding in the wagon has made her a little soft, she's not quite as used to walking everywhere as she always has been. But it's not more than she can handle, if she could find a way up that plateau, she can do this. "Right, Candice?" she asks.

"Chippu!" Candice agrees.

After a short hike, she can see steam rising over some of the rugged folds of rock. Looking towards the city is interesting too. From here she can see not just the commerce and the homes, but mines, and farms all around. She's a bit glad there's a depression to step down towards these pools, for modesty's sake.

If the elf in her even needed proof of nature's providence, here it is. The earth even provides its creatures with hot baths. But, she has to wonder, *How hot?* She can only hope those bubbles are air and not that it's boiling. She timidly dips her foot in to make sure it's not too hot. When it's not, she looks around to make sure she's not visible to anyone before she undresses and she gets in. She opens a pouch of mint leaves Bob had given her to make tea with when she was more unwell, and drops them into the water.

"Stand watch, eh?" she asks the beaver. She wonders if she might make a good chaperone on her 'date' too. Now that she's had time to think about it, she wonders why the hell she said 'yes'. *Non-threatening -- Nothing.* She scolds herself, *It's those guys that you have to worry about most!* she'd bet. It's not like getting propped for 'pleasure' by guys is uncommon for her. Except in Järviby, she gets at least one cat-call at every inn. And she's not even pretty, these guys, *this guy* probably just wants someone to violate, same as the rest. *So what if he was polite?* she scoffs at herself. She sinks herself deeper into the water. She's always wondered how girls let themselves be taken advantage of, now she knows.

She sighs out a big sigh, and sniffs in the steamy, fresh air. "Ahhh... No more alcohol smell..." She splashes her face and wipes it with her hands. *That Hayden guy...* she questions. He asked her even though she smelled, was in torn up, stained up clothing, and seemed to not exactly like her elven features, but he asked anyway. Maybe, just maybe she's overthinking it? *Maybe,* she considers, *Maybe he just is trying to be nice.* Zanvan and even Geric can be 'nice', despite being men. Maybe it's the same with him too.

And if he's not, she'll clober him.

After relaxing for a few more minutes, she gets to washing herself in earnest. As she runs her fingers through her hair and picks the collected dust from her ears, she's reminded that it's only by Geric and Zanvan's hands that hers even still work. That not only makes her smile for her friendship with them, but also that maybe not everything men do is a prelude to violence.

Not every man... she feels her face turn bitter, and her eyes almost start to well up, *Is Shad.*

Coming to the realization that time is passing, she wastes no more time and dries off, and cleans her clothes. They aren't fully dry, even after blasting them with some wind magic, but it'll do. Carefully makes her way back to the inn, trying desperately not to get resoiled along the hike, an effort that proves *mostly* successful. She gets back to their room and finds Geric studying a spell book, which is not surprising. Respectfully, she sneaks by and makes a rouge for her cheeks and lips with the little berries, elegantly accenting her pale complexion. After gently blushing her cheeks and lips, she hears Geric stand up from his chair.

"Going somewhere?" he asks as he closes his book.

She runs her fingers through her still pliable, damp hair, "Yeah, a guy in town asked me to go around town with him tonight." she giggles.

"You?" he asks, rather ambiguous, he could be mocking her or genuinely surprised.

"Yeah." she answers, "Zanvan said to get info, I figured this was a good chance."

"Well..." Geric says looking her over. "You actually look nice, shame you don't have a dress."

She looks at her blouse, torn, wrinkly, and slashed. *Yeah...*

"Say, how about this, see if you can rent something a little nicer, my treat." he continues.

"What, really?" Avrel says with a look of shock. "Why?" It's not like Geric, where's the joke at her expense?

It looks like Geric is trying to think of a reason other than, *'because I don't want you hanging around while I practice my spells'*. He looks at her thoughtfully before having the idea in which he speaks. "Well, it'll probably be pretty cheap I mean, less girl, less fabric; less curves less fitting!" Geric chuckles out.

There it is. Avrel playfully hits him over the head, she's in too good of a mood to take offense, or at least in the pursuit of one. "Oh you!" she coos as she accepts the coin pouch and thanks him as she darts off to find a place to rent a dress.

She figured that was it, now she knows. Still, it was nice of him, but she can imagine him slumping down, sighing something like '*Ahh... Peace once more...*' as he rolls up his sleeves and primes himself to cast some spells.

But enough of that, she's got to keep an eye out for clothing stores. "Keep a look out with me, eh?" she tells Candice.

"Chippu!"

She goes to the first dressshoppe they see. There's not many furs on display, but Candice stays outside anyway. Upon entering, Avrel sees a well dressed lady fixing a clasp on a fancy corset.

"Um, excuse me, do you have any rentals?" Avrel asks meekly.

The lady leans up. "Umm... what exactly do you mean?" she responds. Is it an unusual request?

"Well, I need a dress." she half chokes, even with money, she's not used to shopping like this. "Just for tonight. It can be just about anything, so long as it fits." Avrel explains.

"That might be hard." the lady thinks as she looks her over. "Hmm... well, I have one that I made for someone, she got splashed with hot geyser water and it shrunk, so they returned it. I suppose you *could* have that for tonight. That is, if you give me a hefty deposit." the lady says pointing to a small dress in the back behind the counter. It's a simple dress, thin straps, lightly colored, probably about a medium length skirt. "No offense, we don't get many elven tweens around her that aren't here to make trouble."

Avrel wonders what she means by that, but lest she get angry, she ignores it. Travelling with Geric has given her some practice in that. "Really!? That's wonderful!" Avrel smiles, "Will this cover it!?" she says as she gently pours the coin purse out.

"This is more than enough." The lady says with a look. "I'll take this..." she says taking about three-quarters of the coins, "And you'll get half of this back when you bring the dress back in the morning, does that seem fair?" she asks nicely.

"Yes, please!" Avrel grins "Thank you." She says as she takes back the remaining coins. The lady carefully hands over the dress and Avrel graciously accepts it.

She rushes back to the inn with Candice close behind, and changes into her new clothes, and touches up her makeup and hair. Thanks to her ears, her hair stayed pretty well tucked. But the draw strings on her dress are another matter; Avrel can't reach them, and Candice has trouble gripping them. She comes out from behind the dressing screen, as she tries to pull and tie them with her arcane hands, but she doesn't quite have the finesse for it.

"Geric?" she says, but she also can see that Geric is getting ready to head out as well.

"Yes?" he turns.

"Could you tie this for me?" she asks, gingerly.

He shrugs, and sits the book in his hand down on the desk he'd been sitting at. He pulls the strings a bit tighter than she'd expected, but she's welcome for it anyway. "Not bad." he comments, stepping back and tipping his hat up, "You actually look nice." For a cleric, his eyes linger a bit too long at her neckline.

But he's right, She's never had or worn anything giving her cleavage before. Namely, she lacks the tissue. "So where're you going?"

"I'm going for a walk." he says as he holds the door for her.

"Thanks!" she says as she passes him in the doorway.

"You're welcome." he says. "It's not everyday you look like a lady and not a dirty, long haired boy." he chuckles to himself.

"What?"

"Nothing!" he quickly recoils, she knows what she heard though. And it's probably true.

"Come here, Candice." she says, tapping where she's used to those cumbersome leg armor pads, instead slapping her thigh through some thin fabric. Just for a brief moment she wonders if the skirt is too short, too inviting. She bites her lip a moment but she carries on. She still has her magic. "I'm going alone, I think." she says, not so obviously surprising the beaver. "I'll call you if I need you, how about that?"

Candice nods, almost as if she's okay with the idea as she goes back to a corner and slumps.

She and Geric make their way through the inn to the steps outside, where Avrel sits herself down and waits for Hayden.

"Hey, have fun." Geric says as he makes his way down the steps, and to the steep road. Probably heading to a book shoppe if she knows him well enough.

"I will." Avrel says softly as she smiles. She plucks a flower from the nearby flower-box and sniffs it. Maybe she'll put it in her hair.

Geric disappears down the hill and she sits there as the afternoon sun glows its intense orange over the dusty cityscape, twirling the flower in her fingers. Soon the warmth of the stone steps grows cold as afternoon turns to evening. *I...* she thinks to herself, *Suppose he got lost, he'll figure out where this inn is. It's... on a hill, it should be hard to miss...*

Evening goes on, the sound of a city at dinnertime rings out as evening turns to sunset. She begins to feel cold and considers getting a cowl but is sure he'll come for her soon.

Sunset turns to twilight and Avrel's eyes gloss over with tears as she brushes and shakes the dust off of herself.

Twilight turns to dusk and Avrel begins to cry, shivering in the cold night air. At last she gets up, tosses the dying wilted flower down and goes into the inn.

Dusk has turned to disappointment.

She gets back to her room with Candice at first greeting her happily before she reacts to Avrel's sad face. Avrel has nothing to say as she tearfully whimpers while she takes the dress off and curls up in bed next to Candice. Candice cuddles in closer, offering comfort to her as she cries into her pillow. She doesn't like men, she doesn't want any relationship with one... *So why...* Avrel wonders, *Does this hurt so bad?*

***

Geric is making his way to the downtown of the city glowing with orange, afternoon light. A savory scent leads him to a stand where he buys a roasted chicken leg to chow on as he makes his way about town. Eventually he comes to a cross-street and up ahead he sees a magic shoppe. As he crosses the street, he sees Zanvan and she who is apparently his latest paramour talking on a bench up ahead.

"Hey!" Geric waves to them as he walks over to them.

Zanvan turns and says something to the nicely dressed blonde woman before greeting Geric in return. There's no doubt it's about him, Geric knows.

"What a charming lady you have there." Geric says looking over to her. She blushes and turns slightly in bashfulness.

"What do you want?" Zanvan asks.

"I thought I'd take a walk." he comments with a stretch. "Taste some local fare, maybe drop into a magic shoppe, buy some books."

"Yes." the lady says, "Zanvan tells me you're quite the bookworm."

"I've read a few." he grins. "Might practice a few new spells later."

She laughs, she's extremely feminine and lady-like, it rather stands out in this more rustic place. Right down to that strange, soft clap ladies do when they find something humorous, and cute cheek dimples to boot. *Zanvan's doing well for himself.* he snickers to himself just as a muddy old crone limps by. *Very well.*

After a few minutes of idle chat Geric hears someone shout "Elisé!" from behind him. *Close* behind him. He turns to see a short man running towards her, Zanvan blanches as if he recognizes him and not in a positive way. He's barely as tall as she is. *Not even, actually,* he revises as he sees him next to her.

"Elisé, I'm sorry!" he shouts, dropping to a knee. "I was gonna go out with another woman but I just can't, I love *you!*" the guy cries out to the woman, apparently named Elisé, who blushes beet red.

Zanvan's look of surprise turns to panic after he looks up at the darker evening sky, and back to the short guy. "Geric..." he says with a hint of uneasiness, "Where is Avrel?" he mutters.

Geric thinks for a moment. "She said that some guy was taking her out this afternoon, why?" Geric replies calmly. Zanvan facepalms, first covering his eyes, then he moves his hand up his forehead, then down to his chin, "I've made a huge mistake..."

He has, has he? Zanvan? Geric's interest is piqued.

Elisé stands up and holds the guys really rather small hands. "Dear Hayden." A unisex name too, poor fellow. "You've been my best friend since I returned to this city. If you hadn't supported me, I never would have been able to take over my duties to the Fur Traders Guild after my father's passing... But I don't *love* you." she says tenderly, giving her version of that dreaded speech known to all men who pursue women and not higher knowledge.

Still, despite what he's sure Zanvan and she plan to be up to, she is most lady-like about it. *At least she's not laughing.* Geric knows he would.

"Shite!" the guy, Hayden shouts with a scowl, "That's utter shite! Just this afternoon you said 'I love you!'" he says, angrily standing on his toes asserting himself into Elisé's facial space.

Elisé sighs for a moment. "But as a friend..."

"Ouch." Geric can't help but smile out of utter cringe. It's uncleric-like to enjoy such things, but, well...

"I *love* you, but I'm not *In love* with you." she continues. "My heart belongs to the past." she says defeatedly.

Hayden's eyes turn angry and his face is of one facing betrayal, he slaps away the pretty lady's hands. "You... of all the women I've met... Were the one my heart's chosen one." he cries.

She steps back in fear and sadness. "I... I-" she stutters.

"I *hate* you!" he screams.

That was a quick turnabout!

By now several people have noticed the shouting and have gathered around, only adding to the tension of the situation. Hayden attempts to slap Elisé but Geric catches it even before Zanvan. But then, he is a fair bit closer. In a show of dominance, he tries to force his arm back but is surprised by Hayden's strength.

Somehow, Geric finds himself in a bit of a brawl, for Zanvan's lay's honor of all things. It makes him wonder, whether it's this Hayden fellow or he that is the bigger simpleton.

While he's pondering it, a hard hit to his jaw puts his mind back on the fight. Regardless of why it's his fight, he's in it now, so he might as well smite the little guy.

At first Geric's significantly above average height proves effective at overcoming Hayden's further punches and attacks, however, Hayden abuses his access to Geric's core and lower body to his advantage. After elbowing Geric in the solar plexus, Geric falls to his knees and takes a kick to the face forcing him onto his back.

"Heh." Geric taunts as he lays on his back, "That hit to the head jogged a memory."

Hayden drops his guard just slightly.

"An orken slang for short humans..." Geric snickers as he leans up. "Manlet!"

Hayden angrily casts a spell of force knocking Zanvan back before he can sneak up and subdue him.

And without so much as a lip twitch -- "You! You didn't even mutter an incantation you..." Geric pulls himself to his feet, "You *innately magic bugger!*" he yells while pinching his bloodied nose shut. It's not about the blonde's honor, or securing Zanvan's mood in the morning, it's on for real now. He's not going to lose to some snot-nosed, innately magical manlet!

"What of it!" the magic-manlet asks, "Jealous!? Don't underestimate my power!" Hayden screams.

"Same, kid." he sneers as he straightens his dashing, red hat, "Same."

Hayden readies a spell of his own, but Geric stands tall and holds his arms out in fists in front of him, and quickly whispers an incantation before slamming his fists into the ground, causing a large wave of earth-spikes to shoot out of the ground in front of him. Hayden is pushed down the street and out of sight by the wave of jagged rocks -- Along with a few other things. Maybe a person or two as well. Perhaps a cart or wagon, anyway people usually have insurance on those things.

Oops. he considers just the same that he might have overdone it. Zanvan seems amused. The lady, not as much.

Still, he strikes a victorious pose as he stands back up and strides victoriously to them. "Been dying to try that spell." he laughs.

Zanvan raises a brow. "Obviously." he pats Elisé's hand too.

"Right." he says, taking that queue, and looking at some less than pleased folk down that street. "MmmAnyway... I hope Avrel's date went better than yours has." Geric says sarcastically.

Zanvan looks rather concerned. "Hayden... " he squirms, "*Was* her date." Zanvan mutters.

Geric barely keeps his brows from shooting his hat off of his head, "Aw shite!" he forgets himself, "Why? She'd finally stopped being the gloomy twit she'd been these last weeks!" Geric says bombastically.

"I know!" Zanvan grunts.

"MmmWell I'm tired of the drama" he says with some haste, "I'm going to that magic shoppe."

Zanvan looks as if he tries to forget Avrel for the moment and comforts the lady. It's only a minute until she collects herself. "Thank you, Geric." she says.

"Later." Geric says, bowing with a sweep of his hat before briskly heading out.

***

She closes her eyes and she sees Shad, half naked, alone with just that duck-rat. She opens them and she hears Candice's doting on her friends. All of them men. *To hell with men.* she groans, *Sards all.* She says as she rolls over for the umpteenth time. This is what she gets for trying to have anything to do with them, well, ones besides the two she's with now. She didn't even like or want to like this guy, but she didn't deserve to be left out in the cold, waiting like that. *Blasted...* she just wanted to take her mind off things, was that too much to ask for?

After several hours Avrel finds her heartache and restlessness to be too much to sleep on. Reluctantly, she decides to go out and get some air. She leans off her bed, still in her dress and slips her shoes on, carefully and quietly as to not wake Candice. She glaces out of the window and looks at the soft glow coming from the streets below. She's not sure what she's to do, but she must do something, anything to help her ignore these gloomy thoughts.

Or at least tire herself out with a walk.

She makes her way down the stairs, down the hill and tries to admire this city's night-life. *No Ar-Guards.* she comments to herself, several times. It's a positive, and so she tries to drill it into her thoughts. It doesn't stick, however.

Nor do the colorful paper lamps draped across the busier streets and squares. She can only assumptively put together that the nighttime is so busy because in the mines, there would be no day or night for those workers to go by. A few scents remind her that she never ate supper, but she ignores it, that's one thing she's well trained to ignore, but after a while of listlessly looking for distractions, a bitter, woody scent leads Avrel to an open street bar. A cold ale does sound delightful, maybe even something a little more bitter. She puffs the air out of her slender, small nose as she decides she *won't* let those hulking miners rob that from her. There's an open stool, and it's hers.

"Give me something strong..." she asks the tender as she sits down. That's what tough guys used to say in Argoth, usually then they'd tell their sorry tale. She won't do that, unlike men, she doesn't need to talk down and explain everything to everyone.

Some of the other enclosed bars she passed had loose looking women handing out the drinks, this guy looks more like he's just not cut out for mining. "Sure thing." he says, pouring her a drink. He mashes something into the glass and pours a bourbon over it. She can smell it before he passes it to her.

"Thanks." She sips it slowly, the thoughts of the day swirling within her mind as she swirls the minty herbs in the glass. It tastes hot and cold at the same time. Much like how she feels; burning with anger and resentment, but also cold, mellow, lifeless. She has another.

Then another...

And she allows herself just one more.

After arranging her used glasses into a neat three sided stack, she realizes she's been here a while. And put more than a few of them away. She figures though, that if she has the presence of mind to make a shapely stack of her used glasses, she can't be too impaired.

Over the buzzing in her ears, she hears an older man's gravelly voice. "Hey! Yeah get over here, there's a chick that's just your size, but she can out drink me!"

"I'm half elf..." Avrel grumbles as she looks up at the older man, who looks just as he sounds. At first her angry heart thinks the shorter young man is Hayden and she begins clumsily channeling a flame spell under the bar, but she burns her hand and after flinching, realizes that it's not, just some other block-headed lut. She gets the ale which brought her to this place originally before she takes one final shot of that hot/cold bourbon. And all of a sudden it all hits her. The buzzing in her ears turns all to distant, tiny echoes, she loses the ability to hold her thoughts back from becoming words, and fearing for herself, she disjointedly staggers off of her stool so she can get away from these guys that'll surely have at her. There are a few offers to help her back to her place by those obviously more able than her, but they *won't* have her. She's going to her inn, on her own, and not going to be carried off by some middle-aged, beer bellied, human lech.

    The following morning Avrel's head pounds as she hears Zanvan talking to Bob. Every consonant a cymbal, every vowel a heavy drum. *What are they on about?* she wonders.

    "C'mon Bob." Zanvan urges. "Give me the money, she'll give me a great deal."

    "Nerp! Therks fer the erferr, burt irts nert hernerst!" he says dishearteningly.

    "Believe me." Zanvan promises. "I got to know Elisé really well. I've seen her furs, she's got lots of fur -- lots of animal furs, and she told *me* she'd give me a nice price. Please let me do this for you, it's the least we can do for all the extra you've done for us on this trip." the ranger insists, "It's way more than we bargained for back in Manitäria."

    "Mmmmmmmm…" the gnome drones on.

    For the love of goddess… Avrel wishes her large ears came with equally large hands.

    "Fern!" Bob says finally giving in.

    "Great" Zanvan freaking has to say with a percussive fist in hand gesture, "I'll be back in a while. You're with me." Zanvan says tapping Geric's shoulder, because even that sounds like roaring thunder.

    Geric turns his face up from a book, each page rustling like the howling f winter-storm winds. "Awww, why me!?" he whines.

    "Because Avrel is not gonna be able to." Zanvan barks.

    Got that right… she says, squeezing her eyes tightly, it feels like if she doesn't, they'll burst out of her skull.

    Zanvan's hand brushing his stubble like he's thinking is like fingernails on slate. "For an elf to drink enough to be passed out on the floor, she must have been pretty upset." Zanvan tells him. "She's gonna be pretty hungover."

    She never even made it to bed? *Shite…*

    "Come on!" he orders, loudly and apparently *not* aware that she's awake, not by his tone, nor by the strongness with which he shuts the door behind him.

    Geric grunts in defiance but soon follows, having not even had a chance for further protest. She just thanks goodness that they're gone.

Several hours later, Avrel is still lying in bed, but more awake and lightly casting some frost magic on her aching head.

She hears a knock on the door, and it hits her skull like a club to her forehead. "Ehhhhh...That hurts!" Avrel moans in a pained, froggy voice. "Who is it? I'm decent, guys if it's you..." Her head hasn't hurt like this in quite a while. "Oh Candice... It's like the migrain I had after that day long magic show..." she mutters, more or less intelligibly, Candice understands.

"May I come in?" Avrel hears an unfamiliar woman's voice say from behind the door.

Who the hell? She stirs just a bit, but she can't quite get herself up. "Sure, just don't be too loud..." Avrel replies. It's a woman, so it's probably safe.

The door opens and it's a fair haired, blonde woman bearing a container filled with a hot, bitterly aromatic, brew. "Your friends dropped by to buy some of my furs." she says softly, about time someone did. "They said you weren't feeling well."

"Great..." Avrel says slowly leaning up, successfully this time.

"I'm Elisé, a friend of Zanvan's." she introduces, "He said you might have um..." she pauses, "Well, he theorized that for someone of your lineage to become intoxicated enough to pass out, you might have..." She stumbles, trying to be polite and choose kind words, but all the same speaking in fragments.

"Shite-faced and hungover?" Avrel completes in a grunt.

"Well, yes." she replies with some reserve. "Anyway, I thought... Well actually, Zanvan thought you might want another woman to talk to." she says pulling a chair next to Avrel's bed. Avrel wonders how long they could've been friends, she thinks she recalls Zanvan saying he'd never been here before. But then seeing this Elisé up close, she'd imagine he'd make friends with her pretty quickly.

While Avrel considers Zanvan and the woman's relationship, Elisé pours a cup full of the rich, brown brew. It sounds like a bloody waterfall to her aching ears. "Here" the woman says, wisely, "The miner's around here drink this a lot. Something we learned from the orcs actually, it instills unnatural vitality to get through a busy day. It also can help if you're... Hungover."

Avrel takes the cup and sips it slowly. "Bitter..." she shudders. Funny how something bitter the night before tasted so good.

"You'll get used to it." she assures her. "So what's bothering you?" Elisé asks, gently. It's obvious but very appreciated, the tone of her voice.

"Nothing..." Avrel groans. "A guy stood me up is all..."

Elisé looks sad for a moment and then leans in to receive the cup and refill it. "Geric said you'd been acting, 'As if you were on the rag for a while now'. Elisé says as she hands back the refilled cup. "Before you even got here."

No doubt that's something Geric would say... Avrel blinks her aching eyes, "Why are they so concerned, why would Zanvan try to get a *complete stranger* to talk to me?" Avrel says frustratedly.

Elisé sighs. "I don't know for sure, but I can tell you this -- Zanvan is very good at keeping himself emotionally detached. Or rather, he tries to seem that way."

"And?" Avrel grunts, blanching at the taste of her drink.

"I *think* I know why..." the woman dodges. "But you'd have to ask Zanvan. He seemed really worried about you, even all during our outing last night. He's protective of you, he just doesn't really show it." Elisé says brushing back the hair obscuring Avrel's face. Avrel appreciates the oldersisterly or motherly gesture, but it hurts.

But, it gets her to thinking, it's true; he had defended her against Shad, and has often dropped bits of advice. *But then why can't the guy show his feelings?* But then she answers her own question. Men toxically don't ever show feelings. Not good ones anyway. "Eww... That womanizer doesn't *like* me, does he?" Avrel blanches, gulping nervously.

It's a logical conclusion but Elisé looks as if she very much doubts it, "No, no... not like that. Not at all..." she giggles, "And you're avoiding the question." Elisé says more firmly.

So did you. she almost has a mind to speak, "Well... I bore a lot of antipathy towards my father... And..." Avrel's eyes tear up, "I had so much I wanted to shout at him when I finally met him after so many years... I had this scenario in my head.."

"Are you sad because you..." Elisé interjects. "Didn't overpower him?"

Shite. They bloody told her about all that? "No, I always..." Avrel takes a deep breath through her nose, "I had so much I wanted to say to him... and he was empty... I had this thought that somehow he'd justify everything that he'd done wrong and he'd apologize..." her lower lip sinks, "... And he'd *hug* me, like everything was alright!" Avrel cries out, beginning to bawl. Elisé catches her as she slumps over, handing Avrel a kerchief to sop up her tears.

"Oh deary, don't..."

"...But there was *nothing!*" Avrel admits, "He was just *mad, rabid*... I didn't even know what to do... In my heart... My dreams were broken..." she creaks, gasping for air between her intense, tearful wails.

"Oh honey..." Elisé says as she holds Avrel close. "I... Sort of know how you feel. I never wanted to have anything to do with this fur trading, and bad blood came between my father and I... I never saw him to apologize for the things I said to him... I went east to live in the lake country and never thought any more of him until word reached me that he was deathly ill. By the time I got home... he had passed." Elisé says clutching Avrel tighter as she herself tears up. "But dear, I'm stronger because of it. It hurts but it *will* get better." the woman stresses.

"I just…" Avrel continues to weep, she's held it in for weeks, and in part; for many years. Instead of at least understanding him, or rightfully telling him off, there was nothing. Nothing…

"That's fine, sweetie." Elisé tells her, "Just let it all out…"

11

Geric and Zanvan step out into the morning light, quietly, as to not disturb Avrel who is still lying in bed.

"Rerdy?" Bob asks.

"Ready." Zanvan answers, lighting a morning smoke.

The two settle into Bob's wagon, and after he hears the reins pulled, they begin to pull out. He feels just a little bad about leaving the kid there, but she has that beaver. It was Candice that alerted Geric the moment he came into the room that her master was passed out on the floor. He himself didn't find out until later when he got back from his evening with Elisé.

As good as that first puff in the morning is, he can't shake that it's his fault, to a degree.

They go down into the town, and Zanvan distracts his mind for a little bit while giving Bob directions. After a while, they finally come to an attractive building on the edge of town with gilded letters on a large sign, and more than a few docks for larger caravan wagons.

"Fur Trader's Guild..." Geric reads, forgetting that the kid is back at the inn. "This place is huge, is this a trading center for *just* this town?"

Zanvan laughs. "No, Elisé said this place is the headquarters for all of the Argothian Kingdom." Zanvan's voice quiets down, "That's how I get such good prices for us on the furs we sell, they don't have to pay guild fees so we can bargain better." he smiles.

Geric snickers, "Sounds like not only do you cut her undies but undercut--" he shuts up as Zanvan readies a hand to hit him should he test him further.

Bob pulls them around back which faces into some foliage but also a fairly empty frontier. Upon stopping fully, Zanvan and Geric hop out as he comes around to the front of the wagon, Bob tosses him a heavy coin purse with which to buy the fur.

"E'rr ber wertirn." Bob says as he pulls his cart around to a less in-the-way part of the path around the guild building. Zanvan leads Geric around to the store room in the back where Elisé is waiting for them, sipping tea with a sweet biscuit like a lady, with a couple of crates serving as both table and chair.

"Hello." Zanvan greets Elisé warmly.

"Hello, uh..." Elisé says softly, looking a little confused, looking around behind them. "I thought you said there would be three of you." she says after wiping the corners of her mouth with a napkin.

"Yeah um..." Zanvan stutters, "Avrel, well she took Hayden's bailing on her pretty hard." Zanvan says regretfully.

"Yeah." Geric immediately chimes in, "She's been down for a while, and then Mr. *Love-Master* here thought he could cheer her up." he says as he taps Zanvan over the head.

"I mean... it *did*..." Zanvan replies defensively.

"*Until it backfired!*"

"*I know!*" Zanvan screams harshly back in Geric's face.

Elisé motions for them to stop, gracefully. "Is she alright?" she asks with concern in her voice.

"Nah." Geric confusingly answers, sounding completely unworried, "I think she's just having 'the ladies blues' and she got stood up. She's fine." Geric says with a superficial whisper.

"Actually... I'm worried." Zanvan clarifies, "I realize I made it worse, but she's been horribly depressed since we left Järviby." Zanvan says as he sits on a crate opposite Elisé.

"Well, I mean, she did get her moment to get revenge but then got her arse kicked, that'd make me sad." Geric suggests. "Mistress Erin..." he grumbles. Elisé and Zanvan ignore him.

"Who was this?" Elisé inquires.

"Headmistress Erin?" Geric says again, somehow thinking that saying an unrelated name twice will somehow give it meaning. He raises his finger as he seems to get that, "Oh." He says, "Her father, I think."

"She had a long grudge with her father." Zanvan explains, "I guess. Anyway, through some events we came across him back there. It was... certainly something." Zanvan says coldly. "He drew some sort of arcane weapon and made quick work of her." Zanvan notices a motion from Elisé as he is about to light his pipe. *Right, fine furs*. He puts it back in his cloak. "Not to mention his magic." he adds.

Geric looks to agree, "You ever seen a wee womanlet getting clobbered by some half naked elf writhing in his own sweat and excrement?" he says, offering far more information than the lady needs. "Yeah, he had to put the creep outta his misery."

"Oh..." she sighs. "I imagine it is troubling her." Elisé nods, ever the lady.

"I don't know." Zanvan admits, "I can't talk to her. I always say the wrong thing." Zanvan says angrily as he gets up and faces away from Elisé. He's used to saying things to get women *into* bed, not out.

"Ehh... I'm gonna load up these crates." the 'cleric' says, trying to make himself scarce.

"Zanvan." Elisé states with a softy giggle. "I find it hard to believe *you* would get tongue-tied around a woman."

"It's not like that." Zanvan says before he pauses to consider whether or not he should get into this any further. "She's not a woman to me." he tells her, "Just a little girl. The issue is in her -- To her, Geric and I are just *men*." He admits that she probably doesn't know what that entails in regards to Avrel.

Elisé looks at him coyly. The fact that she's so familiar with him is both pleasant and off putting at the same time. Right now, it's rather unnerving. "Is that *really* all?" she asks, leadingly.

"...She reminds me a bit of my..." He pauses, No, he decides, Elise needn't hear his whole story on that. "My sister, okay? I... I worry about her." Zanvan says roughly. "If she's having trouble dealing with it so much that she drank *that* hard, it's startling and I can't help but want to help her."

Elisé looks ghostly, just for a minute before putting on her more controlled emotional mask, "I can understand, you don't want to pry." she nods. "Has she approached you?"

"No, she hasn't." he scoffs, "She'd never confide in a guy." he again tries to hint. Hell, he's surprised she was willing to go with a walk-about with Hayden. "And now because of *me*, she's in bed with a killer headache." Zanvan scowls as he white knuckles the lip on one of the crates.

Elisé's eyes widen, "I might have something I can give her for that." she says softly, watching his hands.

"Could you talk to her?" Zanvan asks insistently. "She might talk to another woman."

She looks around, to Zanvan it doesn't look very busy, but what would he know? "I suppose..." she says. "I can kind of understand your predicament, women can be hard to read." She breaks into a short laugh, "But then we can read each other and we don't always get along as a result."

Zanvan gives her a quick smile. "Thank you." he removes his hat and kisses her hand. "Oh, I'd better get a start on these." he says, trying to keep his cool.

Elisé grins. "You gentlemen let me know when you're ready to leave." she says. "I've got just a thing or two to get in order first."

"Thank you, very much."

"After you pay, I'll come see your friend." she says to Zanvan. He nods and begins to carry the crate to Bobs wagon.

"Bring rags!" he hears Geric yell from a distance. Sometimes he wonders how he *ever* was taken by his clericly illusion.

After loading the crates into Bob's cart, Zanvan goes into Elisé's office. He's let through by a clerk and pointed to a room down the hall. It's beautiful, much like her personal quarters were; craft wood furniture, some tapestries, a fireplace with a fur rug, and ornate torch lights decorate the room. She's a woman of both taste and means, no doubts there.

"Here you go." Zanvan says, handing her a filled coin purse.

"No, thank *you*." she smiles, "Recently a little boy was attacked by some wolves, one thing led to another and we were overrun with wolf pelts." Elisé laughs. "Selling these all to a Manitärian merchant won't flood the greater Argothia market so much." She figured that out too? It's no wonder she is where she is. Shrewd woman, he'll give her that. "Wolf fur is nice, but it's been taking up a lot of room so it has killed our selection!"

He considers how many crates they'd carried, "How *did* you get so much?" Zanvan inquires.

"Oh..." she says, writing something down, "The family of the boy offered to pay for any and all wolves killed in the area, that combined with all the guys around here who are trappers, led to a rather 'wolf focused' season. I felt bad for the wolves, most were harmless." she says regretfully, "But those with money will spend it as they will, if putting bounties on animals makes them feel better about the death of their boy, I suppose it's their business." she sighs as she stands, closing a ledger. "Anyway! Let me get some brew for your friend, I'll be right out." Elisé says as she hurries into another room.

Zanvan sees himself out and waits in the cart with Geric. After about ten minutes Elisé comes out with a large container and a drinking cup.

***

She looks at the gnome's cart in all its hanging swag, and the adorable driver. "Aww wow, you guys have been traveling in this?" Elisé asks. "How quaint, I love it!" she can't help but smile. It's an older model, a Midrosh Mianderer by the looks of it, but it's well taken care of. The little gnomish driver obviously gives it a lot of love.

"Herp ern!" the driver says invitingly. She gives it a few tries, but it seems he's retrofitted the fold down steps in favor of a tailgate and curtains. Quite nice looking, but it requires more movement than her dress allows her.

Apparently seeing her problem, Zanvan hops out and gently lifts her, sitting her on the edge. She quivers from his strong hands holding her waist. "Why thank you." Elisé blushes.

"Rerdy?" the driver asks.

"Yeah, Bob." Zanvan answers.

"Ger yup!" she hears along with a shake of the reins.

None of them seem to have much to say from the outset, Of course she knows Zanvan, and has met the cleric, but Zanvan hadn't said much about Bob, the gnome. After a little bit more time passes, she finally comments, "I like your wagon." and she knows gnomes, above all merchants love their wagons.

"Wherr thernk yer!" he replies brightly. "Er've herd ert ferr yerrs!"

"Well, it's in excellent shape." she says, trying to project over the rumbling and the clopping.

"Thernk yerr!" he says again, "Yerp." he adds, "Er've herd it ers lerng ers Er've bern irn bursernerss..."

From there, she and Bob discuss business practice and such, how their fields differ, what's the same, philosophies. Zanvan chimes in on occasion, but Geric sits in the back looking rather bored through it all. But she very much enjoys herself, it's delightful to hear his stories, his victories and setbacks; all very different from hers. What she manages, he *does*. It's interesting to see the smaller side of things.

After a while they all adjust as they feel the wagon tip back, indicating that they must be starting up the hill leading to the inn.

As she slides a bite, Zanvan gently hugs Elisé, "Can't have you falling out, now can we?" he smiles at her.

She looks at him slyly, she knows what he's up to. "Of course not." she sighs sensually, "Funny that your hands always find themselves holding me by my hips..." she says with a seductive glance, before her eyes look to notice Geric staring on from the back, blanching. She pulls herself a little bit away from Zanvan. It's not the time or the place, she decides.

Finally the cart levels out and stops as Bob pulls it into the lot behind the inn. The group gets out, Elisé with some help from her gentlemanly ranger, and she makes her way to the door.

"I really appreciate this!" Zanvan waves. Elisé turns and smiles at him before heading through the door.

As soon as the door shuts, she can hear Geric proudly shout "And then they shagged."

She chuckles, she can just picture Zanvan and Bob just shaking their heads. Soon she finds their room, and she knocks on the door.

***

She's in there for quite a while until she comes out looking a little touched. When she turns around from shutting the door, Geric and Zanvan are standing there trying to act casual, though it's obvious she can tell they had been trying to listen in. Geric could half expect Zanvan to start whistling.

But he doesn't, so he takes it upon himself to complete the picture. Except he can't whistle.

"So..?" Zanvan asks, inviting explanation.

"Yes." Geric agrees, "Do tell." He's still betting on the rag.

"She..." Elisé says tenderly. "She felt emotionally hurt from how things went when she confronted her father."

"Why, because she lost a fight with a nutter?" Geric laughs. "Or because one of us *dreadful* men had to finish her fight for her?"

"No!" she snaps at him, "Because she wanted reconciliation, understanding, a hug!" Elisé continues, "Some affection from her father, not vengeance and *certainly* not to *kill* him."

Geric holds his hat lest it fly off with how his head is spinning, trying to reconcile what he remembers of that night to this. Not to mention how the elven womanlet has been acting. "W-w-w-wha-wait..." he sputters, "All this *because she wanted a bleeding* **hug**?!" he shouts astonished and confused.

Zanvan nudges him to settle him down. "I mean... Is that all?" Zanvan asks, he sounds just as puzzled. "Why didn't she just talk to us about it, why did she get all gloomy and secluded?"

The woman rolls her fair eyes, "*Because*, you'd say '*Is that all?!*'" Elisé chides him, passionately. "She wanted love, understanding --" Elisé pauses, her lip twitches and curls a bit. "And instead she watched him die."

"He *attacked* her." Zanvan concurs.

Even Geric feels a little bad about the whole thing in that context, and it does make a lot more sense. Not that Avrel usually makes much sense, but her going after him to fight him did seem extreme. Same daddy issue, different context. Somehow being furious at a parent and wanting just to be acknowledged? He can get that. In *that* context, yeah, he really gets it. And that whiny manlet was just the final bit of weight that broke her after giving her a little boost.

"Think of it, gentlemen." Elisé says, "How many *people* has she herself actually been forced to fight with?" she asks, "How many people has she actually watched die?

Geric facepalms, really he could only say her mother. Obviously though, she'd roast a guy if he so much as copped a feel, as if there's anything to feel. But she engaged Shad, she'd already decided to put herself in between him and Järviby. She failed at that, and her own father would have killed her if not for him and Zanvan.

"You okay, Master Geric?" Elisé asks all properly, he rather likes the ring of 'master'.

"Yeah." he says, giving them a bright grin, "Alright, enough of this dung, I'm going to find some lunch." he says. They have their answer, and this is getting to be a bit much. "You with me?" he turns to Zanvan.

The ranger's arms are folded as he looks down to the ground, then to the lady, "Well, regardless of why she was upset, thanks for helping her." he clears his throat, "How can I repay the favor?" he asks.

Elisé pretends to think for a moment. "I have some fur skins that I could use some help getting processed." she says after some thought. Zanvan agrees and they start on their way.

Somehow, Geric can't help but guess the only skins being stretched will be that of lamb. His mouth waters, *MmmLamb...* With a little mint jelly! He's not sure a rustic place like this would have something more fine like that, but after ministering to the sorrowful elf, if only indirectly, he probably deserves *something*.

"Herr, ber berk arfter dirner, we're learvern thern!" Bob shouts from a distance.

"Alright!" Zanvan replies from a little ways away.

"In the middle of the day?" Geric's surprised just a bit, that ranger has some stamina, especially if they're walking back to her place.

Along the lines of walking, he starts on his way to find something for his palette, worthy of his good deed.

***

Inside the inn Avrel is getting dressed in her normal clothes, having gotten out of that dress, when Candice happily brings her shoes to her.

"Thanks." Avrel forcibly smiles as she slips on her ragged old shoes.

"Chippu?" the beaver squeaks.

"Yeah, my head still hurts some, but I'm okay." Avrel replies, with a pet. "Sorry for worrying you."

It still hurts a little, but she glances out the window to see the later hours of the day. It's at least past noon, maybe more.

"We gotta get this dress back to that shoppe, it's overdue already." Avrel says as she hastefully fastens her shoes. Candice picks up the folded dress and brings it to Avrel in her little paws. "Thanks." Avrel smiles, genuinely as she takes it, "Let's go... And uh... Thanks for being by my side."

Candice just swints happily in reply as the two head out.

Out in front of the inn Bob's wagon is parked, and some of his boxes are piled around. She's worried at first that someone could have gotten into his goods, until she comes around to see him working inside.

"Herr! Goord ter serr yer urp!" Bob waves to them from the back of his cart.

"It's nice to be up." she agrees, "Need some help sorting that stuff?"

"Nerp, E'rm gerd!" he brushes off, good for her, her head feels like it'd pound with that much labor. "Jerst be berk arfter derner, we'rre leaverng thers ervernern." Bob replies.

"Okay." Avrel waves, "See you then." Rudaski is interesting, but she doesn't mind going so soon. That being the case, she pays extra mind to its features as she and Candice head into town. She'd not choose to come back, so she'll make a memory.

Memory... she frys with dread, "Candice, do you remember where I got this?" she asks about four streets down from the hill.

Candice says nothing, but she twitches her nose and begins to take the lead. Despite what Geric says, she's no rat, but her rat's nose comes in handy. It's not long before Avrel sees the dress shoppe in the dusty distance. She crosses a cobbled road and heads for it.

At the entrance she turns to the beaver, with her beautiful coat, just like the pretty hats just out of Candice's sight.. "Uhhh... Candice... Maybe you should stay out here." Avrel says delicately.

"Chippu." Candice replies with a pout, but she on her haunches, intent to stay outside as requested. With an affirming nod, Avrel goes through the door and puts the dress up on the counter, trying to get the attention of the owner.

She can hear cloth being cut in the back, but nobody up front. "Is anybody here?" she says, rapping her fist against the counter.

The shoppe lady comes out from a back room. "Ah, you're back." she greets as she comes through the curtains behind the desk. "I was starting to wonder about you." she adds.

"Yeah, here you go." Avrel says, nudging the folded dress across the counter.

The lady picks it up and inspects it. She begins looking it over for tears or stains, "How did your outing or whatever go?" she inquires.

Avrel looks to the side, "I... was supposed to have had a date but he stood me up." she says softly, trying *not* to think about it while talking about it.

"Eh, his loss." the lady replies brashly, sounding rather token given how the people of this town have viewed her ears with disapproving eyes. It's a tried and true reply for the disappointed heart that she's heard in ever tavern and bar where anyone was drinking away sorrows. Even so, Avrel smiles slightly.

"Alright, I'll get your deposit then." the shoppe lady says as she bends down to look through a coin drawer. "Here it is." she says as she tosses a small coin purse up onto the counter.

Avrel grabs it and steps back. "Thanks." she says with a curtsy. The shoppe keeper nods, and Avrel exits. As she leaves the doors of the shoppe behind her, she finds Candice just outside the door waiting for her. It was more painless than she'd thought. She thought about entertaining a man, and as a man, he showed his despicable colors. Lesson learned, and with the return of that dress, she can wash her hands of the whole thing.

"Alrighty... How about a corn muffin?" Avrel says, bending down and petting Candice.

"Chippu!" Candice squeaks enthusiastically, as if there was a thought that she wouldn't.

Avrel gives Candices nose a tap, and they begin looking, or sniffing rather, for some sort of bakery, and after a trek across town, she finds one. She buys the beaver a muffin, but in all the joy of finding the damn place, she'd not noticed that it's getting rather late.

She does now

"I should probably find some food for myself and head back." It hadn't occurred to her, in a meaningful way, that she'd lost half the day already. Until now that is.

On her way back to the inn she buys a cup of soup from a vendor and gives the crackers to Candice who accepts them graciously. Eventually as the city glows orange as the setting sun shines through the dusty city, Avrel is again back at the inn. Geric is waiting with Bob by the wagon as she goes around.

"Heyr, yer sern Zernvern?" Bob asks.

"No I haven't." she answers, not to her surprise, he's probably off making fowl use of another woman's body. "Otherwise, are we ready to go?"

"Yerp!" Bob says with a nod.

12

After a quarter-hour or so Zanvan comes into view carrying a neat little bag. Geric nor Bob can make it out, but she and her elf eyes are sure it's a bag.

"We pirckt urp yer sterff, we'rr rerder ter gerr irf yerr arr." Bob says as Zanvan comes closer.

"Yeah, I'm ready." Zanvan replies as he promptly gets into the back of the wagon. Avrel follows him, and the Geric and with a shake of the reigns they depart the lot of the inn. Bob's boxes are much better organized now, and she enjoys the added space it provides. She feels comfortable spreading out just as selfishly as the men. And as a whole, the air seems more fresh, no foul pockets of spilled meat crumbs or sweaty odors, Bob cleaned it well. In regards to more pleasant smells, as they head down the road Zanvan unpacks a carefully prepared meal from the bag he'd arrived with. She's curious, it smells too nice to be from a street vendor, and the bag is rather nice as well. *Fur*, and that answers her question.

Geric leans into his space and inspects the food before she can. "Where did you get that?" he asks.

"Elisé gave it to me." Zanvan replies.

"*Nice...*" Geric says with a pat on the back.

Avrel overhears and finally takes a look for herself. "Damn... Zanvan, I think she likes you." Avrel says with intrigue. It's a bone-in beef steak with vegetables, she even had it wrapped in a thin, metal foil to keep it warm.

"So when is she becoming your wife?" Geric laughs while poking Zanvan with his elbow. Zanvan looks at them both with an intense glare that cuts into them, and Geric stops teasing him.

"For your information." Zanvan says strongly, "Her old, white-haired assistant, Blair made this."

Avrel looks at Geric and they both shrug and say nothing else of it. "All the same, she is a very nice lady." Avrel comments.

"Yeah, she was." Zanvan agrees.

She supposes that his choice of tense means he won't be pursuing the relationship further, and it's both sad and infuriating to her. "So who's Blair?" she asks without much else to say.

"Her assistant." he says, just after taking a bite. He doesn't seem to want to continue the discussion further either. Just the shame she floats one of his carrots over to herself and splits it with Candice. She's never had one cooked before outside of a soup or stew, she wasn't expecting the sweetness. In fact, she's surprised how much she dislikes it. What's more, Zanvan seems as if he couldn't care less; it's Geric who's annoyed. She takes a string bean just for good measure.

After a nice ride through town, through the business of evening time bustle they come to a large tunnel in the side of one of the rocky foothills Rudaski is built under. It's where many of the mining carts are set up and head into smaller caves along this same area, but far wider, and roughly paved with cobblestone. Despite all the warmth and pleasantness Avrel found in the more lively parts of the ride, this side of things, much like the approach, is anything but. The stone of the mountain is scarred, and punctured, the air is full of grit and dust, and when once in a while she sees someone, they are dirty from head to toe.

But their path, thankfully isn't into a dirty, dark, and dank dungeon. But just the same, the utter darkness of this tunnel isn't so pleasing either.

"What!?" Avrel yelps as she covers in goosebumps. "Why are we heading in here!?" Now that they are here, she'd prefer that they'd just have gone north, the way they came.

"It's a path under the mountain." Zanvan replies, lighting up an after-dinner smoke. "Saves a lot of time, I'd imagine."

"But…" she protests. "It's dark and creepy!"

Geric clicks his tongue thrice, "It's an old mine that was turned into a tunnel." he comments, it's no doubt something he's read, "How is that creepy? We have lanterns." Geric interjects.

"I suppose." Avrel says softly.

"Make one of your glowing bones." Geric suggests.

Avrel protests, "I'm not afraid of the dark."

It's not so bad when she thinks of those dark, back alleys in Argoth. She never thought that she'd think of those for comfort, either. She's *always* hated them, even as a child. Dark alleys, the way she was always treated, the hustle and bustle of the Goldday rush as everyone heads home for the weekend with their pay for the week, and sometimes hers-- No, maybe she still does.

She gets a few looks from the guys as she lets out a little giggle to herself. "It's nothing." she smiles. They give her an eye but they quickly go back to smoking and reading. She recalls once during a particularly dark day she lit herself a small candle stump she'd found in a rubbish can, the only problem being that it began to burn the inside of her wooden crate. She can smile about it now, but not then. Mother had passed only months before, and she was cold and all alone, without even Candice to keep her company. "Just an old memory." she adds. "You wouldn't get it."

As they make their trek under the mountain, they can sometimes faintly hear the echoes of mining from nearby areas ringing through the crevasses and rocks.

Avrel mostly, but Zanvan and Bob as well. As they go deeper, Bob finds the torchlight to be a little underwhelming, so Avrel channels a soft moonlight-like glow in the front of the cart. Geric has something similar, and they switch off every few hours. A few times into the night, the light attracts some large rats or bats, in all cases they are easily dispatched.

As they all lay down for the night, it's strange to her. No stars, no wind, a balmy moisture, almost dead in its silence but for drips from distant stones, and pitch black. Blacker than anything she's ever experienced, even her elf eyes can only barely make out the far distant pinprick of light. She finds Candice in the dark and holds her tightly as she drifts to sleep.

After a day and a half more of creeping through the darkness in the wagon, they see light from the exit. Avrel notices several small rats heading towards the exit as well, even Candice seems to have spells of staring off in that direction. Candice seems unaware of them though, so she pays it little mind, putting her focus instead into her illumination. When it's not his turn, Geric finds amusement in flicking the small rats off of the cart and seeing how far they fly. She'd hit him if she wasn't busy, and she can't hit him during his cast, lest he lose his focus and have to read off his spell again.

Finally they come out of the cave, their eyes phased by the bright morning light. Apparently their guesses at the passing of time were a bit off. Zanvan swore it would be later in the afternoon, but it's fine. Finally the air is fresh and the sound of the wind sweeps through the greenery, and in the distance she can see the mountain foliage fade to the plains they'd passed through in the weeks long passed.

They continue on until nightfall. Under the stars, they stop to make a proper camp, and cook some meat that Zanvan has prepared for them over the fire.

"MmmmTastes like bacon! What is this?" Geric asks enthusiastically.

Hers isn't the thin strips like Geric's, but it has a peculiar flavor just the same, and not one she can place. Not that she has a wide knowledge of such things. *Gamey*? she thinks might be the word. "Is it something from Rudaski?" she asks. She's been enjoying the potato bread that Bob had stocked up on, but this is interesting too.

"Bat wings." Zanvan replies casually.

"Well, by the Gilded's halo…" Geric shrugs, "They aren't bad!" he smiles "Would make a nice soup. Maybe like a potato and cream stew or something?"

Avrel blanches and looks away from Geric's dish, and prods another of the small, crunchy nuggets of meat that Zanvan had made for her and Bob. She ponders it a moment. Bats, if she remembers rightly, aren't the same sorts of animals as beavers or coypu. They're more like foxes, she recalls, and it's not like they haven't eaten wolf meat.

"Wherrt er thers? Err've nerver herd ernertherng lirk thirs." Bob asks happily. "Irt's serr ternder!"

Zanvan looks at Avrel, and then to Candice, and very briskly looks away and mumbles. "You uh... ever had conies?"

"Yerp!" Bob replies.

"Yeah." Zanvan continues. "It's kind of like that.

Bob eats up but Avrel stops eating and hands her plate to Geric. The closest thing they've encountered to rabbits would be those jumbo rats. She's always been grateful for any food, but she just can't eat that. She grabs a cup of tea she had waiting for her and rinses her mouth out with the tea before she bids the crew a goodnight. She doesn't want to seem ungrateful, and she'd never want to turn down good food, and it's not even the fact that it's a rat that ties the knot in her stomach; it's just Candice. She cuddles her precious water-rat in the back of the wagon as she waits to fall asleep, her mind aflutter. She almost feels just a little relief, maybe even satisfaction. Satisfaction; she can choose to skip an easy meal and not fear that it'll be a number of days before another.

"I'm..." she can't help but hold Candice tightly, "Making my way, Mother." She smiles, it's so simple, but it's just a little privilege she's never had, and a taste of yet to come. And a reminder of her true goal on this job, to be able to choose discriminatorily the things in her life left to her beggars' chances, and reject those who chose to reject her and who looked down on her. Yet those thoughts don't seem as sweet. Maybe it's because she can't imagine her mother being proud of her thinking that way. A mother that made her promise not to turn her magic on another person certainly wouldn't.

Avrel's eyes dim as sleep begins to cut through her lingering thoughts, as her eyes draw themselves shut, she vaguely hears Geric jokingly say "Now if only we could find an excuse to roast that damned beaver."

Joke or not, she holds Candice extra close, and she falls asleep.

"Move, kid." the Ar-Guard said, but Mother was still sleeping. She'd been sleeping more and more over the last while.

"Mother?" she nudged, softly at first. "Mom?"

"Drunkard?" the other Ar-Guard said as he leaned down to sniff Mother's clothing. She sniffed too, just because they were doing it. She thought it was just fruit, rotting on a nearby street on this warm day -- But it wasn't.

"Mother?" Avrel said again, putting herself between the mean men and her lovely Mother, and nudging her once more. "We need to go." she said.

"Move, kid." the Ar-Guard said firmly.

"Move, kid!" the other said, trying to push her from his way with a strong push to her small shoulder.

"Kid?" she hears distantly. Her eyes fuzzily make out Zanvan as they, like the rest of her, wake up. "There's a pack of bison up ahead, we'll need your help if they charge us." he says patting her shoulder. "Come on, get moving."

She yawns and leans up, and looks though to the other side of the wagon. So *that's a bison, huh?* "One sec…" she frys, trying to put to rest the lingering recollections of that dream. She's rather surprised they spotted them, they are far even by her standards. Once she's fully aroused, she meets him and Geric as they peer out on either side of the back tailgate.

"Sweet dreams?" Geric asks. It's midmorning, they must've begun moving without waking her.

"Not especially." she understates. "They're far." she also understates more relevantly.

"Yeah, I don't know." Geric says somewhat lowly, "While Zanvan was getting you they dashed away for a second, almost like they thought something was chasing them."

"Us?" she asks.

"They'd rip this wagon to shreds." Zanvan scoffs, "Something else must've spooked them." he climbs further out and onto the side.

Aside from the big, hulking bison, she can't see anything. The plains look about as uniform and unending as they did when last they were here.

Zanvan climbs back in. "Just be alert." he says.

"Can do." Geric replies, even as he swats to read his book.

Avrel glances around for one more look, it seems they are heading away probably for the best, she doesn't feel very well rested, and fighting an ugly plains auroch doesn't sound like a great way to start the morning.

"Your potion is on the crate behind you." Geric says to her, without even looking. She takes the flask and drinks it down. Judging that Zanvan is taking his smoke and Geric is in his book, she must've missed breakfast.

She's not hungry anyway.

The following afternoon, they happen across another pack of them. They are grazing, and they are close, but not too close. Just enough for Bob to call Zanvan to be alert. Avrel just enjoys watching them. But then, all of a sudden, they begin to charge. She hears it before she sees it, the sound of thunder on the clear day draws her eyes right to them. But yet again, they aren't charging for the wagon, nor are they running from the wagon. That's when the earth ripples and bursts open with a pack of bear-sized marmots, the bison storm across the plain, and some marmots give chase.

"What in blazes?" Zanvan asks, in a rather unsettling way. They kind of rely on his nature knowledge.

"Are they not supposed to do that?" Geric asks, coming up beside him. Avrel can't see past both of them and looks out the other side.

She still can't see anything...

"*Look out!*"

But Zanvan's shout comes too late for her to brace herself as one of the marmots dashes past the horses, startling them and giving the whole damned wagon a jolt. Luckily, all she does is fall on her arse.

"Werrr! Werr!" Bob cries as he tugs the reigns, trying to keep the horses from running wild. Zanvan jumps out of the cart and draws his sword.

"Watch Candice!" Avrel tells Geric who looks a bit more roughed up tha she was, as she quickly follows Zanvan but only to motion to him to stay his sword. He reluctantly complies.

Avrel whips her staff against a nearby rock creating a loud crack that grabs the marmots' attention. For a moment they all look over to her with tranquility, but just as she channels a light spell to try to draw them away from the cart they all at once stampede at her. Avrel tries to react, but has no time and is quickly overtaken by the sheer force of the pack of rodents who knock her over and trample over and around her.

"Help!" she wails as she tries to charge a spell, but loses her focus as a foot jabs into her still healing ribs.

She hears Zanvan draw his sword and he beats the lingering marmots off of her. With one final kick and then a blast of force, they are driven back, and they charge off into the distance.

Avrel lays there a moment, dazed and panting. She was completely caught off guard, but strangely she's not bitten or anything.

"Are you okay?" Zanvan asks as he helps her up.

She pats herself. "Aside from this scratch on my collar bone, I think I'm fi-" she cuts herself off with a gasp as she stands and feels a harsh pain in her side. Zanvan helps her over to Geric who is sitting with his arms crossed giving Candice the cold shoulder, Candice mirroring him.

"I saw that." Geric laughs. "Don't you have some sort of spell that summons a mouse trap? Or maybe a lion titan?"

"I don't know any summoning spells." she mutters, she's not amused.

"Yeah, me neither." he says, patting the spot on the tailgate beside him. He comes at her but stops an inch short, "*May I?*" he asks, snarkily, but at least he's asking.

"You may." she says.

Geric feels her side gently. "Hmmm.. No biggie, you just had a lot of pressure put on your broken ribs. Good thing they are bound up well already."

"It really hurts..." Avrel whimpers as the adrenaline begins to fade and the pain really sets in.

Geric looks through his bag. "Well, lucky for you I got some Orken Wheat Root at a shoppe in Rudaski, so I'll be able to make you a better potion now." he says as he tosses a piece of bark at her that she fails to catch as it bounces off of her forehead onto her chest. "Chew on that it should help with the pain."

"Thanks" she says softly. "I should have just let you handle it, Zanvan." she admits, in hindsight. "I'm sorry." she says as she bites off a piece of the bark.

"I mean, your way worked last time." he says, laying a hand on her shoulder, "It's not your fault they reacted like that. I've never seen whistle pigs charge in packs like that." he says darkly. "Hopefully you learned your lesson though, wild animals are unpredictable." Zanvan says sternly.

Avrel blushes and nods, and after Geric redoes her rip wrap, Bob starts the wagon forward again and they continue on through the plains.

Even after a few hours, she's embarrassed. What's worse is that Zanvan keeps taking glances at her like he knows.

"Hey, so you grew up in a city." Zanvan finally says "It's not your fault that you're not familiar with fighting wild beasts." He says breaking the silence since the incident.

Avrel leans up and weakly smiles in reply. Coincidentally, Geric hands her a fresh vial of potion. "So where in Argoth do you live?" he asks idly. "I never saw you around."

"Well, a-around." she says after some thought. They've never asked directly that she remembers, but why is it so hard to just say nowhere? She hasn't a home, not since she was a child. Not since shortly after Shad left. She looks over to Zanvan who seems to know better. She won't say it, she won't get into it; but someday she won't be ashamed of the crate, the box, or the open stable. And she'll punish the lofty, unhelpful elites who bullied her, and left in those back street gutters. But now isn't the time, Geric is asking as a friend. "Sometimes Candice and I would go outside the city gates to bathe or to get some wood too." she adds.

"Ahh... Cool." Geric says as he closes his book. He wasn't paying much mind anyway.

But Zanvan smiles, he knows. He might even relate a bit, but he chooses to forrige unlike her. She smiles back anyway. "Remind me, kid, sometime when we're stopped for a while I can give you pointers on your fighting. You're not bad considering, but you need help." Zanvan says, tipping his hat down as he lays back to snooze.

"Okay." Avrel says softly as she applies some of the potion to her injury.

As they continue on, they notice harder and harder tremors in the earth. Over the many days that follow, they often see in the distance as more marmots charge through the grass, much to their surprise and relief, none come too close to the wagon. But still, they have to be ready. And Avrel won't argue, she now knows how fast they can turn and run someone down. Relation to Candice's kind or not, she has a job.

The group continues on for several days until one afternoon, only a day's ride from Manitäria, according to Zanvan's latest answer to Geric, they suddenly stop. "Errr... Thert dorsern't berd werr..." Bob laments.

They all find a way to look ahead and all see the smoke rising over the horizon in the city's direction.

"Maybe they're just cooking the royal palace to make stew?" Geric interjects jocularly. Everyone shoots a disapproving leer at Geric. "You tell me, Miss Super Eyes."

She can't see anything. "Pray, what does your Goddess say?" she counters.

He shrugs.

"Bob, do you want to keep gong?" Zanvan asks, but Bob is silent. "Bob?"

"Bob?" she asks too.

"Therre's err stream arernd herre." he says darkly after his long, ponderous delay. "Therr herses cern drirnk urp ernd rerst." he says. He's obviously in no hurry, but also worried.

"Are you sure?" Avrel asks.

Zanvan puts his hand on her shoulder, "If something is afoot, best we see it in daylight first." he says, "If it looks to be better seen at nightfall, we'll still have that option."

She supposes that's true, but all the same, it feels wrong to be setting up a camp while the city burns, for all they know. It's not as if their masculinity isn't letting them care, thank goodness, around the campfire they all ponder what might await them in Manitäria.

"Err herp erfrererrng ers arrighrt." Bob says sorrowfully.

"It..." she says in a draggy fry. "Could always just be nothing." Avrel says trying to cheer Bob up, as he's done for her a few times. "It could be... a fire-mountain in the west spewing fumes... or something." Her geographical knowledge is limited, but even she can't think of such a mountain in this region. She only finds herself being looked at with eyes screaming, 'Just stop'. *So this is how Geric feels...* she gulps.

"Just apply your potion." Geric says harshly.

"Well, whatever it is..." Zanvan speaks up, "We'll find out soon enough." he says reassuringly while she dabs the potion on her wound.

Later that night Candice comes to Avrel, who is reclined against a tree, with a large bundle of berries held in her tiny paws. Avrel graciously accepts and eats them while petting the beaver. *What now?* runs through her mind again, and again. *Could it be an attack?* After all, that woman knight had said they feared an attack by the orcs. She wonders if the others have thought about that. But as she thinks about it more, it doesn't seem right, Manitäria is too far inside of Argoth. Even she knows *that*. She puzzles and puzzles again, not coming up with a positive answer before finally falling asleep against the tree.

"Good Goddess." the Ar-Guard pinched his nose, up under his helmet's nose plate. "The smell."

She thought it was rotting fruit on a nearby street.

It wasn't.

Early in the morning before dawn, Avrel is awakened by the men discussing the smell wafting in the air. *Burning mushroom.*

"Hurry up, kid." Zanvan says, showing a plate of food, "Bob wants to hurry."

She nods and begins to stand as she's stunned by a massive cracking sound splitting her ears, followed by a harsh tremor. She tries to keep to her feet but the tree uproots and begins to fall on her. She screams shrilly to draw the attention of her companions.

"Avrel!" Geric screams running over trying to lift the tree off of her. Zanvan attempts to follow but Bob requires his help to keep the cart and horses under control. She watches helplessly as Zanvan struggles for a minute to unclasp the horses bindings letting them run off, so that he can turn to come help her, because despite Geric's attempts to help the tree still inches closer and closer to fully falling over. She's not hurt yet but pinned, and she can't hold back the weight of this tree.

As Zanvan gets there and starts trying to hold it up, it seems hopeless. All this way just to be crushed by a tree? She won't accept that. Life has diddled and roughed her over enough. No... "No!" Avrel feels her hands tingling with spell magic as her frustration, fear, and anger rise to the surface.

"Hold on!" Zanvan screams as he draws his sword and starts hacking into the trunk.

Suddenly, she feels it erupt in a blindingly bright and fiery flash. She closes her eyes as she feels the energy in her hands burst. Her eyes are shut, but she still hears the boom of it, of the tree exploding, and the core of it being blown off of her. The power still surges through her, until she lies still for a moment, still keeping her eyes shut until the tremors finally stop.

Avrel opens her eyes to a charred crater at her feet, the core of the tree soldering a good distance away, and to see her friends lying on the ground, stunned by the blast.

She crawls over to them and tries to wake them. "Guys!? *Guys!?*" she yells frantically as she slaps and shakes them.

"Yeah!" Geric coughs profusely.

Zanvan stands up and brushes the soot off of himself. "Well, I suppose that works." he says feigning a chuckle. "I wish to hell you'd give some warning though."

"I'm sorry." She notices Geric feeling his head, and then scanning around for something.

"**Nooooooooooooo!**" Geric suddenly screams. She and Zanvan rush towards him fearing something horrible just to see him cradling Rufus's red hat. Or rather, what's left of it.

Avrel looks at her own clothes and sees that they are charred up from the blast as well. She really overdid it, and didn't even mean to. "I'm sorry."

Zanvan laughs lightly as he lights up a smoke on one of the nearby embers. "I think a little less powerful of a spell was in order."

"I'm sorry!" she repeats once more "I didn't even think I was casting anything, it just happened." Avrel stresses. She's a little frightened.

"My hat is dead...." Geric whines, "Now I'll have to wait for Zanvan to die if I want another cool hat!"

Bob comes running over to them but is immediately shushed as Zanvan raises his fist signaling everyone to halt. He jumps down pressing his ear to the ground, Avrel turns behind them facing away from the city after hearing faint sounds only her elf-ears can hear.

But they both hear *something.*

He listens, he listens hard, and she does the same. "More of those freaking marmots!" Zanvan grunts.

"I can hear them too." Avrel sighs.

"I'm just sitting here not hearing anything because I'm not a freak." Geric mutters. "Does no one else mourn this precious hat?"

No. she almost lets fly, but she's still listening hard.

Just then, four enraged marmots burst out of the ground and swipe at Bob who is thrown back several feet by the hit. That's about the only hit they land, however. Geric, Zanvan, and Avrel quickly dispatch all but one of the marmots, who flees towards the city.

"Bob!?" Avrel says as she's trying to get him up.

"Yerp?" he grunts" Er'm firn ...erkkk.." he moans, getting to his feet. They spend the next hour searching for the horse, but once reclaimed and harnessed, they head towards the city at full speed.

The city burns in the distance. The sooty air thickens as they draw nearer and the distant noises not even the ranger can hear continue to grow louder. But she hears them.

"Theory." Geric says, trying to break the long, uneasy silence. "*Giant marmots* decided to roast and eat the royal palace."

He's being a sarcastic sard, but he has a point, "Do you think all the rodents are connected with the smoke over the city?" Avrel asks Zanvan, seriously.

"Hell if I know." Zanvan answers. "I've never spent much time in these plains. It wouldn't surprise me though."

Bob looks disheartened as they continue on. Understandably.

Some way outside the gate they tie the horse and wagon to a tree and continue on foot, unsure of what awaits them inside the city. They've arrived to a burning city of pandemonium; rats, marmots, and muskrats of all sizes run rampant in the city. Large marmot packs tackle and destroy buildings in a way reminiscent to how their cart had been attacked.

"Oh... my..." Avrel says despairingly.

"By the Gilded--!"

"What the hell?"

"Er. Mer. *Gerrd!!!*" the gnome drops to his knees. "Wherr? Wherr courd herve dern thirs?" Bob cries out as he looks onto the mayhem of large rodents chasing down his kin and destroying the infrastructure.

Geric steps forward looking as a dog who has caught a scent. "There is a great bewitchment upon this city..." he says, possibly as serious in tone as she's ever heard him, "I can feel it now."

"Wher arr yerr, ernd whert herve yer dern wirth Gerrrerc?" Bob shouts inquisitively.

"Huh?" he mumbles.

"Sirnce whern herve yer beern ursferr?" Bob shouts in deep stress over the situation.

"Hey, I know my spells!" he defends, "I can feel some of the large-scale spells when I'm in their presence! Somebody or something is *controlling* these vermin!" Geric pontificates while drawing his mace, charging it with lightning. "Nothing to do but kill any possible traitors." he grunts as he walks towards Candice. She will have none of that! She jumps between her familiar and Geric and gives him a lewd hand gesture. "Oh fine, send her away though!" he commands.

Avrel thinks back to the cave, *He might be right about that.* she agrees. "Candice, he might be right, go back to the cart."

Candice shoots a mean leer at Geric before following Avrel's wish.

"Keep your weapons handy." Zanvan says, drawing his sword. Geric's mace is already out, but she pulls out her staff. Bob, unarmed cautiously follows as the group makes their way into the city, dispatching what marmots they can. They aren't sure what they are looking for, but Geric at least seems sure that he'll know it when they find it. She can only hope, she senses some strange aura about the place too, but she hasn't the discernment to know what it means.

In a sea of cracked, bulldozed and crushed houses, Bob screams as they run past a particular burning building. "Ehrr Nerr! Berberrerr!" he shouts. Avrel turns, followed by Zanvan and Geric.

"Bob, what's wrong!?" Avrel yells over commotion. Between the thunder of the vermin and the roar of the fires, it's stinging her ears.
"Merr daughrter Berberrerr's herse!! She mert ber irn there!" he yells in reply.

Zanvan throws off his cloak and rushes in before Avrel or Geric can stop him. They wait frantically for a few long minutes until Zanvan returns, covered in even more soot."There's nobody in there, they must've left." he pants.

"Err thernk goodners." Bob sighs.

Avrel hands Zanvan his cloak. "Alright *Mister Macho*." she smirks. A lesser woman would be impressed, she can admire it, but she knows better.

They continue deeper towards the downtown, starting to grow suspicious of the lack of more gnomes running around in panic. Where they'd expect more, there are none, and as of yet, there's no sign of the rodents consuming them. Strangely, they've seen very few even injured.

At last as they engage a pack of them, they are cornered by several giant marmots that come up behind them. And they are almost twice as big as the ones from a few days earlier.

"Now what?" Avrel asks Zanvan.

"I don't see a way out of this." he mutters.

"So what?" Geric shouts, flashing a light at one of them as it's about to charge. "We surrender? To a bunch of mindless rats?"

"Geric…" Zanvan says, "Do you think they're being controlled?"

The cleric closes his eyes, "Maybe."

Avrel watches as Zanvan lays down his weapon, and concedes. "Avrel." he says. She looks hard at her staff. "Don't pang the damn thing."

She doesn't, she gently lays it at her feet.

"Really?" Geric protests. The marmots form a circle around them and begin to tighten it. He looks to have a change of mind, "You really think they're being controlled?"

"I asked you, *cleric*." Zanvan bites back.

"Now, now." he scoffs.

"Geric." Avrel asserts herself softly, "We still have our magic." she reminds him.

He obviously is against it, but he reluctantly lays it down.

And almost immediately, the rodents start nudging them in directions they appear they want the group to go. *Candice might have been helpful*, Avrel grimaces, but it's too late for that now. She didn't trust Zanvan to go on the offensive before, but now she must trust his instinct to be passive. "I hope we made the right decision." she gulps as they are brought to a large city square where three enormous marmots are waiting for them.

"Just stay close." he tells her.

Geric touches a finger to his lips as he looks around, "HmmmmMaybe I was wrong and there is no skulduggery here and these marmots are just very clever." Geric mutters. "Welp, time to bow to my new marmot-general overlords." Geric says with a shrug.

One so masculine it's toxic, the other so jocular it hurts. "We need to be serious and focus." Avrel barks sharply.

"Hey um... Do you guys see that?" Zanvan says as he points to the tallest marmot in the middle, which has a fleshy, dark-red shield over its head with a glowing magical aura around it.

It looks familiar, or at least the way it was described to her. "No... That can't be!" Avrel gawps.

Geric looks at it, squinting and obviously unsure of what he's looking at.

"Therr Aerggers!?" Bob yells to him.

"Oh... Neat." Geric replies.

Suddenly they hear a piercingly high-pitched laugh as a small figure comes out from behind the largest marmot's ear.

"Oh... *Oh no*...Oh Please **NO!!!**" Geric screams as he sees it, with increasing angst and intensity.

"What is it?" Avrel inquires.

Geric points to the small figure. "Avrel, tell me, what your freaky elf eyes see up there, because my inferior, book-strained human ones see the silhouette of a rat wearing a wizard's hat." the cleric says with distress in his voice.

Avrel looks for a moment, it's a tiny brown rat, indeed in a wizard's hat, he has a little cape to boot. "Oh geez! What the hell?" she recoils. *And why did Geric seem to recognize it?*

"Hahaha!!" she hears the rat wizard announce confidently, though with a rodential warble, "I told you that wasn't the end, *cleric*, and now I will have my vengeance! With the Aegis by my side, and my army of giant marmots, **nothing** can stop me!"

"Oh my god, you bloody varmits!!" Geric screams as he falls to his knees. **"We have places to be!!!"**

Avrel turns to the cleric who obviously knows this-- this thing, "Geric, what is your relation to this?" she asks inquisitively, she's not sure she wants to know, but she's completely lost.

"I uh..." Geric mumbles nervously.

"Hahaha!" the rat squeaks, "I thought it was all over when that falcon took me away, little did I know that a bigger bird would catch him, and then a small snow-dragon from the north would eat him?! And just when I thought I was safe and was left alone in his den, I found that I couldn't remember the counter-spell to my transformation! It can only be your fault for injuring my head!" the rat wizard pontificates.

"Head injuries don't work like that!" Geric yells to him, "You probably forgot it because you're an old man and a pervert with a mouse brain!"

"What?" she interjects.

"Silence!" the rat shrieks, "Lamenting that I'd be a rat forever I stumbled around the icy skeleton corpses in that den until I saw it, the Aegis! At last such a grand magical artifact should come to me! *The Grandiose Wizard: Murinae*!"

"Oh..." that name... "OH! I know you!" Avrel says stepping forward.

"Who are you, tiny!" Murinae demands.

"Isis Lavian was my mother!" Avrel says angrily.

The rat strokes his chin with his hind foot for a moment. "Oh! That hot copper haired vagabond who offered magic lessons on the streets!? I remember her! It's because of her I learned of my **obsession!**" the rat chatters.

"Obsession with what?" Zanvan asks, coolly.

"Magic and seductively sensuous feet!"

They all share a blanch.

"Err'm serry we errskd." Bob says sickly.

The rat's dark eyes turn starry and dreamy, "Ahh... I remember them well, I was about thirteen and she was always poor and could never afford shoes for herself. I learned everything I needed to learn of sexuality due to those lustrous tootsies..." the rat continues as his lusty thoughts prompt him to drool.

Lusty thoughts about *her* mother.

Avrel feels sickened as she screams in reply, "Don't you dare talk about my mother that way, lecher!"

Murinae laughs. "You shouldn't talk to me so, after all, you lack your weapons!"

If the hate in her gaze were any stronger she'd not be surprised it became daggers launched to kill him. *Sorry Mother...* "To hell with the promise." she growls as she quickly quells the tingling in her fingers by shooting a fireball at him, she critically wounds the enormous marmot but Murinae jumps to safety.

"Oh ho ho..." he says with a chatter. "Is that how you wish to play this? Your feet will be my pleasure slaves and you with them when this is over!" the rat chuckles.

Avrel can feel every muscle tighten as angered, agitated arcane power aggressively floods into every cell, tingling not just her fingers, but her toes, her spine, and every stretch of her appendages, "What?" she growls, "Say that again, shaft-sucker!"

Geric is standing there counting on his fingers. "Hey wait a minute, I have an objection!" he says, ever the thinking egghead. "If you were thirteen when Avrel's mother was around, you can't be an old man!" he says, taking a strong posture while pointing to the rat.

"Well... I used magic to give myself an older appearance for my shows!" Murinae says, "Nobody trusts a young-looking wizard." he laughs hysterically.

Avrel taps Zanvan's quiver to remind him that the dumb rodent's only took the his sword. "Shoot the bastard!" she growls, barely suppressing the power gathering in her hands which feel like it could erupt at any second. "Argh, enough of this!" she shouts as she fires another ball of blazing red fire as Zanvan shoots at Murinae.

The rodent merely blocks both with the Aegis he hovers over himself. "Attack!" the rat-wizard yells.

Avrel and Geric quickly cast spells forcing the waves of rodents back, wounding some. "Ahahaha! Get them!" he rallys, "Bring me the cleric and the girl! Nip the others to death!" Murinae commands. Given the space, Zanvan dispatches all of the larger ones with his arrows, toppling Murinae's mount, giving her time to stand back and charge a spell. Avrel screams as she slings a large fireball into the largest group of marmots. Her aim is merely to scare them, but sadly it seems Zanvan isn't so considerate.

"You'd think Argoth's army would be deployed!" Avrel grunts giving in to the fact that some of the creatures must die if that rat is to also.

"I'm going to guess this just started!" Zanvan answers as he puts an arrow straight through one's head before it can tackle another building. At least he's not letting them suffer. "Besides…" he adds, "That doddering old fool would forget that they are charged to defend this place." he chuckles with a snark.

Avrel sees it another way, "That or those bastard Ar-Guards are too busy busting buskers to get off their shiny arses--!" She rolls to barely dodge the claw of one of the very giant ones when she notices something is missing, "Wait." she calls to the ranger, "Where's the rat and the shield?"

Zanvan snipes another, before glancing around, "Where's Geric?"

***

Through all the fire, chattering and chaos, Geric spies the Aegis slowly moving away from the fight, hovering but a few feet from the ground. He grabs a chunk of wood and runs after it until he catches it. He punches the shield over and sees the rat standing under it. "Running away!?" Geric says winding up a crushing blow with his makeshift club.

"Hahhhhh!!!" the rat screams as he throws a bolt of lighting at Geric.

"Arg!" Geric screams. "You stupid rodent-man! I should have squashed you when I had the chance!" But no, he had to be a cleric-like, he regrets as he tries to hold off the lightning with his own barrier magic.

"Yes." the pipsqueak agrees, tauntingly, "But you didn't, and at last I will avenge myself upon you!" he squeaks while intensifying his power. After the standoff of power goes on for several minutes, Geric begins to take the upper-hand as he not only bolsters his spell power, but recalls the words to the perfect counter shield for the varmit's lightning.

"Why marmots and vermin, you scum!?" Geric growls out exasperatedly, leaning down into the rat's space.

"When I came here looking for you, I found that you'd all gone on a silly escorting job..." he chirps, "It was perfect! All I had to do was wait and gather the army of my new kin! And *you* gave me the power to draw them to me! Hahahaha!!" he laughs cockily.

This only fuels Geric's conviction which empowers him to encroach more on the rat.

"No... **NO!!!**" the rat begins to panic, **"*I will not be beaten so! Please spare me! I only want some cheese!!*"** the tiny wizard screams as Geric manages to cup his reflection magic around him, wrapping him in his own lightning storm prison. After a few minutes, all the marmots throughout the city stop their riotous behavior, and disperse as if nothing was happening. Most scurry away towards the plains and the city quickly falls quiet.

After that, Avrel and Zanvan seem to finally notice Geric's epic fight off to the side as they finally rush to him. They arrive just as the tiny magic field with lighting inside slowly flickers out as a tiny rat lays there, his fur charred and his body exhausted.

"You got him!?" Avrel asks, darkly. Her voice is almost as uncharacteristically low as when she tried to beat up that Shad fellow-- in defense.

Geric stands upright, taking a victorious pose. "I guess so." he replies proudly.

"Hmph." Zanvan hums, "I'm surprised. you managed to win that fight using only your defensive cleric magic, I'm impressed." Zanvan comments, giving Geric a manly pat on the back.

Geric is sure to give Avrel a smirk, Zanvan's right and he knows it. *And* he's not some innate knife-ear either.

"Cough-Cough...Kill me." the rat says "I... Only found the will to go on with the drive for vengeance. You took that from me, and now I have nothing to live for so long as I'm trapped in this hideous toothy form..." the rat grumbles.

Avrel runs up and is about to stomp him when Geric catches her. "Let go!" she struggles as he lifts her into the air from under her shoulders. It's funny. "I'm gonna stomp that little bastard's brains out!"

She fails and grunts but can't get free, a veritable rodent to his own stature. "What? Really?..." he scoffs, "You'd stomp the little guy?"

"Hell yeah, I would!"

"Zanvan, hold her a second." he passes her over to Zanvan whom she struggles far less against, but still, he restrains her. It'd be very uncliclike, even for him, to allow her to curbstomp a defenseless rodent. Punch into the air he could understand, but stomping is for spiders, regular rats, and displeasing letters.

"Oh you son of a--!" she shouts.

He gives her a grin, "This is how the good people do!" he says, much to her torture as he pulls out a healing potion and pours it over the tiny half-cooked rat and then pulls out a book on hex reversal. He closes his eyes and chants an incantation as a soft light glows around the rat's body. Geric urges them all to stand back as Murinae's body turns into a glowing white shape that expands into the shape of a man. At last the light dies off and he leans up, looking hard at his own human legs for the first time in many months, with walled eyes that gradually focus inward.

"Oh... My!" he says standing up. "Thank you chiiiip- Umm nevermind. Thank you so much!" Avrel has broken free of Zanvan and is running towards him when Geric catches her.

"Let me at him!" she screams, only barely missing him with a few ill casted spells. Forced to look at him for more than an angry second, she blushes and looks away.

The former rat-man looks confused before he seems to realize that he is naked. "Oops..." he smiles in embarrassment. "Ummm... Well, I'd like to stay and show my appreciation for your mercy, but I think I'd best be going!" he says as he runs off grabbing a piece of debris to hold over his lower front.

"Hey wait!" Geric misses grabbing him, barely holding back the murderously intended she-elf. Zanvan doesn't get him either before he disappears into the dust clouds surrounding them in the vermin's wake.

Bob looks especially confused by the sudden appearance of the naked man, but then, it's been one of those days, Geric figures, one might and should expect anything. *There's plenty of confusion to go around!* Geric laughs to himself. Still, he's not sure about *not* going after that guy.

"Yer cern loork nerr Arvrerr." he says to Avrel. "Arvrerr?" he repeats.

"C'mon it was just a naked guy." Zanvan nudges her "It wasn't the first you ever saw, was it?" the ranger laughs.

Avrel says nothing and just stands there blushing with her hand over her mouth. "Was it?" Geric says getting into her space, he has to wonder, it must've been some shock to snap her from the bender she was on. He has a book with him if she's unclear on anything. "Well?"

Avrel staggers to reply. "He was... Kind of handsome..." she says as she blushes a bright crimson. Her cheeks practically match her hair.

"...What?"

***

"N-Nothing." Avrel gasps, shrugging off his staying hand. Bastard rat threatens not only herself, but mocking her mother; how dare they deprive her of rebuking that! *Idiots*.

"Hard isn't it?" Geric says, patronizingly as he carefully grabs the Aegis that had been left behind by the *former* rat wizard.

What the hell is wrong with me!? If she could, she'd slug herself for even thinking that, or even noticing. She swallows hard and purses her lips and tries to forget that she's done nothing to that bastard.

But damn, Zanvan sees through it too.

"What's wrong, Bob?" Avrel asks, trying to find something else to talk about and noticing his slightly aggravated demeanor.

"Erxcurs me, derd we jerst lert the mern wherr derstrorred thirs cirty gerr free!" Bob shouts.

"Well... Uh..." Geric stumbles trying to think of a response, "I mean..."

Just then a pretty young gnomish woman with two tiny children comes running out from the slightly settling dust, from a less ruined street.

"Heh ferther!" she cries holding her arms outstretched to Bob.

Bob stands and runs to her, "Derter!" he cries with the joy of seeing his family alive as he hugs her.

"Err Berberer... Werr... Er guerrs irts orkey." he sighs.

Avrel can't help but be jealous, but not of him, but the children. A father who shows love, a mother who is healthy, it's a sight, a sight she's not sure she's ever had.

"So... Bob." Geric speaks up, interrupting their hugs, and probably trying to cover his arse for not letting her execute the rat. "Seeing as though we're back in Manitäria, or what's left of it..."

Zanvan elbows him.

"Ner" Bob says, "Yer rerght!" He breaks from the hugging to shake hands with Avrel. "Er gerss thers erss gerd-ber?" he says. "Jerbs dern!" he adds excitedly.

"Yeah..." she guesses, trying to soften her glower for his sake.

"It seems so." Zanvan agrees.

"Do you need any help--" Avrel begins to say as Geric not so subtly makes a slashing motion across his throat, *Blast him.* "Any help? Your wagon is still-"

"Nerr!" he smiles while rubbing his son's hair, "Er'll ber firn!"

Damn. she nods, but she still feels a sense of relief and maybe even accomplishment, but maybe some sadness too, this journey is almost over.

"Heyr!" He says, tipping her chin up, "Keerp sturdererng yer margerk, yer quirt talernterd." he says to her before moving to Zanvan, "Herr, thernks fer guarrderng ther yournger werns, yeour'rr reallerr merd thirngs werk." he says with a handshake before moving to Geric. "Gererc... Yer arr a hieghterst arrshorr, but yer did yer jerb. Ernd, yer bert der werzard." the two look to share a mutual respect for their disdain for each other. Although she's not clear on *exactly* what was said, so she *knows* Geric isn't.

Bob stands back and gives the three a final farewell wave before walking away with his family.

Avrel is very solemn and quiet over his leaving, and can't help but feel uneasy. Maybe Geric only meant to not let her kill the helpless rat, not for Murinae to get away. She stops thinking about it, it'll only get her mad again.

Zanvan forcefully takes the Aegis from Geric with a taut tug and places it in a sack before strapping it to his pack. "Let's just keep this covered, hmm?" the ranger says rather insistently. "I don't know much, or if this is the real thing but I've heard some of the stories about this thing and it's not good." he says.

"The Aegis..." she mumbles. They have *both*.

"Yeah, yeah." Geric says casually, "I'll try to figure out if it's the real deal later." he yawns, with a stretch. "I don't know about you guys, but I'm beat. Let's see if that one inn with decently sized beds is still here."

"First we should go back and find our weapons." Zanvan reminds them.

"Oh, you're right!" Avrel gasps.

Geric feigns his incredible weakness, but follows them as she and Zanvan ignore his silent plea.

And it doesn't take too long anyway, Zanvan's ranger senses help them retrace their steps and within a few hours, they've collected their weapons, the city has settled down, and so they go in search of the inn. The inn is indeed there. A bit roughed up, but intact. Like a surprising amount of the city, it could be much worse.

They go inside, but she lingers a moment, she hopes Candice is alright back at the wagon. She assures herself and heads inside.

"Can we get some beds here?" Zanvan asks the frazzled gnome at the front desk.

"Werr shurr, bert we'rr herve terr charge arr prermiurm sirnce yerr urss morre berds. Wirth sorr merny perrples herms destrerd we're arr lirtter burser." she explains. Maybe the larger beds were destroyed?

Geric leans over her. "Why yes, we need extra beds." he says with a haughty air about him. Haughtier than usual. "Us *tall* warriors who -ahem- *defeated the rat wizard and his army* do need some beds."

"Errmergerd! Thert wers yerr!? Ehr plearrs sterr wirth urrs! Err irnsirst!" the hostess says taking them to some rooms without a moment's hesitation. Avrel finds that she can sleep on a single bed while Geric and Zanvan need a special room with several beds fit together. She'd thought they might relax with cards or something, but they are all exhausted, even though it's early afternoon they rest, enjoying their victory, and the near completion of their quest.

"Move kid." said the Ar-Guard, even as she tried to move her mother.

"Mother's been sleepy lately." the young half she-elf said as she pulled on her mother's lily white arm, mottled with bruises and dirt.

"Alright, lady!" the other Ar-Guard said impatiently, as he grabbed Mother's arm. "Must have a warm heart, Missy." he scoffed, "Cold hands." he commented as he tried to drag her out of the alley and into daylight just a building-corner away.

She fell over stiffly, but her eyes, which had been shut since she went to sleep a day before, fell open. But she was still stiff, and in the light she laid, stilly.

"Good Goddess!"

The smell...

Avrel throws herself out of the tiny bed with so little room to spare, only to remember that Candice waits elsewhere. "Dammit!" she barks to the darkness. "Goddess Dammit!" She fights for a moment, but her eyes finally force out their tears. *Left to rot... Abandoned...* The damn Ar-Guards, and even here they left it to fend for itself, left alone to die. She'll never forgive them. Damn them! All of them. Always there to heckle and harrass but never to help, plenty of money spent for their fancy capes but never so much as a blanket for a woman and her child. *Damn them!* At times like these she wishes she believed in higher powers and eternal fates, just so she could hope their likes would suffer.

She lies back in bed for sometime, thinking a message to Candice who is so close, but so far. But even after, she can't find sleep, her dream and her thoughts make her restless, so finally, she gets up. The guys are just across the hall, and she'd like a look at those relics. It might take her mind somewhere else.

She carefully and quietly makes her way across the room, through the door, and across the hall without so much as a squeak of the door. Between her elven eyes and the torches being used outside, there's plenty of light by which to look through the bags. That is, for the Runeblade, the Aegis stands out on it's own, at just less than two feet, she doesn't need to look hard for that.

The Runeblade is surprisingly plain, and in that plainess she realizes that she might have seen it on Shad's belt as a child and never known. She'd expected more of a sword, or sword hilt than what it is. It's ends look like some ancient copper or bronze alloy with amber and amethyst gems set into either end. It's very round and thicker than Zanvan's bastard sword handle, and lacks any sort of hand guard beyond a simple flanged area around the top after a slight choke. The tail end is tapered slightly and like a rounded off cone. She has to second guess herself as in the dimness as it almost looks a little phallic at first glance. Both sides of the bronzed tips are scarred and dented, with veins of damage running down them as if cracked and renewed many times over. The rest is some silvery metal; aged, pitted, chipped and notched, but not as much as the top but for a few deep gashes on the top side. The more silvery metal looks mildly oxidized, but considering its age, not very; just a bit dirty. She runs her hands along the ribs of the grip, they're barely present after however many thousands of years of wear and polish, but they feel comfortable in her hand even with the general thickness of the hilt. It's about two of her hands from palm to finger tips in length, maybe about a foot, and definitely to be used by a tall, elven warrior.

She sits it down and now takes the Everlasting Aegis from the sack it was shoved into, and suddenly she feels a chill in her, and over her. It's more than just a feeling, or an enchantment, it's the feeling of a dark malevolence. Across its face it looks like some sort of black glass or crystal bound into a pattern almost like muscle-meats, and through it are ruby red and sapphire blue veins and arteries. It's disgusting to look at, but strangely alluring as well. Fake or not, she could believe it was fashioned from the heart of an ancient monster's flesh. She looks along its back which even in the dark seems darker, as if no matter how dark the surrounding, it'd appear black, even in the deepest dungeon. She feels along it, along it's concave form until she comes upon the grips, which she gently fingers. Like the Runeblade, it's fashioned for a man's hand, not her own small digits, but she can grip it well enough.

And as her hand loosely is around the loop of crafted fleshly-glass, dark thoughts creep into her mind. They remind her that she's giving those relics over to these very same people. One of them, rightly hers by inheritance, not that she wishes anything to come of her relationship to him. But still, it should be hers. She has half a mind to take both, if the legends are true, she could easily make them pay.

Oh, how she'd like to.

Oh, but that she could.

Oh, but that these should come to her...

"Avrel!?" Geric says, his voice startling her into turning. "Is that rib bothering you? I--" he clamps his mouth suddenly, "Put that down!"

Suddenly Zanvan stirs and wakes up. "What's wrong!?" he says alertly as his eyes quickly find hers.

But suddenly, she feels tired, drained almost as her vision dims. The guys are saying something to her, but it's incoherent and distant, and muddied as if she were under water or something.

All of which fades away as Geric yanks the massive shield from her grasp. "Seriously, what are you doin!?" he asks, as if he's been going on for some time already.

Her senses return, as sharp as ever but for the darkness of the night. "I'm sorry I--"

"Geric!" Zanvan says, warningly as Geric drops the Aegis with a disgusted mumble.

"I don't like things that move!" he says, "Shields shouldn't move on their own." he shivers.

And without asking, both Zanvan and Geric begin feeling her head. "You alright?" Zanvan asks, waving his hand over her eyes, "You got all glazed there for a second."

She tries to recount everything but already it's fading like a dream. "I--... she mutters, unconvincingly.

Geric grips it as if it were covered in refuse and put it back into the sack and ties it off. "If it's a fake, it's a damned good one." he comments, rushing to the bedside washbowl and rinsing his hands. "What were you looking for?" he demands.

And now, she barely remembers. "I'm sorry..." though she's not sure what for.

Zanvan taps her head, "Listen, if you wanted a look, you could just ask." he says, "But just in case this thing is all it's cracked up to be, maybe wait until daylight, hm?"

Geric wipes his hands on his pants, "Mm*Yeah*." he comes up beside her a minute and looks hard into her eyes, "You just wanted your potion, right?" he smiles.

It'd been the last thing on her mind, but she goes with it. "Yeah." she says, "I didn't mean to cause a ruckus."

Geric rifles through his bag and hands a vial to her, "Should be your last dose, give or take how you feel." he says.

She smiles, "Okay."

'Run along now.' Zanvan's look says, and so she does.

"Sleep tight!" she hears Geric say as she shuts the door and heads for her bed.

As she shuts her own she hears another groggy voice in the inn reprimand him. She lies down, and this time, sleep takes her.

13

    The following morning they enjoy a hot meal together. They don't bring up the night before, so neither does she. Almost as if they're choosing to ignore it entirely, they don't even mention looking at or anything about the Aegis.

    Instead, Geric tells an interesting story of the very morning this journey began, and how he knows of Murinae.

    "So let me get this straight…" she asks, finding parts a little far fetched. "You were hiding under a table when you met him?"

    "Yup!" Geric laughs. "It tried to steal my bacon, so I punched him into the air where he was grabbed by a falcon."

    "And somehow…" The ranger tips up his hat, "The falcon was heading north, got eaten by a larger bird, then got eaten by a small dragon?" he also says in disbelief.

    "I mean, it sounds far fetched." the cleric agrees, "But the Everlasting Aegis was supposedly up in the Northern Chasm, I suppose that a dragon *could* have killed a guy who tried to recover it." he says thoughtfully.

    "Hey." Avrel says pointing at the two men with her fork. "Bottom line, he saved us *a lot* of time."

    They both nod.

    Geric loudly crunches a piece of bacon. "Hey, when we get back to Argoth, you should probably get some new clothes." he says as he chews.

    "Yeah, I know." Avrel smiles, somberly. Her blouse was so pretty when it was new, but it is getting pretty raggedy… Also, Geric's silly hat. "I'll get you a new hat if you'd like."

    "Sounds good!" Geric replies. "I'll hold you to that."

    She guessed him right, and it makes her smile. She'd be happy to buy his elitist arse somthing to wear with all the shite he gave her back when they met. It'll show him.

    "Well." Zanvan says as he finishes his food, "We should hurry back to Argoth, you guys done?"

    Geric is, but Avrel isn't, and she isn't one to rush to eat, even when she was literally starving.

    "I'm sure Candice is waiting." Geric says as he leans in.

    She nods, it's enough motivation to get her to shovel down the porridge.

    Zanvan laughs as he stands, "Good call, Geric." he pats. "Stay with her, make sure she doesn't choke. I'll get our things."

    ***

He watches her eat, until Zanvan returns and hands him his bag. Only then is she actually finished. It's no wonder she's so small, she probably burns off the food by the time she's done eating it. But with their packs gathered and the meal over, the group leaves a tip and heads out into the dilapidated streets of Manitäria.

As he looks around, Geric gets a sour feeling in his stomach. "We shouldn't have let him go." he says with an uncomfortable smile.

"It'll be fine." Avrel assures him in a dark and grim tone. Obviously she still feels pretty strongly about the ordeal.

"Didn't he threaten to sexually assault your feet?" Zanvan says coldly, but noting something Geric recalls as well, and that she needn't, not with that temper of hers.

Avrel closes her eyes and intensely shutters before reopening her eyes. "Yeah... Moving on." she says with disgust, and just a brief death glare at Geric. He's gotten worse though.

The ranger pulls out his map for the first time in quite a while, "We might be able to take a ferry across the Argothian River and just cut straight west." Zanvan says, thinking out loud as he scans the map.

"That sounds good." the half-elf chirps. "We won't have to go through that forest again." she says delightfully.

And he agrees, that forest was a bit of a hurdle. "Wait, why didn't we take this ferry to get here the first time?" Geric says with aggravation.

"Remember that storm?" Zanvan asks, but Geric doesn't, "We would have been mixed up in all of that, besides the destination was that trading post, not here." Zanvan says as he lights up his pipe.

"There could have been information there too!" Geric whines. "There was one stop!"

"Not as likely." Zanvan quickly replies as he pulls out an old map of the area. "I'd wager that that trading post has more ears and mouths relaying rumors than a ferry."

"*Nananamnana*-not as likely *my arse*." Geric mumbles to himself.

"Alright so..." Zanvan says, ignoring him and putting the map away. "Let's see what provisions we can find here and then we'll head for the northwest of the city and make our way towards the river." The three look around at the desolated city, all seeming that they reach the same conclusion. "On second thought, we can forage on our way. Let's go." Zanvan says with consideration.

"Hey wait! I have to call Candice." Avrel says with urgency.

"Well call her then, we should hurry back to Argoth." Zanvan sighs.

Geric leans into Zanvan's space. "Shush! We should just leave it!" he mumbles.

Zanvan brushes him off and looks to Avrel. "Find her and meet us at the northwest gate."

"Sure thing." Avrel replies.

Zanvan makes heads of straight away, but Geric turns back to watch as Avrel finds a quiet alley and takes her meditative pose, calling to her ratty familiar. She sure loves that stupid thing

***

Outside of Manitäria, her patient waiting is disturbed as Bob comes, she guesses he's retrieving his wagon. She stretches and gives her jowls a good flap as she greets him with a smile.

"Err... Ther berver." he says, "Herro."

"Chippu" Candice replies. He's so nice, especially to Avrel, she feels a little guilty for what she took for a snack, but she's sure he'll understand. "Chippu?" she calls to him, but just then, Candice hears the call of her master and wastes no time. She limbers up and heads for the city. Bob smiles as she passes him as he comes around back.

"Hermm... Lerks gerd..." she hears him comment. "Wert, irs thirs cert lorwer? ERR!!! Der bever ert mer wheerls!" she hears him yell in frustration as she speeds away.

He'll be alright.

***

Soon Avrel is greeted in her quiet alley by Candice. Strangely it's almost as if her vision had drifted from herself, and as her eyes open it's a little jarring.

"Chippu?" Candice asks.

Avrel rubs her eyes, "Yeah, I'm fine." she smiles before giving the beaver a hug and kiss on her nose. "I'll fill you in on what happened, we need to find the guys."

Candice looks around and warbles a bit, apparently only now taking note of the damage. "Chippu?" she asks.

"Actually, yes.' Avrel answers. "And it's probably good you weren't here." Avrel somberly giggles.

Avrel recounts their adventure in the city to Candice as best she can, omitting any outright deaths of the marmots at her hand. It works out that she's wrapping up just as they catch up to the men.

And Geric has taken some time to play keep-away with one of the gnome's hats. "Oh Avrel!" he says almost immediately dropping the hat to the gnome below. She watches as the gnome gives him a sturdy kick to the shin, but given the loose, ballooned nature of Geric's attire, it strikes very shallowly.

"I swear," Zanvan sighs, ashamed of his companion as is she, "They aren't going to let you back in this city."

"Eh." Geric creaks as he shrugs, "It's a shite city, especially now that it's all ruined." he grins gleefully.

"Chippu." Candice says, Avrel's sentiments exactly.

"'Scuse me?" Geric chides.

"I agree." Avrel says to her familiar, while making eyes at Geric, coyly.

"Hey now!" he shouts, but Avrel, Candice, and Zanvan hurry on for some distance, pretending not to know him.

She follows as Zanvan leads the way to the northwest corner of the city and begins following the river until late that afternoon. Slicing against the orange reflections on the water, a small building and pier can be seen in the distance.

"Is that it?" Avrel asks Zanvan.

"Yeah." he answers. "But that one is heading towards the western shore, they probably won't come back until morning."

"Camp time it is then!" Geric says, throwing down his packs and rummaging through them until he finds a pot.

Zanvan puts his packs down. "I'll get some wood from that grove over there." he says.

Avrel sets down her pack as well and looks around. "I'll see if I can find any edible roots or herbs." she offers.

"Listen elf." Geric scoffs, "I barely trust what Zanvan tries to feed us."

"Let her try." Zanvan says. "I'll look it over."

She's actually a little encouraged by his confidence in her, at least that's what she hopes it is. Either way, it gives her something to smile about as she heads away from the camp to look high and low for some sort of fruit or vegetation to bring back to them. Finally, after a few minutes, she finds a few mushrooms. Although she's not sure if they are edible, they look like the ones Zanvan would sometimes gather, so she takes them. She also comes by what she's almost sure is wild asparagus not long after that. She doesn't see much else, but she's satisfied with her haul so she stuffs them in a pouch and starts heading back to camp.

As she comes out of the clearing she notices the bright, full moon begins to ascend over the horizon. She caresses her cold arms and bathes in the silver light.

***

"Hey!" Geric calls as Avrel comes into sight. Well, a moonlit silhouette of her boney form anyway. "Avrel, if you've got stuff to cook hurry up!" he shouts. The bonfire is all started, and she's just dazed out across the field. And despite those ears of hers, she acts like she doesn't hear him, she just dances and frolics playfully in the field. "What the hell, Avrel, you-" Geric is cut off by Zanvan with a light hit to the chest. "What the hell is she doing?" he asks with perplexion.

"Elves do stuff like that." Zanvan comments as he throws another piece of wood on the fire. "I think."

He might have guessed that… "But why? She's not even an elf, she's some freaky mixed thing. Most of those elves hated her!" Geric remarks.

"I suppose." Zanvan contemplates. "But what matters is that *she* identifies as an elf. At least at this moment." he chuckles, "You can't blame her, she's got the ears and the eyes, and the impressive magical talent."

"I guess?" he concedes, partially, "I don't see why she has to dance like a fool though." Geric sighs.

"I think it's cute that she tries to accept her instincts like that." Zanvan chuckles.

He's seen more grace, Zanvan certainly has. "Well, I think she looks like an idiot." Geric says, rolling his eyes. "Ouch!" Geric yelps as Candice slaps his hand with her tail before running out to her master. "Should've cooked that varmit for supper!" he growls.

***

The moonlight is like cold breath tickling the tiny hairs of her skin, and yet sinking deep to build up a glowing warmth. Last moon she was in no mood or condition, but for now, she can. It doesn't take the cares away, it doesn't whisk away her dreads, her insecurity, her fears, her angers, her hates, her impossible desires; but still, she finds peace. She dances to a music in her soul across the grasses of the field, ignoring distant calls, and hearing only the music of the moon, and of nature. The nocturne life, the gentle breeze shaking the moonlit grasses into waves of molten silver, it's hers, and she is its. For maybe she *is* elf, and thus, it truly is part of her. This world, this 'Jahoroth' is in her blood. And in that blood; bliss.

"Chippu!" cuts suddenly as the warm, euphoric wash fades to the empty field, and to a bonfire, and to a beaver at her feet.

Avrel stoops down to greet her beaver and notices Geric and Zanvan staring at her from the fireside. She can feel herself flush and she quickly scurries towards them with the acquired food.

"I'm sorry I kept you waiting!" she frets.

Geric opens his mouth wide as if he's about to say something but Zanvan cuts him off. "It's fine." the ranger says, "What did you find?" he asks as Avrel hands him the pouch. He looks through, inspecting the mushrooms closely. "Not bad." he comments as he hands the contents to Geric to begin stewing.

During their meal Avrel has little to say, instead she stews in her thoughts, self consciously. And also having to wonder and fear of any undue enticement she might have given out. Good as Zanvan's been, she recalls his comments about dancing in the rain. But even so, she has to remember that Geric is a man too.

"Hey Avrel." Zanvan asks, sounding as if he's repeated himself already.

"Oh." she answers, "Yeah?"

"What are you going to spend your reward on?" he asks, just another reminder that this journey is coming to its end.

"Some clothes." is at the top of her immediate list. "A place to live... I'm not sure. My mother always wanted to live outside the city near the river..." And after seeing Järviby, she does too, but that conflicts with her other plans. "But I dunno. I like doing my little shows and stuff." She won't bother explaining it all to them.

Geric raises his finger as he swallows a gulp of water, "You could always buy a nice traveling performers wagon." he interjects.

It's a thought, "I don't know, Candice would love the water though." Avrel fantasizes, caught between her dreams of grandeur and her dreams of nature and beauty. "What are you gonna do with yours?" Avrel asks Geric, dodging having to rehash those debates in her head. "Wait!" she says putting a hand out, "Wait, don't tell me-- You'll seed a new chapel!" she laughs. She can't help it, for once she's out Geric'd Geric, and it's hilarious.

To her, anyway. Geric himself shrugs it off, "Actually..." he says, chidingly, "There was this awesome book all about wizardry and old time magic in a fancy book shoppe in Argoth!" he answers with feverish excitement. "I've wanted it for years but it costs far too much due to its rarity." Geric replies.

"Hey that sounds neat." Avrel smiles. "You'll have to read some to me."

"And give away my best chance to supersede your innate shite?" he gasps, "Hell no." he says with a playful nudge. "Zanvan?" Geric asks.

He tips his hat and grins, "I don't know. I don't need a place to live or anything like that, I pretty much can sustain myself indefinitely as long as I have my wits." Zanvan says confidently.

Avrel tries to get him outside of his persona, "Oh come on, you have to have *something* you'd like to buy." she says as she smiles at him.

"He probably is just gonna save it in case he has any paternity suits." Geric laughs.

Zanvan rolls his eyes. "Yeah-no." he grunts.

"You could get a nice elven bow." Avrel thinks out loud.

"This *is* an elven bow." he replies sharply.

"You could…" she almost finds herself envious of his self sufficiency. He has nothing, hardly, but he also needs nothing. She actually draws a blank. He's so damned self sufficient he doesn't seem like he could *need* anything. "…Settle down and have a nice *monogamous* relationship with some nice lady." Avrel giggles, only half serious. Like hell he'd be tied down.

"That'd be the day!" Geric says as he leans into Zanvan's space. "Once a wolf, always a wolf, am I not right?" Zanvan puts his palm over Geric's face and pushes him away.

They settle down as they wait for the food to cook. After a while of watching it bubble, Zanvan tips his hat up and turns to Avrel. "So." he says, "These little 'shows' of yours, besides magic did you dance? Sing or?"

"I'm not dancing for you." she puts down swiftly. "I'm not much to sing either."

"I see." he says as he settles back down. "I only asked because in all this time, I'm surprised none of you have suggested a campfire song." he snarks.

Geric clears his throat.

"*Up Cordol to Her peak Castel he did ride.*
No vision hath he, but still sought for Her light!
For no one should see Her, Her light struck thee blind.
But to he who doth found Her, She saith be ever mine."

She'd never heard Geric so much as hum, much less *hymn*. "That was…" she tries to think of a word, "Rousing." she gulps.

"Well, what have you, Miss Show-Business?" he nudges.

What *does* she know? She hasn't much experience with songs or music as setting too close to another performer is bad business.

"*Oh daughter can I say to you how lucky am I?*
To brave this dark world with you by my side.
To have and to see you with each passing day?
Love her, and cherish her, oh fates I do pray."

Geric and Zanvan seem as uneasy by her song as she and the ranger by Geric's. "That was a lullaby, I take it?" Geric ask, squeamishly.

She nods. "It was." She and Geric both turn to Zanvan. "Well?"

Before he can say anything, Geric puts in his thoughts, "I doubt we'd want to hear him, Avrel." he smirks, "Between the smoking and the whores' diseases rotting his throat, I doubt he can carry a tune." he laughs as he begins ladling out some of the stew.

Zanvan shakes his hand, evenly. He doesn't deny it, hopefully only acknowledging the *smoking* part. They go about dishing out the food when suddenly, Zanvan clears his throat, raspily.

> "*Ninety-nine mugs of ale on the wall,*
> *Ninety-nine mugs of ale-*"

To her surprise, Geric joins in.

> "*Take one down,*
> *Pass it around,*
> *Now we've got ninety-eight mugs of ale on the wall!*
> *Ninety-eight mugs of ale!*"

By now, she can get the idea of how the song works and joins in, between spoonfuls of supper that is.

"*...And now we've got no more mugs of-- Ale. On. The. Wall!*" Geric and Zanvan sing loudly as they raise their empty bowls. She does too, admittedly stunted and getting lost in the numbers. She barely even knows the lower ones going *forwards*.

"We should probably get some sleep, the ferry crossing is probably at dawn." Zanvan says as he rolls out his sleeping mat.

"I suppose." Geric says, nodding in agreement.

"Yeah." Avrel sighs, she's had a slight tinge of a headache since Manitäria, she'd say it was probably all of the smoke, but this is the sides of her head. And it shouldn't be in relation to her time yet either. *Maybe tonight will sleep it off.* she hopes.

And she hopes she can find rest in that sleep.

"*Mom!*" she gasps as she throws herself erect. Her heart pounding, palms sweating and hair matting with the beads of cold sweat on the back of her neck. It's just barely the first lighting of dawn, she notes as she scans around and tries to catch her breath. She moves the hand clutching her chest up and brushes her face before resting in it, "Dammit..." she mutters.

"You okay?" she turns further around to see Zanvan already smoking his pipe, seated on an old tree stump.

"Yeah..." she sighs, "She's been on my mind since..." Since Järviby, since she saw her other parent die. "Nevermind."

He shakes out his pipe, "Well, it's about time to go anyway." he says as he scoots off the stump. "Come on, *Doctor.*" he says with a strange tone.

Geric takes his time, but once he's up they promptly pack up their things and head towards the small building near the pier. It's still a little misty, but clear enough. Not needing the ferry, Candice is already enjoying her swim across the water. And soon enough they are at the little shack right as the ferryman has come out of the shack on the western shore. Both shacks look identical, it's as if he's made a perfect twin of his modest home. Avrel tries to get a good look inside of the eastern shore's shack and compares it to what she can see through the window in the other. It's damn close.

"He' thar!" the waterman greets them from across the river, once he notices them.

"Hello!" Zanvan yells in reply. "We'd like to pass through!" Geric doesn't seem too happy with the high volume, this early, she can't blame him either.

The waterman nods, "Sure theng! Ten pieces each feh enough!?" the waterman asks.

"Sure!" Zanvan replies.

"Hey wait!" Geric interjects, groggily. "This girl here, she shouldn't count, she doesn't weigh very much!"

"Ehhhh..." the waterman stalls.

"Never mind him." Zanvan shouts back.

"He's kind of an idiot!" Avrel shouts jocularly.

Geric and Avrel exchange friendly leers. Maybe, just maybe after last night, she's come to a bit of an understanding with him. He seems to be able to take the sardonic shite he deals, so why not?

"E'll beh right ov'r!" the man replies, grabbing his paddle.

"You'd have done better trying to pass her as a child" Zanvan jokes, placing a hand on her shoulder as he steps back. "Might have gotten a discount *that* way."

Really? "Not *you* too!" Avrel fumes, only half seriously.

Geric laughs bombastically, but the banter fades from there as they wait.

After a few minutes the ferryman reaches their side and welcomes them aboard the vessel. "Yer water weasel just gonna swim, eh?" he says looking towards Candice who is swimming around the flatboat.

"Yes, I suppose." Avrel giggles. She'd have sworn she'd gone to the other side already. *Must've come back.*

They debark and after a few minutes Avrel becomes curious, he, after all, lives on the water and seems to enjoy it. It seems like a quiet and peaceful life.

"So... Why do you run this ferry, mister..?" she asks, not knowing his name.

"Barnabas." he answers. "I used to work as a fisherman in the Great Sea but eventually eh got too old, so I retired to me little shacks an' make my wage on passage." the old waterman explains happily.

"So you were a seaman?" she asks. She's never seen the ocean on the other side of Cordol, she can't imagine its beauty. Sailors, she's heard, are a rough sort, as such, she's never gone out of her way to meet any, even among men they have a reputation, but he seems friendly enough. "I'd love to hear a story if you have any." Avrel asks warmly, excitedly even. Geric and Zanvan both look annoyed by her request, but they'll just have to deal with it.

"Well Eh tell ye, one time oh say, thirty years back I..." The old waterman spins a whimsical story during their crossing until finally they near the western shore. What she'd hoped for, a story of the beauty of the ocean and the adventures to be had there is dashed by a rotten yarn of filth, drunkenness, abuse, and perversity between men. *Now* she knows how those relationships work, but really, she wishes she didn't. "So anyway, that's how Collins died, caught bottom rot from Phil. And as I've said since, eh proper seaman loves the booty, not en the booty!" the old waterman says slapping his knee and laughing hysterically.

Avrel tries to fake a smile and laugh along with him as best as she can. She'd never exactly known how those who'd pair up acted on each other, and she never really wanted to. Now that she does, it does make sense to the character of their carnal and injurious desires. *Men...* she thinks to herself, her teeth gritted in disgust. Though to be fair, Zanvan and Geric aren't the most lively either, but then one's some sort of want-to-be holy man, and the other a consummate bedswerver. "... Wow! That... sure is a story!" she says, "Thank you... *very very* much for sharing that with me." she adds, forcing a smile.

Zanvan and Geric just shake their heads in disappointment. They tried to warn her, it was her mistake, and she sees it now. As she tries to get some pictures out of her head, she notices that they are at the other side, and not soon enough.

"Yep, ol' Barnabas will getcha across." he smiles as Zanvan pays him his fee. "Ye all take care now."

She and Zanvan disembark from the tiny, flat, square vessel but Geric stays behind for a moment. He holds out at least twenty more pieces and offers them to the old waterman.

"Please." he begs, "*Never tell that story again.*" the cleric says as he hands the coins to the old man.

"Heh?" the old man grunts in confusion as Geric quickly runs off to catch up with the others. "It's a good story." he sighs.

Avrel disagrees, and as Candice joince her she lets out a chatter of her own. "No." Avrel answers, "I don't have any questions about *that*." she giggles.

***

Even with all the time saved by taking that ferry, Geric grows impatient, he wants to get back to Argoth. Years he's wanted that book, and soon with just the simple exchange of their procured treasure the funds shall be his. Just as soon as they are there. "Are we there yet?" he whines.

The ranger glances back at him. "Riding in that wagon made you soft." Zanvan says with a smirk.

"Shut up!" Geric says defensively. A better question is why haven't they rented a wagon or horses for themselves.

Zanvan points straight ahead,"We should be able to see Argoth in a few hours." he explains.

"You guys wanna stop for some lunch first?" Avrel says weakly.

Geric quickly agrees while Zanvan does, albeit reluctantly. "I thought you were in a hurry." Zanvan scoffs at him.

"Well…" he grins, "If it's only a few more hours, why not?"

They've gotten good at setting up a modest camp quickly, cleaning up still always takes a bit. Usually deciding whose turn it is takes half the time. It's his, but hopefully nobody else remembers that.

"Who'd have thought we'd actually find the relics?" Avrel smiles as they dish out some leftover stew.

Her question comes out of the blue, but it's crossed his mind too. "Serious question though." Geric asks, chewing his food. "Why the hell did your father even have that weapon?"

She looks like she hasn't thought of that much at all, or, maybe she *has*. "I… I really don't know." she answers. "The point is that we found that he had it before Nerfendor's guys did." Avrel says happily.

"Surprising that we never came across anybody else looking for them." Zanvan contemplates. "If what Lethia said was true, I'd have thought we'd stumble across some adversaries."

"Rat wizard?" Geric retorts.

"Or maybe…" Avrel suggests. "The rumors they heard were false and the orcs *aren't* looking to fight."

"Could be." Zanvan agree, finishing his bowl and lighting his pipe.

"It's funny." the little half-elf says as she puts down her empty bowl. "Now that I know what the Runeblade looks like, I wonder if I ever saw it and never knew."

"What I think is hilarious…" Geric grins, "Is how that one dufus in the red kept asking about your elven connection!" he laughs out loud, "If we'd followed his advice, we'd have gone straight there."

"I mean…" Avrel frys with that pout of hers, "We still *kind of* did…"

That's true, he supposes. Geric quickly finishes up his bowl, he can't have Avrel beat him, and Zanvan looks ready to go. "Don't forget." he says with a plumey puff, "It's your turn to--"

"Yeah, yeah…"

In the wee small hours of the morning they pass the very fountain they all met at the morning they left for their journey. Aside from a few lamps, it's still black out under the waning moon.

"Hey look… the fountain…" Avrel fries out. "You know, I used to bathe in there at night when nobody was around…" she says to Geric.

"That's… great…" he replies. He's taken drinks from there, he won't again. Zanvan is somberly silent and doesn't say anything, he just leads them to an inn and they stay there. At long last, they are back in Argoth.

14

After a few hours of sleep, Avrel wakes up, her dreams are not leaving her alone and she's feeling restless. She tosses a few times, but decides in short order to go outside for a walk. She dresses, not too wary of her comrades' eyes as they're still sleeping soundly in their beds. Lucky them.

It's still dark as she takes a walk about the city, around the inn, and to her old hang outs. *Nothing much has changed in these few months.* she sighs. It's the same Argoth, the same city she hates, yet is at peace to come home too, fickly enough. Argoth however feels smaller; and it's a strange contrast from the feeling of discovery that there was more of a world than this, as now that she's back, it's suddenly less than the whole world to her, and it's all the more striking.

As she strolls through the back alleys, *her* back alleys, through the trash and rubbish, her eyes catch the familiar glow from up above. The sun has risen over the mountain, and dawn breaks hardly, and suddenly. She hadn't realized how so until experiencing dawns further from the mountain ridge, though even Rudaski wasn't as pronounced. She pauses a minute to figure what day it is, certainly in the middle of the week. She counts from Rudaski as best as she can, frustratingly losing her guestimate several times, but all signs point to midweek, maybe Treesday or Watersday. Starsday at the latest, not that it matters much anyway.

She finds her way to a profitable back alley, not far from some row houses that opens to a small court. She's *missed* it, strangely enough. Maybe not the Ar-Guards forcing her out, or offering not to do so while taking advantage of their hold of her, by how and where they hold onto her, but for other reasons. And a few of them are shuffling by now, looking to play the game of the day.

"Hey! Miss Avrel?" one yells from across an alley. "Is that you?" Avrel waves and the kids quickly crowd around her, asking all at once where she's been. She's surprised they're up and at play this early, but it's been a while since she's been used to the sun staying hidden for so long into the day.

She stoops down a little, not by much, to meet them at their level, "I was traveling with some..." She pauses as a smile interrupts her, "Friends."

"Neet!"

"Where?"

"Do a trick!"

"What are those things on your thighs?" one asks as she pats her leg armor.

"Learn any new magics?!"

Avrel smiles. She has, mostly for combat, but that's not to say that's the only way those spells might be used. "Okay, hold on." she giggles, "Settle down and I'll show you a trick." she says putting on a husky stage voice. She's out of practice.

"Yay!" the children cheer before they sit down.

Avrel pulls her weather gem out of her gem pouch and focuses hard on it while dancing around her staff that she has stuck firmly into the ground. After a few seconds, a small cloud begins to coalesce in a ring around the staff. The storm is her anxiety, and her lingering dream visiting so often to jar her from her restful slumber, and as her dance becomes more and more intense, the cloud darkens until finally it strikes the pole. Avrel pulls some of the lightning out and creates a purple ball of light that floats in her hands, copying what Geric had done to the rat. She shows this to her audience and the children are all in awe. Seeing their faces fades the pain, as well as the spell.

"Kids?!" a shrill woman's voice is heard in the distance. "Get in here and eat your breakfast!"

"Oops! We should go!" one child says as he scurries off, then the lot of them follow. Avrel smiles and waves them all goodbye just in time as her stomach audibly growls.

"Heh..." she giggles to herself "I should get some breakfast too."

She heads to a morning market she'd only dared to look at from afar in the past and buys some salted pork, corn bread, and some fresh tea. While admittedly, she's still very thin, maybe a little dirty, pekid, could use some new clothes, it's a world apart from the crossed looks she'd find herself under before. And once she holds up her coin purse, any questioning looks from the salespersons fade. She has it all put in a basket and heads back towards the inn, all the while the ranger's words from so many months back ring in her ears. It makes her happy and she finds a bounce in her step, she can be equal, she can even be *dominant* if she chooses. If she can match that cleric's magic *now*, she could find herself unstoppable for other jobs like this, or in other ways.

Avrel finds Zanvan outside leaning against the inn's wall, smoking. "Hey, where did you run off to?" he asks, nearly as soon as he seems to notice her.

"I wanted to take a walk, I woke up early. Oh!" she holds out the basket. "I got us breakfast!"

"Ah." he puffs, smokily "Nice."

Geric comes running out of the inn, followed by Candice. "Food, you brought food?" he pants.

"Yup!" Avrel says cheerily. She thought they'd appreciate it as she vaguely recalls the innkeeper telling them it wouldn't be offered to them on such late notice.

She hands out everyone's portions, and she likes it. She *really* likes it. Besides the feeling of making her friends happy, it's empowering. She's not begging, she's at liberty to *give*. After Geric takes his, she smirks, *Or not.* she reminds herself, not necessarily in his case, but for other uppity, elitists who've scorned her that are not unlike him.

"Chippu?" Candice squeaks as she rubs up against Avrel's leg.

"I didn't forget you." Avrel smiles as she hands Candice a slice of cornbread. After they eat they get to thinking, she does anyway. "So how are we gonna find Lethia?" Avrel thinks aloud.

"Best bet would be to ask the guy at the bar we were in." Zanvan suggests. "Argothian Guards all have their watering holes of choice, it can't have been her first time in that one.

"Yeah, let's try that." Avrel says with a nod.

"And if it was?" Geric challenges.

Zanvan turns, "Then word will get around." he says coolly. "That having been said..." he adds, "I wouldn't advertise yet that we're in possession of the relics."

"MmmYeah..." Geric agrees, "We'll have some researcher on our arses about it belonging in a museum." he scoffs, "Saw enough of that in the monastery-- Every little chip of arcane crystal, every crest, every relic of the Genesis Wars, they try to snatch up." he chides, "Never mind that using them as intended might *help* people."

Avrel puts a pat of tea into her cup, and heats it with a spell until it's brewed. "Yeah." she agrees as she takes a sip. *Not unlike how some people hoard their money.* she snickers to herself.

Having never done anything remotely resembling this sort of 'typical' paid work, Avrel feels a very strange aura of happiness as they return to the seedy bar where it all began. She'd entered afraid and simply wishing to hide, now, she knows better how to handle herself. She might even stand up to the next Ar-Guard that tries to chase her down over nothing.

"Hey! You!" they hear from across the room, snapping her from her thoughts, "Get that varmit out of here!" the man yells.

Just like so many other bars around Argoth... And, she'd almost forgotten Candice wasn't with them last time. "Wait outside Candice." Avrel says softly.

"Chippu..." Candice replies as she waddles to the doorway. She watches disappointedly as Candice goes, but as she turns back to the bar, Zanvan has already approached the man. She hurries to join in.

"Hey, do any Royal Guards ever come in here?" Zanvan asks.

The bartender gives the three of them a look, "Who wants to know?" he asks, defiantly.

Zanvan's voice turns more aggressive, "We're looking for a woman named Lethia, we met her in here and-"

"Ahh! Are you Zanvan?" the man asks, "And you're Avrel and Geric?" he says just a little loudly, best they *didn't* mention what they had. "Yeah, she shows up once in a while asking for yous. Been in here once a day the last week or so, seemed to be getting impatient."

"Good." Zanvan says coldly. "We'll get a table and wait, send a server over if you don't mind."

"Yeah, sure." the bartender replies. "Stay as long as you want, just order something, I ain't running no social hall."

They wait there for the better part of the day. Between games of cards, Avrel checks on Candice, they get lunch there, and she's reminded how awful the ale was, and still is. As time drags on, she's about to suggest that they leave the address for the inn with the bartender, but just then she hears a clanking sound like armor. Then, the others do too. Lethia, the woman knight, comes in and is directed by the bartender to their table, where they are already waiting.

"Good to see you." she says strongly. "I'd hoped you'd have gotten in touch sooner, with no word I began to worry."

"Well, what can we say we were busy." Zanvan says, puffing his pipe, and seeming to want to take the lead as he often does

"Yes, well let's go outside I'd be interested in hearing about your--" the woman knight interrupts herself, "I see Rufus is no more."

"Who?" Geric asks, looking confused.

"Rufus, the Redshirt." the woman knight, Avrel, and Zanvan all at once say to Geric.

Geric shrugs his shoulders and stares at them blankly.

"You *took* his *hat*?" Avrel says with a tone.

"*Oh*, that loser." he scoffs with a shitey grin, "Mauled by kobolds, such a shite end, only *idiots* could die from an encounter like that." he laughs.

"Uh-huh…" the woman knight responds coldly, "Let's go outside, if you all don't mind." Avrel and Geric follow Zanvan's lead, and he seems not to mind, so they all stand. "Bartender, put this on my tab!" she shouts in her grizzly voice.

They head out and are greeted by Candice's toothy smile as she follows them as they follow the knight. They continue to an empty alley where they can talk privately.

"So, what did you find out?" the woman knight commands, looking around very secretively.

"Not just find out, *find*..." Zanvan says unpacking the Aegis and the Runeblade from his and Geric's packs.

"By The Beast..." she gulps, "*You actually **found** them?!*" she gasps in disbelief, briefly losing her composure.

Avrel smiles, "Yes Ma'am." she says proudly.

"So uh..." Geric says gently running his thumb over his middle and index fingers.

"Oh yes, your pay." she says as she grabs four reasonably large sacks of coins and hands them to them. "Right..." she says, "Rufus is no more." the woman knight mumbles. She looks at the group and thinks for a moment, then her eyes fall on Candice of all people. "Is this... your pet?" she asks, turning to Avrel.

'Candice is my familiar." Avrel replies courteously. "My friend."

"So she's... intelligent?" the knight continues, "And part of your group?"

"Yes Ma'am." Avrel replies again, and notices Geric beginning to sweat as the woman knight bends down with the bag of coins.

"Oh--" he grunts, "Oh no you don't! **NO!**" Geric says adamantly.

"You take exception to this?" the knight barks at him, in a deep snarl.

"I do!" Geric yells insolently. "I refuse to let you pay that bloody beaver!"

"Anyone *else* you think should get this money?" the woman knight says testily.

"...Bob Ethens." Zanvan interjects, putting a staying hand on both Avrel and Geric as they were both about to speak. "He's a merchant in Manitäria."

"Fine." the knight says with finality. "I'll split it one-quarter to three with this beaver and that gnome."

"But!" Geric objects as he watches in horror as the beaver is given the still large sum of coinage, Avrel can only feel pride for her furry friend.

"The rest I'll send to Manitäria, I've heard word they weren't doing well, you're rather thoughtful." the knight says, taking down a note on a piece of parchment. "As I didn't expect actual recovery of both of the relics, a bonus is in order, present this to the Argothian National Treasury Office sometime after a fortnight or so." she adds as she hands them all what Avrel has heard are called 'bank notes'.

"Thank you." the three say with a bow, though Avrel catches Geric glancing disdainfully over to the beaver who is happily gnawing on one of her hard earned coins.

"Shite..." he mumbles.

"These will be placed under heavy protection that none may use them." the knight says as she looks over the relics before rebagging them and hoisting them onto her back. "Thank you for a job well done, The Kingdom owes you much!" she says with a salute. Avrel wishes to engage her but she quickly turns away as Zanvan also tries to engage her.

"**But Ma'am, we never** encountered any... orcs..." Avrel says, briefly trying to get her attention.

"I guess she doesn't care about that?" Geric says scratching his head.

"The point is..." Avrel tries to reason, "The orcs can't use them if they were thinking about it." she shrugs.

"Still..." Geric growls, "Paying the bloody beaver..." he mumbles as he heads back towards the tavern.

"I'll hold that for you." Avrel says, grabbing the bag from Candice as she and Zanvan follow Geric.

"You okay?" Zanvan asks her, perceptively.

"Yeah." she sighs, "I suppose I should be okay with giving away my f-- Shad's weapon."

Zanvan scratches behind his hat, "I just hope they don't misuse those things." he says, coldly, but not without some audible concern, "Hopefully she keeps them locked away, like the knight said."

Foggy memories of not so many nights past flash to the front of Avrel's mind. "Yeah..."

They catch up with Geric and in the tavern, and they share a toast and a decent meal in the tavern and all seems well, their quest is done with pay in hand, and more to come. For her, even though they don't say much aside from recollecting different details of their journey, it seems they say a lot. It seems to her that they may keep in touch after this is over. She *hopes* so.

She hopes so.

Eventually, they come out of the tavern after their dinner and find the chilling evening of the city upon them. Candice quickly returns to her side, as Avrel takes a long look around the street.

"Hey." Avrel says as the guys look almost like they might be about to split. "Do you..." she mutters, "Where should we stay? We should stay somewhere nice, you know, to celebrate, eh?"

They really don't look like that's what they had in mind. "I was gonna get my book." Geric says reservedly.

"Zanvan?" Avrel asks.

He stops, folds his arms and looks down, "I was going to see somebody." he says dimly.

"Oh..." she accepts. *So it's all over?* she wonders. *No goodbyes? Nothing? Is that how* men *handle such things?* "Alright then." She manages to smile, and dip too shallow to rightly be called a curtsy, but enough to show the intent, for what it matters to them. "Come Candice."

She hasn't taken more than a few steps when she hears Geric give his familiar warmup tone as he begins to say something, "MmmHey Zanvan." he projects. "Not far from the bookshoppe, I've heard there's a fantastic bed-and-breakfast. I've heard their food is amazing, but I've never had it because they only offer breakfast to patrons who've stayed there."

Avrel stops and turns back. Zanvan has stopped too. "I'd have thought you'd have a chapel to--" he pauses, "Nevermind." he grunts as he makes striking eyes at Avrel, not lusting that she can tell, just somehow striking. "I suppose." he says defeatedly, "It'll give you time to figure out where you'll stay anyway." he says at her, just short of cruelly, or uncaringly. Although, sometimes in the past his best advice has come in that tone.

He's also right. "Mhhmm!" she hums with a nod.

He gives a fanciful and flourished bow, swinging his hat off and replacing it, "Lead the way, *cleric*."

Geric does lead the way on his long, bloody legs, not to say Zanvan is much slower, but he at least seems to try not to lose anyone when he's leading. She basically has to jog to keep pace with him, and Candice can only waddle so fast.

Just as he'd said, the bookshoppe is actually quite close to the fancy inn. In fact, it's on the same street. She finally catches up as Geric and Zanvan wait outside of the shoppe.

Geric is pressed up against the glass no less.

He looks at it longingly through the window, savoring that it's still there. It's almost cute, or as cute as a giant sard like him can look. Avrel waits outside with Zanvan as the cleric eagerly goes inside. Zanvan sits and smokes, and watches people go by as she watches through the window as Geric takes it off of its pedestal and takes it to the sale's desk. "Ahhhh" he says after sniffing it intensely, I'll start on this baby when we get to the inn!" he says euphorically, that's her best guess anyway, between her elf ears and reading his lips.

The lady running the store looks rather put off by his sniffing of the old book and promptly asks for his payment, Geric proudly presents his money and she carefully wraps the book for him, being careful with it as it's a very old book.

"We've had that sitting in the window for years, I'm a little sad to see it go." the shoppe-lady giggles.

"Yeah, I've wanted it for *some time*, and now it's mine!" Geric grins.

She hears the lady giggle as Geric waves happily in the doorway as he leaves.

He gives it another sniff before presenting it to Avrel, "You smell that, elf-schnoz?" he retracts it and sniffs it again, "Nothing like the smell of a good old book!"

She wouldn't know, but she smiles just the same. She *is* happy for him. "Are we off then?"

Zanvan puts out his pipe and stows it. "Yeah." The inn being within sight, she could lead, but Zanvan quickly takes the lead. It's not a long walk, but about halfway there, Zanvan whispers. "Stop!"

They all freeze for a long moment, Geric had been looking at his tenderly wrapped book, and he does look up.

Zanvan shifts his hat, "Must still be jumpy from all the last couple of months, my bad." he laughs.

Avrel giggles as well, *He should try being a woman.* But she must admit, she thought she heard the clank of an Ar-Guard herself. She probably did, though the street seems pretty empty at the moment, those bastards are always around.

"Come on." Zanvan says as he starts walking again, "I--" Just then Zanvan is tackled by not just a run of the mill Ar-Guard, but a Regal Knight, before Geric is restrained also. She slips under one of the bastard's initial reach arounds, but another gets her just a moment later, and all three of them are restrained.

"What the hell?" Geric yelps.

"Hey!" Zanvan coughs out as the bastard kneels on his neck.

"Excuse me officer, am I being detained!?" Avrel growls, spitting in the open beaver of the knight's helm. He sledges his gauntlet into the side of her head and lifts her to her toes with a chokehold.

"Disarm them!" a gravelly voice commands their restrainers.

"What's the meaning of this!?" Zanvan grunts, windedly as his sword and bow are taken from him.

"If you come quietly..." a knight replies. "We won't bag you."

Zanvan raspilly agrees to it, "Sure!" he gasps, "Sure."

"That goes for you too, tiny!" the gravelly voiced bastard, says pointing at her as she tries to kick her restrainer's crotch plate. Avrel stops struggling and is thrown down, and kneeled on for good measure. His armor alone must weigh as much as she does.

"What's going on?" Zanvan rasps surprisingly calmly

"Come with us." the apparent leader politely asks them. "Your silence and compliance would be appreciated."

Geric, however, struggles while trying to cast some sort of spell and as a result they are all head-bagged, starting with him, then Zanvan, then her since the bastards aren't very considerate of her ears, they wrestle to get the bag around her head. Not that she makes it easy anyway.

"I'll roast you sons of bitches…" Avrel growls out, "Like the pigs you are!" But she can't, her thoughts and focus are going to pieces. She could barely breathe before, but with that threat he doubled down and she can't breathe at all. He's not just letting his natural weight hold her, he's pressuring. Finally the spots over her eyes darken them entirely, and almost as if in a dream she feels the bag being tied over her head. What little breath she had access to quickly grows stale, and it wasn't barely anything at all. "I can't…" she mouths, wasting precious air as it carries no sound. Already the bag is lined with sweat, and feels as hot as the hottest of summer days. "I can't breath." she tries to 'tap out' with her free arm, a gesture she'd seen wrestling boys often use to signify surrender. But her hand is just as soon grabbed and tied to the other.

"Hey, the varmit is getting away!" one soldier yells in the commotion.

The one seeming to lead brushes it off, "Let the river-rat go, we've got the ones that matter." the leader replies, his words echoing airily, dreamily as she struggles to gasp. She fights the weakness, she fights the darkness, but without air, she can't fight it for long.

"Hey…" the Ar-Guard said, as he thumped the butt of his lance against the stone pavement of the alleyway. "I thought I told you to move on, you smelly bindlestiffs!"

Mother, tired as she had been barely moved, her head rolled slightly towards him, but her eyes barely opened. "It's not evening yet…" she said, "Is it?" she asked.

Avrel, of course checked, running out from the shade of the alley to the sunbeams coming down the street. "It's past noon." she reported.

"Are you questioning me?" the Ar-Guard snarled as he turned to her with a sneer.

"Umm…" Avrel couldn't have known what to say. "But it's not evening." she pointed out.

He lifted her up by the remains of her shirt and before she could even yelp, she found herself pressed against the wall of the alley. It took a second before her eyes could get focused on him. "You'd best not question me!" he growled with a glower in her face. His eyes turned down, and he got a peculiar look in his eye. Not unlike that which she'd seen Father with from time to time.

"Stop!" Mother interjected, trying to stand, still half asleep.

He pulled Avrel from the wall and set her down, facing her away from him, and towards Mother. But before she could help Mother up, he put his hands around the scraps of her shirt. "You fucking knife-ears." he scolded into her more than close *enough ear.* "*If you want to bribe us, you should develop faster!*" *he laughed as he turned her loose.*

As she helped Mother up, Mother's muted blue eyes stared at the guard, and in a voice Avrel'd seldom heard, she chided him, "Don't you ever handle my daughter again!"

He wasn't afraid, he didn't blink, he didn't blush. He just tipped his head with a cocky grin and backed off, "If I do, what'd you do about it." he asked, "Treehugger brat looks like a boy anyway." he said as he went.

Avrel's head felt fine, the back of her neck was scrapped a bit, but they'd not yet moved. As they finally did, Mother was very slow, bracing herself on the alley walls. "Avréllïä." she panted, propped over the satchel of things they could call their own.

"Yes, Mother?" Without it having needed to be said, she picked it up.

And Mother spared a hand, and felt the back of her short and quickly tidied hair. "Let's go."

"Let's go!" she feels as if awakening from a sleep lasting ages of the world. Hands on her forehead, on the back of her head, and on the side of her neck. She recalls saying, "It's dark." when a distant voice asks her if she can see. And from there she's lifted up and poked, prodded and all-around roughed up on this trip to who knows where… and an overnight stay, by her best guess. If it weren't that the first thing Zanvan said once they were pulled to their feet was *not* to do anything rash. Otherwise she'd have roasted those pigs.

She still would like to.

They hear doors open from what they guess was the cell they've been in for at least several hours. Pity, Avrel feels as though she'd just managed to nod off when she's grabbed and pulled to her feet. She hears as the others are gotten up and are pushed, prodded, and shuffled blindly towards an unknown destination. They hear some doors, some outdoors sounds briefly, and then more doors. After a long echoing hallway all the clanking Ar-Guards stop, and suddenly, she and the others are thrown to their knees one by one.

"Remove their bags!" an echoing and commandingly articulate woman's voice rings throughout the unknown room where they've been taken.

"Eyes open, scum." the raspy commander grunts as he lifts the bags off of hers, then Zanvan's, and then Geric's heads.

They each take a deep breath for the first time in so many hours where they aren't forced to breathe the stale airs of the bags. Avrel quickly and fiercely looks around the room trying to ascertain her location and her assailants. Nothing but guards in an almost blindly white marble room.

Zanvan tries to stay cool, and leans up a little from his knees. "So, why were we brought here, if I may be so direct?" he says most calmly. He seems to pay no mind to the guards and quite obviously speaks towards the woman's voice.

Which doesn't sit well with the guards, "Kneel when you speak to her, *knave!*" the commander yells as he pounds Zanvan's shoulder until he kneels.

"You'll forgive him Commander, I'm sure he'd suggest I kneel for him." the woman laughs, "You've been caught in mischief before, *ranger*, but never like this." the woman's voice echoes once more around the room.

She's terrified, and is not sure if she can put on a brave enough face to hide it. Even Geric looks downright frightened, but Zanvan? He's cool, and calm.

"Stupid games." he scoffs, "Stop playing and come out, *Catarina.*" Zanvan says with a sly smirk.

The particularly ornate Ar-Guards are all taken aback by Zanvan's disrespect. "That's '*Princess*' you--" the guards all croak, and are about to beat him when the woman reveals herself from behind one of the many stately pillars within the white marble room. Avrel observes her grace in her lavender and white dress. Her neckline is embellished by a small crystal pendant, and while modest enough, the cut is low enough to show her healthy bosom. The cold violet-lavender shade on her dress catches the violet-blue of her cold eyes. Her golden-blonde bangs roll from under her tiara forming three sleek partitions of hair, one down across her forehead, with two coming down on either side to her cheeks. Her hair along her back comes down roughly to her shoulder blades. Her face is elegantly beautiful, she is above all else pristine, and *regal.*

"Stop!" she commands as the commander's boot is inches from Zanvan's face.

The ranger looks up at her, "Impeccable timing, *Your Majesty.*" Zanvan chuckles.

"The *Princess*!?" Geric and she both yelp in surprise.

"All but you, Commander, may leave." The Princess orders. "Commander, stay by the exit."

"Yes, Your Majesty." they all say before they then leave in perfect formation like well trained dogs.

The Princess paces back and forth looking the three over for several long minutes. On some passes her arms are folded, sometimes her hand is over her mouth. But in the end she turns with her head towards them, but down. Her hand on her forehead as if she's thought until she hurts. Avrel would love to know what about.

The Princess's violet eyes pierce as she finally turns her head up and glares at all three of them, resting finally on Zanvan. "My my my, What am I going to do with you, Zanny." she sardonically, and haughtily laments.

"It's been a while since you've had me arrested, Princess." Zanvan sighs.

Avrel flings her eyes to the ranger. The *ranger* who seems to know The Princess of Argoth. "'*Zanny*'?" she asks, demanding of an answer, "Zanvan you *know* her??"

He sweats. "Sort of." Zanvan answers defensively.

"Well," Geric grunts. "Can you use that to our advantage to get us unbound?"

He just grits his teeth, visibly.

227

The Princess stops over him, "My secret police had been watching you when you first took this job, but I never expected you to *actually go through with it!*" The Princess, Catarina says angrily in Zanvan's face.

Avrel's arms strain in her bounds, "What's going on!? We got this job *from you guys!*" she yells.

"Yeah!" Geric follows up.

The Princess gives them each a leer before returning her focus to Zanvan.

"I'm kind of interested, myself." Zanvan says as he still tries to play it cool, his voice is like when he's trying to charm his way into some poor woman's busier. "One of your Regal Knight's was trying to give out a nice little job and we took it, is there a problem with this?"

Her head shakes and her expression is grim. "When given a quest that is *supposedly* from *The King*, or his advisers, I'm a little surprised you didn't contact me!" she scolds, "Not only could I have helped, but *this whole mess could have been avoided!*" The Princess, Catarina stresses.

Geric sinks, slightly. "If you're referring to the incident with the gnomish vassal, I--"

"No, you fool!" she interrupts, "We believe the orcs are planning on some offensive maneuvers and were trying to get the ancient relics weapons that you recovered for them!" The Princess says getting in Geric's face.

"Yes!" Avrel screams maliciously. "That's exactly why we did the job your knight gave to us!"

"**She-wasn't-one-of-our-knights!** *You impudent urchin!*" The Princess booms, "There *is* no Lethia in our corps! She is believed to be Lucia, the daughter of Nerfendör!" she growls at Avrel, her flushed face making her violet-blue eyes all the more intense.

One at a time it seems she and the guys digest and react to what they now are aware of.

The three fidget in silence for a few minutes until Zanvan sighs, "We've made a huge mistake..." he mutters.

The Princess points her finger in Zanvan's face, "*You're damn-blasted right you have!*" she shouts, "If I didn't know you personally I'd send you and your companions to the spear wall right now!" The Princess says, angrily folding her arms.

"No need to lose your composure, Your Majesty..." Geric says defensively. "Orcs are to blame!"

Avrel swallows, "Lethia -- Umm Lucia is an orc?" Avrel questions.

"Did you never notice her olive skin?" The Princess facepalms.

"I for one don't judge people by their skin, or racial traits." Avrel is quick to interject. To be honest, Avrel has never seen an orc, at least not up close. *Besides Lucia.* Or Lethia, rather.

"I mean..." Geric trails off, "She's a soldier, I'd expect her to have tanned skin and scars-*around-her-mouth*-oh-shite." Geric drones on with lamentation. The Princess nods her head with a leer towards the cleric. "Well c'mon, she was wearing a helmet! It's hard to see a face through that." Geric defends.

"Well, too bad." she steps back, her arms folded now, "Because of you not *ever* checking with *any* other officer or, you know, Zanvan could have even contacted me, the very weapons that you were *so nobly* trying to keep away from the orcs were *hand delivered* to them by *you idiots!*" She pauses to swear using words that sound fancy, but Avrel can only assume are ones she's never heard before. "Why didn't you contact me?" she stressfully asks again, "Almost a year of investigations, and for what?' she says, not even to them, The Princess is genuinely anguished.

"You know..." Geric chuckles nervously as he turns to Zanvan and Avrel, "That would explain the lack of any other orcs attempting to stop us."

"Zanny, shut that one up." The Princess commands.

Zanvan sighs. "I'm not exactly his boss you know."

"As *your* princess I am your boss, superseded only by my father, King Markell." she hisses, "You will shut him up." she barks.

Zanvan rolls his eyes, but turns to the cleric, "Shut the hell up."

The Princess resumes her pacing, swearing up a storm. Again she turns towards them, "Well, what do you have to say for yourselves? I have every right to have the three of you beheaded right now for this treason!" she threatens.

"Well..." Geric says meekly. "It was an accident."

Zanvan nudges him.

"We can fix it." Avrel says strongly.

Zanvan butts his whole side into her.

The Princess's violet eyes dart to her, "How?" she inquires.

"We'll catch Leth..." she catches herself, "Or... Lucia before she can get home and do whatever it is she's planning to do with those weapons." Avrel answers.

This prompts The Princess to smile. "I like your friend Zanny, what's her name?" she asks.

"Avrel..." Zanvan sighs, answering for her.

"Well Avry, that's awfully confident of you." The Princess says, belittlingly. "Zanny, are you in on this?" she asks.

He nods reluctantly, "You really think I can say no to you, Cat?"

"Cleric?" she asks.

"Yes, your Highnesssssss." Geric says hissing peculiarly.

She pauses at Geric's antic before continuing. "We can't use our military without provoking an all-out war that would look like we started it. And I don't have such authority anyway. I was hoping we could reach an 'agreement' like this." The Princess says as she motions for The Commander to unbind them. "And Zanny, check in from time to time, I get lonely when you don't contact me for so long." she continues.

"Yes, *dear.*" Zanvan replies.

Avrel's nose crinkles as she looks at them. *Dear...?* she thinks to herself. Hell, why should she give a damn *if* the orcs get those relics? She wouldn't mind seeing the haughty sards in Argoth getting speared by hordes of orcs.

Although, if she doesn't help, it's doubtful she'd see that. *Tomorrow at best...* she figures. She really has no other option, what she'd blurted out of sheer instinct really is the only good choice.

"Alright, let's leave this room and get you guys ready." The Princess laughs before sternly gazing at them with her piercing, violet eyes.. "*You* three have a *lot* to fix..."

15

"Commander!" The Princess beckons the commander as they leave this white room.

He follows them out. "Yes, Your Majesty?" he replies.

"Tell my father I have a plan." she orders. "Fetch a key to the armory." she commands another before she looks at the three of them, "And order a meal for my friends." The Princess continues.

"Friends?" Avrel and Geric remark to each other, raising their brows. Avrel's head's still spinning, trying to catch up one what has happened in these last few hours. It'd finally seemed like all was right. The next thing she knows, Zanvan is tackled, and she's choked until she passes out by those bastards. Maybe she's still woozy from that ordeal. Only air deprivation would have let her so quickly offer to fix this shite.

The Princess points down the hall and tells Zanvan that they are to wait for her there. "I'll be back in a while once I have the key and the food is readied, until then, make yourselves at home."

"Thank you your majesty." Avrel says with a curtsy, reminding The Princess that Zanvan isn't the only one. He bows slightly and Geric nods politely as The Princess turns and gracefully walks away. Avrel mimes them, staying low until she's out of sight before standing back to her full height.

As they then go down the hall as directed, they find a nice parlor waiting for them.

Zanvan takes a seat, easily the most relaxed. "This area is where they would do any sort of political prisoner exchange. This is the room where they might discuss ransoms or something. Or meet with some angry ruffian who happened to be handsome." he casually drops, maybe a hint?

"So..." Avrel asks. "You know The Princess of Argoth?"

"Well enough to call Princess Catarina, 'Cat'?" Geric adds.

"Yeah, what of it?" Zanvan says, lighting up a complementary pipe that was in the room. 'Cat' probably left it just for him.

"It's just..." Avrel says nervously.

"Just what?" Zanvan says testily.

"You two seem to be like, really familiar is all." Avrel finishes. Zanvan says nothing.

"You *like* her." Geric says in an ornery tone, "Zanvan has a crush on a princess, *oh my!*" he continues

"It's mutual, for your information." Zanvan grunts, but smiling just the same. "Smart arse."

Avrel's curiosity had already been captured, but now she's interested, maybe even a little inquisitive. "You're... 'an item'?" she asks. *How?* she wonders.

"Well..." Zanvan hesitates, and she can imagine why.

Just then The Princess enters the room. "Well Zanny, I have the key, we can retrieve your weapons." she says as she gently sensuously embraces him, showing him the key. Avrel doesn't know much of sexual signalling, but she's caressing that key in a *very* suggestive way.

He and his princess exit the room leaving Geric and Avrel sitting there dumbfounded.

"Oh... My... Goddess..." Geric cracks up.

Avrel dryly says the same, but she's not finding it as light as the cleric is.

After a moment, Avrel's face tightens as with her fists which clench to fists. "What a licentious, libertine, lascivious, *manwhore*!!!" she says with incense.

"What are you so mad about?" Geric laughs mockingly. "Dreaming of the lusty-ranger-man for yourself?"

"**NO**!" Avrel grunts fervently, *The very idea!* "He's been shacking up with every loose-brassiered hussy from here to Rudaski!" Avrel furiously fumes.

"Tsk, tsk, truly an inspiration to men everywhere." Geric sighs playfully.

Avrel glares at him ferociously and grunts angrily for a minute. "Are all men rapists or pigs?" Avrel growls to herself, but intentionally loud enough for Geric to hear. She looks him in the eye, "What about 'being a man' means you have to be... to be a toxic, violent, seed spreading brute?" she asks.

Geric laughs -- laughs at her. Likely, he finds her petty, or maybe he finds her funny, it'd not be the first time she's been dismissed because she's so small. Sons of bitches.

"Zanvan you lech!" Avrel yells as she runs to catch up with him. "What in hell is wrong with you!?" she says as she darts in front of him and stands on her toes trying to get in his face. Zanvan is silent with an uncomfortable look on his face. *Good.* "How..." she stutters, "Your Highness, *do you*... Are you two..?" Avrel says, quivering with angst.

"If you mean to ask if Zanvan and I are in a relationship..." The Princess says with a giggle as she leans against Zanvan and holds his arm gently. "Then yes, we are."

Avrel's eyes are like daggers thrown at the ranger, "Zanvan you filthy bedswerver!" she yells, attempting to slap him but being stopped by his catching of her hand. He turns to his woman and they both burst out laughing, Avrel becomes almost as confused as she is angered. "What is wrong with you!? Is *nothing* sacred with you men? Not even your woman's trust when you're away!?" Avrel says as she gets teary eyed. Zanvan holds her hand loosely and coldly tries to explain something to her, but she refuses to listen to him, son of a bitch. "I don't understand you worthless men! Is one woman's *willing affection not good enough for you!?*" Avrel yells as she forcefully shakes her hand out of his. Bedswerving, being a loose belted man, however she'd put it, she has come to accept, but not this. Not if he had some woman neglected in their stead.

Her vision is distorted by her tears as she takes one glance at The Princess. She's just smiling amicably, her hands folded gracefully, and not showing the anger she must have in her. It's stunning, brave, and more than Avrel can bear.

She painfully excuses herself with a curtsey.

***

Just after the mixed she-elf runs away after a crude excuse for a curtsey, the cleric walks up behind she and Zanny. It's rather bold of him, and if she weren't so sure to trust her body to Zanny, her instinct would be to call a guard for anyone coming so close and so brazenly.

"So umm...." the cleric says with an exaggerated clearing of his throat, "As the local cleric and her nearest medical professional, it's my diagnosis that she's pretty mad about something." the cleric says trying to calm the mood with some sort of demented humor.

She and Zanny look upon him with deep disappointment. "Do you even belong to the Argothian Healer's Guild?" Zanny inquires.

"I might." this *cleric* says defensively. "I at the very least do a lot of shopping there, who wants to know? I'm not on trial here!"

Though he and the other two would be if she had any sense. "Alright." Catarina says, brushing her hand to her brows and shaking her head, "Alright. Zanny, I think we need to explain to your little--"

"*Very* little!" Catarina is interrupted by the cleric who impudently speaks over her, luckily none of the castle's staff are around.

"How borish..." she remarks to herself, but loud enough and with enough of her practiced royal voice to shut him up. "Ahem! Your little friend about our arrangement." Catarina suggests. "Also, what is her...?" she asks, with a hint of genuine worry. "The little thing did not seem all correct."

"Long story short." Zanny says putting out and putting away his pipe. "She's a bit of an urchin, trust issues, father issues."

"Hmmm... Quite the gambit..." Catarina remarks, "I can see why she might be such a loose cannon then. Alright Zanny, I'll explain it to her, you two go get your armaments."

"Very wise." the cleric says, with a bow. His voice sounds properly beholden. Perhaps mockingly so. "You see, Your Highness, her trust in men is verily diminished."

Yes, he's mocking. Lucky for him that he's a friend of Zanny's, lest a week in the dungeon be used to set him straight. "Run along." she says, targeting him with the refined, royal, violet gaze. "I shall return." Catarina says as she makes her way in the direction the she-elf had run, leaving the men behind.

Catarina finds her down the hall looking over a balcony. Perhaps she hadn't meant to find one, but not knowing her way around, it just sort of happened. It's one of Catarina's favorite views too.

"Dear?" Catarina says softly.

The small, pasty, stain-haired mixed-elf turns slightly and gasps as she throws herself onto her knees. "Oh! Your Majesty!" the small elf whimpers softly. "Forgive my behavior back there I-"

"It's alright." Catarina smiles, "And call me Cat, so long as no other royals are around. Otherwise you might get beaten." she says so detachedly it's a little chilling, but it must be so.

The small mixed-elf, Avrel slowly gets up. "Yes, Your Highness." They're both silent for a moment, each seeming to wait for the other to speak.

Zanny had said an *urchin*, so it's possible, at least by Catarina's judgement, that she's afraid. "Avrel?" Catarina says invitingly, "That's a sweet name." It's no doubt shortened, so many elven names are.

"I guess so." she blushes, as she falls silent again. Catarina can't help herself, as the mixed-elf, Avrel looks over the balcony, her hair dangling in the slight breeze -- red, truly red down to its roots. She holds a strand still and looks at it, her privilege, after all, she is her subject. A moment later the mixed-elf speaks up. "Doesn't it... bother you?" Avrel says painfully.

"What?" Catarina answers, she's unsure of Avrel's meaning. *Her hair?* she half smiles.

"That Zanvan is untrue?" Avrel stresses. "He's slept with-"

Catarina laughs. "Oh, that. He's really not. I mean, he kind of is, but not really." she says as casually as she can, it's a curious thing to explain, made all the more apparent by Avrel's look of confusion. "Alright, you see this necklace?" Catarina says as she lifts her pendant from between her breasts and shows it to mixed-elf.

Avrel nods, still rather blushed. "That stone is charmed in some way, isn't it?" the mixed-elf says as she looks intently at the jewel.

"Quite..." Catarina nods, "Zanny got a bound pair of these from the elves of the far north." she explains, as she takes it off and lets Avrel look at it closely.

"What does it do?" the mixed-elf's sky-blue eyes strain intensely. "I can see that it has runes in it, but they aren't reading to me." Avrel says sheepishly.

"I don't know what they say either." she says as she takes her pendant back, "But they help me and Zanny remain... intimate, despite our living arrangements being so radically different." Catarina explains as she re-clasps the necklace around her neck, tucking the jewel into her cleavage. Avrel looks at her strangely, but with intrigue. "My father doesn't really approve of Zanny and would rather me marry one of my male cousins or some other well to do person. He's also very old and leaves me and his advisers to do most of his duties, as such, until he passes which is not likely to be more than a few years, me and Zanny use um.. alternative means of... feeling connected." she explains, trying to keep her composition. It's a strange business trying to remain regal while explaining her arrangements to satisfy her desire to be ravaged like an animal by her lover.

"I don't entirely follow." Avrel shrugs.

"When we wear these, we're '*connected*'." she gives a suggestive hand gesture, "I *receive* what he *gives*, in a sense." Catarina explains as she can feel herself blush in mild embarrassment. "And vice versa."

The small mixed-elf thinks for a moment and then winces. "I think I get what you mean." she shudders.

As an elf, it hadn't occurred until now to ask the girl's age. *How old is she?* She'll have to ask Zanny later. "It's a little odd at first but it's certainly allowed us to keep our intimacy across our distance." Catarina laughs.

Avrel lets out the most forced and uncomfortable giggle she's ever heard. "Doesn't it bother you that Zanvan is still... You know, *with* other women?" Avrel says softly.

"Mmm. Not really," Catarina knows she's his best, "I trust my Zanny to not become attached. He gets to live his wild ranger life, I get to feel as though I'm being intimate with him, it's a win-win for us both." Catarina laughs.

"But you're using other women's bodies, isn't that a little... not right?" Avrel says cautiously. Quite obviously the little elf protests, but is holding it back, wisely.

"Well, what they do not know can not hurt them." Catarina brushes it off, besides, her citizens are hers anyway. "Besides, they'd have been seduced anyway, would they not?" she says as she starts to lead Avrel back into the inside halls.

"I suppose." the mixed-elf sighs.

Catarina is quick to dismiss any of the guards that they pass on their walk down the hall to the armory. Each seeing her completely unescorted with some unknown, uncouthly dressed she-elf compulses them to try and fill that void. While it's good to see them following the protocol so quickly and so well, it's not a good time to be adding extra ears to this venture.

Eventually the more ornately decorated halls change to more robust and militaristic. Tapestries change to suits of armor, shields, and walls and walls of spears and lances at the ready.

Finally they come to the castle armory proper.

"Here Zanny." Catarina says as they enter, rightly sure that he's there, waiting for her. Him and that *cleric*. "I have your little friend."

Zanny turns and tosses Avrel a very simple and basic staff. "Here you go." he says.

"Thanks." she answers as she catches it.

It's not a very impressive weapon, if it can so be called 'a weapon'. Catarina gestures welcomingly to the walls, so full of Argoth's finely crafted arms. "If you see something you like, feel free to take it Avrel, same for you, cleric."

"Thanks, but I'm good." the mixed-elf says meekly.

Just then, Catarina's violet eyes catch the cleric as he spies a large, hammer styled mace. "Oh! I like this!" he says, taking it up and swinging it around.

"Take it then." Catarina says with a smile.

"Thank you, Your Highness," he smiles and bows graciously. "I think I might!"

And she knows of course Zanny needs only his bow, though it seems he has a sword as well. It looks like it must be of elven craft, and somewhat new. "Alright, let's get you fed." Catarina sighs, "The sooner you eat the sooner I can set you loose so you can fix the lovely situation you've put us in." she chuckles despairingly.

She leads them to a small and half-way private dining area where four plates of food are waiting for them and several packs of food provisions have been made for them.

"Political prisoner room?" the cleric guesses, correctly.

"If this is where political prisoners' meetings are held, I can't imagine the main castle." the mixed-elf sighs in awe.

"Perhaps you'll see it." Catarina promises, depending of course of how they should return.

She sits with them, and Avrel, who was seeming to admire the quality of the food, seemed to almost freeze as she took the seat at the table's head. But after a moment, she begins to taste it, though her movements are deliberate, and she seems very aware of her table manners. Not to say she's not utterly failing.

The cleric however takes no time to acclimate, and is enjoying himself.

But Zanny, who should be used to it, seems dazed. He's eaten more intimately than this, in many ways, and many times.

"Eat up, Zanny." Catarina says after a few minutes of passive food poking.

"This is great!" the mixed-elf says chowing into it, a compliment to the chef, Catarina's always heard that elf-kind can be hard to please.

The cleric, Geric laughs and nudges Zanny before pointing, with his fork no less, to her. "He doesn't like the fancy food, he likes his bat nuggets and shite like that."

"By the Gilded, Zanny!" Catarina gasps. "I told you to stop eating like that! You'll bring a plague upon us!"

Zanny quickly changes the subject. "So, do you have any clue where Lucia is headed?" he asks.

She smiles over her gritted teeth, if it weren't for his dangerously wild side, he wouldn't love him, she supposes. "Indeed, I'm glad you asked." she answers, letting him have it his way, "My secret police could not catch her before she skipped town, we believe she went south, probably down the river way to the border -- To her home kingdom."

"Yordasvin's borders are very easily reached." Zanny says thoughtfully. "But she'll have to pass through the Shadow Forrest's lakes region."

"I've sent word to the small settlements out there, but I doubt they'll reach them before she's long passed." Catarina says as she sips some wine.

"Then how are we to catch her?" Avrel sighs.

Catarina turns her face more stern as she forces herself to be more serious. "That is up to you three, I pray you'll find a way, for your sake and all of ours." she says in her harsh, royal voice.

"Fair enough." Zanny sighs.

"Please eat." she doesn't just insist, she commands.

The moment they are done, she rises and leads them out. Filling them in on every last detail and order she can along the way. There is so very much to consider after all...

"... And lastly, you must not allow any connection between yourselves and Argoth to be apparent, assassinate Lucia *before* she can return home." she says, fully in the royal voice, with no softness, not even towards her lover.

"And if we can't catch her before then?" Geric, the cleric asks.

She swallows hard, it's not an order she can rightly give. But then, none of this is. "Then do what must be done." she answers. "But again, you cannot leave any evidence besides your swift, unfollowed return which could link yourselves back to me. We're trying to prevent a war, not start one."

"Alright, your Highness." Zanvan says with a bow.

As they come to the gate, she finally calls the guard to them. "Alright, go; for Argoth, and for yourselves." she says as she sends them off with an escort to the city's southern docks.

Zanny and his friends eventually pass out of sight, along with the guards. She wishes she could sigh in relief, but she can't. She sighs, but relief, peace, and calm is yet to come.

When it comes.

***

As they are approaching the docks, Geric leans into Zanvan. "Shhhhh... If all goes well we'll ditch the beaver!" he chuckles. Zanvan says nothing but simply sends him a disapproving glare. Zanvan does question Avrel's lack of concern for her familiar but says nothing when he sees her looking very focused while they walk. Eventually they make it to the small vessel docks where they hear a wharf worker cursing out someone.

"Yeh can't eh just set in ma boat!" they hear him scream as they approach.

"Hey." one of the escort guards says as he hands Zanvan some money. "Her Highness said take this and get a boat, '*The rest is up to you.*'"

Zanvan accepts it, and nods.

"Heh! Where ye goin'?! Ye guards!?" the wharf worker screams as the guards walk back towards the city.

Avrel scoffs, "Typical." she says looking towards the already faraway guards, "*Always ready to help, those guys.*" she says with her usual tone when discussing the Argothian Guard.

Zanvan, Avrel, and Geric walk up to see what all the yelling was about when they come to the small vessel the man is standing over.

"Ahh! Goodie!" Avrel says, clapping her hands together.

"Oh... Goodie..." Geric groans at just the same time, with the inverse emotional responses.

Zanvan says nothing but just shakes his head when they come to see that Candice is happily sitting on her behind, inside the boat, staring snidely up at the wharfman. She's got spunk, he'll give the beaver that.

"Es this varmit yours?" the warfman asks angrily as he points to the beaver's snide, toothy face that is now smiling at her master.

"Nope!" Geric says, walking forward and rolling up his sleeves. "No sir, we'll gladly smash it for y-" Zanvan blocks him with his arm before he can *try out* his new hammer-mace.

"She's mine." the kid says, inserting herself between the warfman and Geric, and the beaver. "And um... We need a boat!" Avrel says softly.

"Well, ye better tek this one, sheh p't tooth marks on the mast!" the warfman says angrily.

"Works for us, right?" Avrel asks, turning to Zanvan and Geric.

Geric pouts while he opens the coin bag the guards had given him. "How much?" Zanvan asks.

"100 gold pieces, not a coin less!" the wharfman says saltily.

Zanvan can't be sure if this is a purchase or a rental. Then again, it might not really matter, with Cat on their side. "98, 99, 100... wow, Cat's gotten cheap on me." Zanvan mumbles to himself as he counts out the coins.

"Gimme!" the warfman says, forcefully taking the coins from Zanvan. "Now go, and get that over-sized smelly coypu out of here!" he yells as he unties the boat as they board. He seems to be in a hurry to send them off. To get rid of the beaver, at least.

Zanvan tips his hat as he steps aboard. It's not a bad sized river skiff, it could probably hold a few more people if it needed to. Although, anyone taller than the kid would bump their head sitting under the small sale. He would, Geric more than certainly.

"Why was the beaver in the boat?" Geric sighs as he settles in.

"Well..." Avrel giggles. "I tried to send her a message to meet us at the docks through our connection, I wasn't quite expecting *that*."

"Nobody would..." Geric says with a grimace.

Zanvan gives a hard kick against the dock and they disembark. It's been a while since he's done anything on even a canoe, but it comes back quickly enough.

The basics at least. And enough to navigate the canals, past the outer delta settlements outside the city walls, until they are in the open water of the Cordol Lake and can start down the river.

But after only a few hours of paddling, Geric grows weary.

"We're never going to catch up to Lethia." Geric whines. "It's hopeless!"

"She has a good head-start." Zanvan retorts. "*Lucia* does." Name blind and whiney as the cleric is, he's not entirely wrong though. If Lucia is heading down the same way, it'll be very hard to catch up to her. "Hm... You see anything, kid?" he asks Avrel who is just stroking the beaver.

She squints and looks out towards the far end of the lake, "Nothing." she answers. "A few fishing boats maybe."

Unless they get a strong wind, they'll never catch her, and the breeze is very calm at the moment. But as he watches Avrel lean back and tuck her hair behind her considerable *elven* ears, he has another idea. "How good is your weather magic?" Zanvan asks, knowing it's probably pretty good.

"I dunno, why?" she replies.

"If we drop the sail can you put some wind behind us?" Zanvan says looking up at the small, folded sails in the middle of the boat.

She looks up, and back to him. "I can try." Avrel says sheepishly.

"Good enough for me, give it a try." Geric groans as he leans back, probably jealous that he wasn't asked first.

Zanvan lets down the sails and Avrel channels some weather magic until a favorable wind starts pressing them forward. And judging by the water around them, *just* them. They might have a chance now. "This is much better, how long can you keep it up?" Zanvan asks, rather impressed.

Avrel breaks from a look of deep concentration. "I don't know, it's not that hard to maintain, at least for now." she says as she grabs a gem in her pouch and clutches that while she tries to lean back.

"Okay, well, if you get tired just let us know." Zanvan says as he lights his pipe, only for it to be immediately blown out. He might have known… "Maybe Geric can take turns with you."

The cleric perks up, "Say what?"

16

As the sun sets, Avrel grows fatigued and finally rests. It's just a wind spell, but given how it was before noon that The Princess sent them out, and likely at least noon by the time she began casting it, she's drained.

"Ahh..." she moans as she lies back, "Can I get something to eat?" she grumbles out.

"No, back to work, slacker!" Geric shouts, making a whipping motion with his hand, "Whoo*pishh* whoo*pish*." he vocalizes, with a flicking motion of his wrist.

"Yeah..." she Avrel frys as she lets herself slump even more, "If you want a slave, get yourself a housewife. Or are you cleric's even allowed to marry?"

"Care to find out?" he says very jocularly, but the thought still makes her want to throw up.

"Bloody-hell no!" she gasps, more harshly than she'd meant, half out of reflex.

He exaggeratedly sizes her up and scoffs, with an equally exaggerated blanch and brushes her off with a "Yeash." Had she not known him for as long, maybe even a few weeks back, she might have lashed out. But she knows he's just playing, and they all sit silently until he notices Candice waddling closer to him -- and opening her jaws. "I was kidding!" he shouts.

Candice leers at him and waits for an agreeing nod from her before waddling back over to Avrel.

"Anyway." Zanvan interjects, "What can I get for you? Cat packed us a lot of good stuff." he asks as he looks through one of the bags of provisions.

'Good' by his standards could mean many things. "Hmmm... Got any grapes?" Avrel asks in a tired sounding fry, it's the first juicy thing that comes to mind. Right now she feels like a raisin herself.

He shuffles through the bag. "Uh..." he mumbles as he looks through, "Well, there's a raspberry filled crescent bread in here." he says as he holds it up so she can see it.

"Close enough." Avrel says, reaching for it. It's bigger and heavier than she'd expected. *And rich* she'd add as she takes a bite. She was never one for truly sweet breakfasts, nor could she afford the fancy stuff like this, but it's pretty tasty.

As she goes for a second bite, she's almost startled into dropping it by an aggravated scream. It cuts into her ears as just a second later, several arrows fly past the boat.

"What the hell?" Geric says, leaping to attention. He mumbles something and raises his arms out forming a barrier.

"I don't know..." Zanvan says in a cold and calm whisper. "Just stay calm and duck."

"Fat chance." Geric retorts as he sits lower.

Zanvan swears. "*Hey! Why are you shooting at us?!*" he screams towards the shore.

"Direct, isn't he?" Avrel comments to Geric. For all he knows it's orcs out there!

"Come to shore lest we bring out the fire arrows!" a voice shouts from the eastern shore.

"Yeah..." the ranger grunts. "Sure thing." Zanvan says, holding his hand in the air, surrenderingly.

Avrel leans up. "Excuse me, am I being detai-" she attempts to inquire before Geric covers her mouth, disallowing her to finish.

"Just blow us shore-ward." he insists.

"Or away?" she asks, looking to Zanvan.

But he nods, 'No,' confidently.

"I'm tired, you guys can row, can't you?" she replies, forcing Geric's hand off of her face.

Geric grabs an oar, "Okay, we'll row, but you try to push us in as much as you can." he sighs. "Hey Zanvan, you too."

Zanvan grabs an oar as well. "Just trust me." he tells them.

Yeah... Avrel scoffs mentally. She hopes he knows she's not going to have the stamina to roast them if they turn out to be orcs, or kobolds, or any other creature.

Eventually they make their way to shore. She's decided to save any strength she has left for just-in-case. She's a girl, it's the woods; it's the smart thing to do.

The boat skids into the bank and they are immediately surrounded by men dressed much in the same way as Zanvan. Tight vests and pants, forest colored of course, and hoods or caps of some kind.

Woodsmen and rangers.

The three are looked over by them for a moment while Candice hides in the boat. Avrel might have been able to as well, had she thought of it before getting out, but she's stuck now.

"Wait..." one of the men says as he takes a less aggressive stance. "Zanvan?" He walks up closer and unravels a mask that obscures his face, "Well what do you know!? It *is* you." he says, patting Zanvan on the shoulder, "What's this rabble you've got following you?"

"I never took you for a knife-juggler." one of the other men over Avrel's shoulders says as his shaded eyes linger on her, long enough for her to feel uncomfortable about it.

"And a cleric too?" the first asks, "Imagine *you* taking an arrow to the knee." he laughs, doing that macho punch to the shoulder thing men do. Usually toxic ones.

Zanvan brushes him off. "Hold on, why the hell are you so defensive, we're in a hurry!" he asks with aggravation.

"In a hurry?" the man asks. "Why? I haven't seen you in a hurry since The King caught you and Cat-?"

Zanvan rolls his eyes. "Yeah yeah..." he says impatiently.

"There's an orc woman we're pursuing down this river." Avrel struggles out.

The man looks a bit surprised, but not unfamiliar to the situation. He gives a signal and the other woodsmen lower their guard. "An orc woman landed ashore when her boat hit a rock and she needed to patch it." he says, "She found Old Harry out that way and when he started questioning her about *why* she was in such a hurry, she cut him down and ran into the woods." he says somberly. "I suppose she's running from you guys?"

"Well, not exactly." Zanvan sighs.

"But basically." Avrel interjects.

"So Gil, when was this? and where?" Zanvan asks.

"A little ways down the river, her boat is still there. A few guys went to look for her but nobody saw her." the man, Gil replies.

Avrel flicks out her index finger, as a thought strikes her, "So she left her boat?"

"Yup." Gil replies. "We've got two guys watching in case she comes back and tries to sneak off. Anyway, you can be sure that if she stays in these woods we'll find her." he laughs.

"Why?" Geric asks.

The man looks at Zanvan with a smile. "Zanvan, you can tell them all about this place, I'll go back and put some stew on in my hut, I'd love for you to introduce me to your friends over supper." he says with a hearty slap to Zanvan's back.

The other woods men bid them farewell and leave them. Just in time too, one more look from one of those goons and she would have lit them up. But Avrel is curious and waits for him to explain what the older man alluded to. "So?" she says perkily.

"This is part of Woodsman's' Ridge, it's a camp that, well... Rangers trade with and woodsmen tend to hang out in." Zanvan explains shyly.

"So it's where you grew up?" Avrel grins.

"Not really." he puts down rather quickly, "I spent *some* time here though."

Avrel looks at Zanvan suspiciously, "And?"

"And it's a place where a lot of rangers hang out, trade stuff, etc." Zanvan says guardedly. "C'mon Gil's waiting." he says as he walks away.

"Who is Gil!?" Geric shouts but receives no reply as Zanvan walks into the treeline. "Oh well, free stew is free stew!" Geric says happily as he follows.

They follow Zanvan to a warm inviting cabin a little ways in from the treeline, scattered around in the dark forest are tree houses and rope bridges between the tall trees they are built upon.

Avrel rather likes it. "This place is... Amazing." she says in awe.

"Eh... It's only because you're an elf, you like anything with trees." Geric says in a sarcastic tone. "This is technically Argothian land, so I have to wonder if this is at all legal."

"Why shouldn't it be?" More over, who cares? They aren't hurting anyone.

"Well..." Geric considers for a moment, "I doubt they pay taxes for one." he says, "Plus the aforementioned unconfirmed use of The King's land. And, bless your tree-hugging heart, but those tree huts *probably* aren't up to code."

Avrel shoots him a glare even as they enter the cabin, she's not even sure what half of what he's said means, but she makes out enough.

Once inside they see an inviting fire-pit in the middle of the room which has a succulent looking venison stew simmering over its coals.

"Come eat up." Gil says invitingly.

She'll wait. Maybe it's Geric's implication that these guys are all below the law, and more than anything it's her witful distrust of their masculine impulses, but she'll let one of the others taste the stew first. Instead, Avrel waves politely to an older man with thick grey hair sitting in a chair towards the back by a window, he notices and looks at her strangely.

"My goodness! Miss Haley I thought you were dead!" he blurts out.

Avrel steps back looking rather unsettled and confused. "Haley?"

"Ummm.. Excuse him." Gil says as he guides Avrel to take a seat around the fire-pit. Zanvan looks uncomfortable as well but takes a seat. Gil hands the older man some very thick glasses. "Terrence, please put these on." he sighs.

"Alright, alright.." he scoffs, "Oh, I'm sorry miss, I thought you were someone else, haha." the older man, Terrence says in a jolly manner. "Wow, no wonder I need my glasses to see you, you're a tiny thing." he says with a chuckle as he takes a seat with them. "She looked bigger as a cream, blue, and red blur." Terrence says, not to subtly to Gil.

"Hmmm... I like this guy!" Geric says, leaning into Avrel.

She firmly pushes Geric back. "So... This is a pretty cool place you all live in." Avrel says trying to ease the situation, thanks to Geric, she's getting used to such ridicule.

"Yeah" Gil laughs. "Most people who come down the river pass through without even knowing we're in here."

Likely as they aren't being shot at... she thinks, and it looks as if the other's had similar thoughts.

"So..." Zanvan says, abruptly in a harsh and serious tone. "Old Harry was murdered by Lucia?"

"Yep." Gil says somberly. "You know him, he loved to fish in the evenings."

It's all very sad, but a certain irony occurs to Avrel which she feels needs to be asked about. "Doesn't a place for rangers to gather kind of *negate* what makes someone a ranger?"

The company of woodsmen and rangers all come uneased, "Well..." Gil sighs.

"I'll tell you lass." Terrence comments before he shallows a large spoonful of stew, "This place is where an ancient battle was held, where the armies of men and the ancient magi, led by the Tiger Warriors finally made a stand against the armies of less civil men and of course, of the fallen elves. So much magic and blood was sprayed across this area that *to this day*, there is deep enchantment to all that grows and lives here." he tells them. "So the legend goes." he ends in a tone most spooky.

"Terrence." Gil says in a belittling way. "Don't bore our guests with your stories."

"No, no." Avrel says with intrigue. "I wanna hear."

A group sigh is shared by the three younger men as the older man is only too happy to continue at the young lady's request. At least *one* of them is a gentleman. Getting explained to by some old man usually is shitey, but being about the woods, she'll bear it.

"So there, after all this time the deep enchantment in this forest makes the trees grow strong and thick, and the animals and creatures all spring with vitality..." Terrence continues for a good quarter hour, "And at last, with the few cabins and woodsmen and the generally good land, rangers began to come here as a refuge and trading post if they were hurt or had goods." Terrence concludes.

"That's actually pretty cool." Avrel smiles. It's much better than the story that the ferryman told them.

Geric has long since just taken to staring out the corner window in his boredom but not everyone learns such things in stuffy monastery classes.

Zanvan of course, smokes the time away. "So are we sure Lucia isn't going to try to get out on foot?" Zanvan asks.

"Are you kidding?" Gil says confidently. "As soon as Old Harry got taken down we sent out messenger arrows in all directions, if she so much as sneezes in these woods she's going to have a new nostril in her forehead."

"That's a lovely picture..." Avrel sighs.

"So, Miss *Not-Haley*..." Terrence asks in his jolly tone. "I take it your father was an elf?"

"Why yes, actually." Avrel smiles.

"And obviously your mother was gnomish, no?" he says, deadly seriously.

Laughter erupts so suddenly from Geric that he blows snot from his nostril. It's the kind of shrill laughter that only comes from pure bliss.

Son of a... she scowls, fighting the urge to let it show too much externally. "I.... uhh...." Avrel leans over, shaking her head. "Who is Haley?" she asks, trying to change the subject.

"What? Zanvan, you never tol-"

Again, at the name, Zanvan looks disconcerted and shuts the older man up with just a leer. Zanvan's eyes grow heavy, burdened even. "I think I'm going to take a look around outside..." he mutters as he stands up to leave.

"Sure." Gil says, showing him the door. As the door shuts Gil looks over to Terrence. "Dammit you need to learn to not just say anything that pops into your head."

"Sorry, Gil." Terrence concedes.

It never stops Geric, Avrel thinks to herself.

"So... Who is Haley?" Geric asks, finally taking part in the conversation, aside from his hideous outburst of laughter.

"Haley was Zanvan's little sister." Terrence explains. "She was small, auburn haired. Without my glasses you looked quite like how I remember her."

"Your memory isn't the best." Gil puts in.

"She was a ranger too?" Geric asks.

"No, she just visited here often, hoping to see her older brother." Gil remarks. "Zanvan really never told you any of this?"

"No." Geric grunts. "Only this week did we even find out that he's in a relationship with the bloody *Princess of Argoth*."

"You men aren't always very open with your feelings." Avrel adds. *Unless they want you.* She almost adds further.

The two woodsmen give glances back and forth, '*How much should they tell about their friend?*' they seem to communicate.

"Zanvan's mother died of sickness soon after Haley was born." Gil explains. "His father took to drinking to cope."

"Zanvan started living out here when he was around twelve or thirteen" Terrence says solemnly. "Haley often visited when she came to that age. They were rarely here at the same time but when their paths did cross you could see how much they cared for each other."

"Well..." Avrel asks delicately. "What happened?"

"One day, about twelve years ago..." Terrence sighs. He doesn't seem to want to go on. "Haley was here waiting for Zanvan since they'd promised to meet that month, the day he arrived she was out picking flowers in the forest."

Gil's thin face is grim. "An orken hunter shot her with a crossbow bolt." he finishes.

It's not what either Avrel or Geric were expecting. "By accident?" she gasps.

"The *first* shot was." Gil says more grimly. "*Supposedly.*"

Avrel's shock turns to deep sadness, as she holds back tears. She cups her hands over her mouth and nose.

"Orcs are such arses!" Geric says disgustedly. "What the hell!?"

"Yeah." Gil comments. "You can understand why Zanvan might be a little touchy on that subject." he says with a glare to the older man in his thick glasses.

"Huh..." Avrel mutters. "I guess I just never pictured him being like that, I just... You know... Macho bedswerver man..."

"Yeah." Terrence chuckles, lightening up just a bit. "Zanvan is quite the ladies man. I think part of that comes from him missing his sister though, despite what you might think, he can be very protective of women he meets, I think you ladies like that."

Avrel sighs, remembering Järviby. "Yeah..." she exhales. Even *she* does, but then, he's the only man to protect her from much of anything.

"So tell me..." Geric inquires, "Did he ever catch the guy who did it?"

Gil and Terrence both shrug.

"He never really talked about that." Gil explains. "In fact, his coming by here became far more sparse after that."

"Yeah..." Avrel can see why. She'd never considered Zanvan's, or Geric's family for that matter. It's never crossed her mind before that Zanvan could have even the slightest clue to what she's been through. *A good for nothing father, losing a mother, a sister.* She can feel herself about to cry. "I'm going to look for Candice." she says tenderly, "I haven't seen her since we came inside."

"Have fun." Geric replies as he begins chowing through the remains of Zanvan's bowl of stew.

Avrel exits Gil's cabin to find Zanvan leaning against a tree, smoking his pipe, acting cool, collected and unaffected. It's different though, now that she knows what he's lived with. Could she ever be like that? It's a doubtful wonder.

"What's up?" he asks, after she is caught taking a peek at him.

"Oh, nothing." Avrel replies quietly, maybe he'd rather be alone. "Have you seen Candice?"

"Yeah." Zanvan says pointing towards the water through the trees. "She's over by the shore, playing with some coypus."

"Thanks." Avrel says as she heads that way, she'll let him smoke, it's his way.

Avrel walks out to the shore to see that Candice is indeed wrestling with a pack of coypus by Lucia's damaged boat. "Hey, what's up?" Avrel says as she sits down on a large, smooth, river rock.

"Chippu!" Candice squeaks before being mobbed by the squeaks of the other coypus.

"Just tell them you're sorry for smashing their den and they'll leave you alone." Avrel giggles. Candice rejects that notion and continues tussling with the river rats. Avrel laughs heartily, almost falling backwards off of the rock. As she's wiping a tear from her eye she notices a strange smell in the air. She stands up and looks around her, but her elf eyes see nothing but moonlit trees and water.

Hmmm. Maybe one of these coypus pooped up wind somewhere. Avrel thinks to herself. But it doesn't smell like shite, not even Candice's which would be close. It's more herby, and more foul.

Just then Avrel hears a twig snap behind her, she turns to look but is quickly tackled by Lucia. Avrel struggles to get her off of herself but is unable to. The orc woman is built like a man.

"Candice! Get the others!" Avrel yells, but Candice instead starts biting at Lucia's feet, drawing her focus away from Avrel, allowing Avrel to get unpinned. "Now go!" Avrel yells as she draws her staff. Avrel hears as Candice scurries up the incline leading to the treeline but then suddenly falls over. "Candice!" Avrel screams as she notices a putrid smelling, green vapor pouring out of the forest.

Lucia says nothing and simply smiles as she unsheathes a glaive. She's not in all of her bulky armor anymore, just in a form fitting undersuit.

"Is this some kind of orken black magic!?" Avrel questions angrily. "A... An orc witch's brew?!" Geric would know, but either way, the smell is nauseating.

"Sort of." Lucia says playfully as she thrusts towards Avrel. "I had to make do with what I could find out here!"

Avrel dodges the stab, and with all her might manages to knock the glaive away.

"Hmm, you're not as much of a knave as I thought." Lucia says jumping back and regaining her composure. "Alright..." the orc says as she pulls out the Runeblade handle and with a brief moment of concentration the arcanium blade flashes and bells into existence, taking the form of a halberd. Avrel tries to keep her wits but the fumes begin to affect her.

"I'm gonna make you--!..." Avrel tries to keep standing but falls to her knees. Lucia laughs but as she's about to cut Avrel down the blade flickers out.

"Death on this is too good for you." the orc frys. She looks around for a moment in the dark, "Where's my glaive!?" Lucia growls in frustration. There's no sign of it, so she turns back towards Avrel and kicks her in the face. Avrel fights the deep feeling of sleepiness as her clouded eyes see Lucia's shadowy figure walk over to their boat, until at last her will is spent and she goes unconscious.

***

Isis watched, helpless to her only daughter as she herself could barely stand. For which, her daughter was paying the price. "Stop!" it took all of her strength to say.

The Argoth Guards put her down, and within a few moments, she and Avrel were off to a new place, a new alley where they'd not be bothered for a while. But Isis knew what was coming, and she couldn't bear to burden her poor child with any more grief than what was to come.

But she knew what was coming.

She had for some time.

She and her daughter found a shady alley near some stands where maybe some scraps would be left over after they are wheeled away. As she took her place, seated against the warm brick, she could feel the rattles in her chest with each breath. She could feel the numbness in her mottled feet, and the coldness in her hands.

"Avrel…" she said, holding her dear girl close. "I know it's hard, but promise me, don't use your magic on people, or living things." she said, thinking of her beloved Shäddäi, whom Avrel's face so resembled.

Avréliä, still so young, gave her the classically childish, 'Oh mom', look.

"Promise me." she begged, "Scream, claw, fight… but no magic."

Her girl tilted her head, but nodded after a moment or so. "Yes, Mother." she eventually complied.

She took a lingering look at her with her dim, dry eyes. She was so tired, and felt that every blink gave her eyes the chance to never open again. "Love you." she managed to smile as her eyes fell shut. She begged them not to, but they couldn't open.

They wouldn't.

No matter how she tried, sleep was talking hold of her, and scattering her thoughts.

Avrel… Her girl will grow up with no father, no sibling, no mother. Isis couldn't bear to think of it, but it was the only line of thought she could hold. Her daughter deserved a home, a family, people that'd love and take care of her.

But it seems… she lamented, That it will not be me. Not for her as she grows older, not for her as she navigates life beyond her youth, not in understanding her father's power.

Not from Isis, ever after that final sleep, even as she heard her daughter calling her.

She would not awaken.

***

The next morning, Avrel wakes to Candice's nervous face as she's shaken and slapped awake by Zanvan. She's aware for several minutes but she can't seem to open her eyes, finally she flails to full wokenness, even awake, the dream's feelings persist. *Mother...*

"Ugh..." Avrel groans out. "You guys ok?"

"Yeah we're fine." Zanvan says, "We were worried about you, your nose must've been bleeding, we feared the worst."

Avrel leans up, feeling sickly she then immediately vomits. "Oh shite! Oh please uggghhh..." she cries out as her gut expels its contents, down to its own bile.

"Yeah..." Geric says as he walks up to her with a potion of some sort. "On someone so small that vapor might have that effect."

There's still some to come. "What the hell was all that?!" Avrel gasps between expulsions. It's like when she learned not to eat forgotten fish.

"Lucia." Geric answers. "She made a black magic brew with some plants in the woods." She knew he'd know.

"Yeah." Zanvan adds. "One of the guys found the source this morning after some of us woke up." He places his hand on Avrel's back, comfortingly.

"Agh!..." Avrel heaves once more, "So she just found some sleep-vapor ingredients in the forest?"

"Yeah." Geric grunts. "We're lucky she didn't find anything *more* toxic."

Avrel feels her innards quiver climatically with one last eruption that takes almost all of her breath. "I think she took our boat." Avrel pants as she *finally* stops vomiting. She hopes 'finally'.

Geric looks in wonder at the vast puddle of vomit and seems oblivious to the fact that Avrel is talking. "How can somebody so small barf *so* much?" the cleric laughs as she crawls to the river bank to wash up.

"It's not funny!" Avrel bites back as she splashes her face with the river water and wipes herself off.

"Yeah, our boat is gone." Zanvan confirms, ignoring the banter. "Some of the guys are already stringing together a raft for us to use." he explains after giving Geric a hard shove.

"Wait, the boat is gone?" Geric inquires. At that, Avrel throws her used washcloth at Geric's face. "Hmm... Sour." he says with a sniff.

Gil walks up with some of the other woodsmen who are dragging a raft to the water. "You're going to have trouble catching her now." he sighs.

"Yeah, we know." Zanvan says sharply.

Gil looks around nervously for a moment. "Avenge Terrence, please." Gil says somberly.

Avrel is troubled upon hearing this, "Mr. Terrence *died*?" she asks.

Zanvan nods solemnly, but says nothing, just tipping his hat down.

"Is that a glaive?" Geric says as he takes what must be Lucia's glaive out of a bush.

"Alright, you three-" Gil is cut off as Candice smacks his leg with her tail, "Ummmm four? Get going." he continues.

"Yeah." Zanvan replies as they gather on the sturdy, spacious raft.

As they shove off and Geric raises the sail, Avrel begins channeling her wind spell, filling the sail.

"Plug that green bitch with her own glaive, cleric!" Gil yells to them as they speed away.

Geric smiles and waves back.

Yeah. thinks Avrel, *and if he doesn't, she will.*

***

Days. *Days* they've been scooting down this river on this half-arsed raft made by a bunch of industrious, forest hobos. Every day they hope that they are gaining on the orken bitch, but somehow Geric can't help but think they aren't. Avrel tries to sleep when she can, but if they want a dark-sider's chance of catching her that's not often. As much as he hates to admit it, his wind spell, at least the one he knows, isn't nearly as good as hers for filling the makeshift sail. They manage to get into a decent routine after a few days. One afternoon, while Avrel rests, Geric and Zanvan are arguing over a wrong turn where the river forked and how they can get back on track.

"I told you to start steering south!" Zanvan exclaims.

"We're on a boat!" Geric replies defensively. "How am I supposed to be able to discern north and south?" *Not everybody is a damned ranger.*

The ranger points towards the sun, "Because we are, and have only been traveling *east*, you ignoramus!" Zanvan says, slapping the face of his map.

"It's okay!" he shouts back as he points further down the river "We'll get off of the Argothian River by Willow Island and head southeast!" Geric wails.

For a moment there is silence.

"Wake the kid." Zanvan says, "She'll need to be the one to steer the winds."

Geric feels the damned rat watch his every move as he approaches its womanlet master. "Hey, this sail isn't going to blow itself." Geric says as he shakes her continually. "Also your beaver was lonely." Avrel awakes from her deep sleep to see that it is midday.

"Ughh... Alright, alright..." she groans. "Damn my head hurt last night. Nightmare too..." she says taking a deep breath. "Only it didn't seem like a nightmare..." she mutters.

"Probably residual effects from that sleep vapor." Geric replies as he hands her some bread.

"Hmmmm..." she grumbles as she accepts the food. "It felt really strange."

"How so?" Geric inquires.

"It didn't feel like a dream." she answers. "I didn't feel even like I was asleep."

He considers it a moment. There's no chance she was projecting or casting a far-see in her sleep, "Orken brews hit people differently." he shrugs.

"Anyway." Zanvan puts in. "No thanks to Geric, we're back on course for the orken border." he says as he lights his pipe, this time being careful so that it doesn't blow out.

Avrel nods, "Alright."

And Geric lies back.

17

One afternoon a few days after they've corrected the cleric's screw up, the kid is loudly rummaging through the bag of provisions, which is significantly emptier.

"Where are my dried mealworms?" she asks. "Princess Catarina had some prepared for me." she frets.

Geric is sitting in the corner of the raft and is dangling a piece of string with a hook on it into the water. Upon hearing Avrel's distress, he carefully and silently pushes the bag of worms out of sight. "Dried mealworms you say?" he tries to say nonchalantly.

"Yeah, they are like dried grubs, a little salt and pepper and they are quite good. Good for you too, not that I had many options growing up, but as a damned petfood it was affordable." Avrel says as she gets more aggravated at the lack of her special food.

Zanvan chuckles, it's funny too, but he really doesn't want to get between them. He never does. "So you'll eat worms, but you didn't seem to like that sauced varmit I made a few weeks back?" he tries to deflect for the 'cleric's' sake.

"My best friend is a beaver" Avrel snaps. "It's a little different."

"Alright, alright." Zanvan says passively.

"Hmm..." Avrel moans with a heavy sigh. "They must've gotten lost when we were in the woods. Damn." She begins breathing through her nose for a moment. "Wait a minute..." she says with a heavier sniff. "Candice, do you smell that? I still smell my worms." she continues.

Geric freezes and breaks into a sweat. "Hahaha, that's funny, I didn't know you'd be able to smell something that was *clearly* left many, many miles upstream." Geric says as he inches the bag up and over the side of the raft. "You... You stinking elves you." he laughs, unconvincingly.

Just then, dozens of manic fish begin jumping around the raft, swallowing up the sinking worms.

"What the hell?" Avrel yelps as she leans down to the side of the raft.

"Damn you fish!" Geric yells as he shakes his fist at them.

Zanvan, smiles and shakes his head at what he's witnessed, this is definitely a thing he can lord over the 'cleric' with next time he requires some motivation. After all, his competitiveness with Avrel only goes so far. "Hurry up." he sighs.

After settling for another type of sustenance, Avrel gets back to filling the sails. He hates to push her, but then, it was her suggestion to go after Lucia like this, she played right into Cat's hand.

"Find any better air spells?" he asks as Geric looks to be ready to lie down with his books.

He leans back up, slightly. "Working on it." he groans before flipping pages.

Zanvan looks down the river, and around. They are far past the Rudaski area now, and chances of catching the orc inside Argoth's borders are slim to one now. "I wish you would." he turns to Geric. After such a delay, he wonders if Geric still has his previous statement in mind.

The look on his face says he does. The cleric looks to Avrel, and back to Zanvan. "Believe me, I am."

That evening, as Zanvan scouts ahead with his keen, hunter's eyes, he can see the river narrowing up ahead. He hopes it is anyway, Avrel would be able to tell, but her eyes are shut as she concentrates hard on her spell. Zanvan looks around for other landmarks, and once he's sure they are where he believes they are, he taps Geric.

"From here we'll have to continue on foot." Zanvan says as he gets the 'cleric's' attention.

"That's nice." yawns Geric.

"I was thinking you might help her steer." Zanvan adds, "The current might be a little hard to get out of."

"Avrel?" Geric tags her. Her response is minimal, and Geric gets that bloody sardonic grin on his face. "Quick! Lucy's on the shore and she's got Candice!"

Avrel flushes an angry red and almost blows them over as her rageful response comes as a swift, angular wind. Zanvan holds tightly to the raft and his hat until the thud of sliding up the river bank.

"Candice!" Avrel leaps off the grounded raft and looks around, her hands glowing with her magic. It's not the help he'd had in mind, but Geric's method worked.

Sort of. "She's here." Zanvan says, pointing to the rodent clinging to the makeshift mast. He watches Avrel's battle-ready eyes dart to the 'cleric'.

"Gotcha!" he grins.

Avrel quite clearly is unamused, threateningly throwing a blast of force away before coming to grab her pet. "So now what?" she asks, gravelly. She sounds tired, if not somehow in pain.

Zanvan thinks for a moment as they disembark. He knows they can't leave it there, the question is what to do with it. Luckily, sparse as most of orken land is with wild vegetation, there are some bushes near the water. "Hey Geric, help me pull this raft over into that bushy area over there." he says as he attempts to lift a corner of the sizable raft.

"Excuse me?" the 'cleric' questions, "I feel like this thing isn't going anywhere, it's too damn big!" Geric says adamantly.

"Try anyway." Zanvan says with a glare.

"Ehhhhh..." Geric groans as he halfheartedly attempts to pull the raft. After a few minutes of straining and loud cursing, Geric grows tired of 'trying' to move the large raft. "Hey Candice, you fat little rat! Eat this for us!" Geric shouts.

"Lower your voice!" he says pretty loudly himself. "The point isn't to get rid of it, it's to hide it so we can use it later if needs be." Zanvan pants.

"Avrel." Geric barks at about the same volume. "Stop standing over there looking at us and do something! Lift it, show us that size doesn't matter, lift it like a ship lost in a swamp, you stupid pointy eared freak." he shouts, stumbling around, seemingly drunken with overexertion.

Yet he wields a mace. Zanvan can't help but note.

"That was uncalled for." Avrel says, trying to keep her lower lip stiff. "Besides, it *is* too big. I don't even think somebody trained in telekinetic magics could lift this easily." she laments.

"So you can conjure storms but you can't lift a raft?" Zanvan scoffs, taking a page from Geric's book.

"Hmm." Avrel hums, touching her curled finger to her lips. She then closes her eyes and clasps her weather magic gem and spins around, as she turns back towards the raft she throws her arms towards the raft. Suddenly a powerful gale blasts past her and takes up and throws the raft into the bushes. It's not as cleanly done as he'd hoped, but...

"Does that work?" Avrel pants.

"Yeah." he admits.

"*I thought you said you couldn't lift stuff!?*" Geric yells.

"Blasted it with wind magic, didn't lift it..." Avrel says as she looks again towards the brush. "However, I'm not sure how we're going to get it *out* of there." she says, scratching the back of her head where the wind tangled her hair.

"Whatever." Zanvan says as he leads them on. "We're almost at Yordasvin's border, let's keep going."

The land grows uglier and deader as they near the orken border. After so many days cramped in that little boat and then the raft, it feels good to stretch their legs.

Him and Geric anyway, the kid ducks behind some brush just as the actual border gate on the road comes into sight. Knowing full well she can see it, they continue on rather than wait on her to do her business. Knowing her, she probably prefers that.

After a few minutes, Geric gets a very puzzled expression on his face as they continue further up the road. "Hey, the river is still here." he points out. "Why did we ditch the raft??" Geric asks, again far too loudly.

"Because, the water is flowing the wrong way here, it's easier just to walk." Zanvan explains. "And shut it!"

"For Avrel maybe." Geric replies sharply.

Zanvan leans in closer. "We also need to keep a low profile." he whispers. "Zipping by on a raft isn't going to do us any favors. -- Nor does mentioning it!"

That coaxes a nod out of him. "Alright." he shrugs.

They come upon the border crossing where a few hulky orken guards are chatting in orkish, and don't seem interested in him or Geric.

"Excuse us." Geric asks assertively. "May we come through?"

The interrupted orc swears in his harsh, orken tongue. "That depends." the orc growls.

"On what?" Geric asks innocently.

The two orcs stare blankly at him and resume their conversation, though having stopped to speak in the common tongue, it sticks.

"So I was like, 'really?' and she was like 'totally!' so I spun her around and-"

Lovely images these orcs are giving them as they both brag about their exploits. Zanvan's got them beat anyway, at least in *country* matters. "Excuse us, we really need to get into Yordasvin." Zanvan speaks up.

"Ehhh, what are ya?" one orc asks. "Merchants from Rudaski?"

Zanvan and Geric look at each other, "Mmm*Suuuuuureeee*." the 'cleric' replies.

"What you looking to trade?" the other orc asks.

Zanvan pushes past Geric before the fool can open his mouth again, "We're here to negotiate the contract on bi-yearly shipments of --"

"Alright." the other orc says as he lifts up the gate.

Zanvan and Geric pass and look for the nearest rock to sit and wait for the kid.

***

"Ugh..." Avrel grunts angrily as she fastens her pant belt. It's dark behind the bush, even for her eyes.

"Chippu?" Candice squeaks.

"Yeah yeah." she frys, "I can watch the moon *too*, I've been a big occupied, and not very private." Avrel laments. "It just really sucks for it to happen when we're on foot like this, Bloaty, my chest wrap feels tight... Ugh.."

"Chippu chippu." Candice chirps.

"Tee-hee *'bloody problem' very* clever." Avrel replies saltily. "C'mon, the boys are waiting up ahead." Avrel says to Candice as she pushes through the brush and gets back on the path.

Avrel eventually comes to the border gate and can see her friends sitting on a rock off in the distance. Avrel stands there for a moment, waiting for the orcs at the gate to notice her. She feels fragile and vulnerable in their presence, they are *huge*. Taller than Geric, more muscular than a professional brawler, and by their conversation, not respectful of women. She wishes the guys were a bit closer.

"So then she's all over my tusks, gripping them tightly and pressing her cheek against it when–"

"Ahem!" Avrel grows impatient and interrupts the orc's story. The larger of the two orcs stands up and leans over her, towering over her by nearly three feet.

She tries not to be intimidated, she has a perfect right to ask for passage through–– Or she would, were her business not to bump off their rogue princess. "I need to get through... please." Avrel shyly mutters out.

"Why?" he growls.

"Well I...Uhh...." Avrel stammers, stepping back, trying to think up a lie, what's worse is how it might look if it doesn't match the guys'. "I..."

The other orc's bull ring twitches as he sniffs intently. "I smell blood!" he shouts as he jumps to attention.

"What are you hiding, she-elf!?" the taller orc growls as he grabs her by the arm and pulls her closer. His hand could practically grip her around her waist if he wanted.

She sweats as she feels a dreadful chill come over her. "Nothing!" Avrel cries out.

"We don't like you she-elf!" the other orc says stepping forward. "Not at *all!*" The two hulky orc men lift Avrel over the window that separates them.

"Am I being detained?" she whimpers.

"Why do you smell like blood!?" the tall orc asks. "You wanted for murder!? *Blood on your hands!?*"

"No I.... Candice!" Avrel yelps. "Get the guys!" With that, Candice dashes under the gate and heads towards Geric and Zanvan.

"Hey!" the orc barks. "What are you doing with that big muskrat!?" the orc asks, tightening his grip on Avrel's thin arms. "We don't like creepy druids either!"

"Nothing!" Avrel pleads, not even knowing what in blazes a druid is. "I don't know what you guys want! I just want to pass through the gate!".

"You are *suspicious!*" the tall orc growls. "Elves cannot be trusted!"

"Yeah." the other orc growls as he pulls her hair. "If you are not a murderer elf, you must be here to preach tree-love and villainize our furnaces!"

"No!!" Avrel yelps, "Although, from what I've heard, you really ought to respect the forests more." she mumbles. *Women too.*

"That's it!" the orc growls. "You're not wanted!"

"Yeah, we'll send for authorities!" the taller orc growls as he points his long, cracked fingernail precariously close to her nose. "You're here to cause trouble and incite riots!"

"Excuse me." Avrel grunts as she begins to struggle, "Does this mean I am being *further* detained!?" It's taking all her restraint not to blast them to hell. Just then Geric and Zanvan, led by Candice, come running up to the border house.

"Fellas, she's with us." Geric says, trying to sound very nonchalant.

"She's a merchant?" the orc asks, his disgusting nail touching her lip, it smells of...

"Yeah sure, she's sold... stuff before." Geric replies.

"But elves don't trade with orcs." the taller orc says cautiously. "Very suspicious."

Zanvan brushes that off, "Oh no, Avrel's only half elf, she grew up in Argoth, she's one of us!" he explains in a paper-thin phony friendliness to the orcs.

"Well, 'one of us' may be taking it a bit too far-" Geric mumbles as he's silenced by Candice's nip.

"Oh..." the orcs say as they relax their grip, then they suddenly burst out laughing. "Hahahahaha!" the tall orc laughs with a spray, "Tiny half-elf lady's too small to kill anyone!"

"Pro-forest protest sign would be too small to read without glasses!" the other laughs with a gargled snorting. "Or too big for her to carry if it was big enough for us to read!"

The taller orc scrunches down and walks on his knees. "Look at me, I'm the smelly elf lady, my only friend is a giant rat!" The comments and laughing continue as Zanvan, Geric, Candice, and Avrel take their chance to leave. She has to purse her lips hard together as she tries not to cry.

Even a long ways off, the orc's borish laughter is still audible to her ears.

"Well..." Avrel sighs after they've traveled a while. "*That* was unpleasant."

"I mean." Geric laughs, "They were kind of right."

Avrel doesn't honor his comment with an answer, not even the slap he so richly deserves.

"You okay?" Zanvan asks her. "Do you need a moment?"

"No." she sighs, "I'll be okay."

"Alright then, lets go."

Zanvan leads them through the ever drier, dustier river valley as they follow the ever more polluted river towards Yordasvin, hoping to catch up to Lucia. But running for that long is just not an option for her. And damn it all if she doesn't need to stop again because of it.

"Ugh..." Avrel blanches, casting her eyes at the river. "This water is so filthy."

"Ehh so?" Geric says brushing her off. "We have full canteens."

"Yeah but..." Avrel sighs. "I'd kind of like some fresher water for *other* things. Candice would probably also like to take a dip."

"Too bad." Geric says crassly. "Your dry beaver will get over it. And keep up!"

"Well *I* need to stop for a minute." Avrel retorts, *Long legged sard.*

The ranger stops and turns with a sigh, but maybe he understands. Goodness knows, he must know a lot about 'womanhood'. "Alright, we'll wait up ahead." Zanvan says calmly.

"Aw c'mon!" Geric laments. "We'll never catch that green bitch at this rate!"

She ignores him and quickly goes off the path into some dead and dry bushes to tend to her sanitary rag as she hears Geric complaining up in the distance.

"Seriously." Geric sounds very annoyed, "She's barely been drinking any of her water, why has she been relieving herself so often the last three days? Remember, same thing happened on 'Berb's' cart for a while!" she hears as the guys' voices fade into the distance.

"Chippu!" Candice squeaks angrily.

"Yes, but he's *my* oblivious kook of a friend." Avrel dismisses. "Though I agree, he's supposed to be a damned healer, he should know." *Maybe even have a potion or something.*

After rinsing her rag as best she can with what water she has left in her canteen, Avrel replaces it and stumbles through the bushes towards the road. She's almost out when she trips over what appears to be a large log.

Huh, this looks almost like finished wood... she thinks to herself. There's no bark on it, and it has a certain sheen to it.

"Chippu!" Candice squeaks.

"What?! Are you sure!?" Avrel replies.

Candice nods and runs and fetches the guys and quickly returns with them.

"What's up?" Zanvan asks when they've made it back to her.

"Candice says that this is the mast from our boat!" Avrel explains.

"Okay... So then where does she propose the rest of the boat is?" Geric says snarkily.

"Hmmm." Zanvan ponders. "I suppose she sank it and hid this part so it wouldn't stick up or float."

"I guess she failed because we still know she's going this way." Avrel says optimistically.

"Yeah." Zanvan says as he examines the brush clippings that were hiding the mast, "This looks somewhat fresh, look." he points, "The leaves still have some green, see?" he explains. "We might be able to catch her." he says, "If it weren't for the bloody river we could try and cut across and intercept her that way." He gets Avrel's attention, "Try to keep up, okay?" he says.

"Okay."

For several more days they continue with a fast pace and with little rest. After the first few, she begins to feel a bit better. But regardless, they pass inns, small villages, and the like with no sign of Lucia. The dirty river roars as they grow closer to Yordasvin, seemingly louder and louder each passing hour that they've not caught her.

Geric eventually questions if they might have *passed* her.

"I'm just saying." Geric shrugs, "Why couldn't we ask around at one of the inns we passed and maybe stay there?"

"Because--" Zanvan grunts as he drops his face to his palm. "*Nobody* can know we're looking for anybody, we're here, and that's all anybody needs to know."

"We've passed others on this road!" Geric points out, "Now what's to say *her highness* might not have been royally pooped?"

"Call it a hunch." Zanvan says lowly, "I think she's looking to get back to her halls as soon as possible."

"Maybe..." Geric blanches as the wind carries its smells and drives them into their faces. "I can only guess they have scented candles or incense in those royal halls." he gags a little, "Because they sure could use some out here."

"Hey buddy." Avrel says, pointing to her nose. "You think it smells bad *for you?*" But at least they agree on something.

"Besides..." Geric admits, "I'm dying on three hours a night."

"The inn would likely have stunk as well." Zanvan replies.

"But they had nice beds." Geric sighs. "Besides, we haven't caught Lucia yet, and according to you, we're not far from Yordasvin! We *aren't* going to catch her at this rate!" he laments.

"Shh!" Avrel shushes, "Keep your voice down!"

Zanvan is silent for a moment and sighs. "If we get to Yordasvin and we haven't found her... Well." he says, very drawn out. "We'll know where she'll be heading."

Avrel feels her stomach turn, "That's..."

"A great way to start a war." Geric finishes for her. It's not what she was to say, but it fits. "Not to mention it's suicide."

"Think about it." Zanvan says, grimly, as he turns to face them. "She's looking for a war, if one's to start, it's by her hand, not ours."

Geric scoffs, "It seems the independent ranger becomes a simpleton for his Princess." he says at Avrel, but obviously only to chide Zanvan.

"You have a better idea, *cleric*?" Zanvan asks. "She's already drawn blood, in *my* woods. Would you let her have them? Would you let them only be the first?"

Avrel looks around at the desolate, bleak wastes that are this land, dominated, not inhabited by orcs; raped, barren, dim and brown. She compares it to the lush Argothian forests, and that alone makes her mind up. "I'm with Zanvan on this." she says. "I don't give a damn about The Crown, or that rotten city, but I don't want these toxic sards pillaging all the splendor I've seen outside of Argoths walls."

Geric sighs heavily, it's clear he knows they can't turn back now. "Fine." he gulps. "Fine."

The men seem to come to a truce, but they are silent and still, even as Lucia makes her way ever closer to her heavily fortified home. "So how much further is it?" Avrel asks, hoping to get things started.

"Hmm..." Zanvan explains as he opens a map to double check. "If I remember correctly, the Yord River meets with a canal from the Grey Lake up ahead. There *should* be a bridge."

Her insides squeeze at the name of that lake, "Why is it called the 'Grey' Lake?" Avrel asks.

"I've heard it's full of ash and dust from their furnaces and such." Geric explains as Zanvan folds up the map and puts it in his satchel. "It makes the water milky and grey."

Zanvan waves an open hand to Geric, giving him credit for his knowledge or some shite.

"Legends say..." Geric adds, "It used to be a lighter silvery grey from all of the silt that washed down from the mountain highlands." basking in his moment.

It's so sad to her as an elf, that every bit of her elven blood seems to want to cry. Suffice to say, she feels her face frown. "That... Makes me feel sad." Avrel sighs.

"Somebody call a dispatch writer!" Geric says, mocking cupping his hands around his mouth as a horn, "An elf is sad over something involving nature." he chuckles.

"But it *is* sad!" Avrel protests.

"Keep it down, Avrel." Zanvan says politely, yet firmly. "I get how you feel but we don't need any more incidents where you're mistaken for an environmental activist."

"Okay." Avrel nods softly. Just then they come to another bridge complex leading over the merging waterways. "Oh mother of mercy!" Avrel yelps as she kneels down, pinching her nose tightly.

Zanvan extends a hand to help her up. "Okay, so the joke goes 'why do so many orcs have bullrings?'" he asks.

Geric shrugs, "Because when you're that ugly, why not?"

Avrel and Zanvan both give him a disapproving glare. "Well actually…" Zanvan says dryly, "The answer is supposed to be, 'because they'll do anything to keep from smelling this,' but you soiled it." Zanvan laments.

Avrel whimpers. "Like they soiled, what was a beautiful lake and river?"

At that a nearby orc traveler raises a brow and stares at Avrel disdainfully. Before she can cover for herself, Geric grabs her and starts rubbing his fist into her hair, "Oh… Avrel, you…" he says with a phoney smile, "Goofy little elf! Haha, very funny!" he says, trying to play down Avrel's comment before releasing her. He no doubt draws *more* attentions to her with all that, but she doesn't say anything,

The traveler passes by, callously bumping Avrel as he passes.

"I'm not going to like this place, am I?" Avrel asks Zanvan in a low tone.

"Probably not." he admits darkly, "But you'll have a couple days to prepare yourself before we reach the city gates. I suggest you."

Avrel nods, and stretches as she's sure they'll be off in a moment. "Yeah." she sighs, "But how bad can it be?"

She's never seen so much metal. From even a few miles away there is soot and a foulness on the air, but closer, past many of the smaller houses outside the walls is the wall itself. Argoth's walls seemed high, ugly, and a cage, but they sparkled in the sun. These are black-iron, dull, and intimidating.

It may be the ugliest structure she's ever seen. After the last few days, she's begun to understand why the elves and orcs don't get along. This wall; this obtrusive, monolithic, eye-sore of a city wall absolutely cements that point. It's made from giant forges spewing shite into the air and water, it itself is ugly and built purely for durability, it has no natural aesthetic, no shimmer for the light to dance upon. Just pitted, aged black iron, standing like a hole of utter blackness against the barely alive landscape around it.

"…They *really* have a thing for iron." Avrel comments as she disgustedly marvels at the large wall around Yordasvin.

"Yeah come on." Zanvan says as he leads them into the city. Just inside, it's suddenly far noisier. Unlike the area outside the wall, there is considerably more commerce and loud carts and wagons. And a lot of yelling.

After they pass a line of shoppes, Zanvan yanks her and Geric into a dark alley. He takes them deep in, and looks cautiously all around. "Ok, so we need to find an alibi; ideas?" he asks.

"We're sleeping in a nice cozy inn." Geric suggests. "One that doesn't smell like the rest of this city."

Avrel nods, she guesses an 'alibi' is like an excuse or something. "And you're off with some woman." Avrel scoffs.

Zanvan thinks for a moment, his teeth gritted. "I suppose Geric's is our best shot, check into an inn, and sneak out."

"Yeah!" Geric says victoriously.

"Alright so…" Avrel tries to build onto the idea, "We check in, and what? Pretend to get plastered and then stagger into our rooms?" Avrel asks.

"Yeah." Zanvan agrees "The getting drunk part sounds good too. We should sign under different names too…" Zanvan thinks for a moment.

First he points to Avrel, "Uhh…" she's never had a thought about another name. "Faithe?"

Then he points to Geric, "Mattheos?" the cleric shrugs.

Then he points to himself, "Rai." he says, "And until we're out of here, those are the names we will use unless we are amongst ourselves." Zanvan says authoritatively.

"Alright." Geric moans. "Let's find an inn, I'm beat…"

"Yeah…" Avrel says, tired and groggy. "We should actually rest before tonight."

Zanvan nods, finally admitting that they've failed to catch her. "Yeah." And so he leads them back into the bustling, smoggy city.

The streets to which the view in the trash-ridden alley is preferable. "This place is so disgusting!" Avrel whispers. "There's not a tree to be seen, just sooty buildings everywhere."

Geric sighs and pretends to ignore her. But she catches him glancing around, and judging by his expression, the billowing pipes exuding hot gas and smoke from the many ironclad workshops aren't the prettiest of sights to his eyes either.

Geric looks around at the crowd in the city square. "MmThey may be green monsters, but I can't seem to hate this place." Geric says jocularly to Avrel, she knows that the manner of his smile means a joke at her expense.

She might as well hear it. "What? Why?" Avrel replies perturbedly.

"Everyone is so *tall*, it's great." Geric says with a scuzzy grin.

"Yeah, uh huh." Avrel replies trying to hide her obvious offense, she's not in the mood. "Can we look for an inn, *Mattheos*?"

"Over there." Zanvan points, "Best part is, that street leads to *where we're headed*." Zanvan whispers, while he shows it on a map. "I think…"

"Yay." Avrel whispers enthusiastically.

"Alright, let's go!" Geric whines. "I've been stricken with tiredness."

Avrel leans down and picks up Candice, who also seems very tired, "Yeah." she agrees, "We all could use a rest."

Zanvan nods as he puts away his map. and leads them to the inn.

18

Shortly after they check in and place their packs in their room they all take a few hours to rest and prepare their things for later that night. Geric reads a bit, Zanvan smokes, and she strokes Candice, falling in and out of a nap. Everytime she drifts off, her dreams, all too real, show her the gravity of what she and her friends are undertaking.

"Zanvan." she asks groggily after one such vision. He leans up and gives her attention, but just as soon she doesn't want to discuss it. They're men, they're not like her, and they wouldn't understand.

"Nervous?" he asks anyway.

She recounts the most recent dream to herself; a memory of fending off Shad with a magic blast of white and rainbows much the same as a blast he shot at them in Järviby, of how as a *child* she was able to do that, of how she wonders if she could use the power to take out this wicked country's wicked princess... She is nervous, she is afraid, but not so of their mission, of this idiotic plot that stemmed from the ill-fated result of that simple job; she's afraid of the pieces begining to line up for her. What that man in Järviby said about Shad, of those unnamable spells, of how her mother begged her to promise not to use her spells on others. Are they all related, she wonders. "Just a little?" she gulps.

"Vvüt you Vvizsh to discúss it?" Geric says in some bizzare accent. Orkish she would guess.

"Nah." she sighs, but she actually would. Not with them though, not at this time. "It's fine."

"Well." Zanvan runs his fingers through his greasy hair before replacing his hat, "Let's go."

Geric springs up, closing his book with a smack, "Yeah, who knows, they might even have something edible!"

"I hear orken beer isn't bad." Zanvan opens the door, holding it for Geric and Avrel, and Candice. "Ales too."

She wonders if he's already acting or not. "Well, I like a good ale." she smiles, "Anything is better than cheap piss-water." Though if she's honest, she's accustomed to it enough that she's used to the cheap stuff.

After the steps to the main street level lobby, they head down into a cellar where a taproom tavern is. Unlike all the many taverns they'd visited, diversity of race was lacking. All orcs, arm-wrestling, hooting, hollering, sounding angry even as they make merry. And all of them are very loud.

"Sheash." Geric mumbles, "And I thought the place at the lake place with all the elves was... Well... Only full of elves." he scoffs, lowly.

"Well..." Zanvan whispers as he leans down, "It's more that the elves are cautious of outsiders, whereas dealing with orcs is often just avoided." Just then, a few tables down two orcs begin fighting, mercilessly tearing into each other.

"Can't imagine why." Avrel giggles nervously. She snidely takes a slow sip as she watches them fight. *All the toxicity of men*, it seems, *is amplified in these orken guys.* she thinks to herself, finding them almost laughable. And then one's shirt is torn off, revealing a pair of muscular breasts, and upon another closer look, the other fighter is a woman as well. She grits her teeth as she looks away, *It's humiliating and demeaning to watch fights like that anyhow.* she scoffs to herself.

"C'mon drink up," Zanvan whispers. "Remember, it needs to look like we went into our room and passed out."

"If I drink much more..." Geric yawns. "I'm not going to be able to... Do whatever we're going to be doing."

"Slip them to *Faithe*." Zanvan suggests. "She's an elf, she'll hold her liquor well." At that comment, Candice leans up and sniffs Zanvan's shot glass. "...Works for me." he sighs as he lets Candice have it.

"Take one for the team you miserable rat." Geric mumbles.

"Okay guys" Avrel giggles quietly. "Me and Candice have got this, just pretend you're getting shitefaced."

After several rounds they've all put on their best drunk acting while Candice is bloated and burping in her seat. It's reasonably convincing. He overhears a few orcs comment to their partners on the boisterous travelers showing such little restraint. Most wish they'd just shut the hell up over there. The feeling is mutual, even without her acting drunk, there were a few giving her dirty looks. Several have already found creative sleights against her, most of which Geric has taken delight in. *Big, green sards.*

Finally, she hopes they've made their point, as if she drinks much more she will start to feel its effects. She signals this to her friends and she, Geric, and Zanvan all share a hearty laugh, and boisterous, slurred chat as they stagger out of their chairs and up towards their room. If they *were* drunk, the two flights of stairs would be cumbersome. Near the top steps, Geric trips Zanvan, sending him tumbling down until he catches himself. Geric speeds to the room while she waits for him at the top of the stairs. She'd have offered to help him up, but her arms are full of her drunken beaver.

Once inside their room, Zanvan is furious. "What the hell, cleric!?" Zanvan shouts.

Geric grins with a closed eyed shrug, "I figured it'd be more convincing if you stumbled." he replies.

"Okay whatever." the angered ranger says after a long, silent glare. "Grab your things and get ready to go." he says, picking up his quiver.

"Thanks for taking one for the team, Candice." Avrel says softly, "I'll find you a nice aspen tree once we're back home." she says with a pet as she tucks her beaver into a nest made of blankets. The little thing looks horribly sick.

"Alright so what's the plan?" Geric asks.

"Sneak in and find Lucia." Zanvan says confidently. "Figure out where the items are and then sack her. Grab the relics and run for it." he adds calmly.

Avrel sighs. "That still sounds a little easier said than done."

"Well..." Zanvan grunts. "Under the circumstances that's the best I've got. It's not like I know the layout of this castle, but if we can get in, the hardest part will be past us."

"Yeah." Geric snorts, "Aside from offing--"

Zanvan whips his hand into Geric's gut before he can finish. "Shush!"

"Alright." Avrel and Geric both nod.

"Don't take anything you don't need." Zanvan says grimly, "Don't leave anything you'll be needing in the future." he tells them as they holster their weapons, but leave their bedrolls and other general supplies behind. Not that she has much, but it pains her to know that it might be left behind. But, it's only a bedroll and a few things like that. Hell, Geric is taking his stache of books, but then, any spells in there might be useful, so she understands why.

"Let's be off." Zanvan says as he opens the crude window to a smelly and dark alley.

The three sneak out of the window and head towards the castle. Crisp moonlight runs along the large and wide street heading straight in for it. It's dark out, very dark as the sooty clouds block much of the moon and starlight, but still, it finds its way. The castle itself is erie in this darkness, standing like a black shadow against the dull grey of the polluted sky with it's diluted light.

As they approach a lamp-lit courtyard, they hide in even deeper shadows than they have been. The gate is shut, and the wall is tall and the only wooden access door is blocked by a trio of orcs in dark, unpolished suits of iron armor sitting around a small fire.

"Shh." Geric hisses as he shows a vial before tossing it into the fire. It makes a quick and colorful flare in the flame which arouses the orcs, but just as quickly as they stand up, they fall over.

Zanvans sneaks up and quietly dispose of them. "I'm glad you mixed a sleeping potion this afternoon." Zanvan whispers, patting Geric on the back.

He smiles and holds up a few more of the small vials. "Hey, we should wear these." he says as he joins Zanvan by the knocked out guards. "We can get in there much easier if we do, none of this sneaking shite." Geric suggests.

"Good idea." Zanvan nods. They strip the orcs and she searches their packs. Avrel finds nothing of value. As they suit up, Geric and Zanvan easily get into the suits of armor, Geric's fits exceptionally well, Zanvan's fair. Hers though...

"*Faithe*, how are you doing?" Zanvan whispers as he looks over to her, apparently having paid no mind to her struggling to put it on.

"This isn't going to work!" Avrel grunts. "It's so big, it's loose around my leg pads!"

Geric covers his mouth vent with his hand to keep from laughing as Avrel shuffles in the armor that is *clearly* too large. She of course can only see by looking out the mouth slit, as the helmet portion is practically balanced on the top of her head.

"*Faithe*, my dear." Even Zanvan is cracking up, at her expense of course. "You look like a bewitched set of ghost armor, it's actually horrifying." he chuckles.

Geric can no longer control his laughter and begins to lose his composure.

"Shut up!" Avrel yelps in a whisper, that proves useless as her whole metal assembly jingles.

"*Kesh yoush!!*" a tall orc comes out of a door in the castle, "[You slackers get in here and stop lazing around! *And stay at your posts!*]" she hopes he's saying.

Zanvan replies in a convincing, affirming growl as they all salute.

As the orc leaves they all sigh in relief. "Well, I feel better knowing the guys we drugged weren't doing their jobs well anyway." Avrel giggles softly, nervously. It means so far they've *only* overcome some slackers.

"We should be careful though, they're not speaking common..." Geric whispers. "I can--"

"Yeah... I think most official business will be done in common, fingers crossed" Zanvan whispers back.

"I should have found a spell of understanding..." Geric sighs apologetically. "But I-"

"Too late for that." Zanvan dismisses, "But now's our chance, let's get as close to the throne room as these guys can and wait for her there." he commands as they try to orderly march into the castle.

Once inside it becomes a matter of trying to look like they are patrolling or some shite while they are actually looking for Lucia. Big as the place is, they haven't the slightest clue, but they eventually make it to a less ugly area that looks almost more regal and castle-like. Zanvan seems to be hoping that it's the same as in Argoth's castle. A big if, but it's the same guess she'd make.

Once in a while, Geric also makes suggestions.

Once in a while, Zanvan heeds them.

"Hey!" or something like it is growled through the hall from behind them. One at a time they turn, Zanvan and Geric with little effort, but even by this point, Avrel can't manage to turn without a lot of effort and noise.

The orc storms over to them, his armor is far financier indicating a far higher rank. "*Vver akk yoush guh'ook!?*" he sprays harshly at them, the amount of air he's blasting, she just begs the forces of nature to not let the air blow their visors open.

"Uhhh..." Zanvan moans, before saluting.

"*Vvook...*" the orc leans right into him, and then turning with great suspicion in his visible eyes as he turns towards her in her loose, and half-collapsed armor. "*Akk yoush?*"

He lifts his hand and is about to throw off her helm, which is more upn her neck armor than her head. It's over; it's done. They'll be caught and nothing can stop it.

"Drék" Geric says, holding up his hand, and with a perfect roll on the orc's harsh sounds.

The orc stops and turns to him.

"Shäk ikk múrrä..." Geric says with a shrug, "Níkkish- Étk'ka... zhísä-dúltár."

"Söh?" the orken officer, or whatever is rank, says with a spying eye. Geric laughs, still emulating the orc's dark tone, "Häl, häl." he says, brushing his hands in the air, "Shä ikk díshkäh'kó föta ikk gráudäk."

The orc relaxes, smiles even. "Söh?" he grins, his internal teeth just as ugly as his tusks, "Güt!" he stoops to Avrels level, and gives her one of those soft shoulder punches guys do before he pats the top of her helmet. "Vvekk Vvish!" he says before backing away like he might be going.

Avrel scrambles to recall, she's seen those Argothian sards salute a bunch, but she's drawing a blank. She just puts her flattened hand like a visor over her brow. "Umph!" she grunts, painfully low.

The orc gives a patronizing smile, obviously her salute is wrong, but he's letting it go. "Üntär Vvey!" he says waving them on. She'd guess it's the same as the Ar-Guards saying '*Move along*'

One they are away from him and in a quiet corner, she takes a moment to vent. Staring by slumping against a wall and sighing out all of her air.

"Are you okay?" Zanvan asks.

"It's heavy." she pants. She turns to Geric. "You know orc-talk!?"

He shrugs, noisily. "I know enough." he says casually, "Some of the best potion recipes are in orkish."

Zanvan is unamused as well, "Why didn't you say anything before?"

"I tried." the cleric shrugs again, just as loudly. "And you didn't ask."

"Alright, alright." Zanvan relents. "What did you tell him anyway?"

"That she's a new trainee." Geric answers, he sounds like he's smiling.

But the notion begins to dawn on her, Geric would have had to have explained her height. "At what age do they start taking trainees in?" she asks as she stands tall.

"Oh I dunno." Geric sighs, "Maybe like ten or so?"

She *might* have known. "Of course." she sighs.

"Hey." Zanvan tags each of them, "Let's not get caught again, hmm?"

"Right."

"Yeah." Geric and she each sigh.

They duck out of the little cavity in the hall and begin their false patrol once more, keeping an eye out for anyone or anything that'd suggest where Lucia could be.

After a few minutes of trying to get their bearings, they find themselves in a great hall and they notice Lucia up ahead, arguing with another orc in superior armor. "There she is!" Avrel points. Zanvan swats down her hand and shushes her, she realizes that she'd almost brought Lucia's attention upon them. They casually stop out of sight but in elf-ear shot. Avrel relays it to Geric, and he translates.

"It seems..." Geric begins to say.

"Vfehr ahkk dah." she repeats.

"Yeah." Geric confirms, "She was expecting a small escort to meet her at the gate.

Zanvan tips his head. "Wonder who *that* could have been."

"Well, hey I--" Avrel begins to ask when suddenly, Lucia is staring right at them.

"Qäsh ishk yoush!?" Lucia growls. "Who are you!?" she repeats in a powerful royal voice, this time in common, thankfully.

"We- Ahem!" Zanvan gargles out as he kneels. "We are the guards your father requested, Your Highness."

"Ó'kän thö Vvish mírthté!" Geric growls, in *support*? He kneels as well, Avrel does too.

Lucia scowls, stretching her mouth scars as she grinds out some guttural string of sounds. "Vvólló" she commands with a wave as she walks away. Geric quickly takes a place behind her, it seems she said to 'follow'.

As they fall in line, Geric quietyly translates for them what she'd said. "*Ugh... I told that stupid old man I'd see him when I was ready. Whatever, come'.*"

They follow her, nervously unsure of how to proceed with their objective, clunking around in their heavy armor. But one thing seems obvious to Avrel, Lucia hasn't been in the castle very long. She's still dressed as she was on that night in the woods.

Maybe they still have a chance. That is if there are no more steps to climb; the orc princess has led them up *several* and to a large, ornate hall, and opposite the way of a set of immensely huge doors.

"[Let me grab a few things from my room, tell my father I'll be in in a moment]." Lucia commands, as quietly translated by Geric after she enters her quarters. Geric turns towards the partially open door, he's thinking what Avrel"s thinking and sees this opportunity and begins inching towards Lucia with his hands outstretched ready to throttle her.

"Yoush thersh!" a guard from the throne room comes up behind them as Geric quickly retracts his arms and tries to act casually. Again, it sounds more like a coughing fit than language, but Geric seems to understand. The guard commands *something* in a low, thunderous growl.

Geric turns to her and Zanvan "Vólló." he says as he takes up the rear of this orken guard.

She and Zanvan fall in behind him as he leads them away from Lucia and towards the gigantic doors. As they open, they see it for what it is. Avrel follows timidly into the throne room. A red tile path cuts through the obsidian floor to the throne as beasts and gargoyle sculptures serve as gas lamps, impressively looking as though they are breathing flames.

"Thesh Myströsh kahmes! Vväll in!" the orc commands.

Avrel finds herself next to Zanvan, with the red path between them and Geric, and the other orc. Lucia comes into the room bearing the large sack the Everlasting Aegis had been kept in and holding the hilt of the Runeblade.

She's dressed differently, no longer in the undersuit of Argothian armor, but It's Lucia for sure. Her clothing is as gaudy and ornate as one might expect an elite to wear, certainly fitting of a princess; yet, there's a militaristic look to it as well. She is a warrior, she is a princess, they are in *her* hall, and she has ancient weapons of war.

***

The womanlet elf and the two men are long gone. smiles Lucia as she stretches her shoulders in the light of a new day. After days of travelling down the river, why shouldn't she have taken a rest? And what a fine rest, from a fine, upstanding family. They knew not that she was their princess, yet they took her in. And by all appearances, they are most rightfully traditional; as evidenced by how the man of the house had been walking. He must've fallen short of his duties, and she, like any respectable wife, homemaker, and mother fixed it right away. Such is the way of the Yordlands, should the bond of balance between them be broken, should the man, the warrior, and conqueror of the household fail, no self respecting bride would not challenge him to Säkkdúm.

It's a beautiful system, really; for either the man regains his honor, or she shall treat him like the sub-man that he's given the impression that he is. And of course, the duel, little more than a public wrestling match, is fun for these smaller villages. It brings pride to the woman's lot, and keeps the man in his, should he not fight with all his might or should he lose, his honor as a man is forfeit. Moreso once the wife obtains her trophy, a trinket, a 'garment' to wear, and to punish him with. For if men will not be the best of men, they must be shown what it is to be the least of women.

And through such social pressure preserved in tradition, the warrior creed of her people will never die. The values of fathers should not be lost on sons. Nor mothers to daughters.

This is why YordäsVvin prevails, and why Argoth will perish.

At least in theory... Lucia sighs.

A young girl comes up behind her, and tugs on the torn fragments of her white cloak. "Momma says that the break-feast is ready!"

Lucia smiles. The children, *the future* of her kingdom. What a bountiful future she'll bring them. "Thank you." she says, patting the beautiful little girl.

Lucia had almost become tolerant of Argothian food over the last while, but she's always preferred the commoner's food of her home, of the Yords. Jäk steak, with the skin, and fur still intact, and an ostrich egg. From soldier, to iron smith, to fieldworker, no other plain break-feast imparts such strength.

Certainly not the puny eggs of a hen, or the crisped fat of a domesticated boar.

Boars...

She looks at the family, this perfect nucleus of society living, breathing in a small, sooty backwater on the way to the castle and city of YordäsVvin. The children, all five of them smiling with their uncut teeth, the girl's not, or sadly, merely not *yet* removed to match the mother's. Even such things find their way even to the most traditional households.

But Lucia, she will fix such things.

What does it say about her society? She wonders along the road, the iron walls of YordäsVvin within sight. So many like her are barely born from the womb before their tiny infant bodies are strapped down, and a sensitive and proud part of their body is cut from them, leaving them permanently scarred and mutilated. All for what? Women have endured it for aesthetic reasons for generations, but damn these new, pacifist idealists growing like spots of consumption in this land, even now men are having it performed on them. And, society is slowly not referring to it as mutilation for their sex. For that *is* what it is, it has been for women for so long, and so it is also for men. Lest another generation grow to forget this, and view either or as merely a cosmetic right of passage for the young.

Had she tusks, Lucia would bear them proudly. She's not ashamed if they are strange or ugly, they would be hers, they would be an added layer to her intimacy, and they would be a reminder of orken superiority. They aren't the pearlescent and glowing, thin figures of elves, they aren't the dainty, unambitious, profligates that are men; they are orcs. They are warriors.

It took a cult of *men* to remind her of this. To remind her of the great power of orcs past, of war, and bloodshed, and of great, dark magic.

But she does not desire to regress, to the contrary, the orken nature is one of progress! Of this, she is most sure. Her kind, from the eons of time were blessed with the knowledge that the people of this world must progress.

Progress beyond the peaceful coexistence with pantheonic beasts in harmony with the forests!

Progress beyond settling lands peacefully, and with little ambition of *change*.

It's every true orcs' knowledge and *duty* that they are to take all that the land can give. And she shall remind them of that.

She enters the gate with little ceremony, despite that she should have been expected. That will change. She shall put on her warriors clothing, not some flowing princess's attire when she presents the old profligate council with the future. Rudask, Mithrashoth, all the ancient mountains full to the brim with metals shall be theirs. The tradition of the orcs, and the power of the relics she now possesses will cut and burn across the lands of the lazy and useless Argothians. The forests will feed the furnaces, the waterways shall feed turbines and mills, and the true nature of the orcs will show.

More than warriors, more than conquerors; they will bring about a revolution of industry like none other seen this side of the Great Sea. They shall rival, no, *surpass* the ignorant and pacifists of the Minarchy of Astaroth. They shall become what such an industrial and forward thinking people could have made on this fresh new world had they not acquiesced and become neutered by their beholdance of elves.

These stupid grunts barely knowing the layout of the royal halls, they don't know the power within them. The power to join into the mightiest fist of power with which to smash the old world and to bring upon new machines that will put the greatness of the YordäsVvic ironworks to shame; but they will. By Night Star, by The Father of Orcs, and by the Lost Daughter, they will.

After 6,000 years, it's time the orcs fulfil their destiny.

Even these shambling morons behind her will have their time. she smirks to herself as she waits for the throne room doors to open. The most fortified city in the known world, they shall fear no counterstrike, no teaming fortress, no last defense of their ancient home. They shall strike out hard, and fast, and be victorious, weather it takes the second half of her life to see it through or not, victory will be theirs.

Much she's thought over on her long journey from Argoth, and even long before. She fears not those she left behind, let them conspire all they want. She has the Aegis, she has the Runeblade, and they are of little consequence now.

She'll do her part to take the orcs to war, but by *her* lead, by *her* plan.

"The Mistress comes!" she hears the court announcer bark as the door creaks open. "Fall in!"

As she steps inside and down the long, red tile path to the throne, her impudent escort finds themselves spots on either side of the line of guards. No matter, if nothing else, the likes of those are good arrow fodder. She holds her head high, for she has done as her father had asked, more even. And, she is most familiar now in common tongue, not that it shall be the language of this court ever after.

***

"May the Moon and Sun long bless you, Our Princess Lucia." some announcer guy announces. "And may many blessings stem from your return to this mighty court!"

Please keep speaking common... Please keep speaking common... Geric whispers in his head. Not for himself, but for others. Also, understanding a single person is easy enough, but a whole room of these gravelly, green, groaners might not be so easy on the ears.

"Father!" the orc princess bitch growls, giving Geric a sigh of relief, "You sent me out to find a way to bring glory to our kingdom! And glory I shall bring!" she cries out. "Though you rushed me in here, may these four sworn troopers bear witness along with you and your counsel that I, Lucia, Daughter of Nerfendör, have found a means to bring ancient glory back to YordäsVvin and orken-kind!" The orc princess, Lucia smiles proudly holding up the sack and the hilt. At this time, Geric takes note of Nerfendor, not the great evil looking warlord type he was expecting. He doubts the others feel any differently, rather, he is a kind faced old orc with a white beard and a forlorn, aged body.

"Dáttör..." he growls with a predictably old sounding voice, "Daughter, what is this... artifact you've brought so triumphantly to our court today?" the old orc king asks softly.

"I have brought the tools with which we can reclaim our ancient glory as the warriors we were bred to be!" Lucia exclaims as she uncovers the Aegis.

The King and his counsel all gasp in horror as they see the shield and recognize it for what it is. "Dáttör!?" he slips again, though, much like the elvish word, Geric can tell what he means, "What have you brought!? That evil thing cannot bring us glory, our ancient allegiance to The Beast only brought us despair and ruin!" the old king exclaims as he jumps from his seat, pointing his boney and geriatrically wobbly finger at Lucia.

"Father, our glorious days have been all but *lost* because of our straining to become a peaceful people!" the she-orc bitch turns towards the other members of the council, "Let us cast off these chains that bind us and raise our swords once more! Reignite the flame and battle hunger that brought our race into being! With the Everlasting Aegis: The Heart of the Beast, and the Runeblade which slew him, none can stand in our way!" she says joyously. "Let our mighty and worthy people bring industry to these forested lands and rich mountains!"

Geric can't help but feel bad for the old-coot king, his daughter may be a warmongering gash, but he seems kindly enough in his reaction. He doesn't seem too on board with her ideas. He nudges Avrel, no, Zanvan-- Whoever is next to him, and mutters to them, "Heh, the old guy's not so bad, what do you say we just knife the bitch and hightail it." he chuckles.

"**Bäch däkk déVval'la!**" he blurts, in orkish, and not in either Zanvan or Avrel's voice. "[**What did you say!?**]" the guard screams as he draws his glaive and points it at Geric, rather quickly.

Both the old orc king and the bitch can't help but notice, and turn. Anyone would, the slightest movement in this armor creates quite a racket. "What's going on over there!?" Lucia asks with frustration.

"[This trooper was discussing his plans to kill you, My Mistress!]" the guard replies as several other guards come in from the other corners of the room.

She raises her brow, the low corners of her scarred mouth rise to form a smirk, "Bring those three before me." she commands. Geric can feel himself sweating under the armor, he hopes it's rust proof. "Father, who are the three that you sent after me this evening?" Lucia asks the old king.

Not good.

"I uh... I don't remember sending anyone." he replies seeming rather confused.

"*By Shéól!*" Lucia growls, her arm trembling in the air a moment like she might swat the old codger, "The security in this castle is as fortified as your **senile old mind!**" she screams. Geric, and the two armored people who are *actually* Zanvan and Avrel are lined up in front of Lucia and forced to their knees. "You three, who are you?" she asks but receives no reply. "You are YördasVvin's sworn troopers who have taken an oath to King and Country, have you not!? Your names!" she growls ever fiercer.

The small half-elf whimpers in fear or something, drawing Lucia's attention. Maybe it's just the weight of the armor.

"Aren't you a little *short* for a sworn trooper?" the orken princess asks as she grabs Avrel by the beaver of her helmet. Lifting the helmet off she reveals the rosy haired half-elf. "Well..." Lucia frys as she takes his and Zanvan's helmets off as well. "I never thought I'd see you three again." she grunts. She purses her scarred lips into a smug, pinched expression before relaxing to a smirk. "All the same, I'm glad you're here." the orc bitch turns towards the coot king, "The road to glory for this dying empire is the road paved in blood! If you doubt our eventual victory I ask you to bear witness to the power of what I've brought before you!" she exclaims, desperately.

"Lucia." the old king says disheartenedly, "I beg you..."

Just then an explosion knocks Lucia back as Avrel slips out of her loose armor and blasts all the guards back, giving him and Zanvan space to free themselves and strip off the cumbersome armor.

"Lucia!" Avrel yells, "Your father doesn't wish to lead you into war, give us back the relics and think no more of it! We can put this all behind us!"

"You are such a foolish girl" Lucia smirks as she activates the Runeblade. "My plan never was for my father to lead us." And having it take the form of a javelin, she throws the runeblade, skewering Nerfendor to the back of his seat and popping his heart spectacularly. The bitch can aim.

The surrounding knights and guards all step back in horror as Lucia laughs over her father's lifeless body. "The King is dead!" she shouts at them, "Long live the Queen!"

"Ikk mäkkdúr!" one has the gut to point out. She did, after all, just murder him with an excellent spear toss.

"[Too long has this damned kingdom sat in disrepair at the hands of old men!]" she growls, "So let it be the future of Queens! Too long has this cursed place abandoned its princesses!" she belts as she raises a dark aura around herself.

The old king's counselors run at her, seeking vengeance but she uses the Aegis to push them away.

Geric has just gotten his back plate off and can reach his glaive when Lucia has finished equipping the shield to her forearm. And with a bit of a disconcerting mushy sound, its hideous veins begin merging into her flesh and her skin begins turning a shiny, obsidian black in the affected areas.

"What the hell?" Avrel steps back, horrified.

"That's messed up." Geric gawps.

Zanvan, no longer restrained by the orcs, sheds the last of his loose, orken armor and takes up his sword. He attempts to strike Lucia in this seemingly opportune time to strike her down, but his sword clashes with her as if he were swinging it into a boulder and it flies out of his hand.

She doesn't seem too keen on the whole process either, screaming and flailing until the majority of her body is assimilated.

"Well... This seems bad." Zanvan says reluctantly as he steps back. The whites of Lucia's eyes turn ruby red as her irises turn a blazing fire orange. Her body distorts into a monstrous form as she becomes unrecognizable.

"She's actually becoming The Beast?" Avrel yelps in fear as Lucia begins moving again and savagely lashes out at her father's counselors, crushing them in her massive claws.

"Lucia stop this!" Avrel screams, stepping out of one last iron boot.

"There is no Lucia." Geric gulps, "The evil of that shield has consumed her entire being." Geric says as he and the group backs off. "The Aegis was made from The Beast's heart, it must still have his presence within it."

"So that's why…" Avrel mumbles out.

Geric takes a deep breath, he's thinking the same thing -- that night in Manitäria.

"Great." Zanvan scoffs, "So at least we know about the thing that's about to kill us. Any ideas on how to kill it?"

The monster turns from the shredded bodies of the king's counsel towards them and begins charging, Runeblade in hand. Zanvan and Geric dodge it but it catches Avrel and forces her into a corner, where it takes all of her strength to hold her staff locked against the Runeblade. As the monster is about to cut Avrel down after breaking her guard and knocking her out against the wall, Geric manages to sweep in and catch the blow for her, taking a bit of it's painful arcane effect into his limbs.

"Hey, pick on someone your own size!" Geric yells in defiance, it wouldn't be a fair fight were Lucia her normal size.

The monster's blows quickly shatters his glaive, forcing him to pull out his mace. Zanvan jumps in and attempts to help but is just as quickly thrown back into a support column.

"Hey, hey guys!" Geric yells as he blocks and dodges the wild swings of the monster. "You can like... Use spells or arrows or *some shite*!" He receives no reply as both of them are still stunned. Geric casts an earth spike spell that knocks Lucia's monstrous form off balance allowing him to make an offensive strike. The monster however blocks his strike with the Runeblade, sending an intense shock of force into his hand. "Ahhh!!!" he gasps, "Oh right, that shite... Avrel, you stupid elf, why would you guys make a weapon like this!?" he yelps as he jumps back. "Oh right, I'm the only one here who didn't *instantly get clobbered!*" Geric chuckles, they're still not back to their feet.

He again has no choice but to swing his mace against the Runeblade despite the shock that feeds into his wrists. It's not so bad when he parries, and so he does his best to dodge. Still, it's not entirely non-present on the monster's attack strikes. But she leaves herself open. The shield, which seems to be slowly migrating to her chest on her monstrously mutated body, is exposed, and since all he's got is a hammer, it looks like a big nail of hope to him.

***

Avrel comes to.

Amidst fleeting dreams and a sense of eons having passed, she sees Geric valiantly fighting the beast. Geric at last swings his mace with all his might, aiming for the Aegis that is merged into Lucia's shoulder, but it is blocked, and while his swing manages to force the Runeblade from the monster's hands, Geric's left hand and forearm bursts.

Geric's blood and particles of his flesh shower her as she's still slouched behind him, as she realizes what she's just witnessed, as she sees not just the flesh but the bloody stump, she lets out a blood curdling shriek.

"Oh come on." he scoffs, like an idiot, turning to give her his typical, shite eater's grin. "It's not like it's *your* arm." he adds, right before being swatted at by the monster and thrown across the room. What little of his armor that he hadn't removed flies apart from the hit.

Avrel wipes the blood from her eyes and quickly dashes and attempts to recover the Runeblade. She has a chance, only because Zanvan has regained his composure. She ducks low as he begins trying to hit the monster with arrows, but they simply bounce off of her black crystal-like skin. But, with Zanvan's arrows at least *distracting* the monster, Avrel manages to find the Runeblade hilt among the now substantial pile of rubble and debris. She clasps it to her chest as the gems along its sides begin to glow. The blade, however, has yet to form for some reason. But time is short, and the monster's red, ruby eye has caught her, and despite the arrows has its sights on her.

As Avrel takes a fighting stance, a mist of what appears as glowing dust condolence to form bronzen, glowing, crystalline quarterstaff shafts from either side of the hilt. She's ready to take a swing when she notices that Zanvan's arrows have stopped, *Is he alright?* She turns to look.

Until Geric chides her. "You gonna look at your fancy weapon or are you gonna smack that bitch!?" he yells from afar.

The monster is only a few feet away from her now, and ready to swat her the way it'd swatted the cleric. Seeing it's side exposed, Avrel lays into the side of the monster with a wide power swing. It delays the sweep long enough for her to dodge.

"Avrel, give me time!" Zanvan yells from across the room. "I have some elven arrows that might work!"

"Okay! Make it quick!" Avrel yelps as the monster digs in a pile of debris before raising up Geric's hammer-mace. "Oh shit..." she gulps.

***

Zanvan opens one of his packs and pulls out a handful of arrows that bear a subtle glow to their heads. He can only hope the elven incantations and craft can piece the armored skin of that thing.

"Hey! Over here you freak!" Zanvan yells as he fires an arrow at the monster's head. Avrel swings aiming to follow up the strike to the monster's head but misses. And the monster, in dodging the strike, also dodges Zanvan's arrow.

Avrel backs off and charges briefly before unleashing an iceball that hits the side of the monster's face, freezing out one of its eyes. After letting out an ear piercingly loud shriek, the monster swats back at Avrel and slams her shoulder with

Geric's mace. Avrel falls to the ground as the monster presses the mace into Avrel's wound with her beastly strength as the kid cries out, paralyzed from the pain.

Zanvan is across the room, he can't jump in with his blade, but he takes a clear shot and fires an arrow at the monster's back. He hears a loud snap and Avrel screams intensely as her face flushes beet red, it seems her collarbone finally broke under the pressure. She drops her hilt and recoils as his arrow whizzes into the back of the monster's neck. The kid scrambles to get back up and strikes the monster in the head, sweeping from its blind side. Letting another arrow fly,it strikes directly into the monster's spine causing it to flail around.

Until it pulls it out.

Zanvan is now Lucia's monster's focus as she charges at him. He manages to fire several arrows at the Aegis that has now migrated and formed a chest plate over Lucia's heart, but to no avail as they simply bounce off. He primes himself to leap out of the way, but Avrel, with his sword, uses her short stature to her advantage and slides in between and under the monster's legs and attempts to stab it in the heart, only to find it impenetrable with his sword.

Damn... he grunts, seeing as though it's elven, he'd hoped it would be effective. But it still is, the monster's charge misses Zanvan as he leaps out of the way at the last second. The kid's attack did slow it slightly. He prepares for a followup swing, but Avrel shoots a lightning spell at the monster's hand to keep it from swinging its mace at him, buying him time to get some distance and kite this monster. He prepares his aim, and takes a few shots, but he notices the kid focusing intensely on her spell.

And the monster is open for as much a volley as he can muster.

***

Avrel intensifies the spell, she can feel its power growing as she throws all of her hate and anger into it. Every ill memory, every moment of deep sadness, her hate for this rotted and disgusting land, of the Argothian Guard which this orc bitch masqueraded as; everything. The monster writhes in pain and the mace is thrown out the nearby stained glass window. The ranger turns and rapidly shoots several arrows that hit Lucia square between her glowing ruby-red eyes.

Avrel takes up the runeblade hilt as her glowing quarterstaff and plunges it into the monster's gut as she leverages it under the chest plate, but too late she realizes she's nowhere to dodge as a punch thrown by Lucia's monster.

And she is thrown by it.

Zanvan, the monster, and the Aegis plate all recede until a sharp and sudden stop shocks her, dazing her, and she fails to fight off the darkness.

Avrel wakes a moment later from her daze to see Zanvan kiting the monster across the room.

"Wait a minute..." Avrel groans to herself as she meditates, clasping the Runeblade to her chest. Again a glow condenses around the hilt, but the shape of glowing magic shifts into a halberd before solidifying into its crystalline state. Avrel smiles briefly and then charges after the monster.

Meanwhile, it seems Zanvan has all but run out of his elven arrows as he attempts to dodge all of the monster's attacks, making use of her depleted field of vision, he stays to one side only.

Avrel spys a broken column leading like a ramp to just over the monster and with a running start, she takes a grand leap off and spears the monster's chest through its back, pinning Lucia's monster to the ground. It lets out a wail and slumps, Avrel then retracts the Runeblade into a short dagger and drops down and works to cut the Aegis from Lucia's body. She can hear as Zanvan grabs a large rock and pounds it into the monster's skull until she can hear it cracking the obsidian-like shell open after several blows, causing her flailing to subside somewhat after flaring up a moment, as Avrel tries not to be crushed by it.

As she cuts the shield-like plate away from the monster's body, she sees a hideous veiny web that connects the shield and Lucia's heart where they'd seemed to have merged. She cuts and pulls, but she's both too slow and woo weak to do it alone.

"Zanvan! Help me!" Avrel shouts.

He jumps down and they both tear the shield like structure from the monster's chest. He pulls it away as she repeatedly cuts the vine-like veins constantly regrowing and regenerating after every injury to their snaking web of connection.

The monster writhes violently, knocking both Avrel and Zanvan to the ground but Avrel quickly recovers and plunges her dagger into Lucia's exposed, tainted, deformed heart. The monster lets out one final shrill screech that shatters the rest of the windows within the throne room.

As Avrel and Zanvan huddle on the floor with their hands over their ears the monster's breath slows until at last it halts, the rhythmic blood gushes cease as its ruptured heart ceases to beat, and Lucia slowly shrinks back to her normal size, and her skin fades to her attractive olive tone from the obsidian black, her naked body ravaged from the fight.

The Aegis's tentacle-like veins dry out and wither as it regains it's shield-like appearance.

Lucia is dead.

The threat is gone.

Avrel steps back and catches her breath and moistens her dried tongue and lips. She *killed* Lucia. She *killed* this wicked monster.

Or, they did rather, but it still aches coldly in her chest. She looks at her cracked, scuffed hands, the fingertips blistered from her own spells-- and then to Lucia's broken body.

She's *capable* of this, should she turn her magic on another person. *She.* Violence, she must admit, is not solely the domain of men. Her magic, which she'd promised to never turn on another human being, allows her to do this. Did her mother know this? Is this what she'd feared? Or what she'd hoped to avoid? Avrel's eyes fall to the blood covered runeblade hilt. Is she the same monster her father was? Or will she be?

Could she be... Worse? Is that potential there? She'd thought, being a woman, she'd be above that, above *this*.

Her eyes float over to all the destruction caused by Lucia's hand, her father, his council, her very own knights.

Is she?

All of this aches in her like an icy knife as she catches her breath.

And before suddenly, as the adrenaline begins to subside, the pain of her wounds begins to overwhelm her. She clutches a swelling knot on that straight and prominent bone that runs from the base of her neck to her shoulder. And just by the shoulder, she feels it grinding and burning. But the searing pain at least clears the reflective thoughts in her head as she takes a moment to breathe it out.

She recalls from the plateau, in and out, slowly-- not letting the pain override her. Though, it still very much wants to.

"Hey." Geric says drowsily as he waves his profusely bleeding forearm stump around. "Not that anybody cares, but your friend whose hand got exploded is probably bleeding to death over here."

Zanvan though comes to her as she huddles over, cradling her left collarbone. "Hey, you okay?" he asks softly, more tenderly than she's used to hearing from him.

"Yeah..." Avrel whimpers, holding back tears.

"So guys...." Geric waves once more. Zanvan helps Avrel up as they walk over to Geric. She instinctively turns away, but slowly forces herself to look. He just smiles between bitter grunts, "As our resident cleric, I find it extremely unfortunate that I'm the one who's in dire need of medical attention." he laughs, dryly.

"I can't heal it..." Avrel concedes, "But I can stop the bleeding." She knows it's going to hurt, but it's all she can do. She's no healer.

"What?" Zanvan asks, "You've got something we can use as a tourniquet?" he says, almost turning the brim of his hat into the path of her spell.

"**Yerrrahhh!!!!!!!!!!!**" Geric screams as Avrel's fire curls around his wound, singeing the hemorrhaged vessels closed. "**Jeeeeezzzzzahhh! By the Guh-- By the Siv-- Bloody hell! I was going to *ask* if you could do that anyway,** *why not give a guy some **warning!?*** " Geric agonizes, in between blowing on his stump.

"I thought..." she murmurs. She thought it'd be easier.

"It's fine." Zanvan pats her.

Geric nods, though making a face. "Doing this for your damned bitch..." he growls, "How is it that *you* get off with scraped knees?" He *tries* to put on his usual sardonic arse smile, but his eyes look ready to pop straight across the room.

They three turn around as they all hear a hard pounding on the doors from the hall outside the throne room. A hard and desperate pounding, and shouting in a deep orken gargle.

"We need to get out of here fast." Zanvan says, lowly as he helps Geric up.

"The window." Avrel points. "Maybe there's a way down?"

Zanvan runs over to check, and she grabs their personal items.

"Yup, c'mon." he says, waving them over.

Avrel helps Geric over as the three look out to the courtyard below. As they get to the side of the window, Zanvan leaves them. He picks up the Aegis and puts it in a spare sack.

It's a long way down. "Funny, it didn't seem like we went up that many steps when we came up here." Avrel remarks as she looks through the broken window.

"Dawn is breaking." Zanvan says as he looks around the ledges of the window. "We need to get out before it's light or we'll *definitely* get spotted." he trails off a moment. "Alright... Okay, if we follow this ledge that way, we can get down to that area there..." Zanvan points around, "And then..." he trails off again.

"And then what?" Avrel asks impatiently.

"Well... I was going to say we climb down that bricky siding there and then make for that water way but..." Zanvan looks over to Geric's wounded arm, "I don't think climbing is going to work." he sighs. The knocking on the door turns fierce, as they scramble out onto the ledge. As they carefully crawl around the ledge along the path Zanvan had directed they hear the soldiers running around the throne room, panicking, lamenting, and rueing what had apparently transpired.

What they've done...

19

As they crawl down the sloping ledge and away from the throne room, they come to a lower flat roofed part of the castle and they get off the ledge and onto it. They hear an alarm horn blowing from within the castle and the kid and the cleric begin to panic.

"Where to now?" Avrel frets.

"Well... Down there." Zanvan says uncomfortably as he points to the water several stories below.

"*How am I going to climb down there with one hand!?*" Geric shouts.

"Shhh!" Avrel yelps.

Zanvan looks around for an alternative but after a few seconds of deliberation he grabs Geric and Avrel and promptly jumps off the building, carrying them down with him.

Avrel and Geric scream the whole way down until at last they all three plunge into the water. Once their initial panic subsides, Zanvan leads them quietly into a tunnel leading under the castle. It wasn't the kindest way to get them to do it, but he knows better than to have given them time to debate it. Even so, it's not without their complaints.

"Shhh..." he warns, "If we head this way we can easily get back the way we came here... I think. The map is a little wet." Zanvan says as they head into the dark, smelly tunnel.

"What is this place?" Avrel says, pinching her nose.

Zanvan rolls his eyes and half-smiles uncomfortably, "It's a waterway that leads to where we need to go to get out of Yordasvin, let's leave it at that." Zanvan says reluctantly. She doesn't need to know what's in the water. But it seems she does, as the kid shudders.

"Well..." the 'cleric' sighs, "At least the water isn't so deep here, it's pretty hard **swimming with one hand!!**" Geric yells as he tries to swipe at Zanvan but misses due to the lack of a full forearm. He then slumps over in disappointment.

"Hey." the kid chirps. "We could find some empty liquor barrels and float down the river in those." Avrel suggests after a while of wading through the tunnel.

"That's a stupid idea." Zanvan scoffs. "Even if you could fit, me and Geric wouldn't. Besides, wouldn't people see the barrels and be suspicious?"

"Hey I mean..." Geric snickers, "Avrel wouldn't need a whole beer barrel, just a large mug." he replies, cracking up at the end.

"Shush!" Zanvan says, noticing that Geric is being quite loud.

"MmmWell, excuse me!" Geric snaps back, "Mr. *I-Came-Out-Of-That-Fight-Without-A-Scratch*, some of us people find that humor masks the **heinous pain of an exposed bone that has been cauterized by being blasted with fire!**" Geric rages.

"Alright, alright..." Zanvan says dismissively.

***

Eventually they come to the end of the tunnel where it leads out into a milky, polluted complex of webbed streams. The sewers have been ugly enough, but seeing the water in the daylight is worse. At least in the open, the air isn't so foul.

Zanvan points. "I think if we keep down that way we can get around the city walls unseen."

"You think." Geric grunts. "Or, we get seen and shot by one-hundred angry orcs."

Zanvan has gotten us this far... Avrel thinks to herself. "Just follow his lead..." she sighs acquiescently. They continue around the interwoven streams until they unite to form a small river. So far without being spotted. Zanvan is so casually stealthy, it honestly makes her a little self conscious, elves are *supposed* to be. She's tried watching how he walks and wades, but can't quite emulate it herself. But it doesn't matter now, she *can* walk softly on dry land. More so than a lumbering lummox like Geric, anyway.

"Alright." Zanvan smirks. "Here's the fun part, leaving the shadow of the iron walls and heading into the open." he says, peering around a corner.

He's gotten them this far... she reminds herself, hell, he got them all the way through the original job. "Is going back the way we came such a good idea?" Avrel still asks.

"I mean..." he sighs, tellingly. He doesn't sound thrilled either. "It's that or climb over the mountains."

Geric groans, "Scratch that." he says waving his stump.

Avrel points over to the large group of soldiers on patrol. "I don't know how we can make it around here, look at all the guards on the bridges."

"Oh shite." Geric agrees.

"It'd be easier to sneak around if orcs actually kept some forests around." Avrel says with disgust.

"We could bum rush them." Geric says straightly.

Avrel and Zanvan non-verbally agree to ignore his suggestion.

"Or..." the ranger pauses, "We can try swimming under the water...How long can you hold your breath?" Zanvan asks.

Suddenly the guards scramble and appear to be pursuing someone.

"Okay!" he barks in a raspy whisper-yell, "Let's run for it, get under the bridge, *now*!" Zanvan orders as he leads the way. The three stumble and wade, and swim until they manage to get under the bridge unseen. Zanvan climbs up and peeks around to see if any guards remain. "Hm... Looks like they're all gone." Zanvan says quietly.

"*Eeeek!!!*" Avrel gasps, her scattered mind finally remembering something it should have thought of sooner. "Candice is still in Yordasvin!" she starts sweating profusely.

Geric smiles. "Good!"

"Avrel, we can't go back." Zanvan says firmly holding her arm.

She resists. "But!"

"She'll find you." Zanvan reminds her, comfortingly. "You know that."

She *does*. But she could have called out to her already. She could kick herself for not thinking of it. But then, it's not everyday she's sneaked into a castle to kill a monster. She gulps, *To kill a... person.*

"And if not, who cares!" Geric adds, unwantedly.

Avrel is pained but she concedes with a nod to Zanvan. She'd hit Geric were it not for his state.

"Let's get going." Zanvan says, softly. "The coast is clear." he adds, waving them along as he climbs up onto the bridge.

She climbs out of the gully just fine, but Geric needs help. "Hey." he grunts as they pull him up by his good hand. "You know what else is back in Yordasvin? My arm."

"Nah." Zanvan replies. "You and I both know some of that landed in Avrel's hair and down her blouse."

The sardy cleric chuckles, "*There's space for things to get lost in Avrel's blouse?*"

She catches her hand before she can act on her impulse. "I've never slapped a cripple before." Avrel says saltily.

"That's good!" Geric replies.

They follow Zanvan as he dashes as fast as he can down the road. But as she mulls it over, she arrives at a decision. Some ways. down she slaps Geric across the cheek. More his chin really, but it's the most she can reach. "Eh? I believe in equal treatment to all, you know?" Avrel smirks. He seems unamused, but they continue on, Zanvan is not willing to give them a moment.

They are able to go on rather easily until at last they encounter the squad of soldiers they'd almost confronted before. Her heart pounds, she sees very little way to avoid them. She still keeps her pace, but stiffly as her fear tenses her up.

However, Zanvan, still keeping a quick pace, still takes a confident and easy stride. She tries to as well, for what it's worth.

"Hey you!" one growls out.

Another snorts like a bull. "Where are you going in such a hurry?" the particularly tall orc asks from in the back.

"Hehe…" Geric chuckles nervously. "One might ask you the same thing."

"You!" one barks familiarly, she recognizes him as well, "You are those two 'merchants' and the puny elf lady!"

"Y-yeah…" Avrel stutters nervously. "We *are*.. We uhh… *Sold stuff* and we… Need to *go* now?"

She can't believe it, but it's the same as the keen nosed sard from the border guard, because hell if he isn't sniffing out Geric's bloody arm. "Why is the big guy's arm gone!?" the orc asks.

"We're merchants…" Zanvan pauses as he considers possible excuses. "We uhhh…"

Avrel does too. *Demo accident. Angered buyer…* she gulps as nothing comes to mind. Even the stoic ranger looks nervous.

"I sold it!" Geric puts in. Avrel and Zanvan both facepalm at Geric's comment.

"You sold your arm!?" the taller orc grunts in disbelief as the other orcs stance more aggressively.

"It…" Geric shrugs. "It was handy!"

The orcs aren't buying it, like shite they would, and they come closer with their weapons drawn.

"Well…uhhh…" Avrel stutters, before making a split second decision. She lets out a scream as she throws a fireball at the guards, the blast knocking them all over.

"Boring conversation anyway." Geric chuckles as he begins to rush off.

But she pauses. The tips of her fingers where they already were burned a bit sting once more. She just threw the spell out, no thought, no hesitation. Is it right? It's as if the more she breaks her promise, the easier it is to do so, it seems. It makes her wonder, *What am I to do with this*? Her mind floats to Argoth and the unfairness she was always subjected to, she can't help but wonder what she could do, if she chose to.

She grins, no Ar-Guard will dare bother her again, that's to be sure.

"Avrel!" Zanvan shouts.

Her deep thought breaks and her eyes look around. Up ahead they spy a small brown figure scurrying up the road towards her. "Candice!?" Avrel yells.

"Chippu!" she answers, leaping into her arms. All of her bitter thoughts melt as she holds her precious friend.

Until the orcs moan, reminding her of why they are running. "Never..." one growls, "Trust elves!" He's trying to get up.

"Avrel, come on!" Zanvan calls.

But the orc still tries to get to his feet.

"Stay down!" Avrel says softly and apologetically, "You don't understand and I don't want to hurt you." The reality is she'd like to treat every one of those sards how they treat their environment, but she doesn't have the time. "Come on, Candice!" She puts the beaver under her arm like a loaf of bread, and runs for it the way she's often had to when in the possession of one.

The guys catch up in no time with their long-arsed strides. Geric in particular gives her a glare, after staring at her beaver. "Done pissing around?" he asks. His voice is full of pain, so she leaves him to be.

The three run well past the pile of stunned orcs and then after some distance, Geric raises a barrier to cut them off as they pass over a narrow bridge. "That ought to hold for a while." he laughs.

"Candice!" Avrel yelps as the beaver leaps out of her hold and turns towards Avrel, squeaking playfully.

"Yeah, come on!" Zanvan tags both she and Geric, "There's worse things than orcs on foot we need to get clear of."

They sprint across the bridge, and onward through Yodasvin's desolate landscape. All the while she wonders what Zanvan was referring to, but at the moment she hasn't the breath to ask. Not when she's trying to keep up with them and their long legs.

They keep up the brisk pace and after many, many days on the run, the group comes to where they'd left their raft, such as it was.

For their enginuity, Avrel can only be speechless, if not a little proud for Candice's sake. She can't rightly tell what Zanvan's thoughts are, but Geric's are loud and clear. And he hasn't begun to speak yet.

"**Oh my god, you bloody beavers, I've got places to be!**" Geric screams. "**Was this your doing!?!?**" he says, grabbing Avrel's beaver.

"Chippu." Candice squeaks snarkily.

"She says, 'no.'" she translates, feeling a little superior for it too. "But she finds it damn funny." Avrel laughs.

Zanvan rolls his eyes "Dam... Funny...." he sighs as his eyes roll over to it. A beaver dam. Beavers or some similar breed, they don't look quite like Candice or others she's seen closer to Argoth, but they have the same tails, teeth, and overall shape.

And apparently, the same affinity for using any available wood, such as that of a raft hidden in some brush, for damming rivers.

"We **need** to get **home!**" Geric says as he quakes with rage. "This!" he holds up his arm, only mildly bandaged, "Needs proper attention!"

That she'll concede. Just when her ribs were really healed up, she went and broke something else, and her potion is running low.

"Okay well…" Zanvan says as he thinks. "We could turn north and head to Rudaski."

Geric leans in and whispers to Avrel, "He wants a booty call at a time like **this**!?"

"I heard that!" Zanvan snaps, "And *actually*, Elisé might be able to help us." Zanvan says calmly after steadying himself.

"Uh huh…" Geric says sassily.

Avrel kind of agrees, but Zanvan has a point too. "Just come on." Avrel says, siding with Zanvan. "We can get you properly bandaged up there. I'm sure they have mining accidents."

"Yeah." Geric groans. "Except it's half healed already!" he protests.

"Good". Zanvan chuckles darkly, "Then we'll get you a fashionable sock." Avrel giggles uncomfortably as well.

They continue northwest until they come to a river crossing, Zanvan is careful to check back, and often climbs up tall stone pillars and boulders to make sure no orcs are behind them. Both he and Geric told her of an elite orken group of horsemen, the Death Riders. Zanvan only knew the name, and that they are to be feared, but Geric and his insight too. It's said that they crushed an entire army of dwarves by riding down the side of a mountain. That was ages past, but still, it's frightening. She wonders though what she could do if she needed to, but also hopes that she'll never find out. Now that they are back in Argothian territory, she's a bit more at ease.

"Ugh… I'm hungry…" Geric moans, laying himself down by the river bank.

"Eh?" Avrel agrees. "Most of what we had was ruined from that whole running around sewers and waterways thing we did." she sighs, delicately caressing her stomach. "Zanvan, do we have anything left?" she asks weakly.

He looks through his bag. "There's this big… raisin?" Zanvan says curiously as he lifts a tiny piece of dried fruit.

Avrel sighs. "I think that was an apple…"

"Hmmm…" Zanvan hums, "Stem should have given that away I guess. Alright, you two stay here, I'll find us something before we cross." as he leaves some of his bags with her, Geric, and Candice.

"We're completely out?" Avrel asks.

"Yeah, Avrel." Geric says in a weird tone. "We're just a'boot oot." he pauses to lean up, "Eh?"

She's not sure what he's trying to say, or whose voice he's supposedly imitating. "Eh?" she frys, questioningly.

Zanvan straightens his hat, "We can talk about Avrel's accent when I get back. I'll see what food I can find."

""My accent?" he asks. "I don't have a--"

"You doon't have *éh--*"

"Oh bugger off." she swats, but not quite making contact with him. He snickers before lying back down, and falling silent. She lies down in the grass beside the water too, not too close. They've been near streams and rivers all this way, but the soft sound of this one is trying to lull her to sleep. It's *clean* water after all, maybe that's the difference. After a little bit, she dozes off.

She awakens with Candice curled close into her side, her dark eyes looking quite emotional. Candice can always tell. "I'm alright." Avrel says with a pet.

Her eyes drift to her sardonic friend, his fancy white cleric robes all tattered and soiled.

And his arm.

He healed hers, he nursed hers, and spent a lot of time, thought, study, and arcane stamina to make sure hers healed well. There's nothing she can do for him though. Just like Shad, it seems her power is only to harm.

No. she tells herself. She is her mother's daughter, even if her spells can't help her care for her friend, she still can. For what it's worth, Avrel finds a cloth in Zanvan's pack and moistens it with the river water. She chills it, and places it on his forehead. She sits, kneeled by his head for a long moment.

"Silly Geric..." she sighs, "Why would you be the one injured? You're supposed to be our silly party's healer." she mumbles softly. "And you're too proud and stupid to admit you have a fever." Avrel says with a sad smile, male arrogance at its worst. "You knew what happened to me when I fought against that weapon, and you, despite your constant teasing, still defended me..." Avrel says as she tears up. *And also at its best.* "I'm so... So, so sorry..." she mutters as her lower lip sinks. *Maybe...* she gulps as she admits, *not everything of the male ego is of an evil.* She feels strange for even thinking of such a thing, but maybe it's the truth.

He stirs. "Hey... hehe... MmmmWanna... make some magic?..." Geric mumbles as he twitches, fast asleep, "Hehe...mmmMorrr...d Nice book you got there...Can I see smmmm... Pages..."

Avrel smiles softly as she finds one of his books in a leather container in his pack and places it in his right hand. "Here's my book." she whispers playfully in his ear. She watches uncomfortably as he seems to try to hold the book open but it keeps falling out of place due to the lack of a second grip, so she withdraws it and puts it away.

As she sees Zanvan approaching in the distance, she takes the cloth off of Geric's head and pats him on his cheeks. "Hey, wake up." she repeats a few times until he comes to.

Zanvan comes with an armful of small fruits. "Here, it's all I could find."

"Yay." Geric sighs as he takes one, giving her heart a start.

Just how asleep was he, actually? She'd rather not know. "Thanks." Avrel smiles as she takes one as well.

Zanvan's eyebrows flash quickly, "If only our food had been stored in the same type of pouch as Geric's books." he sighs as he chomps into a fruit.

"Well, they weren't." Geric replies saltily.

"So how are we gonna cross this river?" Avrel asks as she pops a grape in her mouth, finding out too late it's the kind with big, hard seeds. "It looks kind of torrid with all the rocks sticking out." she says before spitting them out.

Zanvan looks at her, "I don't suppose you could freeze it?" he inquires.

"Well, I could." she considers. "But then that would dam it up and then it might cause it to overflow upstream."

"And we've had enough with damming!" Geric puts in, leering at Candice.

"Good point." Zanvan agrees, with her she assumes. "Well, there is a trade route between Rudaski and Yordasvin, so I guess we should just go further north until we find the actual bridge." he shrugs, reluctantly. Or at least, there *was*.

"But the river bends east *here*." Geric points out. "You can see the mountains Rudaski is built under from here."

"Have any *better* ideas?" Zanvan asks testily.

"Actually, yeah." Geric retorts. "Have the damned beaver do what beavers do best, aside from annoy me."

"...Which is?" Avrel asks.

"Have her gnaw down a tree and we can cross on that." Geric replies excitedly.

"Oh..." Avrel says as she looks around. "That's a good point, are there any good trees around here?"

"Over there." Zanvan says as he points to a large, sturdy looking tree.

It's very big, and Geric can't help. "You think we can drag that?" Avrel asks.

"Yeah sure." Zanvan says as he walks towards the tree. "Come on Avrel, Candice."

Avrel looks at the tree, proudly holding its own against the elements. For once, she sees a certain irony in the form of her familiar. "Seems like a shame to--" she's cut off by the sound of Candice's ravenous gnawing.

"You were saying?" Zanvan chuckles. "Really though, between this and the bar, and her felling that tree for Bob, Candice certainly has been useful."

She can tell he's trying to be nice, but still, "Helpful." she corrects. "She's not a tool to be used, she's choosing to help."

He seems unfazed. "As if I can keep the minutiae of your magicks straight." he scoffs, and fairly enough. She tries not to question his areas of expertise.

After a few minutes the tree is felled and Avrel and Zanvan slowly drag it over to the side of the river. Admittedly, Zanvan does most of the work, even with her trying to add leverage with an extra mage's hand, the cleric's would be better.

"Hey." Geric scoffs as they return. "That rat was useful!" As Candice walks by she slaps his bandaged stump with her tail, causing Geric to groan intensely and curse her. Zanvan and Avrel are still too labored to reply, and work on carefully laying the tree across some rocks in the river to help hold it in place.

"Hmm..." Zanvan mumbles. "We're gonna need more trees." It only reaches about halfway, maybe a little more. Still, Avrel's not so set on cutting down more.

All the same, Candice dashes over towards the treeline and they end up repeating the process several more times until the logs roughly span the whole way across.

"Next time--" Zanvan grunts as he wipes the sweat from his brow. "I think we'll just take one log and paddle across, this was ridiculous."

Avrel splashes her face with water. "I feel bad for the trees." she says softly.

"Chippu." Candice informs her.

"Oh." she sighs, "I guess that's not as bad."

"What?" Zanvan asks.

"She said some of them were sick anyway." Avrel relays.

"Speaking of sick..." Geric stands tall, "Let's get to civilization, please."

They cross, and wary of any lingering pursuers, but before they carry on, Avrel blasts the log as to not leave the passing. From there, they strive on long into the night.

***

They continue on, foraging their way until after a few days they come to the familiar dusty air and irrigated farmlands around Rudaski.

"Ahh..." Avrel sighs as they enter. "I never thought I'd want to see this dusty shitehole again."

It could use a few more trees, but after some parts of Yordasvin, he wouldn't complain. "Avrel." Zanvan says as he unties the Aegis from his back. "Take Geric to an inn, I'm going to see Elisé."

"Yeah uh-huh." Avrel replies sassily. But she sticks by Geric as they head to the west side of town. Zanvan follows the sun the other way, and heads east.

It doesn't prove hard for Zanvan to find the Fur Guild's building again, and he enters into the lobby. "Hello, is Elisé Essgrante here?" he asks an older man at the front desk.

"I believe so, Miss Elisé is almost always here." the gentleman says before he glances back at a door somewhat caddy corner to his desk. "Who wishes to see her? She is a busy woman and I'm guessing you haven't an appointment. " the man asks, and explains. Needlessly.

"Tell her 'Zanvan'." he smiles. "--She'll want to see me."

"Very well." the man says as he walks back and opens a door briefly before closing it.

"Yes, Blair." she answers, before he says a word. "See him in." Apparently, she's heard the whole thing, and Zanvan can't help but admire women who aren't afraid of being on top of things.

"Third door on the right." the man points as he returns to the desk.

"Thanks." Zanvan says, tipping his hat courteously. The older gentleman tries to seem like he doesn't care, he rather obviously does though.

He enters the door to the right and there she is, hard at work. She throws down some surprisingly aging reading spectacles as she notices him. "Zanvan? Whatever are you doing here?" Elisé asks with joyful surprise in her voice.

"A lot of stuff has happened." Zanvan replies. "But I was wondering if you could do me a favor."

Elisé blushes and looks at Zanvan coyly. "What kind of favor?" she asks. He hadn't realized he'd made *that strong* of an impression.

"I need you to hold onto this." Zanvan lifts up the sack containing the Aegis. That's no doubt hardly what she'd expected. "It's the Everlasting Aegis, and it needs to go away." he says imperatively.

She's a little taken back, saying 'he *actually found* it!?' with her clear eyes. "What's wrong I thought you were trying to find it." Elisé asks with concern.

"We did." Zanvan explains. "As it turned out, the orcs' princess was trying to get a hold of it so she could use it in warfare."

She looks a bit confused still, not that he'd blame her. "Oh dear." Elisé comments.

"Yeah." he nods "It turned her into a monster, me and my friends dispatched her, but at great cost."

"Okay?" Elisé asks with a puzzled smile. "So why do you come to me?"

"Do they ever close off mining shafts?" Zanvan asks.

"Yes." Elisé responds. "*Sometimes.*"

"Please." Zanvan says with a harsh and serious tone. "Take this and next time they do, cast it in there. Let this thing remain hidden in a deep pit forever." he says holding up the large sack.

"Well…"

"Please." he insists as he holds it out to her.

"Sure, Zanvan." Elisé smiles. "I can do that."

"For Hazell's sake don't touch it." Zanvan tells her. She takes the shield from him and sits it beside her desk, as she then slowly comes back to him, to tenderly embrace him.

She breathes hotly, over the back of his ear, "Have anything that I can?"

***

"Hey Geric, I brought us a roasted chicken." Avrel says cheerily as she enters the room at the inn.

Geric is startled awake. "*The chicken!?*" he yelps as he leans up. His usually tidy hair is in a bit of a fluff.

"Yeah, and some bread." Avrel smiles.

"Oh… Yay." Geric says enthusiastically. Avrel hands him a leg, she had almost handed him a wing, but well, she doesn't want to invite trouble. "Is Zanvan coming?" Geric asks tiredly.

Avrel thinks for a moment and then rolls her eyes. "Probably." she giggles wryly.

"Uh huh…" Geric says shaking his head.

"I can joke too, you know." she says as she slices off a piece of breast meat, puts it on a slice of bread, and sits next to Geric.

"Frankly." Geric says, awkwardly reaching his stump for the sandwich before switching to his hand, "I'm surprised such slangs are even in your vocabulary."

"I grew up on the streets." she reminds him. "I may not have a firm grasp on their exact meanings, but it doesn't mean I don't know a lot of words."

"Foul ones, apparently." he chews.

"Well, yeah." she nods, controlling how far her eyes roll, "But that accounts for most of what you men threw at me." And instantly, she sort of regrets that instinctive chide. She very much regrets it as her eyes fall to the hand he gave up on her behalf. "Sorry." she forces herself to mutter, but her pride won't let her do it audibly.

She takes her portion and offers Candice a piece of bread, which the beaver eagerly takes. It's not often, but it's times like this she wishes she wasn't poisoned with the reality of knowing the darkside of men; of knowing the toxicity below their surface, and their chivalrous deeds. She can acknowledge the good it does, but that doesn't vindicate all the evils that comes from it. Not to her mind.

Still... she considerately sighs to herself. Sometimes she wishes she was simple and basic enough to just accept things as they are; to spread her legs for the least awful man she can find and be done with it. It'd make things simpler. Simpler for sure, but in the end, she's not ever going to fall for their barbaric traps.

Aside from her thoughts and Candice's nibbling, the room falls pretty quiet, until after a while, Geric snickers.

"What's up, Geric?" Avrel asks, expecting something objectionable.

"I was just thinking." his grin confirms that it's coming, "The chicken breasts you are eating are bigger than your own!" the cleric laughs heartily as he slaps his knee with his stump, immediately causing him intense pain.

"Serves you right!" Avrel barks as she leers at him, but all at once, grateful to him for helping solve her internal debate.

Just then, there's a knock at the door, and Zanvan enters the room.

The cleric shoves the rest of his sandwich into his mouth, "What's up stud?" he asks in an ornery tone.

"Uh huh." Zanvan says with a calmness Avrel's started to notice he has after such 'encounters'. "So Elisé said we can hitch a ride on an express wagon that's heading to Argoth that leaves tomorrow." Zanvan says as he sits down and lights his pipe.

"Works for me." Geric says as he grabs and proceeds to chow on a hunk of leftover bread.

"Oh." Zanvan says as he tosses a rather fancy fur sock to Geric. "And Elisé wanted me to give you this."

"...Amazing." Geric sighs.

Avrel leers at him. "I'd have thought you'd be overjoyed."

"How did she come by it?" Geric asks, test fitting it.

"Miss matched sock." Zanvan sighs smokily. "Apparently, it gets pretty cold out here during the winter."

Avrel gently feels it, "Wish I'd have had some of these growing up."

The cleric pulls away, "Mine!"

"Anyway." Zanvan says, taking one last huff before putting his pipe out, "She said it's leaving very early, so we'd best call it a night."

Geric doesn't seem too keen on it, but unlike him, she didn't nap all afternoon. She does however make a second sandwich for herself first.

Early the next morning they pack up and meet at the Fur Guild building for their ride. Zanvan helps load some of the goods into the wagon, and Avrel tries her best too. Candice and Geric understandably just watch and wait. Once all the lighter things she can handle are loaded, she joins them. After a few more minutes, Zanvan joins them and smokes until they are ready to leave.

Once they are given the okay, they get on board the wagon. There's not much room, but they have a nice spot by the back curtain, where they can see the scenery, or hop out should they need to. The wagon lines up with a few others in the back of the guild building, and just as the cart pulls away from the storeroom Elisé comes out and waves goodbye.

"Don't worry Zanvan!" she calls as she walks to one of the loading platforms, "I'll take care of the *thing*!" she shouts to them.

Zanvan brushes past Avrel to lean out and wave back.

"Thing?" Avrel asks as Zanvan leans back. Avrel glances back, her elf eyes don't see any evidence that she's in trouble. "What *thing*?"

Zanvan seems to catch onto what Avrel's thinking. "No." he puts down. "I left the Aegis with her, she'll throw it in an abandoned mine shaft when she gets the chance." He lights his pipe again, "That way *nobody* will find it." Zanvan explains.

"Oh." Geric replies.

So he wasn't just lying with her, "That's actually a pretty good idea, I guess." Avrel sighs. She's just glad he didn't leave her with a bastard. She rummages through her pack for a minute, "If none of you care…" she says, "I'm keeping this though, no evil spirits in here." Avrel giggles as she holds up the Runeblade hilt.

Zanvan waves it away, aquiescently.

Geric scoffs. "Yeah, it was just used by a crazy guy who made a whole village's water supply full of horrible biting fish!" He cracks his neck, "Besides, I thought you hated your father."

"Well, it's mine now." Avrel retorts. "I won't let Shad deprive me of it." she inspects it, closely and in the light for once, imagining how much of the world such an old thing might have seen. The legacy of the elves, of long ancient magic, and of this blade. All the forms it might take, and has taken. All the worthy elves who have held it, and all that it has passed from and to.

She can't help but smile and the romance and memory of it. Elven legacy, *her* legacy. She is both, but she is elf-kind.

"Hey Avrel--"

A tap on her shoulder scatters her thoughts as she spasms in a startle. Suddenly two shafts of arcanium shoot out, piercing the sides of the wagon, startling everyone else. "Hehe…he…" Avrel giggles nervously as she tries to get the crystalline shafts to dissipate. After they do, she nervously shrugs as Candice and the guys leer at her.

"I had figured it would be right for you to keep it." he sighs, "I'm second guessing that now."

After a few minutes of awkward staring and silence, she asks, "So what did you want?"

Geric puts on his arm sock. "My stump looks like a fox's tail." he giggles as he playfully wiggles his arm. "I thought you and your elfy nature-lust would like that."

She feels his head, his fever isn't *that* high. "Hehe…" she giggles for his sake.

Minutes later, the wagon falls dark, and they pass into the cave as they leave Rudaski.

After a fortnight or so of riding through a cave, plains full of giant whistle pigs, and deep forests, they at last pass over the Argothian River on the same bridge that they had crossed when their journey began. From there, the merchant wagon let them off at a trading square, and from there, the castle isn't far. Even so, it's dark by the time they reach the castle. After a short delay at the gate, waiting for messages and orders to be relayed, they are taken into the castle and lead to a room to wait once more. There's some fancy rich person type snacks there, but not much, and it's growing later. The wagon was its own respite from the mad rush out of Yordasvin, but still, she's tired from the road. They all are, by the looks of it. Geric's fatigue is more obvious than Zanvan's, but both show it. Catching her reflection in one of the silver plates, she realizes that she shouldn't judge. If the circles under her eyes were any darker, she'd look like she's wearing witch's paint.

Finally, and only after she's let her hunger drive her to taste the rather gross looking, gooey, fishy pellets on thin crackers, a handful of heavily armed guards in bright, shiny armor come. "Leave your weapons." the lead one barks.

She has no choice but to swallow the putrid saltiness with so many witnesses present. It's like no fish she's ever tasted, but a dry cracker sops the rest of the taste away as she pays heed to the fancy Ar-Guards.

Zanvan sheds his bow and sword, and she just leaves the runeblade hilt in her pack which she'll leave in the room. Geric hasn't a weapon, she only now realizes.

"Come." another of the guards orders.

She picks up Candice, and they go.

The halls are beautiful, which is to say, even more so than what she'd seen of the castle before, and far more so in contrast to the orken castle. Deep royal blues, and gold lined tapestries depicting legends and history, Avrel can tell it catches Geric's tired eyes. Also, the patterns and cloth murals contain a lot of violet in the same shade as Princess Catarina's eyes. Further along, they are led past rows of head sculptures, almost all of human men, but a few women, all wearing the same crown. Finally, a door at least two normal doors tall opens, slowly by men at some sort of crank on either side. As it opens, a long red carpet leads their way to the royal throne. There, The Princess and The King, King Markell sit upon a dais. It's all Avrel can do to not let her nerves eat her alive.

But she meets eyes with Zanvan who has glanced down to her, and he's calm. *Well...* she thinks as she gulps, *If they're okay with him, I suppose I'll be alright.* She holds fast to Candice, and follows the guards forward until they drop to their knees. Zanvan and Geric follow almost immediately, but she almost forgets herself before following suit, clumsily.

The Princess stands, her hands gracefully holding each other. "Greetings friends." she says in a very distinguished, round, and snooty royal tone. The guards rise from their knees only to give another standing bow. Zanvan and Geric follow, while Avrel panics, losing her grip of Candice, and curtsying as best as she can remember how. *Candice's is better than hers.*

But for all her worry, it seems that the surprisingly elderly king is fixated on Geric's lack of hand motion in his bow. And then simply to the lack of a hand. Despite being old, shadowed by wrinkles and folds, and framed by thick, grey eyebrows, his eyes are the very same violet as The Princess. It makes it easy to see where The King's gaze lingers. "Ohhh Goddess blind me!" he yelps, half causing Avrel to choke on her spit, "That man is missing a hand!" he says in a disturbedly spastic way.

The Princess tries to look composed, but her attention twitches. "No, Father." she corrects softly. "This is about what we *just* discussed."

"Yes, yes, yes..." he dismisses.

Zanvan steps forward, "Your Highness." he starts, "We pursued Lucia and ultimately faced her in combat when she awakened the evil spirit within the Everlasting Aegis." he says solemnly. Almost gentlemanly, Avrel never knew he had it in him.

"She ate your hand!?" The King says confusedly, his violet eyes almost popping out at Geric.

"What?" Zanvan gasps, "No... no, Your Majesty, Geric's hand was shattered by the power of the Runeblade's intense magic." he says, trying to keep his composure.

"A shaving accident?" The King says before his almost nonexistent lips flap idly, "What kind of man shaves his arms?" The King again asks in confusion.

Avrel's not sure what to think, but her stomach was already in knots and seeing this spastic old man who is supposedly the ruler of this kingdom is only pulled the knots tighter. No wonder all those people live in the woods.

"Oh my Goddess!" Geric rises up and says testily, drawing attention from the guards. "My hand exploded!"

"*Explosion, **where**!?*" The King says as he seems to panic.

The Princess rushes to him and quickly calms him down, "Father, let me handle the rest..." she says, soothingly, "Go on."

"No, Your Highness." he corrects. "We recovered the Aegis upon her defeat and discarded it where it can never be found." Zanvan finishes.

The Princess smiles. "Rise." she commands, "Were there any other casualties aside from Geric's arm?" she asks.

"Well... You see..." Avrel says nervously after Zanvan seems reluctant to answer.

The cleric clears his throat, "She transformed into this hideous monster in the orken throne room and she... MmmKind of shredded them all to pieces."

"Oh... Goodness." The Princess says as she places her hand aside her cheek. "Did any guards witness this?" she asks with concern.

"Everyone in the room was killed except us three." Zanvan replies.

"Well." she says, letting go of a deep breath, "If that's true, I'm sure we can work things out then." she replies after thinking for a moment. "Still, this could be troublesome..." she says as she gets up off of her seat and turns around. "Guards!" she shouts. Avrel fears the worst upon hearing that.

"Yes ma'am!" two guards say as they step forward.

"Escort Geric and Avrel here to our 'Honored Guest' chambers so they can rest." she says in a commanding tone.

That doesn't sound good! It sounds euphemistic to her cynical ears. "Ummm." she tries to get Zanvan's attention, but he's calm, showing no fear.

"Ranger." Catarina says with a confident, domineering voice. "I want you to come with me and give a full report on your journey." she says, coming down from their dais to meet him, and presenting her hand. Much, it seems, to The King's displeasure.

"Yes M'lady." he grins as he leans forward and kisses her hand softly.

"Report." Avrel whispers to Geric, "Yeah, right."

Geric has trouble containing his laughter as they bow and curtsy. She picks up Candice on her standing up, hoping to not be run through, should it be a breach of etiquette.

"Come." a guard says, "This way."

And she still worries that it could be a trap. The temptation is there in the back of her mind, reminding her of her power. She can and will use her spells, should it come to that, but she will follow for now.

And much to her pleasure, she is led only to a suite with a fluffy bed, a bathing tub, and some food.

Despite the luxury of it all, sleep and rest don't come so readily. She can't help but feel uneasy, guilty even as she lays in bed, in a fortified castle, and her mind wanders to her mother.

Her lovely, loving mother; who no one else in this castle would have ever given a thought to. Avrel picks Candice off of her feet, and spoons her as she rolls over to lay on her side. She holds Candice tightly and she closes her eyes, and tries to find more comforting thoughts than that fragile, broken and lonely excuse for her family.

"But..." Thinking of family doesn't only bring to mind her mother, not anymore. She opens her eyes slightly to look at Candice, and to think of Zanvan and Geric; her friends. She's not alone anymore, she reminds herself.

Early in the morning, the purple of pre-dawn creeps into the archway leading to the balcony attached to her room. She hasn't slept much, but all the same, Avrel decides to get up. She puts on her cleaned, but still tattered clothes and walks out onto her balcony. There's a faint glow just haloing the mountains to the west, begging for the sunrise.

And she wonders, *What now?* It's the same thought that'd awoken her again and again throughout the night, and the perfect counter to the peace she'd finally made to herself for the evening. She looks out over the courtyard below where guards still stand stiffly erect, ready to act on a moment's notice. *What now?*

Get a proper place to live, she's assumed to be the answer ever since taking the job. Avenge herself on all those that looked down on her status, she always thought; and will eventually do, but something tugs at her heart in the immediate circumstance. What about her, and her friends?

Pacing while taking glances over the balcony rail eventually grows old, and so she undoes the latched gate on the one side, and climbs some spiral stairs made of beautifully crafted metal fitting of a royal castle. She doesn't know where it leads until she comes up to it; a terrace, with a view of not just a sliver of the mountain, but of the whole range so far as the eye can see, which as an elf, is quite far. And the other way, the sprawled city of Argoth still sleeping under the shadow of Cordol.

"You can see all of the city from here." Avrel sighs, pleasantly. From up here, it's not so ugly.

"Yeah." she's almost startled into making a swing for it, but she catches her heart in her throat as she recognizes it as Zanvan's deep, morning voice. "It's something isn't it?" he asks. Obviously he hasn't warmed it up with a smoke yet.

She nods as she notices Geric coming up the stairs too. It seems all the suites are connected to this terrace, *and* that they all have decided to come here. "Mmm." he hums as he yawns, "You should tell The Princess to use thicker blinds in those guest rooms." he says, "I wanted to sleep in."

So had she, but the light wasn't the issue, for her. *Speaking of light...* she notes as a golden spark lights like a candle atop the mountain, "Hey Geric, isn't that the Cordol Monastery." Avrel asks as she points towards it.

Geric tiredly turns and squints his tired, human eyes. "Y-Yup." he sighs.

Zanvan leans against the rail and lights his pipe. "I told you the view from here was excellent." he comments to Geric. They must've passed each other already this morning.

But Geric, while taking glances at the glowing structure, seems wildly unamused. Dejected, in fact. "Sure is."

It's a good few minutes as Zanvan puffs his pipe, and she and Geric look over the view when Candice waddles to Avrel's side.

And a moment later, slaps her ankle for attention. Avrel turns, and looks down, but not before catching a glance at The Princess and a pair of guards. With less hesitation than she feels she rightly should have, she falls to a curtsy.

"Hello Zanny." The Princess says chipperly as she makes herself known to them, and they drop as well. "Avry, Geric..." she pauses and looks hard at Avrel's beaver. Her finger twitches, ready to point with the name on the tip of her tongue. Finally a guard leans in and whispers to her, "Right." she says, "Candace?"

Candice. Avrel almost corrects, but decides not to. It's close enough.

"Can...dice" she actually corrects herself, much to Avrel's shock. "While I rarely consider domesticated *vermin* to be my subjects, I do my best to know the names of my people that I meet." she smiles as she walks past Avrel and goes to Zanvan. "Showing your friends the view, I see?" With but a look, she dismisses her guards. Avrel feels it too, and she's *not* one of The Princess's brainwashed pigs; it's those eyes.

"View just got better." Zanvan says as he caresses her shoulder.

Frankly, Avrel still can't get over seeing Zanvan; rugged, bedswerving Zanvan acting *genuinely* romantic and affectionate towards a woman. The juxtaposition is almost nauseating.

"So." The Princess says as she feels up his stubbly jaw, for reasons beyond Avrel's comprehension, "What are you going to do now that you all have your reward?" she asks Zanvan, tenderly.

"The thing I do best." he answers as he exhales a ring of smoke. "Live." he smiles. "You know I don't really need material wealth, I just want experiences."

"Yeah." The Princess blushes, "Adventures and experiences, like that *last one*." He'd pulled away coolly, but she just follows. "Even if it's a *tad* painful?" she giggles softly.

Zanvan smiles confidently as he rolls his eyes, and simply keeps smoking away. *He tosses her a bone and then acts all aloof and distant?* By Avrel's reckoning, it's kind of shitey, but it's not her relationship.

And she doesn't want one anyway.

But, along the lines of looking distant, it seems that both Avrel and The Princess notice Geric looking over to the monastery and glancing disappointingly at his still very much swollen, if at least properly wrapped, stump.

"Avry." The Princess asks, "Tell me, what are your plans?"

"Well... I..." She pauses a moment, '*showing up the elites who spit at me, or ignored me*' might not sit well here. "I want to make a home for myself." Avrel sighs as her hair blows in the breeze "And Candice." she adds.

"Geric?" The Princess asks.

"...I don't know." he says depressingly

He should have squeezed in a joke by now. 'Good news is you can buy an affordable, *small* house.' she'd have expected him to say. *Oh dammit...* she's internalized it.

The Princess looks disheartened and takes a few steps back and stands silently for a minute. "You know, across the sea they have all kinds of contraptions with technology we've barely touched." she comments casually. "One fool came all the way across to beg us to invest in a cart that he said could pull itself!" she laughs heartily, turning back towards the cleric.

"Neat." he sighs, dimly.

She then walks up next to Geric and leans against the railing with him. "Funny thing..." she says, "He had a hand that was made of clockwork-type parts." she coyly sighs.

"Yeah, so..." he sighs dismissively, "Mmm*What?!*" Geric then asks excitedly.

The Princess nods. "Yeah, apparently they know how to do that over there, it must be expensive though." she comments, "I suppose for your efforts, I could finance that for you." she adds.

Geric sits in deep thought for a moment.

Avrel goes to his side. "I'll come with you, if you want to go." she says shyly, compared to how she approached.

"Really?" Geric replies, surprised for some reason.

"Sure." she giggles. "I don't have a home yet, *I suppose* I can wait." Like hell she'd miss on another adventure, assuming Zanvan is to go too.

The Princess walks by Zanvan and gently caresses and holds his arm a moment as she walks past. He mutters something, and she continues past. He then leans forward and takes his pipe from his mouth. "How far do you two think you'll get without me to keep you two from starving, getting lost, or otherwise dying miserably?" he asks with a confident smile. "Anyway, if you two are going, I might as well go." he says as he smiles confidently at them.

"Wonderful!" The Princess says, turning back around at the top of the stairs. gently folding her hands together. "I'll go see if I can arrange your passage, the Admiral ought to be able to sail you away within the week!" The Princess says excitedly. "You three…"

Candice squeaks, making her presence known.

"Four -- will like it. I imagine you'll do well with a relaxing boat trip to and fro." she smiles.

"Well." Zanvan says before breaking into a short laugh. "This ought to be much simpler than our last little journey."

"Yeah."

"Yeah." Geric and Avrel chuckle with him.

But for Avrel, it's not a chuckle merely of humor, it's *happiness*. What now? This! A new journey of sorts, to some place a long ways off, across the sea. The sea itself, not a thing she's ever seen before, and she's to *cross* it.

An elf, she's to cross it -- with her friends.

Epilogue

The dark room, hidden far away from prying eyes, is lit only by red candle light, such as it always is for their meetings. And dark is the mood. She of course was made aware even earlier, as soon as Leth missed her last rendezvous with Kain. But all of them were scattered, each doing their part, or merely going about their lives as they do outside of this great task. Only Kain was able to even attempt a pursuit of that orken usurper, and he hadn't a chance. It matters little, however, they know what has happened.

Aäron is waiting at the head of the table, and of course she's at the far end, but even in the darkness of the room and the distance, there's enough candle light to see his displeasure, even from under the shadow of his hood..

And if she couldn't see it, it wouldn't matter much at all, the room is thick with his dark aura. He doesn't twitch angrily, he doesn't fidget, he just waits.

Along with the rest of them.

That is, but for Kain, and of course, Leth. But still, Aäron just sits there, gently resting his chin on his knuckles, just waiting for news to come. Within a few more minutes, it does.

Kain scurries into the gathering chamber in a hurry, rushing to Aärons side and kneeling. "It's as we thought, Master."

Aäron turns with a dark glare.

"She made it back to Yordasvin, and tried to use the Aegis." Kain says sheepishly.

Aäron's eyes are cool as he turns away from Kain.

"We're not blind." she says for herself, darkly. This they knew from his seeing stones, vague as the images they show are, that much was already apparent. "What of The Aegis then?" she pushes, in Aäron's silence.

"The orken guard pursued the intruders as far as their border." Kain says weakly. "But it wasn't recovered in Yordasvin, or along the way. The contact in Rudaski said that they entered with a large, flat sack, but did not appear to leave with one."

"Ha!" Gilead lets out abruptly, ever the cantankerous blowhard. "Shame the orcs didn't pursue further, they could've taken care of things then and there."

Aäron's lips twitch at last, he's listened enough. "That neophyte is nowhere near ready." he dismisses.

They all agree, given their passive silence after his simple, decisive dismissal. The silence is almost deafening, but for a tiny sneeze, from one of the tinier cloaked figures. And after, the silence resumes for several minutes.

Gilead stirs. "I still don't see why you let Leth carry out even what was *supposed* to be her plan." He has balls, but it's going to be his undoing.

"I do agree." says one of the others, she can't quite tell who.

She debates whether she should explain it, or to let Aäron. He makes the decision for her. "Lethia and Rufus's plan was not folly, left to happen idly under a loose watch." he insists as she stands and hears over the long table-head. "I might remind you that *several* of you failed your own tasks on this matter, and that the loss of so key a member so early into the layed out events helped very little." He's letting a little of his anger show now, but just a little.

Quaid now speaks up, "There were a lot of things that could have gone wrong." he says, "If that little elven quim had just given Rufus his lead, we could have-"

"I know." Aäron cuts him short. "But." he says as he sits back down, and leans back quite calmly, controlledly, unfazed. "Amidst the mere *partial* failure due to Lethia's betrayal, we now have several key things now to our advantage." he *smiles*. "For in the myriad of things put into motion under Lethia's tainted plans we still now have that which we wanted. You--" he points to Kain, "It would then seem that the Aegis, our Lord's Heart is in Rudaski?"

Kain nods.

"And the *elven quim*..." he turns towards Quaid, "We now know for sure that she is the living daughter of Kriegsön, no? How was it Lethia called her? 'A daintily small and underfed urchin, with whorishly stained hair.'?" he recalls. "Lethia, or shall be correct?-- Lucia's betrayal ultimately has very little bearing on our plan moving forward. She was to bring the orcs to war under our guidance by her standing as their warrior queen. Consequently, her death may serve just as well for rallying the best of orken savagery." He stands tall and begins walking around the table. "We can recall the others searching, now in vain, for His Heart and move along. Lucia means nothing."

"What of the girl?" Jabesh bravely asks. "Does she not have the elven blade?"

Aäron stops over her own shoulders to stare down the dissonant, brushing his greasy hair over her. "The elven blade was two-fold. We've seen that it's able to cut The Beast, all the more easily when his renewed flesh is freshly formed. This, and that it would have been most helpful with the dragons' dens northward, but we've little need of that now. The Aegis is now likely somewhere in the Rudaskin region."

Jabesh and Quaid both nod following a muffled thump from another chamber, and they go to fetch it, as they always do.

And she feels Aäron begin to shift his gaze down to her. "And so now, rest assured." he says placing his hand on her shoulder. "Mildred has been working tirelessly on one of many contingencies. Kriegsön's daughter might not have fallen to Rufus's knife, as we'd hoped after delivering us to her father, but she will yet be dealt with."

Dred she wants badly to correct. "Yeah, she's played her part so far. And I'll see to it that we have an answer to any more interference from her." she smiles as she flips off her hood, careful not to smear her necromancer's face paint, nor pull on her ponytail. It was after all, a tool of Aäron's that allowed Leth to set up her plot, but now, it'll be by her magicks that things are made to happen.

"If nothing else…" Aäron says with satisfaction as he continues his way around the table, "The fire of her blood will consume her before too long." He turns with a jerk, "Tamar!" he barks, scaring the most timid of them out of her wits.

Not that it takes much, the poor thing. "Y-yes." she says, raising her hood hastily off of her golden bangs and bob-cut hair.

"Bring the bread and wine." Aäron grins.

Understandably, her heart sinks. Tamar's eyes glaze over, and her head drops, "Yes, Master Aäron." she gulps as she stands from her seat and takes her leave.

A moment later, the door flies open, and Jabesh and Quaid have with them another young woman. One would not think a scream muffled with a gag could be bloodcurdling, not after so many times, but it always is. The obvious words of comfort would be that it'll be over soon, but that would only be fitting were she to be subjected to a natural death where her soul could pass on.

But, Dred reminds herself, *It's a means to an end…* Just as is the nature and purpose of her own dark magicks.

"But Mildred!" Aäron says to her excitedly as the woman is thrown onto the table, "We shall be ready, for our blood does *not* burn." he reminds her as he draws his knife from a flap in his robe, "And by her blood or the spilling of it, that wretch's fate will not be so different from this one."

The young woman makes eye contact with her, the only unhooded women in the room that she would have a chance to see.

"So let us not be troubled with her for now." he grins as he takes an aura into his hands, "When Argoth is remade, should she show herself, the tide will already have begun to carry her away." he says as he passes both the knife and the aura to her.

Dred agrees, for she accepts that which *must* be done.

###

Avrel, Zanvan, Candice, Geric, and Trishia the mute, invisible fairy will return in Episode II: A Long Ways Off

This is a work of fiction. Names, characters, places and incidents either are products of the author's vivid imagination or are used fictitiously. Any resemblance to actual events or locales or persons, living or dead, is entirely coincidental.

<u>About the author...</u>

Æthan lives in south-central Pennsylvania at his family home with his two cats.

When not creating artwork or writing his literary shitposts, he's likely to be laughing hysterically at capybaras in hot springs, or watching anime.

CPSIA information can be obtained
at www.ICGtesting.com
Printed in the USA
LVHW070841220121
676908LV00057B/329